praise for pity party

'What a read!'
MARIAN KEYES, author of *Again, Rachel*

'Deeply moving and very funny … I loved it'
LOUISE O'NEILL, author of *Idol*

'The funniest book you'll read this year'
LAUREN BRAVO, author of *Preloved*

'Pity Party is perfection'
LINDSEY KELK, author of *Love Me Do*

'Unbelievably good'
LUCY VINE, author of *Seven Exes*

'Thought-provoking, charming, cathartic and
hilariously vivid'
SARAH KNIGHT, author of *The Life-Changing
Magic of not Giving A F**K*

'Crackling with energy, humour, warmth, and quirk'
JENNY MUSTARD, author of *Okay Days*

'Every line in this book is a wonder'
CAROLINE CORCORAN, author of *Through The Wall*

'Wonderfully funny. Her best book yet'
NINA STIBBE, author of *Man at the Helm*

'Daisy Buchanan makes me laugh out loud'
KATHERINE HEINY, author of *Standard Deviation*

'I laughed, I cried, I screamed, I devoured every
page … a laugh-out-loud balm'
NIKKI MAY, author of *Wahala*

Daisy Buchanan is an award-winning journalist, author and broadcaster. She has written for every major newspaper and magazine in the UK, from the *Guardian* to *Grazia*. She is a TEDx speaker, and she hosts the chart-topping podcast You're Booked, where she interviews legendary writers from all over the world about how their reading habits shape their work. Her other books include the non-fiction titles *How To Be A Grown Up* and *The Sisterhood*, and the novels *Insatiable*, *Careering* and *Limelight*.

pity party

DAISY BUCHANAN

SPHERE

SPHERE

First published in Great Britain in 2024 by Sphere

1 3 5 7 9 10 8 6 4 2

A CIP catalogue record for this book
is available from the British Library.

Hardback ISBN 978-1-4087-2562-7
Trade paperback ISBN 978-1-4087-2563-4

Typeset in Sabon by M Rules
Printed and bound in Great Britain by
Clays Ltd, Elcograf S.p.A.

Papers used by Sphere are from well-managed forests
and other responsible sources.

Sphere
An imprint of
Little, Brown Book Group
Carmelite House
50 Victoria Embankment
London EC4Y 0DZ

An Hachette UK Company
www.hachette.co.uk

www.littlebrown.co.uk

For Dale, who makes me brave

I believe that the purpose of death is
the release of love.

LAURIE ANDERSON

Prologue

Ben's funeral happened on a Wednesday. As I stood in church, between his mother and my best friend, trying hard to think sad thoughts, all my brain could manage was *This really feels more like a Friday.* I kept drifting off, listing my weekend chores – thinking about sorting the bed linen and laundry, and wondering whether I should go for a run in the morning – before remembering when it was, and where I was. *Get it together, Katherine. You're paying seventy quid a year for the Headspace app, and you can't stay focused during an* actual *funeral. What's wrong with you?* It was the saddest occasion imaginable. My brain knew that. But the rest of me wouldn't play along. Why were we doing this so quickly? Grief came in stages; this was well documented. It seemed all wrong to bury Ben during the shock/denial bit. In six months, I'd be ready to cry my eyes out. Now, I felt as though I was at a very dull pantomime. Every time the vicar referred to Ben in the past tense, we should have been on our feet, bellowing, 'OH NO HE ISN'T!'

The vicar coughed, and I caught his eye and smiled. It's OK, I wanted to tell him. This is a very dusty church. Coughing is an occupational hazard. I felt my own cough building at the back of my throat. What funerals needed was a dedicated coughing section. A little pen where we could all sit and pay our respects, while choking quietly. And when I thought about it, 'paying your respects' was such a weird expression. It made grief sound like an overdue library fine. I didn't know how to apply it to Ben. In fact, other than the guest list, nothing about this funeral seemed to have anything to do with Ben.

'Ben loved sports. But he also loved spending time with his family, and having a laugh with his friends . . . ' said the vicar. The unironic use of the phrase 'having a laugh' should automatically place you on some kind of register – alongside 'kiddies', 'nom nom nom' and 'what about yourself?'

'He was a beloved colleague, and he liked to unwind at the end of the day with a glass of wine . . . ' I knew that Constance had provided the vicar with a long, detailed essay about exactly who Ben was, as a son and as a person. And it appeared that the vicar had chosen to ignore the essay and read aloud from his own Tinder profile.

I snorted, and Annabel must have thought I was weeping, because she took my hand in hers and squeezed it. Unfortunately, her hand was full of wet tissue. I gulped, not because I was choking back tears, but because I was trying not to think about the fact that I was now covered in Annabel's cold snot.

The dust motes drifted, pale gold in the winter sun. The vicar was saying something about Ben's kindness to animals, and his beloved pet rabbit, Buster. *Who was Buster?* I couldn't remember Ben ever mentioning a rabbit. Was Ben an animal lover? I suppose he loved to eat them.

Feel sad, I told myself. *You're supposed to be devastated.*

But it was impossible to focus on Ben, because he just wasn't there. It felt as though we were all waiting for him to arrive.

'And now, Benjamin James Ralph Attwell,' said the vicar. 'May you rest in peace. Amen.'

Constance sighed, and it was my turn to reach for her hand, warm, in a soft black leather glove. I tried to force my face into an expression of sorrow – knowing the best I could manage was my own version of upside-down mouth emoji – and looked at her. If I couldn't locate the right sort of sadness at this moment in time, I could be sad for Constance. Her lovely little boy, her daredevil, her darling was up there, and we were here. It was tragic. It was mad. My first tear gathered and rolled as she muttered, 'I told that idiot a thousand times. It's pronounced *Rafe*.'

The tear evaporated. It felt more like a sitcom than a funeral. Any minute, Ben would turn up at the door, covered in seaweed, saying, 'Well, this is embarrassing! I fell in the drink and came to on the back of a milk float in the Isle of Wight. I don't know which poor sod is in that box, but it's not me.'

I could see him, in his shorts and his hat, holding an almost full box of Peroni. 'What?' he'd say. 'The shop was on the way! It took five minutes! Do you want one?'

Then he'd say, 'What are you all doing in church? I never went to church! In fact, the last time was ... '

'Our wedding,' I'd finish. 'Same people, same venue. No gazebo this time, sorry. No vodka luge.'

As a wife, I'd failed Ben in so many ways, but this was the last straw. He'd really wanted a vodka luge at his funeral. I'd only just remembered, and now it was too late.

Because when your healthy, happy young husband says

something like that, you laugh. You try, and fail, to imagine the two of you in your seventies, eighties, nineties. You can't begin to imagine the reality of living and ageing. You can't comprehend the evolution of your marriage. I never pictured Ben's funeral because I was distracted dreaming of the children we'd have, the homes we'd live in, the places we'd explore. I could still see the French farmhouse we'd retire to. I could smell the bunches of dried lavender, tied up and gathered into glass vases. I could feel the warm terracotta tiles beneath my bare feet. That place, and those feelings, seemed much more real to me than this church, and Ben's coffin on the altar.

I couldn't remember saying or even hearing the words 'till death us do part' on our wedding day. Even though in later moments, I sometimes felt trapped and tested by their meaning. I remember thinking that although marriage was supposed to be sacred, and serious, it was so much fun. Most of the time. And I made a promise. Technically, Ben did not break his. He did what he said he would do. He stayed married to me until he fell out of his boat and drowned.

Constance chose the last hymn. We said goodbye to Ben while bellowing 'For those in peril on the sea'. She gripped my hand tightly, and before the end of the first verse, she buried her head on my shoulder. 'What was I thinking?' she said, sobbing. 'What was I *thinking*? He'll never be in peril on the sea again.' She was using her 'outdoor voice'. 'This song doesn't work!' she called out. 'This is a *shit hymn*!'

Without looking around, I could tell that people were staring.

Straight away, Annabel swivelled, trapping us under her

4

long black coat in something between a bear hug and a headlock. Constance almost toppled, and pushed against me, to steady herself. The three of us started to sway.

'FUCK THIS SONG,' shouted Constance, from under the coat.

'It's so sad, so very sad,' said Annabel, noisily, through tears. 'So SAD,' she said, again, drowning out Constance, who was trying to scream obscenities at the vicar. Although it was hard to tell who each noise was coming from. The three of us had formed a solid mass, we were a triumvirate of weeping women, renting our garments and crying over the same man. We must have looked like some kind of Old Testament monster. Or a public demonstration of how to fail the Bechdel test.

Concealed by the coat and under the cover of darkness, I could cry for Ben, and I could cry for me. I felt sick. I growled, I sang, I tried to scream the final 'sea'. But everything got stuck. Everything felt tight, and hot, and itchy and trapped within me. In approximately 120 seconds I'd have to get out from under Annabel's coat. I'd have to stand by the door, and smile sadly, and think of something nice to say to the vicar, and shake everyone's hands, and make space for *their* sadness. When I hadn't been able to begin to find room for mine.

The wake was almost festive, all warm alcohol and flaky pastry and 'Do you remember ...' Ben's brother Sam was discovered video conferencing with Dubai on the toilet – the telling off from Constance was so evocative of an Attwell family Christmas that I had a brief craving for brandy butter. There was much laughter, followed by panicked apologies. Everyone kept telling me they were sorry, everyone kept reminding me that it was 'OK' to 'feel sad'. After a while, the word 'tragic' was used so frequently that it lost all meaning. 'Tragic' became the name of a town in Cornwall, or a new kind of cryptocurrency scam. It didn't sound permanent enough for me to take it seriously. How could any of it be permanent, when I was so certain that my favourite face was about to appear at the door, and I'd hear their voice saying my name?

Of course Ben didn't show up. Funerals weren't really his vibe. And I'd forgotten the vodka luge.

Chapter One

Top banana

It's not over yet. I could still have a good day. Everything depends on the Banana of Portent.

Starting the day with a firm, ripe banana means that everything is going to be OK. I'll be able to keep breathing, keep smiling, and do some semblance of my job. A stiff, green, crunchy banana is a bad sign. It means a telling-off from Jeremy, a sharp word from Akila, or one of those meetings where I zone out, my briefing notes start to dance before my eyes and I have an inexplicable urge to burst into tears and start singing 'I Will Survive'.

This week, I really need to turn everything around. Things haven't been going so well for me lately. So I'd made a plan. As I keep telling Grace the Therapist, I can plan my way out of anything. There is no disaster that can't be overcome with a brand-new notebook and a pack of highlighters.

The plan looked like this. Get up two hours early. Meditate for twenty minutes. Journal for twenty minutes. Drink some fresh ginger tea while sitting in the garden and contemplating the beauty of nature. Get dressed, in a crisp white shirt and my smartest trousers. Arrive at work an hour early. Get ahead on the research for the Woodland Trust. Or at least, become less behind with the research for the Woodland Trust.

The trouble is that I've had to make some last-minute changes to the plan. It's not a problem. In fact, it shows I'm strong, and resilient, and that I have great problem-solving skills. The new plan is as follows. Meditate for two minutes – then accidentally fall asleep for an hour. Wake up panicking. Sack off the journaling, then waste three minutes thinking of a convincing excuse I can give Grace the Therapist when she asks me about this next week. Try to remember whether I own any crisp white shirts. Empty out drawers and find glorious, smooth piece of clean white cotton. Attempt to put it on. Discover that it is a tablecloth. Waste two minutes wondering why I have a tablecloth, and how it got into the house.

Panic, and wear musty-smelling vintage sundress that is too tight in the armpits. Waste another minute testing the range of the dress by trying to spell out YMCA with arms. Put knickers on. Realise knickers are inside out. Take them off. Put them on back to front. Brush teeth while wondering how many times I can use the words 'development' and 'strategy' in today's company catch-up session before Jeremy realises that I don't know what I'm doing.

The new plan still allows plenty of time for a nutritious breakfast. I never skip breakfast because I'm incredibly good at self-care and because Constance, Annabel and Grace won't shut up about it. So, I always start my day with a delicious banana. Did you know that it's possible to chew, swallow and digest a banana while writing an email and running for a bus? Nature is healing. And the packaging is fully biodegradable! I'm not wasting any single-use plastics.

I open my front door. I take a single step out into the world. My right foot is on the outside doormat. My left foot is on the inside doormat. It is going to be a good day. It has to be a good day. I smile, I peel, I bite.

I gag.

And then I stumble off the doorstep, reach forward and throw up.

Trying to forget the fact that I've just puked in the recycling bin, I shut the door behind me and start to scuttle down the street, while scrolling through the podcasts on my phone. There must be something here on positive thinking. Something that reminds me that I'm in control. Bananas can't predict the future. Nothing that happens to me today at work could possibly be so horrible that it makes me throw up in a dustbin.

The thing is, even when I hate my job, I love my job. Admittedly, it hasn't been great for the last few months, but that's on me. I feel as though I've never worked longer or tried harder – but I'm operating from within a thick fog.

Some people have claimed that this is because I'm grieving. 'You don't need to keep battling your way through the fog,' Grace said, the last time I spoke to her. 'Why not let it envelop you, for a while. Trust that it will lift when you're ready. You don't need to *do* anything, Katherine. Right now, you can just be.'

Usually, I reply politely, with, 'That's an interesting idea.' I'm sure it works really well for other people. But I've always loved to be busy. I was brought up by my grandmother, whose catchphrase was 'the devil makes work for idle hands'.

The awful thing, the shameful thing, is that I know this can't be grief, because I'm not sad enough. Of course, I can't mention this to Grace, or Constance, or Annabel. I really wish I felt too upset to go to work. I should be haunting my own house, brought to my knees with pain whenever I find a stray sock under a sofa cushion. But, in all honesty, I keep forgetting that Ben has gone. Before he died, he spent so much time working late or away at sailing competitions.

Instead of crying, I'm sleeping. I should be lying awake all night, unable to bear the fact that there's an empty space in the bed beside me. I told Grace I was 'sleeping like the dead!' (I laughed; she didn't.) Before Ben died, I'd usually wake up at three or four in the morning and lie awake with a pounding heart, thinking about the usual things – mostly the climate emergency, whether I needed to start making my own bird food, how to persuade Constance to get an electric car – but now, I can sleep for up to twelve hours at a time. Sometimes I go to bed as soon as I get home from work and pass out until morning. Sleep is supposed to be very good for you, so I must be doing something right.

But during the day, I keep forgetting where I am. Little things keep going wrong. Last week I made Jeremy a coffee, and then I poured it straight down the sink; I got taken off a pitch for a new client, Go Green! – who make domestic compost toilets – because the name of the woman in charge is Marge, and I kept calling her Lisa; and none of my recent campaign ideas have been met with enthusiasm or even mild interest – just blank stares. And the occasional horrified gasp.

It's strange. I've been at Shrinkr for eight years, and I've always been able to anticipate what everyone wants and needs from me. It's my dream job, helping businesses to implement solid sustainability policies and incorporating their ecological credentials into their branding, and I'm *good* at it.

At first, Shrinkr operated on a small scale. A shoestring. If you went into an early meeting, you would have struggled to spot the CEO – it was just a lot of people in dungarees, saying, 'Did you read that thing in the *Guardian* about kitchen gardens?' We mostly worked with people who went to festivals and sold vegan sausage rolls out of wheelbarrows. Now, we're working with Marriott and Microsoft. It's exciting. It's a lot of pressure. But it's a calling. In a tiny way, I'm changing the world for the better. I'm part of something important. And I still have a couple of old clients, making power bars out of parsnips.

I've proved myself over and over. I've had promotions, and glowing appraisals. I have won awards for my work. I was so proud of it. They *needed* me.

Now, I need them.

I haven't missed a single day of work since the funeral. I mean, *I'm* not dead, so I've got no excuse not to come into the office. HR weren't thrilled – we had some painful conversations about 'burnout' and 'overdoing it' and 'taking time to recalibrate' – but I know myself best, and I know that if I stop, I'll never be able to start again. I have to work through this. I can't wait until I get back to normal. Who knows how long that will take?

When your husband dies, you hear the same three words over, and over, and over. Not 'I'm so sorry,' or even 'How are you?' It's 'Take some time!' People are still, constantly, offering me time, as though it's theirs to share with me, to bestow upon me, like a bowl of roast potatoes. I must make sure I take some time! As much time as I need!

I'd rather have the potatoes, to be honest.

As I told Jeremy and Annabel and Constance and Grace, the only sensible thing to do with grief is to literally work my way through it. Time is the enemy, and I'd rather not have any to spare.

Fortunately, today that is not a problem. When I reach the revolving doors of the Shrinkr building, I'm eight minutes late. By the time I step out of the lift and into Reception, I'm twelve minutes late.

'Katherine!' Jeremy is waiting and ready to pounce. He's in his pale pink shirt, which means he's about to meet a very specific sort of client. The kind that will say, with a straight face, 'We're completely organic – but we're funky with it.' The kind that knows Jeremy from family parties, because he went to school with their dad.

'Good morning!' I say, smiling. 'Nice to see—'

He grabs my elbow and wrinkles his nose. 'What are you doing? What are you *wearing*?'

'It's vintage,' I say, tugging at the dress. 'And it's hot out there. I'm going to make a coffee. Do you want one?'

He frowns. The colour on his cheeks and his forehead deepens, turning from vermilion to carmine.

'Oh my God. Have you forgotten? You've forgotten!'

'Of course not,' I say, slowly. 'There's no way I would forget! In fact, maybe you've forgotten that I'm really good at remembering!' What am I saying? I sound ridiculous. I force a laugh until it becomes quite clear that Jeremy wants to kill me.

'Mayburn,' he says, menacingly. 'The Mayburn team is expecting us, in the boardroom, in fourteen minutes. They're really looking forward to seeing your presentation, which you assured me, *less than twenty-four hours ago*, was finished, and polished, and triple checked.'

'Mayburn. Absolutely,' I say.

Oh, God. I *do* remember Jeremy saying something, yesterday. He was very stern, and very intense, but even though I could sense the meaning behind the words – he definitely wanted me to do *something* – I didn't quite catch the task itself. He was standing by the window, and there was a butterfly behind him. The poor thing had somehow got trapped between the layers of glass. I think it was a red admiral. I didn't know how to get it out. Maybe I should check to see if it's still there. I wonder if I could get hold of a chisel, and make a small air hole ...

'Absolutely,' I hear myself repeating. 'Totally prepared.'

Mayburn. May Burn. Is that ... cars? I think that's cars.

Now I remember. Because when the project came in, and we were invited to pitch, I said that I didn't think we should be working with a car company at all. But I was shouted down with phrases like 'flexible' and 'open-minded' and 'six-figure budget'.

'I'll be with you in three minutes,' I say, and walk to my desk. The very worst part of my job is lying in wait for me. My assistant.

'Morning, Lydia!' I say, cheerfully. 'How are you?'

'All ready for Mayburn?' she replies. 'You're cutting it a bit fine. And that's a brave outfit choice for the big meeting!'

Lydia is mean, but accurate. However, this is a bit rich, given she's wearing red salopettes and a lime-green beanie.

All the better to clash dramatically with her trainers, which are road-traffic-accident orange. Apparently, they were made by a group of period poverty activists in Guadalajara. They have a Velcro fastening. They don't look like the kind of shoe you could buy from a shop. They look like the sort of thing that would be prescribed to you, after a horse stood on your foot. They cost £400. (I found this out when she spilled kombucha on them.)

'Yes,' I say. 'So ready. Really excited, actually. Do you have any revisions for the deck before I go in?' Just because I can't remember making a presentation doesn't mean there isn't one. Just because Lydia has never completed an assigned task on time before doesn't mean she won't surprise me today.

'You didn't send it over, remember?' she says. 'I asked you about it yesterday, and you said it was all sorted.' There's a gleam in her eye, and I don't like it. I suspect she knows exactly what she's doing – or rather, what I haven't done. And she has no plans to help me out. Even though I've lied to save her so many times that I've started to think of her 'dentist' as an imaginary friend.

'Ah, yes,' I say. 'Of course I did. Sorry.' This isn't Lydia's fault. I can't hate her for not reading a deck I didn't send. I am a good person, and when other people challenge me, I respond with compassion and patience. Lydia is a human being. May she be well. May she be happy. May she be free from suffering. May she be less insufferable. Oh, hell. Never mind.

'You've been forgetting a *lot* of stuff, lately,' Lydia says, her voice pregnant with concern. 'Do you think you have early onset dementia? I saw this YouTube series about how your brain cells start dying, once you've turned thirty ...'

The thing about Lydia is that she's the rudest person I've ever met – but whenever I call her out, *she* gets offended. On this occasion, it's easiest to pretend that my old age is also making me hard of hearing.

I lean over my desk, without sitting down, and take a deep breath. There must be a presentation here somewhere. There has to be. The mental fog is thickening. I try to picture myself doing the work, coming up with ideas. I look around for open notebooks, scribbled memos. I retrieve a large piece of rice cake from the leaves of a cheese plant. Now is not the time to panic. If I keep a cool, clear head, I'll be able to deliver *something*. To be honest, with the bigger clients, the messaging tends towards the generic. I can do this in my sleep. It's an hour of smiling and chanting. I know the magic words Energy, synergy, strategy, integrity, liberty. Harrods. Selfridges. John Lewis. Shit. *Focus, Katherine.*

I search my emails for MAYBURN. Here we go. Mayburn Presentation. Aha! I sent this to myself three weeks ago. I'm ahead of the game! I completed it, way ahead of schedule, and then moved straight on to my next task. Of course I did.

'Wish me luck!' The relief is coursing through my body. As if I'd have forgotten! Everything is going to be fine.

Chapter Two

His holiness, the Dalai Llama

When I get to the boardroom, Jeremy is waiting for me. He stands up when I enter. He's flanked by a pair of white men, in identical pale pink shirts. 'Katherine, finally!' he says. His smile doesn't reach his eyes – in fact, it barely reaches his teeth. 'The woman of the hour is gracing us with her presence. Katherine, I don't think you've had the pleasure of meeting the Mayburn team in person!'

'Arlo.' Arlo says his name, then looks me up and down, and I know he's thinking, *Six. Possibly a seven if she was wearing a bit more make-up, it's hard to tell what her tits are like.* He lingers on the hem of my dress and spends a good twenty seconds shaking the hair out of his eyes before he deigns to shake my hand. His trousers are cut to reveal quite a lot of bare ankle. This man is more tassel than loafer, figuratively and literally.

'And this, would you believe it, is Jeremy!' says Jeremy. 'Har har har!'

I stare at Jeremy, trying to find something on his face to connect with. He's completely nondescript. His hair is neither grey, nor black, nor brown. There is nothing of interest here. No spectacles, unremarkable eyebrows, nothing in the plane of his cheeks or the curve of his lips that would make you look twice. And yet I know all about him, or I could certainly make a few educated guesses. His great-grandfather invented the petrol pump. He lives in Richmond but keeps a five-million-pound apartment somewhere in the city. He's never done his own laundry. If he wanted to, he could probably send out a company-wide email with the subject 'You're invited to a naked cocaine orgy. Bring guns', and he wouldn't get fired.

'Jeremy, goodness!' I say. 'Another one! Hello! What a coincidence! Did you know that we have three Jeremys working in Shrinkr senior management?' And they're all white. There's only one woman, and one black person, and they're the same person. Akila – the person I'd like to be when I grow up. And she's a reason to get it together for Mayburn. If I can be half as confident and composed as she is, I'll nail this.

'Right, the presentation!' I dim the lights, open my laptop and click on the email attachment. The word 'MAYBURN' fills the wall. I'm relieved to see that the Shrinkr branding is present and correct. I'm sure that the contents will come back to me, any minute.

'So, we're thrilled that you're potentially interested in partnering with us to deliver both an internal Corporate Social Responsibility strategy, as well as some new environmentally focused branding,' I say, and click to the first slide. This also says 'MAYBURN' and under it 'something here'.

'Katherine, are you sure this is the correct presentation?' says Jeremy.

'Absolutely.' I smile. 'Because "something here" obviously means ...' I think quickly ... 'Yes! Planet Earth. There is something here!' I sweep my arm across the room to indicate the table, the chairs, the gurgling water cooler. 'Nature's beauty is all around us. And ...' If I keep talking, I'm bound to say something with a bit of substance. '... and a key Mayburn brand value is appreciating the Earth. People buy your cars in order to explore the planet. They want to be brave and drive to beautiful places. So we think "something here" really underpins that value. It's about protecting our greatest shared asset, while enjoying the asset of a Mayburn car.'

Jeremy – Mayburn Jeremy – looks perplexed. 'Well, a car can't *be* an asset, because it always depreciates in value ...'

I click to the next slide. It's a quote. '"Look at situations from more angles, and you will become more open" – the Dalai Lama.'

Oh my God. I have absolutely no idea what this means. I don't know what I was *thinking*. I breathe in and breathe out. If I concentrate really hard, I can travel back in time to the moment when I put this mad draft together – and work out where I was going. I can paint a picture with words. I can still salvage it.

'So obviously, when people are driving a Mayburn car, they're on a *journey*,' I say. If I speak really slowly, I might be able to buy myself enough time to string this into something meaningful. 'And why do we go on journeys? Because we want to grow, and change.'

Jeremy – *my* Jeremy – is mouthing something at me. I think it's 'Are you stoned?'

'These beautiful words from the Dalai Lama really

anchor the strategy,' I say. 'Because – because – broadly, we need to rethink travel.' Oh! I have it! 'I mean, the best and boldest way for Mayburn to change the world, with their customer base, is to drive less! So we're thinking about different angles – essentially going *beyond the car!*'

Everyone looks stunned. Clearly, I've said something revelatory. They're totally shocked. As am I, to be honest. This is going surprisingly well. I may be a conceptual genius.

Eventually, Arlo speaks. 'Yah, no, that Disney thing, it's not working for me. It's confusing me. It's not really Mayburn.'

'I'm sorry, did you say Disney?' I say. I can't have heard right. 'What do you mean by Disney?'

'The talking llama thing,' says Arlo. 'I mean, there might be some copyright issues there, for starters.'

'Talking ... llama,' I say. If I stretch out the syllables, Arlo's words will start to make sense.

'The Dalai Llama, yah?' says Arlo. 'From *The Emperor's New Groove?*'

'No, his holiness, the Dalai Lama,' I whisper. 'Spiritual leader of the Tibetan people.' And a funny thing starts to happen. The walls begin to move. I grip the table for support, and it seems to slide into goo as my fingers fall through the air. 'The Dalai Lama is a holy monk. Not a ... cartoon!' I can't seem to regulate the sound of my voice, because I'm not sure where it's coming from. I'm either whispering or shouting. 'WHY IS IT SO HOT IN HERE? Did someone move the carpet?' Everything I can see shimmers and flickers, before turning to black.

When I open my eyes, I'm flat on my back. I can count four faces floating above me. Jeremy, Jeremy, Jeremy – and Akila. Mercifully, Mayburn Jeremy is absent.

I touch my forehead, which is slick and slippery. I try to wipe my fingers on the skirt of my dress, and encounter soft, white wool. 'My cardigan,' says Akila. 'An emergency blanket.' It might be my imagination, but her eyes seem to flick across the Jeremys and their suit jackets.

'Oh my God,' I moan. 'Did I faint? And when I fell, my dress ...'

Akila shakes her head. 'Don't worry about it, you're not very well.'

My Jeremy snorts. 'Believe me, showing your knickers to the Mayburn team was probably the best way to end that meeting.'

Oh no. Oh, no.

I sit up, slowly. Akila looks at the Jeremys, rolls her eyes, and then goes to the water cooler. She pours a cup, and hands it to me. 'How are you feeling?' she asks.

It's rare for me to get this much direct attention from Akila. She's my work crush. We all want her, we all want to be her. I've fantasised about bumping into her in the coffee shop, or chatting in the lift, and impressing her. Showing her that I'm tenacious, talented and incredibly cool under pressure.

So of course I burst into tears.

'Katherine, do you feel well enough to sit up? Do you think you need to go to hospital?' asks Akila. 'Do you think you're able to get into a chair?'

Using my elbows, I push myself into a sitting position. As I sip the water, I try to work out how I'm feeling. 'I'm fine, I think. Just a bit hot.' If I'm about to die of anything, it's shame. 'I think I must have fainted.'

'We're sending you home,' says My Jeremy, brusquely.

'No.' I shake my head. 'That's really kind, but that's not necessary. I think I just overheated. Anyway, I need to apologise to the Mayburn team, and I've got some important Woodland Trust notes to pull together ahead of the meeting tomorrow ...'

Akila squats down and offers me her hand. 'Listen, we've all been talking – I think you should be sitting up for this.' I let her pull me to my feet. I wobble for a fraction of a second, before I manage to grab the chrome frame of a heavy boardroom chair. As I slide it out, I stub my toe.

'Are you sure you're OK?' Akila asks again.

'Fine! Never better!' A bead of blood is forming under the strap of my sandal.

Akila sits beside me, and the Jeremys arrange themselves into a corporate constellation. Senior Jeremy is at the head of the table. Odd, posh Jeremy sits opposite him – because he doesn't believe in formal professional hierarchy. (Other women in the office have told me that he doesn't believe in monogamy or biology either. Not a fan of the condom, Posh Jeremy.) And My Jeremy sits opposite me, and glowers.

The trouble with bad bosses is that they're like bad boyfriends. One day they're all over you, then suddenly, they've completely gone off you, and it's impossible to work out what you did, and when you did it, no matter how desperately you beg them to tell you. He's shuffling a sheaf of papers. I thought they must be something to do with Mayburn, or even his next meeting, but he's opening them and looking straight at me. Shit.

'Katherine, according to the information I have here, you took three days of compassionate leave after your bereavement.'

'*Four*,' I say, insistently. 'Because as soon as I came in on the Monday, I went straight home again.'

The most senior Jeremy starts to speak. 'It's clear to all of us that you haven't been yourself lately. Since the, ah, unpleasantness.'

'What unpleasantness? You mean, in the meeting?' I rub my head, I think I can feel a bump forming.

'No, you know,' says Jeremy. 'The awful, terrible, thing, a few months ago, your poor husband, the event …' When I don't acknowledge Ben, he turns to Posh Jeremy, frowning, and hisses (though notably still loud enough for me to hear): 'That was *her*, wasn't it? Didn't we send some M&S vouchers?'

My Jeremy clears his throat. 'You had a meeting with HR, and it was recommended that you take at least a month off before making a phased return to work, with part-time hours. You were also supposed to be having monthly meetings with HR, and regular check-ins with your line manager.' Jeremy taps the papers against the desk and clears his throat. 'When did you last see HR?'

'Look, you don't understand,' I say. I look at my foot. The blood has started to forge a path towards my big toe. 'I don't need HR. They make things really awkward. I mean,' I say hurriedly, 'I'm sure they're great when you need them, for tribunals and things! Proper things! But with me, it's all boxes of tissues and "how *are* you?" and the head tilt.'

'The what?' Posh Jeremy looks up from his phone, from the end of the table.

'You know, the owl thing.' I demonstrate, slowly turning my chin 90 degrees, and resting my head on my right shoulder. 'It's what people do when they feel awkward but know they should say something sympathetic.'

'Listen, Katherine,' says Akila, 'the point is that everyone here wants to give you all of the support that you need, but Shrinkr can't do that if you don't ask for it.'

'I don't need any support, honestly.' I fold my arms. 'I'm seeing a therapist, and I'm happy to be at the office as much as possible. Work is the best place for me. In fact, I should say thank you,' I say, hurriedly. 'For the distraction.' Because when I'm in this building, I can pretend that nothing bad has happened, and none of my problems really exist. I'm definitely not in denial. I'm just grieving efficiently. Productively.

'Katherine, the quality of your work has deteriorated significantly over the last six months,' says My Jeremy. 'You've always been incredibly detail oriented. But now, basic things aren't getting done. It's as though we can't get through to you. Lydia has said that she's getting very little from you in the way of input, and it's your job to manage her.'

'That treacherous ...!' I exclaim, before putting my hand over my mouth. I'm *furious*. It's not as though Lydia ever did anything I asked her to when I was at the peak of my powers.

'You've been under a lot of stress, Katherine. All of this is completely understandable. But we're recommending that you take a mandatory sabbatical. We're giving you two months off, with full pay. We don't want to lose you,' says Akila.

It's over. My whole career is over. I can feel the panic rising in my chest. 'Listen, I know I've not been at my best, but I promise I can work harder. I can turn it around. I'll get back to my desk immediately, and stay late tonight—'

'Katherine, you need to trust us,' says Akila. 'You're not

well at the moment. You owe it to yourself to take the time to get better, and frankly, you owe it to all of us. This time is a gift. Use it to process, use it to recalibrate. Go away somewhere and relax. I can't imagine what you've been through, but I also think that as long as you're at the office, you're not really going through it.'

'We've already arranged for HR to send all the relevant forms to your home address, so you don't need to see them again. You can go now,' says My Jeremy, almost kindly.

I smile. I nod. I smile again. I look at the group of people staring at me. My boss. His boss. My role model – No. 3 on *Forbes*' list of Ten Women to Watch Right Now. And a man who stands to inherit the Duchy of Northumberland.

I can see myself through their eyes. I'm bright red and dripping with sweat. This dress stinks. Perhaps it's cursed. Maybe people kept giving it away because it's unlucky. You try so hard to do the right thing, the sustainable thing, and shop second-hand, and this is where it gets you. I smell of forty years' worth of bad dates and disappointment. I can't be the first woman to wear the dress, then have a breakdown.

There are so many things I want to say. I could tell them that Shrinkr won't last a week without me. They'll be sorry they did this. I'll get a new job tomorrow, a better one. Maybe the Dalai Lama himself will hire me. I should just quit. That's what they all want, isn't it? I stand up, preparing to say something cutting. Something deadly.

'Please, take good care of yourself, Katherine. Rest. We want you to feel better,' says Akila, and her kindness undoes me. Quietly, meekly, for the second time that day, I throw up in my own mouth.

Chapter Three

'She has always been a bit weird'

I can't believe they want to get rid of me. And they're *paying* me, too, so I can't really complain. I can't sue them. Why do bad things always happen to me?

First, I lose my husband. Then, I lose my job. Then, I hide in a toilet cubicle to recover my composure, and I have to pick the one with no toilet paper. Typical Katherine. Usually, I come prepared. I always have a pack of tissues in my handbag. But all I can find is receipts for stuff I don't remember buying. There's one from Chicken Cottage in here. I don't even eat meat. Weird. Maybe I've been the victim of a reverse thief? Someone stole my wallet and hid their old papers in it. It's got to be some kind of incredibly complex identity theft scam. There's even a Chicken Cottage napkin in here. Damn, they're good.

I'm about to get up and wash my face, when I hear voices through the door.

'She's a bit crap, isn't she?' says Holly, a newish recruit that Lydia seems to have adopted. I'm not being paranoid. She's definitely talking about me. 'And weird.'

'Actually, she never used to be crap. If anything, she took everything too seriously,' Lydia replies. I hear her opening the cubicle door beside mine. I lift my legs up, trying to stay hidden. 'Although, since her husband died she's been all over the place. She was not ready for that Mayburn pitch this morning, and she's had a lock-in with senior management since. I think they might have fired her. But yes, she *has* always been a bit weird.'

'Oooh, will you get her job?' asks Holly. I can hear her *peeing*.

'Hope so,' says Lydia. 'The pay rise would be nice. Although she does have all the shitty clients. I'm not sure I could be enthusiastic about hedgehogs, or earwigs, or whatever that stupid woodland thing is.'

I hear flushing and giggling, and then the sound of the hand dryer. Eventually it stops. I hear the door opening again. I think the women have left.

It takes me a minute to get to my feet. I'm shaking. I splash water on my face. I breathe in. I breathe out. I still smell of vomit.

I want to march back into the office and fight for my job. I'm the only one in the building who really cares. I believe in Shrinkr's mission statement. I believe in hedgehogs. They can't keep me out. I can't wake up tomorrow morning and have nowhere to go, and nothing to do. It's unthinkable. If I'm not in the office, I don't have a point. I don't have a purpose.

But I have to go home. My shower is there. My toothbrush is there. I'm in no position to fight for anything, smelling like this. I'll go home, wash, nap, and make a brand-new plan.

I can hear a voice in my head. *Katherine, babe. Calm down. Just concentrate on getting home. Get some rest. Don't worry about anything else.*

'Piss off, Ben.' I say it out loud. Lydia is right, I suppose. I have always been a bit weird.

Chapter Four

The party

Grace had been insistent on hearing about how Ben and I got together. She kept calling it our 'origin story'.

'Going back to the beginning gives us a bit of framework. In this room, with me, you can relive those happy memories and contextualise them in a safe way.' Then she chewed her pen. 'I'm a Marvel fan, and I think a lot about how superheroes all have tragic origin stories, or complicated ones. The rest of us develop coping skills and strategies in the way that these characters develop superpowers. If we talk about how you and Ben met, it will tell me more about who you were inside the relationship, and how you can cope outside it.'

I'd shrugged. 'The usual way, you know. He was a friend of a friend, I guess.' Because I was hardly going to tell my therapist that I'd been drunk and dressed as a bunny girl, wearing Annabel's second-best bra.

Like all the best love stories, it began with an act of emotional blackmail.

It was October, a month I always looked forward to, and longed for. The skies darkened. The temperature dropped.

And I felt able to embrace my true nature. My mother died when I was little, and I never knew my father; as ridiculous as it sounds, I sometimes suspected that he had been a vole or a dormouse. October was my pre-hibernation period. I liked to fill the freezer with stew and stockpile my thickest jumpers and longest socks. Finally, after the social tyranny of summer, no one expected me to spend my spare time in a beer garden.

Also, I'd broken up with Sean a few months ago. I'd barely noticed that I was going out with Sean, to be completely honest. It was one of those vague, post-graduation things where I was drunk for months at a time, and when I looked up I was sober, hungover, and going out with the world's dullest man. It was a human version of continental drift. I couldn't even call it a fling. That made it sound passionate and impulsive. I suspect that we were unwitting victims of a series of two-for-one offers. We'd go for two-for-one pizza on a Monday, and then buy our two-for-one cinema tickets on a Wednesday. Then, after about six months, we were informed that the restaurant had finished the deal and we had to pay the full price. That was when Sean said, 'This isn't really working, is it?'

But the break-up was great, because it meant that Annabel could sometimes be persuaded to stay at home and eat ice cream with me. All I had to do was look wistful, and say, 'I'm just feeling a bit sad about Sean,' and I'd be excused from the rooftop rave in Clapton, or whatever it was that she had planned for us. But she *loved* going out, and she longed for me to love it too. Annabel loved autumn as much as me – but to her it meant sequins, fairy lights and cocktails that tasted of cough medicine.

She'd walked through the door, letting in a cool, sweet blast of woodsmoke, and said, 'RIGHT.' There's a certain sort of person who announces their arrival by saying 'RIGHT' – they are usually very good at making their friends do things they don't actually want to do.

Her bright green coat was still buttoned. I was hovering near the kettle, but she opened the fridge and pulled out a bottle of Pinot Grigio. 'Hallowe'en is almost upon us, and we're going out out.'

'Where did that wine come from?' I said, confused. 'I didn't think there was any left. That's not like us, not to finish a bottle. Anyway, we can't go out tonight.' I wrapped my arms around my body, and squeezed myself, for warmth. 'It's *Bake Off.*'

'Not tonight. Saturday. Tom and the uni lot are having a Hallowe'en house party. A proper one. I think Hot Ben is coming down for it, do you remember? He went off to Hong Kong for a bit, something to do with his dad. It's going to be a real reunion.' Annabel sipped her wine. 'Do you want to be a French maid, or a bunny girl?'

'Can I be the girl in pyjamas and a dressing gown who goes home at 8 p.m. to watch *Practical Magic*?' I whined. 'Anyway, Bel, I was never really *in* that group, they're all so full on.' I decided to play my only card. 'And I only just broke up with Sean! I need more time.'

'You did not "only just break up" with Sean,' said Annabel. 'I'm pretty sure that *you dumped him* just after the clocks went forward. And they're about to go back again. And you told me the sex was very bad. If you go to this party, your odds of having great sex will increase significantly. Plus, I won't go without you. And I *have* to go, because this might be my very last chance to get off with Tom.'

'Annabel, how many times have you got off with Tom before?' I started to count and ran out of fingers. 'I make it at least fourteen, if you count the ball when he had to stop and puke in the fountain. You told me that he sucked your chin! And what about the chewing gum thing?'

'What chewing gum thing?' she asked, confused.

'You know! When he left his chewing gum in, when he was going down on you.'

'Are you sure that was me?' Annabel frowned.

'I had to help you get it *out*! Do you not remember the lube? The gloves?'

'Oh, yeah.' She nodded. 'And one day, I shall do the same for you. I'm pretty sure that's the sort of thing that happens to everyone at least once. You're a very good friend. And if you come to the Hallowe'en party, the universe will deliver you a karmic reward.'

'Fine,' I say, finishing my wine. 'I'll go to the stupid party. But I reserve the right to leave when I want. And don't get off with Tom if he's chewing something.'

'I can make no promises,' said Annabel. 'And we're going as bunny girls. I'll sort the costumes.'

The date of the party loomed, as though it was an exam. And when I started to think of it in those terms, I cheered up a bit. Firstly, all I had to do was pass, by going to the party. Secondly, this was a rare chance for me to do something nice for Annabel. I owed her. I felt as though I was going to be forever in her debt. When my grandmother died, a lot of people said 'Just let me know if you need anything!' and I never heard from them again. Annabel just kept coming over with home-made soup. It was the loveliest shock. I didn't know her that well, then. I thought she was the person you called if you wanted to get hold of some drugs. Not chicken and noodles in a Thermos.

On Saturday, at 5 p.m., I heard a knock on my bedroom door. It was Annabel, in a cream silk dressing gown, holding her curling tongs and a bushel of ears. 'Happy Hallowe'en!' she shouted. 'Or as I call it, Sexy Christmas! I've come to zhuzh you! I have extra false eyelashes, *and* I've brought an extra bra for you.'

'Why? I have plenty of bras!' I said, confused.

'You do. I've seen them all, and that's why I brought reinforcements. Now, what are we thinking? You've got those nice black high-waisted shorts, maybe with a pair of fishnets ... '

'What black shorts?' Annabel opened a drawer, and rummaged around for a bit, before pulling out a pair of knickers. 'Dude, I'm *not* wearing those.'

Eventually we agreed on a compromise. Our hair was sprayed, tonged and sprayed again. I wore Annabel's bra with my emergency job interview trouser suit and went as Business Bunny. Annabel wore two pairs of false eyelashes, and very little else, and went as Classic Bunny. 'If we don't pull tonight, it won't be our fault,' she said. 'You can keep that bra. Your tits look excellent.'

She looked in the mirror and hoicked hers up – a quick pat and jiggle, evoking a certain sort of man in a certain sort of pub fondling his car keys after finishing his pint. Passing a thumb along the BMW logo, for luck. Annabel had BMW breasts, no doubt about it. Not subtle. But coveted volubly by many men. Their value was indisputable.

I looked down at my own. It didn't matter what Annabel said, I felt pretty insecure about them. What was that car they made everyone drive in the Soviet Union? Or the one with three wheels, that chases Mr Bean?

She grinned at me. 'Come on. Tonight, Katherine is back. We have just enough time for a very quick glass of wine before we have to get the bus. Stop fiddling with your ears. You'll mess your hair up!'

'Do I have to wear the ears at the bus stop?' I said, sulkily.

'Trust me, you'll feel underdressed without them.'

She was right. We were on the top deck with another three bunnies, a sexy cat, Dracula, and someone who claimed to be Eddie the Eagle. (He said his actual skis were in his brother's loft, he'd spent most of the afternoon constructing the cardboard ones he was carrying. Everyone on the bus admired the skis. We were all complicit in the same lie, but it really seemed to help Eddie's self-esteem.)

The bus journey started to feel quite cheerful. When we got stuck in traffic, a different Bunny produced a bottle of wine from her handbag and passed out disposable cups. At first, I shook my head. 'Single-use plastic is the number one cause of environmental—' Annabel elbowed me hard in the nipple. The pain sliced through my coat, my suit jacket and the borrowed bra. 'That's really kind of you, me and Katherine will share!' She grabbed the cup and passed it to me, whispering, 'Dude. It's Saturday. Have a night off, for the love of God. Or Jack Skellington.'

The wine was warm and syrupy, and I knocked it back. 'Sorry,' I murmured. 'You see, this is why I didn't want to come tonight. I always say the wrong thing. You were born to be social. I'm missing the magic gene.' A seed of fear started to sprout in my gut, its tendrils rushing up to my throat and trailing all the way down to my toes. I felt anxious in my ankles; that was a first. 'What if I'm in the corner, all night? What if I try to be brave and start a conversation with someone and they laugh at me?'

'You don't need to be brave.' Annabel shook her head. 'You know these people. It's just the old uni gang.'

'That doesn't help.' I winced, thinking of the 'old gang' – dirty pints and drinking songs and boys that would break off in the middle of a conversation to take their shirt off if they thought they heard the *Baywatch* theme. Even if you were in Starbucks with them at three o'clock in the afternoon. 'I'm not sure that anyone from the old gang would piss on me if I was on fire.'

'That's because you didn't get to know them. You were either hiding behind your hair, or hiding in the toilets,' said Annabel. 'You're a hidden gem. And now you're going to dazzle everyone who didn't get to know you before. You're one of a kind, a classic.'

'You're drunk.' In fairness, I wasn't really sober enough to make any accusations. What was in that wine?

'I know, but ... OK, how about this? You're my friend. I can see how great you are. When you go out and hug the wall and don't talk to people and act as though you're not a pleasure to spend time with, you are insulting my good taste.'

She reached into her coat – I assumed this was a last-minute bra shuffle, but she pulled out a small silver flask and passed it to me.

34

'What is this?' I wiped my mouth with the back of my hand. 'It tastes of bark.'

'Not sure,' she said, before swallowing and grimacing. 'It was a fiver from the shop at the top of the road. I think the man said something about wormwood. Now, Katherine, listen to me. What do you think everyone else at the party is doing right now?'

'The macarena? Cards Against Humanity? Spooky pinata?'

'They're drinking.' Annabel didn't say 'duh!' but she was definitely thinking it. 'Most of them probably started at lunchtime. No one is going to be in any fit state to judge you. If you say something stupid, they won't care and they won't remember. You could probably meet a guy and deliver a ninety-minute lecture about the climate emergency, and he'll wake up and think he had a bad dream about the apocalypse. Obviously, try not to do that.' The bus started to turn a corner, and she pressed a bell.

It was easy for her to say. My apocalypse was imminent. It roiled behind Tom's front door.

Annabel knocked at number 42 – which suggested that life, the universe and everything could be found within this house. Was that a conversation starter, or a nerdy detail that only a weird girl would know? I might meet the Douglas Adams fan of my dreams, or I might be directed to the Dungeons and Dragons party that was happening two doors down. (I'd never played Dungeons and Dragons, but maybe I should start.)

'Waaaaaaaaaaay!' We were greeted by a skeleton wearing bunny ears. 'Annabel! And, ah, Annabel's mate!'

'You remember Katherine!' Annabel stood on her tiptoes

to kiss the skeleton. I waved, wiggling my fingers, feeling exactly like a minor member of the royal family who had been sent to open an abattoir.

'Drinks!' said the skeleton, grabbing Annabel's thigh and pushing her through the hall. 'Was that Tom?' I whispered. 'And was he making a spooky noise, or is that just how he says hello?'

'No, that was Tommo,' said Annabel. 'He lived with Tom in second year and tried to start that business, do you remember? He was going to sell shots that came in spherical containers. The idea was that the bars would install marble runs . . . I can't think why it didn't take off. And that's how he says hello.'

The kitchen was full of bunnies. The sitting room was full of bunnies. When I put my coat upstairs, I noticed that every other person in the line for the bathroom was wearing white fluffy ears.

'I didn't realise that the bunny thing was an official theme,' I shouted to Annabel.

'It isn't!' she replied. 'Ann Summers was doing a two-for-one. I wish I'd known, I bought ours from China. The shipping cost a fortune.' She brought her hand to her mouth. 'Shit! I mean, I looked in all the charity shops first, and I tried to make some ears . . . '

'It's OK . . . ' I sighed. 'What's done is done. We'll just have to be bunnies again next year. And the year after that.' All I ever asked of Annabel was that she remembered her water bottle and turned the lights off before she left the flat. She treated me like the environment police.

'Honestly, K, you should have *seen* my attempts. The first one looked almost human. The next one was close, more of a hare ... ' She broke off and looked at me. 'I think I hear the "Monster Mash".'

She grabbed my hand, and we took the stairs two at a time.

I love the 'Monster Mash'.

It's the best song to dance to because you don't have to be sexy. You don't have to be anything. The beat is irresistible. I've tried yoga, breathwork, tantric YouTube, meditation, you name it, and I can confidently say that nothing puts me in my body like the 'Monster Mash'.

We walked into the sitting room – the one place in the house that anyone had made any attempt to decorate. A line of bat bunting fell from the middle of the ceiling to the floor. I assumed it had come loose, but maybe it was meant to evoke chaos and decay. The sofa had been pushed back against the wall and shrouded in a white sheet. It looked like a ghost sofa, *and* it was protected from spilled drinks. I recognised the red, chilli-shaped fairy lights that were hung over the mantelpiece, from every student bedroom I'd ever been in. The room was choked with the ghosts of parties past, suffocated by them. This was just a repeat of every single college Hallowe'en party I'd ever been to.

For a moment, I felt depressed. We were supposed to be growing up, maturing, *blossoming*. But in the year since we graduated, I'd gone backwards. I'd made the big move to London, but I wasn't really living. When my nanna died, I promised myself that I was going to really *live*. No one was there to criticise me and complain, to say my skirt was too short, the room was too warm, and everything was too expensive. I was free. I was going to be more Annabel. Instead, I'd hidden under Annabel's coat – not just metaphorically.

I'd let myself drift into a relationship based on a mutual fondness for pizza! Pizza wasn't even my *favourite* food!

At student parties, I'd always been a mouse. But tonight, I was a Bunny. So I grinned at Annabel, jumped up and down, and started doing an extremely stupid dance of my own invention, with slightly less self-awareness than the inflatable waving balloon men that live outside used car dealerships. I rode the beat, evoking Wolf Man, and Dracula's Son. There were jazz hands and spirit fingers. And maybe ninety seconds in, I realised that I was being watched.

This could not be good. Was everyone looking at me? Were they all laughing? Like a child, I squeezed my eyes shut, feeling my face growing redder and redder in the dark. But I kept going. I was Moira Shearer in *The Red Shoes*, cursed to keep dancing until the music stopped. But with zombie arms.

Then I felt a warm hand on my elbow. It slid to my wrist, encircling it, before raising my hand above my head, and leading me into a spin. Annabel? The hand felt too big for Annabel's. It scratched slightly, but not unpleasantly. The skin under the knuckles was ever so slightly rough. I looked up over my head and followed the hand to a muscular arm, a broad shoulder, and a smiling face.

'I LOVE THIS SONG!' said the face.

The chillies were giving out just enough light for me to take it in. Floppy hair, a full mouth, small eyes – horribly handsome, but happy handsome. I imagined that he was in the habit of approaching strangers and shouting out his enthusiasms. Had we been in an art gallery, if I'd been standing in front of Whistler's Mother in a state of quiet contemplation, I'd have forgiven him for yelling 'I LOVE THIS PAINTING!'

Even so, my first instinct was to run away. Or to say, 'I think you want my friend Annabel. She's the hot one.' But I bit my lip. We had at least a minute left, and this beautiful boy wanted to dance the Monster Mash with me. I already had more in common with him than I did with Sean. So I said 'ME TOO!' and hopped from foot to foot, bouncing and wiggling. And when the song finished, I took a deep breath, crossed my fingers, and said, 'DO YOU WANT TO GET A DRINK?'

'I WOULD LOVE THAT! I'M BEN!' He picked up my hand, as if to shake it, and he did not let go.

In the kitchen, we found some bottles of beer that were almost cold, and Ben produced a bottle opener from his pocket. 'That's very organised,' I said.

'I'm not usually like this, but I moved house today. This was one of the last things I unpacked, and I thought it might come in handy,' he explained.

'Happy moving day!' I replied. 'Is that why you've got all of that fluff on your jumper?' I picked a white wisp off his elbow.

'No, that's my costume. I was supposed to be a mummy, but most of the toilet paper fell off before I got here.' Ben tapped the top of his head. 'Tom gave me a Frankenstein mask, but I seem to have lost it. Shall we go outside?'

Out in the fresh air, I groaned with relief, like a zombie who had died all over again. We sat on the garden wall. I unbuttoned my jacket and spread it out so we could both sit on it. The cool air felt delicious on my skin. 'Ahhh! That's better!'

It occurred to me that I could feel quite a lot of cool air

on my skin. And then I realised why. 'Shit!' I jumped to my feet. 'I'm topless! I forgot!'

Ben burst out laughing. 'How did you forget?' He stood up. 'I suppose I have to be a gentleman and let you put your jacket back on. Damn my good manners.' He lifted the jacket off the wall and draped it over my shoulders. 'There are so many things I want to say, but the polite thing to do would be to compliment your tailor.'

At the other end of the garden, I saw three bunnies smoking. They were all wearing stockings, suspenders and nipple tassels. 'I suppose, even without the jacket, I'm kind of overdressed. How do you know Tom?'

'Not that well, to be honest. I was in the same year as his brother Miles – I knew Miles from school, and we ended up at uni together. I got back from Hong Kong a couple of months ago, and now ...' He shrugged. 'It's as though I've forgotten everything I ever knew. Everything I say sounds strange. When I told Tom how cool it was that he lived at No. 42 ...'

'Life, the universe and everything!' I said excitedly. '*The Hitchhiker's Guide to the Galaxy*!'

'Exactly!' Ben nodded. '*You* know! Tom just looked at me as though I'd started speaking in an alien language. Which is apropos, I suppose.' He smiled and took my hand again. 'I don't even know your name.'

'Katherine,' I said, after a moment. I'd briefly lost track of what Ben was saying, because I loved listening to the sound of his voice. It was so *warm*. It was almost posh, adjacent to posh, but really without any accent at all. He sounded as though he never stopped smiling. He sounded like someone who would watch his whole house fall down around him, and then say, 'Well, we can't stay in, so we might as well go out for lunch.'

'Katherine, how do you know Tom? Do you live in London? What do you do?' He gestured to the jacket, the ears. 'I assume you're in the rabbit business.'

'I don't really know Tom, either,' I said. 'But my friend Annabel is embroiled in a long-standing flirtation with him.'

Ben laughed. 'I love that! You sound like an Agatha Christie book. Tell me you're a 1940s BBC announcer.'

'I wish,' I said. 'I just started a new job at a start-up called Shrinkr. They work with businesses – trying to get them to implement better sustainability policies, so that when they boast about being environmentally friendly, they're telling the truth.' Even though it was dark, I knew Ben could see me blushing. 'Sorry, I'm a bit of a nerd about that sort of thing. It's my big passion. But I've only got a six-month contract. Maybe I'll be returning to Rabbits Incorporated before I know it.'

'That's really cool,' said Ben, putting an arm around my shoulder. I allowed myself to relax into his warmth. Nothing like this had ever happened to me before, and it was thrilling. This was flirting! I was doing it! It turned out that it didn't have to be a complicated series of confusing signals and second-guesses. I realised that I almost always felt slightly scared of something – but beside Ben, all that free-floating fear dissolved. I couldn't believe this was happening. And at a Hallowe'en party, of all things!

'It's brilliant to be doing something you love, and something that's changing the world for the better. I don't think it's nerdy at all.' He grinned. 'I wish I could get paid for my passion. I'm a sailor. Sadly, I have to work in stupid insurance to pay for the gear. That's what I was doing in Hong Kong. My dad's out there – not that I ever saw him, we were all working fifteen-hour days.'

'Well, I suppose you have to pay for all the, um, gilets,' I say. 'Is that what you need, for sailing? I've never been.'

'I'll take you!' said Ben.

'Oh! I'd really love that!' I said, startled. What did I do now? Did I tell him that I'd meet him at the nearest reservoir at 10 a.m. sharp next Saturday? 'Anyway, you said you've just moved house! Where have you moved to? What's it like?'

'Well, to my mother's consternation, it's in Peckham ...' Ben's hand was still on my shoulder when I heard a woman saying his name. Another bunny was walking towards us, wobbling in vertiginous heels. 'Ben,' she said again. 'You promised me a da-ha-hance.' Even factoring in her extreme drunkenness, she was a perfect doll. Full lips and feathery lashes, ice cream scoop breasts, pearlescent in the moonlight, falling out of a pink corset.

Beside her, I felt like Humpty Dumpty. (I wasn't helping myself by sitting on a wall.) I stood up, and forced myself to smile, pretending to straighten my jacket lapels. I felt very sober, and very cold. *It's not her fault she's gorgeous*, I told myself. *Don't be jealous. Don't be a bitch. Don't point out that half of her false eyelash has come unglued.*

For a happy hour, the natural order of the universe had been reversed. During my brief time with Ben, I'd felt so happy. He was funny and kind – and I couldn't pretend that I wasn't shallow enough to be affected by his extreme handsomeness. But it was his voice I'd fallen for. I wanted to bathe in it. I would have gladly paid him to make a podcast, just for me, maybe with very detailed technical sailing information.

But Bens didn't end up with Katherines. Ben was Ken, and Barbie was standing right in front of me, asking to da-ha-hance.

'Ben, it was so lovely to meet you, but I'd better find Annabel,' I said. 'I'm going home.'

I watched the pocket rocket fall into his arms. Oh well. I thought of Sean. Better to be alone than badly accompanied. I'd had a fun conversation with a lovely man. I was building up my social muscles. At least I could say I was in slightly better shape, party wise. This meant I'd feel a bit less awkward when Annabel inevitably dragged me out so she could get off with Tom on Bonfire Night.

Where was Annabel? There was no sign of her in the kitchen. I tried the sitting room, and I couldn't see her, although I noticed the white sofa sheet was now covered in red wine. She wasn't in the toilet queue, and she wasn't in the bathroom, where I held back the hair of a bunny ballerina, while we waited for a zombie bunny to come back with some water. As I looked in the cabinet for mouthwash, I heard a familiar moan.

'I think someone's having sex!' said the ballerina. 'Listen!' she shushed us, before puking loudly.

Aha. I could just about make out the moaning. If that wasn't Annabel, it was someone who had studied her technique.

'I think that's my friend,' I said, awkwardly. 'Do you think I ought to go and see if she's OK?'

'Honestly, I wouldn't worry.' The zombie had returned with water. 'She's clearly having a brilliant night.'

Having established that the ballerina was OK, I crept out through the hall, towards the door. 'Annabel,' I called. 'It's OK, you don't need to stop, but I'm going in ten minutes. Let me know if you want me to wait – if I don't hear from you, I'll assume you're, er, staying over.'

'HANG ON! I'll be out in a bit!' she called. 'Oh! Oh! Oh!'

At least she hadn't said, 'I'm coming.'

I decided to wait downstairs and give her some privacy. As I descended the staircase, I walked straight into a tall man. 'Katherine!' said the man. 'I've been looking for you!' We stood in the middle, neither up nor down.

'You were looking for me?' Even though I was a step above Ben, he was still taller than me. I didn't feel like Humpty Dumpty any more. 'I thought you and that girl . . . '

'Miles's ex,' he said. 'She's not taken the break-up very well. Listen, I need to get home. My Uber is coming in two minutes. I literally need to make my bed, and I don't know which box my duvet is in. What's your number? I want to take you sailing!' He handed me his phone, and I typed the number in. 'See you soon,' he said, and kissed me very softly on the mouth before bolting down the stairs.

It was as though his lips were laced with a small electric current. I felt jolted, disturbed by a delicious burning sensation. I stood on the stairs for a little longer, smiling and prodding my mouth like an idiot, until Annabel almost knocked me over. She was missing a bunny ear.

'Katherine, what are you doing? Come on, let's go. I think I've finally got Tom out of my system.' She patted herself between her legs and made a face. 'Literally, if I'm honest. I had to have a bit of a rummage. He did the chewing gum thing again.'

Chapter Five

Best friend therapy

'But they haven't actually fired you!' says Annabel, as a
dollop of hummus falls from her Kettle Chip and onto my
sofa. 'Sorry!' She rubs at the hummus and licks her finger.
'You're getting paid holiday, basically. Lots of it. I don't
understand why you're so upset. I think this is a good thing.'

'Leave it,' I say, as she rubs the stain into the weave of
the fabric. 'It's fine, I'll get some bicarb. They've made it
pretty clear that they don't want me there at the moment.
I might as well be fired. It's so humiliating.' Every time I
close my eyes, I get the worm's-eye view of the boardroom
floor – I can see Akila and the Jeremys standing over me,
ready to peck me to death. 'This is the worst thing that's
ever happened to me. It might be the worst thing that has
ever happened to anyone.'

Annabel holds my gaze and raises her eyebrows. She
doesn't say anything. She doesn't have to.

'Oh, you know what I mean,' I say. 'Not the worst thing,
but the most painful, shameful, embarrassing, awkward—'
My flow stops, because Annabel has pushed her hand over

my mouth and shoved a Percy Pig in there. 'Hush now, Katherine. It's OK. I got the vegan ones.' She holds up the packet, to show me. 'Although are you actually vegan right now? I lose track.'

'I'm on a good streak at the moment!' I snap, swallowing hard. As much as I try to keep my diet green, every six months or so I have a run-in with some cheese. I bury my face in a cushion and groan. 'I think I might be beyond sugar. Beyond help. The kitchen recycling system will go to wrack and ruin. Lydia will steal my job, and she'll be really bad at it.' I can't make Annabel understand just how bad it is. 'It's as if Shrinkr have asked for a trial separation, before divorcing me,' I tell the cushion. 'I'm nothing and nobody without my job. I work so hard, and I feel as though I'm being punished for it.'

'Deep breaths. No, not like that, slow and steady. You're hyperventilating. Give me that.' Annabel takes the cushion away from my face. 'Katherine, I promise this isn't a punishment. No one is saying that you don't work hard. Maybe think of this as an emergency stop. You need a break, urgently. Your brain needs a break.'

'Don't you dare tilt your head,' I say. Something feels sharp and strange at the back of my throat. 'If you tilt your head at me, I'll throw you out, and make you buy me a new sofa. Annabel, I need my job. Otherwise, I'll be sitting in my empty house, every day, all alone, and I'll go mad.'

'Then *don't*! Why don't you go on holiday!' Her eyes light up. 'In fact, I'll come with you! We could go to Sandals! We'll go to Jamaica, the Caribbean! I think there's a sale on, no one wants to go in the summer. The best thing for you would be a week in the sun and a load of rum-based cocktails. We'll take a load of trashy novels and get tans. You won't know yourself!'

The trouble is that I know myself all too well.

'Annabel, you're aware of my rules,' I say tightly. 'No amount of rum-based cocktails will get me on a long-haul flight. Didn't you see that programme about the amount of waste generated by all-inclusive resorts? And they treat their employees appallingly!'

Annabel rolls her eyes. 'Not this again. Fine, we'll go to a youth hostel. Are there still youth hostels? We'll get a train to Skegness, no, a series of rail replacement buses. And you can wear a second-hand cagoule, and camp in the grounds to protest the fact that the building was constructed by a slave owner in the sixteen hundreds.'

I pick up the cushion again and squeeze it. 'I know I'm a bore, but the planet—'

'Won't heal itself. I know.' Annabel prods the hummus stain. 'The thing is, since Ben ... you've been completely obsessive. I love your principles and your passion, but you've got to give yourself a break. Anyway, didn't you and Ben go to the Maldives on honeymoon? I thought you loved it. I don't remember you coming back and complaining about the resort staff being oppressed and overstocking the buffet.'

If I closed my eyes, I could feel Ben's hands, smooth and warm on my bare back. I could smell coconut sun cream. I don't understand how humans can travel to paradise, but not through time.

'That's the other thing,' I say, picking up a Percy Pig and putting it down again. 'Those places are romantic. You need to be in love. And you know I adore you but it's not the same.' I pick Percy up again and pull his ear off. 'The thing about my job is that it isn't perfect – but it's all I have left. I'm not sure who I am without it.'

'Well, now you have the opportunity to find out!' says Annabel. She sounds infuriatingly cheerful about it. 'You haven't given yourself any time to find out who you are without *Ben*. Katherine, I miss him. I want to talk about him, to you. I think about the two of you, all the time. Dancing at your wedding. And do you remember that awful camping trip when we all went to the Lake District? Leaving in the middle of the night when our tent blew away . . .'

'Of course I remember.' I just don't want to remember. I don't want to think about Ben, sliding his hand under my jumper, and how he murmured, 'Are you awake?', and I knew *exactly* what he wanted to do . . . and how we were interrupted by screams, as the wind whistled around us. Ben bursting into laughter at the sight of Annabel clutching a single pole, looking confused. 'But you're as bad as Constance. It's too soon, it's too raw. I'm not ready yet.'

And it wasn't all giggly sex and camping trips. There were arguments – and worse, silence. But I can't tell Annabel that.

'What does Grace the Therapist say?' Annabel reaches over and squeezes my forearm. 'She must have some really good ideas about how to sit with these emotions. We instinctively push the feelings away, when they're painful. Just allowing ourselves to feel them takes a lot of practice. And I was watching this video with Dr Soph, and she made some super interesting observations about grief, and guilt . . .'

Guilt. Just hearing the word injects acid straight into my gut. If only I'd stopped him from getting on that boat. If I'd been a better wife. If he'd wanted to stay at home with me, and not gone out into the storm. If we'd had a kid, and something other than me to stay home for. If, if, if ...

'So you're saying that this is all my fault,' I say, sharply. 'Of course I feel guilty. And now, I'm failing to keep my life together, and I feel even more guilty. What do you want me to do with that?'

And now I feel even more guilty for lashing out at Annabel. I'm the worst person I've ever met. I wouldn't want to work with me, or be married to me, or be my friend either. No wonder I'm here. And then, I hear Ben's voice. 'Cheer up, love, it might never happen! Bloody hell, Katherine. You're like something out of the Old Testament.' And then he might tickle me and tell me he was going to turn me into a pillar of salt and feed me to a lion, and we'd realise that between us our basic Bible knowledge was almost non-existent.

If I concentrate very hard, I can see his outline, the shape of him, the weight of him creasing the sofa cushions. The rise and fall of his shoulders. I can remember the way his skin felt under my fingertips. And then ... that throat-sharpness returns. I blink, and there's nothing there. I can't even manifest a ghost.

Annabel looks hurt, and it takes me a moment to re-member why. 'I'm sorry,' I say. 'I shouldn't lash out at you. That's another thing to feel guilty about. You know what might help?' I say, sitting up. 'I could use this time to do some volunteering. I'll try the local charity shops or food banks.' Already, I feel slightly more cheerful. 'The impor-tant thing is to use this time wisely! Learn some skills! Give back! Find people who need help!' I smile at Annabel, but she doesn't return it.

'I'm looking at someone who needs help,' she says in a gentle tone that makes me clench my fists again. 'Listen, have you ever heard of the Hoffman Process?'

I rack my brains. 'Um, I think I saw it. Does it have Jeff Goldblum in it? He's a professor, and he builds a time machine … ?'

'No!' Annabel shakes her head. 'It's not a movie. It's a personal development course. It's a week of very intense therapy to help you heal from grief, shame, anger. You work through your issues in a group. Sienna Miller did it.'

'God, it sounds …' Miserable, embarrassing, self-conscious, hellish? 'Interesting,' I say, politely.

'I've been looking and there are loads of similar courses …' Annabel is an absolute fiend for personal development in any shade or flavour. Long before Ben died, I felt as though I was 'in therapy' by proxy, because Annabel told her therapist all about me and then passed along what her therapist thought I should do. (We both briefly took against the therapist when she suggested that we read a book about co-dependency.)

'Right. Great! If it's good enough for Sienna, then it's good enough for you.'

'Not for me. You, Katherine. You should do a course. A retreat! Go and stay somewhere, and, you know, heal. This seems like the perfect time!'

'Ah, steady on.' I would rather go on an all-inclusive holiday to Australia. A steak-themed one. 'I'm sure I could just stay here and read some books. There's a new yoga studio down the road. I can do a one-woman retreat! It seems a bit extreme to go off somewhere and do therapy and things with a bunch of strangers. It will be full of people with actual, real problems.'

Annabel gives me a funny look.

'Anyway, places like that get booked up months in advance! Even if I wanted to go – not that I don't want to go,' I say, hurriedly. 'I can't imagine anywhere would be able to fit me in at such short notice. But maybe I'll book the Hot Man Process for next year.' That gives me plenty of time to break my leg, or contract appendicitis or do whatever I need to do in order to wriggle free.

'It's Hoffman. And you don't have to do that specific one. Just think about it,' she says. 'Please. For me.'

'Ha! I remember this from the co-dependency book,' I say. 'You're using manipulation to get your way.'

'Oh, as if. You are. You've somehow manipulated me into letting you finish the Percy Pigs.' Annabel narrows her eyes, and I know I've won for now.

The trouble is that I have a sneaking suspicion that she might be right. I've been pedalling as fast as I could. I thought I'd outpaced this, but even I can't deny that the wheels have fallen off. But what good could any of this do, really? My grief isn't *presentable*. I can't sit down with a group of rich women, and say, 'My husband died, and I feel sad, but I'm sure I'll feel better after a bit of yoga.'

And I can't tell the truth, can I?

That my husband died, and at different points, every single day, I feel furious, ashamed, numb, frightened, alone – and *relieved*.

That I'm worried I'm better at being a widow than a wife.

And most of all, that I'm jealous of Annabel. Because she never argued with Ben or cried because of him. All her memories are happy camping.

Chapter Six

Beginnings

When I woke up on the Sunday after the Hallowe'en party, I was glowing with hope. I hugged myself under the duvet and wriggled my toes. Who knew what the Sundays in my future might hold? Brunch with Ben! Bracing walks around the park with Ben! Hot chocolate, and games of Scrabble, and old black and white films with Spencer Tracy ... I paused. I couldn't quite remember who Spencer Tracy was, and I was terrible at Scrabble, but no matter. Maybe I'd have a new boyfriend soon, just in time for Christmas. Everyone knew that this was the perfect time of the year to get together with someone. When you're part of a couple, you can wear a woolly hat and there's always someone there to reassure you that you don't look like a thumb.

On Monday, I thought about Ben, surrounded by boxes in his brand-new house. Of course he was far too busy to send a message. On Tuesday, I started paying close attention to the local news, just in case there had been any kidnappings, or reports of an insurance executive from South London going missing. On Wednesday, I wasted an hour trying to find Ben on social media, and another three hours finding Miles's beautiful ex, and accidentally liking a picture of her on her holidays in Mauritius, wearing a white bikini. On Thursday, I decided that I was going to be single for ever, and I was never going to have sex again, and I couldn't work out whether it was because of my nose or the way my thighs looked in trousers, but I had to do something.

I was in the toilets at work, standing in front of the mirror and trying to send Annabel pictures of my legs, when the message came through.

> Hello, Katherine! This is Ben from the party. Can you come sailing on Saturday morning? BXX

'Oh my God!' I shrieked, and a voice called, 'Are you OK?'

'Sorry,' I called. 'I didn't think anyone was in here. I got a text from a boy.'

'What boy?' called the voice. 'It's Susannah from Marketing, by the way. I'm on my phone trying to get tickets for Taylor Swift, but if anyone asks, my IBS is really bad. Anyway, what did he say? What are you going to say?'

'He wants me to come sailing on Saturday!' I said.

'Oooh, sailing! That's a great date idea. I just turned down a date with a woman who wanted me to come and watch while she got new headshots done. A sailor sounds like a keeper.'

'Is she a model?' I asked, curious.

'No, she's a YouTube forager,' said Susannah. 'That's the other thing, she said something about wanting to cook for me but let's face it, I'd be getting nettles. Shit! I'm number three in the queue. Anyway, good luck!'

'Good luck with Taylor!' I said. My phone buzzed again. Oooh, Ben was keen.

It was Annabel.

Did you mean to send me 8 pics of ur legs? XX

I went back to my desk and composed a text. It only took an hour.

Hello, this is Katherine! Hope things are going well with the new house! I'd love to come sailing! XX

I pressed send and then cursed myself for ruining everything. Even I knew that the more exclamation marks you used, the less sex you had. But Ben replied within two minutes.

Send me your address and I'll pick you up. Wrap up warm, bring snacks. BXX

I sent the message to Annabel, who immediately asked if I had waterproof mascara.

Early on Saturday morning, I found myself standing in front of Annabel's bedroom mirror, putting on a pink beanie, and then taking it off again. 'Do you think the pink is too girly? My skull is a weird shape. Is he going to drive me somewhere and murder me?' I asked.

'I doubt it,' said Annabel, from under her duvet. 'He

wouldn't have mentioned snacks. Although I guess murdering must be hungry work.' I looked out of the window, I paced around the room, and I put the hat back on. 'Katherine, stop it. Calm down. If you need something to do, you can go and make me a cup of tea.' As I left the room, she called, 'And if you must bite your nails, take off my ski gloves!'

As I waited for the kettle to boil, I was startled by the sound of a horn outside. Then my phone buzzed.

Sorry I'm late! Had some car trouble – if I stop the engine, it might not start again. Can you come out? XX

I ran outside, and there was Ben, handsome, smiling and nervous. 'Katherine, this is really embarrassing but the passenger door just stopped working. I can't get it open. Do you mind getting in the back and climbing through?'

His car made me less nervous, and it made me like him more. A little red Honda, probably not quite as old as it looked, filled with wetsuits, pens, wrappers, cups, jumpers, magazines, bits of rope. 'Is this model called the Honda Hoarder?' I asked, as I tried to tuck and roll my way to the front of the car. He laughed.

'I keep meaning to clean it, but ... ' He shrugged.

'I like it,' I said, decisively. 'It's cosy.'

He smiled. 'Most girls hate it. My mother keeps threatening to disinherit me. Or worse, bribe me with a new one. She'll get me something shiny and ludicrous for my birthday, and inevitably I'll fill that with Whopper boxes too and my life will not be worth living.' We pulled away, heading for the road.

'What's she like?' I asked. 'Other than, um, into cars?'

'God, what a question!' He shrugged, eyes on the road. 'What's anyone's mother like? She's great, really. Intense. She can be a lot. Curious about people. Clever, I suppose. And funny. And kind. She's a journalist, not a war reporter or anything, lifestyle. Perhaps overly fond of shiny tat. But good fun. What about yours?'

'Um,' I said, as we waited for a set of lights to change. 'Oh, I've never been this way before! Has there always been a Subway there? Should we get sandwiches?' I could not tell him. I didn't want to be Tragedy Girl with him. Not yet.

'Katherine, I don't know you very well,' said Ben, narrowing his eyes and leaning forward as the lights turned amber. 'But you seem like the sort of girl – woman – who answers questions, who doesn't play games. But that was a swerve if ever I saw one. Why don't you want to talk about your mum? Is she ... I don't know, what's the most embarrassing thing a mum could be? Is she a televangelist? A Tory MP? Has she recently been featured in the *Daily Mail*, wrestling in a satin thong?'

I looked straight ahead and modulated my voice carefully. 'She died when I was very little. Car accident. She was a teenager when she had me, so she wasn't around very much. I didn't know her. I don't remember much about her.' That wasn't strictly true. I can remember shiny hair, soft lips kissing my forehead. I didn't know what shampoo my mother used, but I did know that whenever I smelled apple and amber, I was assaulted by the ghost of a memory. 'I was brought up by my grandmother,' I explained.

'Shit.' Ben threw up his hands and we swerved slightly.

'Sorry, sorry. Sorry!' He shouted the last apology in the direction of the Ford Mondeo he'd been trying to overtake. 'Shit. I'm so sorry. I didn't realise – I didn't think.'

'That's OK,' I said, because that's what I always said. 'I don't know any different.'

'So, what's she like? Your grandmother, I mean.'

I started to laugh. 'Oh, Ben. You're going to love this. She's dead too.'

'She's not!' We swerved again, almost killing a man on a motorcycle.

'She was really old. She was almost forty when she had Mum, it was a total surprise to everyone, apparently. Her husband, my grandfather, was even older than her, and he died when my mum was little.'

I was aware that Ben was studying my face. 'Eyes on the road, fella. Just because my whole family was wiped out doesn't mean we have to be. She had heart disease. It was ironic because she was a real health obsessive. She never smoked, which was unusual for a woman of her generation. She'd have one sweet sherry at Christmas.'

I was going to tell Ben that I thought she died of stress. Bringing me up had been very difficult for her, and I didn't think she liked me very much. But I caught the thought just in time, and stuffed it back where it belonged, in one of the darker crevices of my brain.

This was not first-date chat. I couldn't tell him I was so unappealing that my own grandmother couldn't stand me.

'Oh, Katherine,' said Ben. 'I don't know what to say. I'm sorry. I'm so sorry. So it's just you these days?'

I laughed, awkwardly. 'I'm fine, honestly. I've had a long time to get used to it. Annabel – that's my friend, who was having the thing with Tom – she's like my sister, really. We live together. I don't feel lonely.'

Ben grinned. 'I remember you telling me about her! Did she get with Tom at the party?' I loved him for remembering – and for his unconcealed enthusiasm for gossip.

'She did,' I said, 'but I think it was a bit of a nostalgia thing for them both. She's not planning the wedding, or anything.' I blushed. That was a stupid mistake; you must never mention weddings on a first date. I might as well have said, 'So, Ben, what are your favourite baby names?'

But he looked thoughtful. 'I think a lot of my mates are getting those final flings out of their systems at the moment. When I was in Hong Kong there was a real ex-pat mentality of being wild and single, for as long as we could, and it wasn't for me. I just kept having the same conversations with the same women in the same bars, and I started to feel like I was sleepwalking. That's one of the reasons why I came home. I really wanted to meet someone, and I knew it wasn't going to happen out there.'

He turned around and smiled at me, and my heart leapt. Mostly because in that moment, he'd made me feel like the only girl in the world; partly because we'd just come within inches of hitting a truck.

We drove a little further, and he told me that his parents were divorced, that his father had sailed a little bit at school, and he started at weekends, because it sounded better than piano lessons. He'd been seven or eight then, and he'd sailed almost every weekend since. 'I mean, not every weekend,' he'd explained. 'But if I spend more than two weeks away from the water, I start to feel edgy.'

As we turned off the main road, down a series of narrow

lanes, I felt Ben changing. It was subtle, but unignorable. We sped past fields, and his shoulders dropped. His breath became slower as the sky became brighter and wider. Eventually, we pulled into a little clearing. I gasped and sang out, 'I can see the sea!'

He grinned. 'Technically, this is just a lake. But it might be one of my favourite places in the world, and I wanted to bring you here. It's much calmer than sea sailing. I thought this would be a good place for us to start. But it's a bit rustic. You'll get wet.' He caught my eye, and blushed. 'I mean—'

I couldn't resist. 'I hope so!' I said, and then I nearly ruined everything by turning red and laughing so hard that I snorted. Ben wiped his eyes. 'Let's not be coy,' he said. 'I mean, I've already seen your bra.'

'Technically, it was Annabel's bra.'

'I see. In that case, I feel a lot better about asking you to wear my trousers.'

I climbed out through the back door, and Ben produced a pair of navy salopettes from the trunk. 'I'm giving you my best ones, these are the most waterproof, but they might be a bit big.' He held out his arm to steady me, as I climbed in. 'I'll have to get you your own pair. Maybe pink, to match your hat.'

My eyes widened, and he misinterpreted my look. 'Sorry, I've been away too long. This was supposed to be romantic – but I've just realised that I've driven you out to the middle of nowhere, to go on the open water, and I'm already assuming that you're going to want to do it again.'

'Ben, it's not that I'm not sure of you,' I said. 'But I'm really not sure about this hat.'

'I am,' he said, and then he kissed me, very softly. Again, it was chaste, but electric. I felt my foot lifting behind me. Unfortunately, it was tangled up in the salopettes. We staggered backwards together, and Ben held me tight, and kissed me again.

This time, there was nothing chaste about it.

I wanted to keep falling against him, into him. His lips were so soft, and so firm – I couldn't stop kissing him, but I almost wanted to pull away just to tell him how good it felt, how extraordinary. Yet, I couldn't bear to let a sliver of light get between his body and mine. I resented every layer of clothing that separated us. And there were *so* many layers of clothing. Still, it seemed wilder and more erotic than any of the actual sex I'd had. It felt like a first kiss; a beginning. It woke me up.

I can't remember who pulled away first. I do remember that we held hands and looked at each other for a long time. I think I heard bird song. I think the blue sky was tinged pink.

Eventually, Ben said, 'Your salopettes!' and helped me with the other leg. 'We'd better get out onto the water now,' he added. 'Because I want to remember this day for ever, and I want to say that we actually went sailing. This can't be the day that we drove for hours and ended up making out in the back of my ancient Honda.'

'Can't it be both?' I said. 'We'll probably need to warm up soon.'

We walked out to a little jetty. A white rowing boat was tied up beside it. 'I'll get in, and help you down,' said Ben. 'This is very much Sailing 101. Am I right in thinking that you've never done this before? Technically, I'm a qualified instructor, so I can give you a lesson, if you like.'

'Oh wow!' I said. 'Who do you teach?'

'I haven't done it in a while, but before I went away, it was mostly under tens. Some of those kids were *fearless*,' he said, as he untied us. 'I can't wait to teach my own ... er, never mind.' He picked up an oar and propelled us towards the middle of the water. 'Sailing is so good for you. It keeps me calm. I honestly believe that anyone can do it, as long as they're enthusiastic.'

'Aren't you terrified of all that responsibility?' I asked. 'What if someone drowns on your watch?'

He laughed. 'I'd honestly never thought of that before. But now you're here, Dr Death – maybe that's something I should be concerned about.' He grimaced. 'God, sorry. Was that in the most appalling taste?'

'Yeah,' I said. 'But it made me laugh.'

We lapped the lake, talking nonsense. Ben told me that he'd spent most of the week trying to find the box that contained his towels. I spotted a cormorant, and he was very impressed. 'You know birds!' he exclaimed. 'It's like being on a date with a young, hot David Attenborough.'

'I should warn you, I do the other stuff too,' I said. 'I don't just identify animals, I get quite strident about habitat loss. I've got strong opinions about glaciers.'

'We want the same things, then,' said Ben. 'I care about sea levels. It's in my own selfish interests that the sea stays exactly where it is. But now – I care double. You're already making me a better person.'

I smiled and tugged my hat over my ears. I felt too nervous to say it out loud, but I didn't think Ben could be a better person. He was perfect. Instead, I leaned forward.

'If I kissed you now, would the boat topple over?'

'Why do you think I made you wear a life jacket?'

His cheek, against mine, was wet with mist. I remember noticing the slow creep of lake water soaking through my boots, and not caring. I remember the weight of his gloved hands, clumsy but tender on the back of my neck. The boat wobbled, but we stayed afloat. It was cold, and wet, and perfect. I wouldn't have felt happier if we were being serenaded by a singing crab.

This was not dating as I knew it. No bad white wine, no unsolicited dick pics, no monologues about Crossfit or crypto or conspiracy theories. This was true romance. It should feel terrifying. I barely knew this man. I didn't really know where I was. But when I looked at the reflection on the water, two figures in a little boat, I felt as though I'd finally found a place in the world. And in Ben's face, I saw home.

Chapter Seven

It's not not *an intervention*

As I stand on the doorstep of my mother-in-law's house – technically, ex-mother-in-law, I suppose – I'm filled with two conflicting sensations. A sense of peace, maybe even hope. Perhaps something bordering on awe. But this is laced with a strong feeling of impending doom. At this precise moment in time, everything is going to be OK. But something terrible is lurking around the corner, just out of sight. Something very bad is going to happen.

Why am I like this? Why can't I have appropriate emotions? Obviously, I have no business feeling randomly cheerful. I'm a heartbroken widow with no job. Anyway, *who* feels 'cheer, but laced with dread'? It doesn't make any sense. There must be something very wrong with me.

'I'm opening it, darling!' Constance yells over the electronic chimes, and as I open the door I realise she's got Classic FM on at full blast in the kitchen. I can hear the *Jurassic Park* theme. That explains my emotional state. Not a profound existential shift, nor a sense of impending doom. Just impending dinosaurs.

When I dump my bag on the kitchen island, Constance is in full conversational flow. I suspect she started talking to me before I pressed the doorbell. She squeezes me briefly, and then turns to tea. I'm carried away, a very small pebble swept up in the soothing slipstream of her chatter – it's a strangely effective accompaniment to the dinosaur music. I nod along to ' . . . delightful chap in the shop,' the following words are muffled by the urgent chuckle of boiling water, then a click, then 'absolutely hooked on this imported Ceylon . . . ' a splash, a tap, a drip, 'killingly pricey, but what can you do? But then think of poor Jill, and her side return!'

Triumphantly she places a bone china mug in front of me. I pick it up, sip, and burn my tongue, which is an effective way of preventing the pointless impulse to ask, 'Who is Jill? And what's a side return?' Still, despite the searing pain on the roof of my mouth, I can tell that the tea is delicious. Exquisite, even. I try to smile through the pain, but Constance pounces.

'A splash of milk would cool it down,' she says, opening the fridge. 'Mind you, it kills the flavour.'

I shake my head. 'No, thanks, I'm fine. You know I don't drink milk in tea.' As I have been telling you for, ooh, well over five years now.

'Oh, but I got some special new milk in for you.' She plucks a carton from inside the door. 'It's hemp! It doesn't taste too bad, but it doesn't get you high. More's the pity.'

'Honestly, this is lovely.' I take another sip, squirming as the heat of the tea hurts my tender tongue. Constance and I have been locked in the same holding pattern for the last six months. She performs an act of kindness that is both deeply touching and incredibly irritating. I try to politely decline it, and immediately start drowning in guilt – I swear I can feel it filling my lungs. Also, I usually sustain a minor injury.

She looks at me. I look at the hemp milk, dolefully. She sighs. 'Well, maybe just blow on it?' She points a peach-tipped finger at me, the Lord Kitchener of hot beverages. 'Anyway, what happened at Shrinkr? Annabel said you were in a bit of a state.'

It doesn't matter how well you get on with your mother-in-law – you do *not* want her to befriend your friends. Because they will gang up on you, and they will gossip about you. I lost this battle before it began; it turned out that Constance and Annabel had been messaging for years before they met. They're both in the same giant *Real Housewives* watch-along WhatsApp group.

'Well, I'm officially on sabbatical,' I mutter, avoiding her eyes. Just saying the word evokes the exact, awful sensation, all over again. My body is in a bespoke chef's kitchen in Holland Park; my soul is collapsed and sweating all over a scratchy office carpet. It's so humiliating. 'Anyway ... ' I look around, searching for something shiny and distracting I can throw her way. 'Did you see this interesting leaflet about ... ' I pick something up from a pile of papers and squint at it. 'Conservatory extensions! I know you have one, but you could always extend the extension! Your whole house could be a conservatory, with a bit of imagination!'

She narrows her eyes. 'Katherine, you *hate* conservatories. You made me a graph showing how bad they were for energy efficiency. I had to install a heat pump, just to calm you down. You're avoiding the subject. I've been in the workforce for decades. I know all about office politics. You cannot bullshit me.'

Constance cannot remember how I take my tea, but she knows exactly how my brain works. Damn her.

'It's not great.' I sigh. 'It's totally shameful. I made a mistake. I completely failed to prepare for a big presentation – but because my memory has been so bad, I didn't remember not preparing, if that makes sense? And I was rude to the client.'

I hang my head, expecting a telling-off. It would be a relief if Constance shouted at me. I deserve it. I still can't believe that I let myself down so badly.

Instead, she puts a warm hand on mine, and nods. 'It happens. You want to know my symptom of the month? Prosopagnosia. Face blindness. It's the worst when I have to go to product launches.' She giggles. 'Trust me, if you want humiliating, try saying, "I'm so sorry, I *know* we've met, but I can't quite place you" to Posh Spice.'

Whenever Constance laughs, Ben comes back, very briefly. It's joyous, and then crushingly sad. 'Have you talked to Jonathan about it?' I ask. Constance has been seeing the same old-school psychiatrist on Harley Street for years – she started long before Ben died. As far as I can tell, he's around nine hundred years old, and he costs about nine hundred pounds a session.

'He said all the usual things. It's a trauma response, it's probably temporary, maybe it's because of my age. Maybe she's born with it, maybe it's the menopause. I am so, so sick of feeling completely insane, and not even knowing what is making me insane. Do I need more hormone replacement therapy, or Ben replacement therapy?'

'Fuck.' I exhale. It's a way to say 'I love you' – Constance adores it when I swear in front of her, so I try to make an effort, even though it makes me feel a bit tense. In my eyes, she will always be a proper grown-up. I have to bite my lip to fight the inexplicable urge to apologise, call her Mrs Attwell and take myself to the headmaster's office.

'Anyway,' she shakes her head briskly, 'what are we going to do about you? Have you made a plan? You need a plan, a bit of structure. Otherwise, you'll be sitting around basting in your own self-pity. Feeling sorry for yourself, like Foxe's Martyrs.'

'Foxe's Martyrs?' I repeat, perplexed. 'Is that a Christmas biscuit?'

'Oh my God,' murmurs Constance. 'Look at the pair of us. I honestly don't know who is making less sense. *Foxe's Book of Martyrs* is exactly what it sounds like – an extremely long and tedious sixteenth-century directory of people who elected to live in misery and suffering, for spiritual reasons. And it often reminds me of someone who is sitting at this kitchen island.' She raises her eyebrows. 'The one useful thing Jonathan has always told me is that we can't subject ourselves to one source of pain in order to protect ourselves from a worse pain. We can't suffer in advance. We can't really control anything at all.'

I know she's right. But it's devastating to hear her say it. This is worse than hearing a priest telling you that they don't believe in God. Constance is a Type A Planner. She's an obsessive, detail-oriented perfectionist. This is her grief talking. It's raw and frightening, and I don't know how to reach her.

Unless . . .

'OK, you can control me,' I say, hurriedly. 'I mean, maybe you can help me make a plan. I was thinking about trying to volunteer at one of the local charity shops. Or maybe I could go away somewhere.'

Constance looks a bit brighter. 'Yes! Southeast Asia! The Himalayas! You could help the Sherpas!'

'I think the Sherpas are fine,' I say. 'I'd be more of a hindrance. I don't want to go far. There's a barn owl sanctuary in Kent where you can stay on site, in a little hut. I think you need experience to work with the owls, but I could clean the cages and sell blackberries in the farm shop.'

Constance winces. 'No, Katherine. You're in a crisis state. You can't self-actualise when you're covered in owl shit. Annabel had some good ideas, actually. We've been having a bit of a powwow ...'

I don't like where this is going. 'Don't say powwow,' I mutter. 'It's cultural appropriation.'

'Katherine, *please*! Would you just take one day off from your incessant ... Katherine-ness. Anyway, Annabel and I have been discussing what you should do. Because this time off isn't a punishment. You're not well, and you've got to get yourself better. This break could be the best thing that ever happened to you.'

I will not cry. Crying will only make it worse. I bite down on the burned tip of my tongue.

'We understand why you threw yourself back into work,' she continues, gently. 'But you haven't given yourself any time. We're all in a lot of pain, we're all recalibrating. I know how you're feeling, trust me. I know you're scared that if you give in to this, the hell will never end. But it won't end if you won't start.' Constance grimaces, and her voice wobbles. 'I think about Ben all the time, and it makes me feel better. There isn't a right way to grieve, but you do need to find a way.'

I stall for time, fidgeting with my wedding ring. It feels weird to wear it, but I suspect I'd feel even stranger if I took it off. 'I'm sorry,' I say, pointlessly. 'It's so hard. And I wish I could be more of a comfort.' Because I know I'm not a model daughter-in-law, or even a model ex-daughter-in-law. It would be easier if Constance went into full Queen Victoria mode, not eating, not sleeping, and only wearing black. I'd happily take charge of tissues and laundry. But she only wants to mother me. And I make a very poor substitute child.

'It would help if you stopped apologising,' Constance says quietly. 'Sorry. Honestly, I'm as bad as you are. I'll make some more tea.' She snatches my mug, which is still three-quarters full.

'But I've got loads left, and you said it's very expensive—' I'm interrupted by the doorbell. Constance drops the mug. '*Who* could that be?' she says, loudly. Which is weird because it's usually DHL or FedEx, and she usually says, 'Oh, for fuck's sake, I put a note on telling them to leave it in the porch.'

Instead of opening the door with her phone, she walks towards it, flinging it open in a manner I can only describe as theatrical. 'Annabel! What a *lovely surprise*!' she booms, enunciating very carefully. Has she recently taken up amateur dramatics? She's never got over understudying Amanda in her sixth form production of *Private Lives*.

'Constance!' Annabel kisses her and walks into the kitchen. 'Why are you being so odd? You invited me.' She hugs me, and then looks stern. 'Katherine, we need to talk to you.'

'Is this an intervention?' I say, jokingly. No one smiles. Constance looks thoughtful.

'I suppose it's not *not* an intervention,' she says, eventually.

'We thought it was time for us to join forces,' says Annabel.

'Why?' I ask. 'What have I done?' I feel sick. They're disowning me. I've always been absolutely certain that one day, something like this would happen. The dinosaurs are loose, and I'm going to get my head bitten off.

Annabel and Constance are both looking at me with exactly the same expression. Deep pity. They are standing side by side, and their head tilts are identical – as though they're a pair of Roadrunners working together and watching Wile E. Coyote fall off a cliff.

'Stop looking at me like that!' I say. I notice my arms are crossed tightly across my torso, so I unfold them, and try to neutralise my face and my voice. 'I'm sorry, I'm sorry. It's just been a difficult few months. I promise I'll sort myself out.'

'A difficult few months is what happens when your boiler breaks. Or you sprain your ankle. Or someone nicks your credit card and it takes ages to get the fraud department to sort it,' says Constance, gently.

'Or, you're in a hen party WhatsApp group and someone you don't know volunteers you to book nine flights to Mallorca,' says Annabel. 'Or you get thrush and a UTI at the same time. Or your neighbours have the builders in, and you're woken up by random banging at 7 a.m. every day even on Sundays.'

'Or someone goes into the back of your car, and they've got crap insurance.'

'Or they change the ingredients in your favourite cleanser

and suddenly you break out like a plague victim, and you're googling adult acne and the spots are visible through two layers of Double Wear.'

'Or there's a smell under the stairs, and it gets worse and worse, and you keep calling out Dyno-Rod and you spend *thousands*, and it turns out to be an old sandwich in a gym bag.' Constance is visibly reliving a very specific past trauma.

'Or ... or ...' Annabel does not want to be outdone. 'Your ex's new girlfriend is some sort of yoga expert, and you find out from Instagram stalking that she's actually friends with Adriene.'

'Really? Months?' Constance looks sceptical. 'That would piss you off for a weekend, maybe.'

'Constance! Annabel!' I throw my hands up in exasperation. 'Can we get my telling-off over with?'

'This isn't ...'

'That's not ...' They talk over each other, and then Annabel takes my hand. Constance takes the other one.

'After I saw you yesterday, I had a bit of a think,' Annabel says. 'Katherine, I've known you longer than anyone. And I'm scared. No one would expect you not to be affected by what has happened. We're all sad. We're all devastated. But you're a shell. You've gone from being my passionate, caring, amazing friend to a robot woman. You seem numb. It's as though you've burned through your internal wiring.'

Her voice seems to catch, and she takes a steadying breath.

Constance gives her a small nod, and she keeps going. 'I see you fading away. Becoming completely obsessive. It's scary. Sometimes it's as though you don't want to be here with us. Shrinkr has been a sponge for all of your energy. Over the last six months, you've cancelled so many plans because you "have to work".' She wiggles her fingers and wrinkles her nose. 'Sorry about the air quotes. But I've been scared for you. And I think it's great that you're on sabbatical. Because you need this time. And I wouldn't be a good friend if I didn't urge you to use it well.'

Constance mouths something at her. It might be 'well done'. She addresses me.

'I think Annabel is right. We've been looking at some options, places you can go, where you can get the right levels of support and attention. You desperately need a change of scene, a break in your old routine, but still, you know, with structure. Someone to make sure you eat your breakfast,' she says. My treacherous stomach rumbles. I've gone right off my morning banana.

'You never eat breakfast,' I grumble.

'That's different, I'm over fifty and I'm doing intermittent fasting,' replies Constance.

'Just to be clear, am I hearing what I think I'm hearing?' I realise I sound shrill, and I don't care any more. 'I'm boring and annoying and inconveniencing everyone, so you're sending me away?'

'That's not what we mean at all!' Annabel sounds desperate.

'This thing you were talking about yesterday,' I say, feeling my fury build. 'Is it for ... are you making me go to a place for crazy people?' I've shocked myself. 'Sorry, sorry, not crazy, you know what I mean. Mentally unwell.'

'Katherine, for goodness' sake.' Constance grips the back of a stool. She looks as though she'd like to throw it at me.

'We're not sectioning you. We both think you should spend a week or two in a nice place with a pool, where you can eat properly and talk about your feelings. And yeah, they all have fucking art therapy, but that part's usually optional!' she says, and Annabel puts her arm around her.

'We thought the Hoffman Process might be a little intense, and you were right about the waiting lists,' says Annabel. 'But we've found a few places that look promising.'

'I've sent out some messages, and called in some favours,' adds Constance.

That bloody *Real Housewives* group chat. It's the West London mafia. Everyone in it is far too well connected – these women can get anyone anything on demand, from a blow dry to a place to bury a body.

'Hold on! Wait!' I say, frantically. 'I don't want you to call in any favours, Constance. You've done enough! I can't be your nepo-baby-in-law.'

'Oh my God.' Constance spaces out the syllables, like someone in a sitcom. For a second I think she's going to push the stool over with me on it. But she marches towards the kitchen window and sighs heavily.

'Lion's breath!' says Annabel. 'Let it go!'

'Why can't you just let me do something nice for you?' she shouts, at the window. 'This is just like the time I got you the vintage Saint-Laurent purse for Christmas!'

'But I love the purse!' I say, quickly. 'It's one of the nicest things anyone has given me, I always use it on special occasions.' I think back to the moment I opened it, and feel another wave of shame, crashing out of my heart and drenching my whole body. How guilty I felt about the money spent, the effort made, the level of thought, and care, and attention she'd put into a gift that *really wasn't me*. I knew I wasn't good enough for it, even before I'd got all of the wrapping paper off.

'Katherine, *there are no special occasions*. You're saving your whole life for best, and it's such a waste! And you're so … you can't … you won't … I can't … ' She turns away and makes a sound I've never heard from her before. A sort of mewing.

I feel like the worst person in the world.

'I promise I'll think about it,' I say, eventually, but even as I say it I'm mentally calculating how I can distract them both until the crisis passes, and the plan is forgotten. I might be able to spin this out until it's time for me to go back to work. Or maybe I'll run away to the owl sanctuary. I can keep everyone happy, and everything will go back to normal.

Chapter Eight

Girlfriend

After our sailing trip, I accidentally stumbled upon a fool-proof way to drive a man wild. Total indifference.

I liked Ben very much. *Too* much. I felt myself falling hard for him, and my instincts told me that was dangerous. It wasn't that I didn't trust him, specifically. It was the whole situation that made me feel cynical. If relationships had auditors, ours would have a team of accountants rolling up their shirtsleeves, clearing their throats and peering over their spectacles. We should have aroused the suspicions of the authorities. We didn't quite add up.

Ben was cheerful, uncomplicated, handsome and wealthy. He looked like something usually pictured beaming from a ski slope, advertising muesli. Surely boys like Ben tended to go out with girls who were jolly, blonde, matching.

In the end, I decided that my ordinariness must have made me seem momentarily exotic. I did not begrudge Ben a spot of romantic tourism. Maybe I'd be the one before the one, a final fling before he settled on his preordained path. Probably a girl he'd known since he was eight, a junior tennis champion who looked like Margot Robbie.

So every time Ben's name flashed up on my phone, I answered it ready to recite my rehearsed responses: 'I understand, it was fun, I wish you both every happiness.' And I didn't call him, ever. Because I was pretty sure that the second I started to believe in the relationship, everything would blow up in my face.

I wasn't playing hard to get. And I didn't need to, because Ben called all the time.

Annabel would watch in awe as my phone beeped and buzzed on the table, and I did not rush to pick it up.

'I don't understand,' she said. 'How is this happening? How are you so relaxed?'

'Oh, I'm not relaxed,' I said. 'I'm fatalistic. There's a difference. The writing's on the wall, my card is marked. This cannot last. I'm Ben's weird blip. It's dating inflation. Soon there will be a market correction, and I'll never have sex again.'

Annabel shook her head. 'I thought you did a module in economics. I don't think that's how it works. Anyway, how *is* the sex?' she asked, slyly. 'You've been very quiet about it. Well, I suppose I don't know how loud you are at Ben's house!'

'Oh, God, it's . . . fine! Good!' I said, with some difficulty. 'You know . . .'

'No, I don't. That's why I'm asking.' Annabel tented her fingers and leaned forward.

'You should have been a political journalist, you missed your calling,' I said, grumpily. 'I can see you torturing ministers on live television. That would be a much better use of your powers.'

'Katherine, it's just sex. Are you happy? Are you satisfied? Is he giving you your giddy-up?'

'Erm ...' I let my ellipsis hang in the air and looked around the room. 'I suppose Ben is very tender. Considerate. But quite ... slow? I would like him to be a bit less slow if I'm honest. But it has its moments, definitely! It's not like I'm any kind of sex expert. Or sexpert, ha!'

'So tell him,' said Annabel. 'Ask him to go faster.'

'I think he's trying extra hard already, because I'm not very experienced. I'm sure his other girlfriends were good in bed.' I couldn't bring myself to say what I really thought, out loud. That I just wasn't built for mind-blowing sex. That 'fine' was the best I could hope for, with anyone. And that what I sometimes did, in secret, alone, was separate from proper sex. I was a freak in the sheets, but in the wrong sense.

'There is no such thing as good in bed,' said Annabel, decisively. 'Don't be nervous! Relax!' She shrugged. 'If you're so sure he's going to dump you, you've got nothing to lose. Fuck him like the world is ending and you've got a week left to live. Although as it happens I don't think you've got anything to worry about: you're spending four nights a week at his house, he texts ten times an hour, he calls at least twice a day. I bet you fifty quid that you'll be moving in with him after Christmas.'

After I'd been seeing Ben for five or six weeks, I got the message I'd been dreading. It was just after 3 p.m. I was looking out of the window, brushing crumbs off my desk. The sky was dark grey – it was one of those days that never properly got light – and I was trying to pull together campaign ideas for a tiny chain of hospice shops. They wanted a blog post to encourage people to buy and wear second-hand clothes, instead of dumping their old clothes outside the shop and running off to buy new ones.

Chewing my lip, I typed the words 'clothes swap amnesty'. Did that sound a bit worthy? I liked the idea of it – taking your old jeans, with the strange fades, and deliberate rips, and weird seams and flared legs, and leaving with a perfect pair that were new to you. The trouble was that the nature of the enterprise meant you'd be choosing from a pool of bad jeans. No one would ever say, 'Great, just what I've always wanted, a pair of stonewashed jeans that say "angel" on the arse in diamanté lettering. And I'm sure someone else will snatch up my old bootcuts, someone must be desperate for denim with a high lycra content that went weird in a hot wash!'

In desperation, I added, 'soft furnishing workshop' – maybe people could be persuaded to make cushion covers out of their old jeans? 'From your bum to your bed!' No, that was awful. My phone buzzed and the screen lit up. I grabbed it, glad to be distracted.

> Can I see you tonight? There's something I want to talk to you about. BXX

My heart sank. This was it. We'd had a good run. And Ben was being as kind and considerate as ever. This was the perfect dumping time. Christmas was a couple of weeks away, it wasn't so close that he was going to 'ruin' any festivities – and he wasn't going to do it in January, and make a bleak, bare month even worse. In fact, this was optimal, because if I really wanted to, there were people to see and parties to go to. I could go out every night, get blind drunk and get off with anyone and everyone.

I suspected I wouldn't want to, though.

I fired off a quick 'sure' to Ben, who suggested that we meet at Covent Garden. *Smart of you, Ben*, I thought. *It's well lit, there are lots of people. I'll go quietly. I won't make a scene.*

The remainder of the afternoon went slowly. I failed to think of any good ideas. My worst one was the old clothes tombola – hiding twenty quid in the pocket of a piece of clothing, and enticing shoppers to try to find it. This reminded me that by the end of the night, Annabel would owe me fifty quid. I'd have no pleasure in collecting it. In fact, maybe I could donate it to the hospice in lieu of any useful campaign ideas.

On the Tube, sweating profusely in my coat, I opened my notes app on my phone and started a list titled 'Reasons why it will be great to be single again!' I'd see more of Annabel! I could catch up on my reading! I'd have time to make cushion covers out of my old jeans!

By the time I'd arrived at my stop and emerged from the lift, I had six and a half bullet points and was feeling marginally better, until I saw Ben on the other side of the barriers, beaming. Oh, God. He was really excited about getting this over with. Maybe he had a new girlfriend already, and he was going to see her next. I imagined him speaking to her: 'I've got something to take care of, it will only take ten minutes.'

'Katherine!' He waved at me. Damn, I fancied him so much. I wanted to be immune to this textbook handsome man, with his golden skin and lantern jaw. But put any man in a cashmere coat and a big thick scarf, and I was done for. There was a tiny smudge of blue biro on his cheek that made me feel lustful and tearful in equal measure. I wondered if he'd have sex with me one last time. It would be amazing. I could be noisy and demanding and I wouldn't have to worry that he'd dump me afterwards because he'd already—

No, Katherine, I told myself. *Leave it. You may have a big cry in an hour for a treat. Now, keep your dignity.*

He threw his arms around me before I'd put my card away. I was aware that we were marooned, an island in a sea of harrumphing commuters. 'Sorry, sorry,' he murmured, pulling me away, and out of the exit. 'I'm just so happy to see you!'

I let him take my hand and concentrated very hard on putting one foot in front of the other. This was really odd. Even I had to admit Ben was not behaving like a man who was going to dump me. But maybe he was just trying to ease into it.

We headed towards Long Acre, ducking into an alley and turning into a corner. Ben led me to a little pub, and we walked up the stairs, to a quiet room. 'Perfect,' he said. 'This is my favourite place in London. I'll get the drinks!' He bounded back down the stairs. He was definitely dumping me – he hadn't even asked what I was having. I thought about running after him and telling him we didn't have to sit and drink and draw it out, I didn't need him to tell me I was a great girl, and it was just a shame that the timing wasn't working out, or that I'd meet someone else soon.

Trying to distract myself from the impending doom, I looked out of the window and saw the mass of sparkling lights. I wondered about the people hurrying below. At least one other person out there was getting dumped tonight. And someone else was probably about to go on a very first date with the person who would turn out to be the love of their life, and they had no idea. Someone else would have been fired – brutal, at this point in the year. And everyone else was everything else in between. Happy, hungover, exhausted, cold, desperate to get home, dreaming of annual leave, thinking of their itchy tights, their overdrafts, their families, the contents of their fridges.

And I was just another girl, tucked away, offscreen and watching. I was completely average. Ben would break up with me. I'd be sad for a while and then I'd probably be fine. Up here, I realised, I was alone, but not lonely, or tragic, or weird. This relationship had been a rite of passage. Ben had softened my edges. I wasn't as scared to be in the world as I was before we met, and I'd always be grateful to him for that.

I kept forgetting what was about to happen, I was entranced by the street below. Curled up in my seat, I watched the world through the window.

'I knew you'd love it here.' Ben put a pair of steaming mugs on the table, before blowing on his hands. 'Oooh, it's weird, isn't it, how hot drinks somehow get hotter, the longer you hold them for? Your hands seem to get more sensitive, not less.'

He pushed a mug towards me, settling down opposite. 'I can't resist mulled wine. It might be horrible but let me know what you think. You don't have to finish it if you don't want. I'll drink it if it's undrinkable.'

'Ben, if it's undrinkable, neither of us should drink it.

81

Clue's in the description.' Out of habit, I blew hard, and took a cautious sip. 'It's OK, actually. It's very sweet. Thank you.'

'You're very sweet,' he said, and I thought, *Oh, here we go.*

'And on that point, I have something I wanted to talk to you about,' he began. 'It's a bit ... well—'

'I understand,' I interjected. 'It's been—' just as he said: 'Would you spend Christmas with me?'

'—fun. Sorry, pardon? What did you just ask?'

Ben's gaze dropped to the table, and he rubbed at his forehead with his palm. *Oh, damn.* I wasn't in love with him, but I was definitely mid-fall. 'Um, my mum wants me to bring my new girlfriend home for Christmas, and *I* want to bring my new girlfriend home for Christmas, and what I'm trying to say is will you be my girlfriend, and will you come home for Christmas with me?'

I didn't know what to say, so I took a gulp of mulled wine. Seconds before I swallowed, I thought *this is going to hurt.* I felt the ghost of pain searing the back of my throat, and the roof of my mouth.

'Christmas?' I spluttered, sounding exactly like Scooby-Doo.

'Sorry, maybe it's a bit soon. And I guess I'm assuming ... you might have somewhere else you want to go? You don't have to, if you don't want to ...' Ben trailed off. We made eye contact, for a moment, and then his gaze fell back to the table. He seemed so vulnerable. The joy had drained from his voice.

'It's not too soon at all!' I said, hurriedly. 'I'd love to come! Sorry, I burned my tongue on mulled wine!' I leaned forward and kissed him, breathing in his scent of cold and spice, coffee, wine, woodsmoke.

I moaned, as quietly as I could. I didn't have to be brave and strong about this. I could exhale, relax a little, let myself belong. I could be Ben's girlfriend!

He pulled away and took both of my hands in his. 'My mum loves you already,' he said. 'She can't wait to meet you. And we couldn't let you be a Christmas orphan!'

'What?' An alarm was going off inside me, *somewhere* – but I wasn't especially interested in locating it or working out what set it off.

'Sorry,' Ben said, hurriedly. 'I shouldn't joke about it. But she's even more obsessed with Christmas than me, and she's gone fully Charles Dickens about ... you know. Your situation. I think she wants to buy you the giant piano from *Big*.'

'I've already got one of those,' I said. 'But tell her the only thing that will make up for my *tragic lack of family* is a puppy. No, a basket of puppies. And I still want a Barbie Dreamhouse. Nanna wasn't a Barbie fan.' I smiled, but I couldn't quite keep the defensive edge out of my voice. *If she wants to make me into some kind of pitiable charity mascot, I won't go.* Then I chastised myself: *Be nice. This is a kind woman who wants to help you when she hasn't even met you.*

'Look, I don't want you to think that's what this is about. I told Mum about you – just that I was seeing a girl I really, really liked. She said please, please invite her for Christmas, this is all I've ever wanted from any of my sons, et cetera, you know ... so I said I'd ask you, but I wasn't sure if you'd come. And she said, "Oh, she'll probably want to be with *her* family, or are you going to hers, which will break my heart", blah blah.' Ben rolled his eyes. 'And I said, as delicately as I could, that your situation meant probably not.'

'It's OK,' I said. 'But you really don't have to do this. I won't be alone, usually I go to Annabel's. I don't want to crash your family celebrations because you feel guilty, or . . . anything.'

Ben stood up and lifted me off my chair. He pulled my body close to his. His lips felt soft, and firm, and he kissed me hard. I felt breathless, and I started to get dizzy, but he kept on kissing me. My mouth, still raw from the burn, felt extremely sensitive, like a single, exposed nerve. I let him hold me up, I let my body melt into his.

When he pulled away, he was smiling. 'I think I'm falling in love with you,' he said. 'I know it's too soon, but I couldn't not tell you.'

'I love you too,' I said, automatically, before I could draw breath. 'I really do.'

In that moment, beside Ben, I made sense. I belonged.

Chapter Nine

The healing journey

The following evening, Constance calls a second crisis summit. Annabel and I are summoned back to her kitchen island to weigh up our options. They make a terrifyingly efficient team. I suspect that if the COP organisers drafted them in, the climate crisis could be solved within a week. No digital stone – or hot stone massage – shall be left unturned, on their watch. I hover awkwardly in the background: if I must do this, to keep them happy, I can at least encourage them to choose something sensible and bearable and manageable. Somewhere I can go for a week or two without becoming brainwashed.

'I like the sound of the Wellness Oasis Order,' says Annabel. 'It's a secular nunnery with an ashram-style intensive meditation programme ...'

'It sounds like a cult,' says Constance. 'It's literally an acronym for "woo".'

'Programme participants, or "surrendrants", undergo a series of cleansing rituals, and follow a strict vegan diet,' says Annabel, reading from a website. 'Surrendrants are free to leave at any time, but we do recommend a stay of three months, and a minimum donation of ten thousand—'

'Give me that,' says Constance, pulling her laptop away from Annabel. 'Aha! "Southend 'Guru' Ravi, real name Kevin Gunderson, sentenced to ten years following a trial for financial fraud. Sexual assault allegations have also . . . " Ugh, no, that's horrible.' She shudders, and squeezes my hand. 'Katherine, you are not going there. Look, how about Morton Grange?'

She clicks on a tab and pushes her laptop across to me. The screen is filled by an azure pool. It would be like swimming in Chris Hemsworth's eyes. For a moment, I let myself get lost in a fantasy of sunrise yoga, fresh fruit breakfast buffets, cool cotton bed linen . . . When I come to, I realise Constance is saying something.

' . . . And apparently, she went there to recuperate, after they threw eggs at her, at the Tory Party Conference. I mean, we'd all like to throw an egg or two, but if it's good enough for Lady—'

'Stop!' I say. 'It looks lovely – too lovely. We all know what I'm like, I'd be obsessing over the carbon impact of heating that pool. There would be loads of four-wheel drives in the car park, too, I can picture them. And if I see a Tory, I can't throw eggs, can I? It wouldn't be vegan.'

'She has a point,' says Annabel. 'Although, Katherine, I was just reading that in terms of environmental impact, you're better off with an egg than an avocado.'

'Don't start her off!' says Constance. 'If Katherine didn't eat avocados there would be nothing left of her – she'd just be a Greenpeace T-shirt floating in space.'

'I have never owned a Greenpeace T-shirt,' I say, primly. 'And I will eat eggs, if I know the chickens.'

'Ooh!' says Annabel. 'Then this next one might be great ... "Cadwell Manor specialises in Holistic Integrated Wellness. This retreat is designed to provide a respite from the world, while putting our guests in touch with the Earth."'

'I saw that,' says Constance, doubtfully. 'It looked a bit crunchy. At Morton Grange, you get a pillow menu ...' She reads from her laptop. '"Cadwell Manor offers guests a combination of guided activities designed to promote psychological and spiritual well-being." It doesn't even *mention* the pillows.' She frowns at Annabel, and keeps reading. '"The programme, created by noted psychotherapist Hema Bhal – as featured by Goop – includes erotic meditation, scream therapy, guided journaling ..."'

'Bloody hell,' I mutter. 'No, thank you.'

'Hold on, this sounds quite good, actually ... "A nature lover's paradise, Cadwell is situated in five acres of wilderness, with its own lake, and is visited by a wide range of bugs and butterflies. It was recently featured on *Countryfile* after a sighting of some rare water voles,"' Constance finishes triumphantly. 'Come on, Katherine, that's got to be right up your alley.'

'Let me see!' Annabel muscles her way back in. '"Our aim at Cadwell is to start the healing journey,"' she intones, speaking in the voice she'd use if she ever had to be on a podcast. It's very irritating. '"This is a space for the lost and found. We can't promise to fix you, but we can promise to help you to discover the tools that will allow you to heal."'

'They've said "heal" and "healing", that's rubbish copywriting,' I say, grumpily.

'It's got great reviews,' says Constance, shrugging. 'The name is ringing so many bells. Wasn't there some sort of notorious seventies party there? With that woman who died – who's the one who wasn't actually in Fleetwood Mac, but looks like she should have been? She was married to Mick Jagger, or the other one. You know – he went mad on tour and drove a lawnmower into the sea, in Guernsey?' She taps something into her phone. 'Tamara de Witt! Yes! She's five on "seven rock 'n' roll ghosts who haunt English country houses".'

This is my chance. Constance has mentally left the kitchen, and she's travelling through tangent land. If I ask the right questions, I'm free! 'Has Annabel heard your Mick Jagger story?' I ask, innocently. 'Annabel, you know Constance got backstage at a Rolling Stones concert at Madison Square Gardens . . . '

Annabel catches my eye and raises her eyebrows. Traitor. 'We need to focus,' she says. 'Let's call Cadwell Manor and find out when they can fit you in.'

'OK,' I say. 'Sounds good. Although I bet they get booked up really far in advance. Still, maybe they'll have a cancellation, or something!' Of course they won't have a cancellation. Their waiting list must be backed up for *months*! And I'll look sad, and Constance and Annabel will think that I'm reluctantly bowing out of their evil plan, my hand forced by circumstance rather than – I withhold a shudder – scream therapy.

Constance taps frantically at her phone for a few seconds, before looking up. 'I've got the Real Housewives on it. Christa says she went to school with Hema. She's going to send me her number.'

Annabel nods, approvingly. 'I believe there's nothing that can't be solved by the right group chat. Christa just sent an aubergine and an exploding head – I guess she's a big fan of the erotic meditation.'

Damn. I guess I like the sound of the water voles. But I could do that here, at home, with some YouTube videos. And I suppose erotic meditation could actually be— I shut that thought down as quickly as it begins. Nothing good can come from thinking about that.

Chapter Ten

Found family

Ben did not understand how I could be terrified of meeting Constance. 'Oh, you'll love her,' he'd said, as he swung the Honda down darkening country roads, past signs to places with names like Little Mistledown, and Hinton in the Hedges. 'Everyone does.'

I'd sighed, thinking *Yes, Ben, that really isn't what I'm worried about.* We flew over potholes, as the box of chocolates bounced on my knee. I could feel my thumbs getting sweaty against the cellophane. In my head, she was a steel-haired dowager countess, who was going to examine my shoes and mind for scuffs. 'Isn't that last season's skirt length?' I imagined her scoffing, as I stood in her doorway. Even though I was wearing jeans.

I knew I was being ridiculous, of course. In fact, I'd googled her, and she looked like Ben: blonde, golden, cheerful – no evidence of the sour pout I was imagining. Plus, her last column had been a hymn to getting hammered at Christmas parties and not bothering to take your make-up off before you go to bed: 'We all do it. Let's be real, the best that most of us can manage is a pint of water and two Nurofen before bed. Here are five cleansers that will help to wash away your hangover, the morning after the night before.'

All at once, Ben stopped singing to Chris Rea and spun us ninety degrees into a large gravel drive.

'You told me your mum's place in Dorset was a cottage!' I said. I'd been picturing a child's drawing, a sort of two-up, two-down affair where a Victorian woodcutter might live. But the house sprawled before us. You could fit at least three cottages in it. It had separate outbuildings.

'Yeah, it is,' said Ben. 'Wellacres Cottage. Let's go! I'm ready for a whisky Mac.'

I fumbled for the door handle. Oh, God. Oh, no. This was terrifying. Maybe there was still time to make my exit. I could leave all my stuff in the car, and then do a runner when Ben was in the toilet. Or I could pretend I forgot ... what? Contact lens solution, or mysterious medication, and I could drive home to get it, and by the time I'd come back, I'd have missed Christmas ... I gripped the chocolates harder, making an indentation in the lid of the box.

'Yes! You're here!' A tall, blonde woman was dancing across the gravel. 'Darlings! Oh my God, you're Katherine!' and I was being hugged, being pushed away, and squinted at, and being hugged again. Thornton's Continental Collection fell to the gravel.

'Shit, sorry!' said Constance, stooping to pick up the box. Already, she made me feel as though I was receiving special attention from the Head Girl. It was simultaneously blinding and warming, like being subsumed by a sunbeam. 'Are those for me? How did you know! I love ironic chocolate!'

I knew because Nanna raised me to believe that a box of chocolates was a passport, and you'd be denied entry beyond any domestic threshold without something sweet tucked under your oxter.

She grinned. 'I'm so sick of all of that single estate bullshit, aren't you? Like, fine, sure, it's important to drink good coffee – but when it comes to chocolate, let me live! Give me a bag of Buttons and leave me in peace!'

'Actually, developments in the production of fairtrade chocolate ... ' I started, but she was holding me by the elbow and looking at me again.

'I think we've got the same jeans on,' she said, laughing. 'Are they the Frame indigo boyfriend cut?'

'Um,' I said, stalling for time. I knew there was a right answer to this question, and it probably wasn't what I was about to say. 'Not sure. I got these from the Trinity Hospice shop on Upper Street.' I looked into her shining eyes and waited for her face to harden. Constance wouldn't approve of old clothes. She was a glossy magazine person. She'd think I was smelly and dirty and throw me out of her house.

But she grinned. 'Oh my God, you're a genius and I hate you,' she said, laughing. 'This is my curse, Katherine. It's like lightning striking. I'm surrounded by brilliant women who have a real gift for finding vintage and preloved. It's like they're psychic. I'm also the sort of person who buys things full price, the day before they go in the sale ... anyway, come in! It's freezing! Drinks, then we'll sort your stuff out.'

'Speaking of big idiots,' said Ben, tapping Constance on the shoulder, 'you haven't hugged your child yet!'

'Come here!' I stood aside to let them embrace. I knew

Constance was whispering something to Ben about me. I caught the word 'she's' but not the adjective that went with it. I tried not to think about what it might have been.

And yet when I walked into the house, I felt my shoulders drop a little. It was warm, in every sense. I could smell woodsmoke – it was Ben's smell, dialled up to 10. I breathed it in, and felt my spirits lift, before remembering that I'd just been reading a report about the environmental impact of wood burners. Should I say something to Constance? No, it was Christmas Eve, and I was a guest in her home. I'd wait. Someone was bound to give someone else a jumper, and I could say, 'You can wear that and stop using the wood burner! I've heard that in one week, a wood burner could generate more CO_2 than a whole convoy of lorries driving from Luton to Newquay!' And everyone would say, 'Wow! How fascinating!'

Still, I loved the brightness generated by the firelight, the way the tension in my body – and there was a lot of tension – seemed to dilute and unfurl. I'd been punctured, and I didn't mind at all. I relaxed even more when Constance came in, carrying the chocolates. She placed them on the table with a flourish.

'Right, obviously there's fizz in the fridge, and we've got drink drinks in the drawing room. I'll get my useless son to make you a whisky. Unless you want a,' she snorted, 'cup of tea?'

Ben appeared beside her. 'Let's have whisky, it's cold. And what do you mean, "useless son"? Your other son is much more useless.'

'True,' said Constance. 'My other son is being antisocial on his laptop, so you're definitely the favourite. Still,' she said, meditatively, 'Sam has flown in from afar! You just had to take the M3.'

'Sam is out in … Dubai?' I said, cautiously, as though testing myself. Ben had been vague about his brother, and I couldn't quite gauge their closeness. It didn't help that Ben didn't seem to understand what Sam did – but then, I didn't really have a grasp on what Ben did either. He had just been promoted to 'operations manager' – and was now responsible for insuring insurance companies, which made me think of a set of Matryoshka dolls holding sets of risk assessment forms.

Every time I asked him to explain, he'd get about eight minutes in before saying, 'Jesus, I'm so bored I want to cry. Insurance isn't sexy, is it?'

I knew Sam had gone into finance, and that when Ben described him as 'an aspiring Loro Piana hat guy' it was not meant as a compliment. However, I also knew that Ben and Sam were still playing a childhood game they had invented called 'green car' – one boy had to let the other know whenever they saw a green car. That was how I remembered about Dubai. Sam sent Ben a lot of pictures of very expensive green cars.

Constance rolled her eyes. 'Well, right now he's upstairs, emailing and video conferencing with various people in Dubai, because obviously they don't do Christmas.'

'Poor Sam!' I said. 'He must be exhausted. Does he not get any proper time off at all?'

'He loves it!' Constance picked up a glass and drained it. 'Phew, that was a lot more whisky than Mac, I'd better watch it or no one will get any supper. Yeah, Sam is just like his dad, he loves work, money and not much else. Mind you, Peter has kept me in real estate, so I can't complain too much.' She laughed. 'Sorry, Kath, you did get the useless son. Sam likes bucks; Ben likes boats. All he needs for perfect happiness is to be close to a large body of water.'

I smiled, shyly. 'He's taken me out, once. We've not been back since, though. I guess it's getting a bit cold.'

Constance raised her eyebrows. 'For Ben, there's no such thing. So – assuming you've not been pacing a widow's walk, and shaking your fist at the ocean – he's been hanging out with you on dry land? Not waking up at bollocks o'clock and making you drive out into the dark, wearing a pair of waders?' She smiled, warmly. 'I knew he liked you a lot, but – he likes you so much that he's not constantly running into the water? Wow!'

I felt awkward. I didn't know what to say. 'I know we're near the coast here, so maybe we'll go out . . . ' I trailed off. Constance was implying it was a good thing that we hadn't been out there together much, but if Ben loved boats and Ben loved me, wouldn't his greatest love be me on a boat? Our morning on the water had been magical, at least, to me. Why hadn't he suggested doing it again? Had I done something wrong?

I took a sip of whisky, and tried to focus on what Constance was saying. 'I do worry about safety, especially at this time of year. It's not so bad in the summer, but when it's dark, visibility is awful, there's a lot of wind. I know I'm being silly, but I'm his mum. It's my job to be silly. Or sensible. Annoying, either way.'

I couldn't tell whether she meant that she was annoying, or that the duties that fell to her were annoying. But I really liked her. She was kind, she was welcoming, she was unlike anyone I had ever met before. She was much less complicated than I expected her to be. Even in just a few short moments it was obvious to me that she loved first. She loved more than she worried, and let love guide her. And I realised that once she had decided she loved you, there wasn't much that either of you could do to change that. She hadn't invited me because she wanted me to prove that I was worthy of her perfect son. She wanted to love me because Ben loved me. In the warmth of Constance's kitchen, I felt wanted. My body seemed to crunch and click into place. There was fabulous food, and extravagant gifts – but it was Constance's emotional generosity that meant the most. In her home, I had the best Christmas I'd ever known.

A year passed, with terrifying speed. I had a small promotion, which meant I was allowed to start running some of my own client meetings. Before my first one, I felt sick with anxiety for seventy-two hours beforehand, and during it, I became so nervous that I spoke like Donald Duck for the first ten minutes, but otherwise it went well.

Ben was promoted again, and I understood even less about his job than I had done previously. There seemed to be more operations to manage, but he was happy enough. Every other week, he went sailing, and maybe every other month, I went with him. To my disappointment, he never took me back to the lake, with the little boat. Ben was happiest when the water, and crew, were fast and furious. I wanted to love it as much as he did – but secretly, I liked the idea of the sailing much more than the sailing itself. I told myself that if I kept trying, it would click.

But I never got to grips with the salopettes, even though

Ben bought me my own pink pair. And that was the least of it. There were so many layers. Extra braces and harnesses and things made out of rubber. I felt like a toy – you could push me over, and I'd bounce straight back up again – and eventually, I realised that was simply a manifestation of the typical sailor's emotional state.

But I knew it meant a lot to Ben, so I made the effort, especially when it came to his sailor friends. I really wanted to like them. Well, to be completely honest, I wanted them to like me. I don't think they disliked me – it was more that they were genuinely, completely uninterested. I tried to pay attention, to figure out the strange language, the crucial difference between one kind of knot and another. It seemed as though sailing had its own code, deliberately created to confuse outsiders. The sailors weren't interested in irony, or silliness, or even the superficial chat I could get away with at work, the can-you-believe-Dua-Lipa-might-be-doing-a-West-End-musical, or 'Oh-my-God-did-you-see-that-thing-in-The-Infatuation-about-the-noodle-bar-in-Pinner? Life-changing dim sum in Harrow, who'd-a thunk it?' The only time I heard any of them laugh was when they were talking about someone named Grungo who drank nine pints one lunchtime and then fell off his boat. (In the spirit of full disclosure, I laughed too.)

There were moments, on the water, when I thought I'd got it. Being lost in all that great big blue on blue, while a white noise wind blows everything else out of your body. The razor-edge cold that made everything smooth and numb, fast and thrilling. There would be seconds of pure, magic euphoria. Then I'd fumble my knots, get in the way, and feel stupid and useless and I'd hear Grungo bellowing, 'Katherine, did you touch the halyard again?' and the joy would drain straight out of me. And I'd wait for Ben to defend me, to tell me it was an easy mistake, to gently explain the right way to do things, like he had that very first time – but it never came.

Elsewhere, he was chivalrous to the point of being old-fashioned. If someone jostled my stool in a pub, he'd be on his feet, with a stern 'Mate, watch it'. I'd be thinking that it was starting to get a little chilly, and before the words were out of my mouth, I'd feel the weight of his cashmere coat being draped around my shoulders. Once, he drove all the way to Bristol to pick me up when a meeting finished late and all the trains were cancelled.

But on the water, he was different. He wasn't like his friends, exactly. He was never boorish or aggressive or cruel or critical, and he never fell off a boat. But sailing was his drug, his trance state. It was an addiction. No, I was never going to find him passed out in a gutter, under a pile of ships in bottles. He wasn't going to risk his life in a Clapton back street, having found a guy who could cut him a deal on a wetsuit. But he needed sailing, more than anyone or anything. And, out there, he didn't need me. He didn't really see me at all.

Privately, I started to worry that this was a problem.

'I know it's good for us to have separate interests,' I said to Annabel. 'But maybe he needs to be with someone who loves sailing as much as he does. Someone who really understands it. And him.'

'No one loves sailing as much as Ben, though,' said Annabel. 'Not even the people he sails with. From what you've told me, most of them use it as an excuse to give themselves alcohol poisoning and spend five hundred pounds at Helly Hansen. Have you talked to him about it?'

'No,' I said, dully. 'I don't really know how. I think he's pulling away. He seems less ... not interested, exactly, but something is off. The other day, Christmas came up, and he got really weird. Offhand. Like, "You are coming, aren't you?" I think he's just assumed I'll come, but he doesn't care if I'm there.'

Annabel frowned. 'I don't think that's offhand, at all. He expects you to spend Christmas with him. He feels secure with you, your lives are entwined. That's a big deal.'

'Maybe,' I said. 'I suspect he feels obliged to invite me because I don't have anywhere else to go. And I'm scared to ask him about it, in case I rock the boat. No pun intended.'

'Look, Ben is a grown-up. We both know he's able to handle rocking boats, literally and figuratively. I think it's normal to feel a bit insecure. This is your longest, happiest relationship, and you've got nothing to compare it to. But you could make two mistakes here. You either make yourself miserable and sabotage it slowly by not talking to him, because you're afraid to breathe out and communicate,' said Annabel.

'Very good,' I said, grudgingly. 'But I'm fairly sure that you copied it off Esther Perel. What's the other mistake?'

'Actually, it came up on Oprah's podcast,' said Annabel. 'The other mistake is that you sabotage it quickly. You blow it up because you can't bear the uncertainty of being a vulnerable human in love. Just talk to him.'

I sighed. It was much easier to talk to Annabel about Ben. 'I'll try,' I said.

'Honestly, I don't think you have anything to worry about. He tells you he loves you all the time,' said Annabel. 'I've heard him. And I've heard you say it back. And you spend nearly every night a week at his. Why you're still paying rent on this place is beyond me.'

'I dunno,' I said. 'Moving in is a big step, and he's never mentioned it. And if anything does go wrong, which it almost definitely will, I still live here officially, so ...'

Annabel punched me in the arm. 'Hey! What about me? You're supposed to say that you're staying here because your beloved bff, aka me, will get lonely without you ...'

'Well, obviously that too! Anyway, what about Andy?' I said. Annabel had recently started seeing her personal trainer. Well, sleeping with him. 'You might want to move in with him.'

'Ha! It's just sex, as well you know. How are things on that front with you and Ben? That's usually a fairly reliable barometer for the state of the union.'

'Actually,' I said, flushing, 'pretty great, I think. The quantity could be improved upon, but I have no complaints about the quality.' It was a half-truth; the sex was good, but it was so infrequent that I was starting to forget how good. I was trying not to worry about it too much.

For the last couple of months, I'd noticed that Ben often seemed too tired, anxious, and distracted. 'Work stress,' he'd say. 'Sorry.' I'd ask him if he wanted to talk about it, and he'd shrug, and tell me it was too boring. 'No point depressing both of us.' I knew he was under a lot of pressure in the office, and I didn't want to turn the bedroom into another place where he felt forced to perform. But I craved his touch, and when he didn't reach for me, I felt as though

I'd done something wrong. Secretly, I was ashamed of myself. I couldn't even tell Annabel. It's one thing to share embarrassing confessions about doing the wrong thing with the wrong person. It's another to admit that there isn't anything to report at all.

Annabel shrugged. 'It's been a year, this is the natural sexy drop-off point. Of course you're having less sex, it always slows down a bit. You're scared, and you're over-thinking things. This is classic Katherine – your brain is always looking for something to be anxious about. This is new, and lovely, it's terrifying for you. You're waiting for the shoe to drop. And if it doesn't happen soon, you're going to throw them in the lake yourself.'

'That's a very confusing mixed metaphor,' I said, primly.

'It's not, it's from "Hounds of Love". Anyway – let's save this conversation for when you've been together for ten years, and you've found his ... I don't know, Teenage Mutant Ninja Turtle themed porn, and you're contemplating divorce and you don't know what to do about your joint ISA. For now, just relax. Let yourself love and be loved.'

'Did you see that on a cushion somewhere?' I said, grumpily. 'If you buy it, I will burn it. Live laugh love. All you need is love. Love is the drug. Keep calm and carry on shagging. If you like, I'll do that for you for Christmas as a cross stitch.'

'Perfect! And would you rather have a Campaign for Nuclear Disarmament logo, or "save the whales"? I'll do it double-sided, I'll get a jumper from a charity shop, and unpick the wool, and ...' Annabel was laughing too hard to speak, and I started laughing too. I felt a lot better.

*

As Christmas drew nearer, I did talk to Ben. I said he seemed a little withdrawn, and had I done something wrong? Could I do anything better? And he shook his head and apologised and blamed 'boring work stuff'. The day afterwards, he sent me flowers – tightly budded ranunculi and winter roses, with a card that said: 'For Katherine, who does everything right'. In retrospect, that was worrying, but at the time it was reassuring enough for me to get into the Honda and drive down to Dorset, singing Chris Rea all the way.

I'd seen Constance maybe seven or eight times since our initial meeting. We'd been for 'supper' at her place in Holland Park (another lesson in poshness – we had courgette cacciatore and lemon tart, not biscuits and hot chocolate in our dressing gowns). The more I saw her, the more I liked her, especially when I allowed myself to forget that she was Ben's mother. I'd never spent proper time with a real adult before. Not one who swore, and gossiped, and laughed, and genuinely didn't care about whether you used a coaster.

When we hit the gravel, Constance was out on the drive before the car door was open, waiting for me to emerge. 'Oh, Katherine,' she said, gathering me into her arms and squeezing me. 'I'm so excited.'

'Great!' I said, mystified. 'Um, for Christmas?'

'Yessssss,' she said, and looked past me, trying to make eye contact with Ben. 'For Christmas!'

She led us into the house, hopping from foot to foot. 'Is it OK if I go to the loo?' I asked. 'You go first, if you need to?'

'Yes! No! Great! You go, actually. I need to have a quick word with Ben!' she trilled, all but shoving me into the boot room.

I sat down and picked up an old copy of the *London Review of Books*. I tried, and failed, to understand a paragraph about European monetary policy, and flicked forward to a piece about a new encyclopaedia of drugs, which reminded me that Constance's old friend Eva was coming for Christmas. I hadn't met Eva yet. She was Ben's godmother – a model turned artist who'd had a wild old time in the eighties and nineties. I giggled. That's what's up with Constance. She and Eva must have spent the afternoon reliving the bad old days. I thought quickly. Would I need to sort out dinner? Technically Christmas Eve wasn't a bank holiday, the shops might still be open. Maybe I could order a curry? This was a chance for me to be useful, and help!

Unless . . . oh, God. What if Constance wanted us all to take drugs with her? What if this was why Ben had been so weird with me? What if the police came? I stared at the magazine, panicking. What if the house got searched and this article counted as evidence? I flicked through to the back pages, leaving it opened on the classified ads. 'Nothing to see here, officer, I'm just thinking about renting a country house for sixteen people in the Dordogne!'

'Katherine,' called Ben, through the door. 'Are you OK in there?'

'Coming!' I shouted. I scurried back into the kitchen, in time to hear Constance say: ' . . . think you should just get it over with.' Then she saw me, and turned red, and then I turned red. Then Ben turned red. He picked up a bottle of champagne and said, 'I'd better put this back in the fridge. Whisky Mac?'

I remember very little of dinner that evening. Just Ben, every so often, touching my elbow and asking if I was OK, and me, trying not to cry. When it got too much, I hid in the loo and concentrated as hard as I could on European Monetary Policy. Did Constance really want Ben to dump me, in front of everyone? She really wanted him to 'get it over with' at Christmas?

Eva was fun, and kind. I have a shameful memory of listening to her talking about the sculpture she'd been working on for the last few months, and then panicking and asking if she preferred acrylics or watercolours. She squeezed my knee, and said, 'Oh, love, you look knackered. I'm the same, I always feel peaky after a long journey. And these bumpy country lanes don't help.' Sam had brought his new girlfriend. He left her at the table, and disappeared upstairs, muttering something about the markets. I thought about running after him and asking him to explain the LRB article. His girlfriend, Brooke, told a very long story about going to Fendi and accidentally ordering two pairs of boots.

At about nine o'clock I said I wasn't feeling very well and went to bed. 'I'll be straight up,' said Ben. But when I woke up, twelve hours later, I couldn't tell whether he'd been in the bed with me at all.

I sat up and considered my options. A good cry would help. I'd feel better afterwards – unless I started and couldn't stop. You never have to see these people again, I told myself. Just get through the next forty-eight hours. At least there was plenty of alcohol in the house. Constance was a generous pourer and it was Christmas. I could start at breakfast, and no one would object.

Standing under the shower, I thought about Christmases gone by and how bad they'd been. Would being dumped be worse? I'd survived being fourteen, when Nanna had caught me sneaking out to a party on Christmas Eve – and sent me to my room until Boxing Day. And being eleven, and made to peel pounds and pounds of potatoes when my period pains were so bad that I could barely stand. ('Your mother was the same,' she'd said. 'Always making such a fuss. Hard work is the best thing for it.')

I could remember being six or seven, and being allowed to watch *The Muppet Christmas Carol* – it was a treat I'd been longing for, and looking forward to for weeks. But when the moment came, it made me weep for reasons I didn't have the vocabulary to explain, back then. I suppose I saw all of that love on screen, and I ached for it, and felt the lack of it, and I could see that Scrooge had become Scrooge because he had been starved of love, too …

I had to get a grip. I held the showerhead up to my face and permitted myself a small bout of sobbing. OK, so this was another bad one to add to the list. Here, I'd experienced the most love I had ever known. It would hurt horribly to lose it.

Dressed, and determined to be brave, I made my way to the breakfast table. 'Good morning!' I said. 'Happy Christmas! Did everyone sleep well?'

Something strange was going on. Firstly, Sam was there, looking at me, and, for once, not tapping at a phone or rustling papers. In fact, everyone was there but Ben. It was as if they were waiting to begin a play, and my first line was everyone's cue.

'Where's Ben?' I said, trying to keep the tears out of my voice. It seemed shameful to still, technically, be his girl-friend and not know where he was.

'Katherine! Down here!'

Everyone's eyes moved to the same spot. It took me a second to follow them. Ben was kneeling by the side of the table, in front of an open window. Like me, he was holding on to a small, wrapped package.

Ben's face, I realised, had started to feel like home. All that old gold, the tawny warmth of him, bright eyed and hopeful. He looked at me the way he had at the beginning. He didn't seem distant or distracted.

'Katherine, I love you,' he said. 'You make me happy, and I want to look after you. You're the sweetest, kindest person I've ever met.' He started to look panicky. 'I had a big speech planned and I've gone completely blank. Will you marry me?'

'Yes!' Constance jumped in the air, and I was aware of the pop of a cork. 'Oh, fuck, sorry! Not me. Katherine, you will marry him, won't you?'

'Of course!' I said, and dropped to my knees, beside Ben. I threw my arms around him and burst into tears. I was the happiest girl in the world! Relief coursed through me like a general anaesthetic. As Ben slid the ring onto my finger, I made myself a promise. From now on, I was going to stop leaping to conclusions, and assuming the worst. I was going to trust Ben and trust myself. Everything was going to be different.

Chapter Eleven

For your #journey

The universe has got it in for me.

Cadwell Manor had a cancellation. According to Constance, Hema Bhal is beyond desperate to welcome me to the world of Holistic Integrated Wellness. She's going to take a personal interest in my healing journey and she's especially keen that I experience the full benefits of Erotic Meditation.

'I think Christa told her that I'm a journalist, and she's hoping I might run a piece,' admitted Constance. 'That woman knows how to lay it on thick. Still, this is fantastic! I didn't want to say anything, but I was worried that it might be tricky to find something at short notice. Maybe this was meant to be!'

The last few days have reminded me of the run-up to my wedding. Constance and Annabel are bustling. I've been a fixture at the kitchen island, perched on my stool, drinking my very expensive tea and awaiting further instructions. Then, every so often, one of them will run in and say 'energy bars!' or 'you need new underwear!' before running straight out again.

The shopping has been relentless. I keep trying to tell them that I really don't need any new underwear, or tiny shampoo bottles, or a new suitcase. But I can't summon the energy for an argument, at the moment. Maybe they're right about the energy bars.

It's only a week. How bad can seven days be? I'll make friends with the chickens. I'll find a way of getting out of the erotic meditation. Then, I'll come home and maybe I can persuade work to take me back. I'll tell them I've been fixed. I'll stroll into the office, wearing a badge that says I GOT CURED AT CADWELL MANOR!, and everything will go back to normal.

Anyway, this time last week, I was in the middle of the worst day of my life. No, obviously the day Ben died was the worst day of my life. Or the day my mum died. Last Monday was a different kind of worst – the shameful day, the day the sky fell in, and the walls tumbled down, the day when everything went wrong, and it was all my fault. The horror is behind me. It can only get better from here. And at least I can't get fired from Cadwell Manor.

'Keys! Keys! Where are *my bastarding* keys? Oh, found them! We're leaving in five!' Constance calls, from the kitchen. 'Don't forget to go to the toilet!'

'I've just been!' I say, trying not to shout, erasing the whine from my voice and suppressing the urge to follow with 'You do know that I am thirty years old?'

She emerges from the doorway with an armful of packets. 'We'll stop on the way for lunch or something,' she says. 'But it's good to have snacks. Can you grab some bananas? And I bought us matching keep cups!'

I can't help myself. 'I already have one in my bag! You

have at least eight in your cupboard, I've seen them. You're treating them like single-use plastic, which doesn't help the environment one bit. "Keep" does not mean, in this context, "Keep buying these cups".'

Her face crumples, and I immediately feel terrible. 'Sorry, sorry, it was a lovely thought, I'll go and get them.'

As I step into the kitchen and see the matching pair, a lump forms in my throat. I like being part of a pair. I liked it. I didn't notice that almost everything comes in twos until I didn't. What if I'm always the odd girl out again from now on? I'm so uncoupled, so adrift, that I need to team up with my dead husband's mother. It's like at school, when thirty-three of us had to get into twos, and no one wanted me to make three with them, and I had to conjugate *avoir* with the teacher.

I pick up the cups, which are Tiffany-box blue, with gold, cursive writing. One says 'Katherine' and the other says 'Constance', and both say 'for your #journey'. It's a classic example of Constance being completely thoughtless, and profoundly thoughtful. It's cheesy, and cringy, and it's so kind it makes me want to cry. If I start, I won't stop. I have to grip the side of the kitchen counter very hard, and say, in a false, bright voice, 'Ooh. Now, where are the bananas? Must not forget those bananas!'

The cups are too tall for stacking, so when I return to the hall, I'm clasping one in each hand, a banana balanced on each shoulder like epaulettes, a monkey major. Constance takes a cup and turns it, checking the name. 'These looked great online, but they're a bit naff, aren't they? It's impossible to buy anything that doesn't have a hashtag on it these days,' she says, and I know it's an apology.

'I actually love mine, this is the only keep cup I'm going to use from now on,' I say. I'm sorry, too.

She starts to set the alarm, and I walk down the steps, scanning the street for her enormous, ridiculous black jeep. Automatically, I start to do the climate maths for the journey ahead: can I persuade Constance to give up meat for a month to offset the petrol?

'Katherine, it's open!' calls Constance, striding towards me. Like a baby, I stand, dumb and motionless, as she opens the boot, puts my case in and closes it, before giving it a reassuring smack with the palm of her hand and raising her eyebrows. There's something about her face that briefly evokes Benny Hill.

'What?' she says, as I look at her quizzically. 'Peter always did that before a long drive. I don't know why I still do.' Her mouth turns down for a fraction of a second, and I think about Ben's dad. I don't think Constance has any regrets about the end of her marriage, but I suppose she has been muddling through, too, trying to find the rituals that make her feel less adrift, a former part of a pair.

'Right! Let's go! Road trip!' she cheers as we clamber into the car. 'Woo!'

I start to turn the radio on, readying myself for a blast of Classic FM, but Constance hands me her phone. 'I made a playlist,' she says, sounding pleased with herself.

Perhaps unfairly, I'm always surprised by Constance's singing voice. She's good. Tuneful. She has a lusty contralto, she sounds as though she might be a cousin of Bonnie Raitt. At our engagement party – and I still haven't worked out why we had karaoke or whose idea it was – she picked up the microphone and I felt sick with terror for her, for me. She'd had a lot to drink. I'd appealed to Ben. 'Should someone . . . intervene?' He smiled, shook his head and said, 'Trust me, she's fine,' and Constance belted out a showstopping rendition of 'Walking in Memphis'.

The nice thing about being side by side, in the car, is that you can talk about nothing, and everything. It's a safe space for big questions. As I hear Amy Winehouse singing the very first line of 'Rehab' – a playlist choice that feels a little on the nose for me – I start to think out loud.

'Sometimes, I think about Amy and Ben. Dying young, I mean. Completely different circumstances, obviously. But . . . ' I'm not entirely sure where I'm going with this, and I'm already regretting voicing this thought, but it's too late to stop now. 'When I hear this song, I just can't link the life or the warmth of it with death or ending. And I think it's the same with Ben. Sometimes I see an old photo, or something reminds me of him, and I find myself wondering where he is and when he'll be back. Does that make any sense?'

Constance murmurs, in assent. 'All the time. It's horrible, but it really helps to know that you're feeling it too. I wonder whether we should both have a couple of sessions with Jonathan, when you get back. Together.'

'Sure,' I say. 'I mean, it's really kind of you to offer.' I would rather go to an orgy with Constance than go to therapy with her. Is there no end to this hell? This week is supposed to fix me. I thought that if I agreed to go, I'd be excused from grief, and fit for work again. It wasn't meant to be the beginning of bonus grief. Post-graduate grief. I need to change the subject. 'I can't believe I'm doing something like this,' I say, because I really, really can't. 'It seems so indulgent, and so strange. I should be getting punished for what happened at Shrinkr, not sent on a luxury retreat.' I wince, realising I haven't even thought about how much this is going to cost. 'I bet it's horribly expensive, too. Do I pay at the end, or do I need to pay you back?' There's no way I'm going to be able to afford this. I hope there's an instalment plan.

'Fucking hell, Katherine, this is a gift! Let me do something nice for you! I thought we were past this,' says Constance, then, 'Oh, God, sorry, sorry! Not you!' as she bashes the steering wheel and accidentally honks at a woman in a Fiat 500. 'Whoops! She looked so pissed off with me.'

'No, I think that's just her face. It looks like she had a Groupon eyebrow microblading accident,' I say. 'I'm sorry I'm being such a brat, I'm just nervous, I suppose. Honestly, I know I'm not going to fit in. I'm worried ... ' I clasp my hands, pushing my palms away from me. Making the church, then the steeple. Who are the people?

'What else is new?' She stops at a red light, and I watch the people crossing the road. Everyone here has the Groupon eyebrows. Are they all related? Is it a cult? Maybe it's my eyebrows that are wrong?

As we drive on, the landscape changes: from mostly chicken shops, to mostly bridal shops, then motorway, grey and green, under a big blue sky. The heat seems to make the air shimmer. Constance gets overtaken by an aggressive ice cream van, which makes her jump, and she accidentally turns on the windscreen wipers. We pull into a services for coffee, and as we queue at Pret with our matching cups, Constance says, 'I wonder if they'll think we're sisters' and

I can't work out if it makes me want to hug her or storm off and sulk in the car on my own. Perhaps we are sisters in spirit.

Walking back to the car, I think about the strangeness of where we are, a liminal space. All these people in transition, in motion. I know there's something very wrong with a world where so many motorway service stations are necessary. These are palaces of plastic, running on pain, temples that only exist thanks to a succession of bonfires. Filled with millions of Constances, who drive everywhere with no conscience, believing that bringing their own cup will make all the difference. Part of me wants to climb on the roof with a megaphone, so I can yell, 'YOU SHOULD ALL TAKE PUBLIC TRANSPORT! YOU SHOULD ALL MAKE YOUR OWN SANDWICHES!'

But another part of me loves the car, the way it makes me feel soft, and quiet, and private. And the way this space is designed for adult children, warm, womb sleepy, confused, craving sugar, milky coffee, and well-maintained toilets.

Amy is right: they are trying to make me go to rehab. I'd rather get back in the car and remain on an eternal road trip, driving, talking, stopping, never really arriving, staying in slow motion for ever.

We pull back out into the stream of traffic.

'Constance?'

'What?' She checks her mirrors, and we overtake a green VW Beetle.

'Green car!' I shout, unthinkingly. Then, 'What happens if I hate it? If I really hate it, if I actually can't bear it, if I freak out, if I want to leave?'

I sip my coffee and wait, hope for her to say, 'I'd drive

straight back and come for you!' There must be a hotel nearby. Maybe she'll stay over tonight, just in case.

She sighs. 'Um, I dunno? You'll scale a wall, or something? If you're ill, I'm sure they'll let you leave, but basically, you have to suck it up. Crack on. Remember that this too shall pass.'

'Right.' I don't like that answer. 'I've got an idea! Why don't you stay with me? I bet Hema would be absolutely delighted, and you could write about it, they'd probably let you stay for free . . . '

'Is there something in your coffee? You're being very needy for you, Katherine. You're usually so stoic.' She thinks for a minute. 'Sam was a little clingy, before he went to boarding school. But he was sixteen and only ever actually away for four nights at a time. I was surprised, because he was . . . well, you know, Sam.'

'What about Ben?' I ask, knowing the answer.

She laughs, but she looks a little stricken. 'Exactly as you can imagine. Hovering outside the car, saying, "Come on, if we don't get a move on, we'll miss the cake!" They did a sort of high tea on Sunday nights. He loved the whole thing. Thrilled to get to school. Thrilled to come home again.'

'One of the things I miss the most about him is how much he liked things,' I say. 'And as soon as he decided he liked something, that was pretty much it.' Just like Constance, really. I don't think I ever noticed quite how similar they were when Ben was here. 'Occasionally it drove me crazy, but most of the time it was hard not to be as happy as he was.'

'Yeah, it was,' she says. 'Less so when he was ten and his favourite things were the Crazy Frog song and SpongeBob

SquarePants. Oh, God! And when he was a teenager, all of his friends got into *The Matrix* – I never cared for it, I thought it was pretentious and nerdy and made for adolescent boys. I suppose it was.'

'I've seen the pictures,' I say, smiling as I thought of the framed photo on the wall in Dorset depicting Ben with a group of mates in sunglasses and pleather trench coats. Even Sam, looking slightly superior, hovering in the background in his *Matrix* outfit.

'That's how I knew he was going to marry you,' says Constance. 'I knew long before Ben did. As soon as he phoned and said, "Mum, I've met this girl," I thought, *Aha! It's happened!* and I made him bring you home for Christmas.'

Twisting my hair around my little finger, I pull it into a tourniquet, until I see the skin turning white. 'And you weren't worried? You didn't think "that bitch better not break his heart"?' I say, trying to lighten the heaviness.

'I think I liked you straight away through the phone,' says Constance. 'In that way, I suppose I'm quite similar to Ben. I've never really thought about it before.' And she flicks her indicator, and we turn, and turn again, driving under verdant canopies, trees bending and stooping to kiss. More liminal space.

In ten minutes, we'll be there. In twenty minutes, I'll be out of the car. In thirty or forty minutes, Constance will have left me. She'll hug me goodbye, she'll tell me that she'll see me soon, and then I will be completely alone.

It's just a week, I tell myself. A mint-coloured Ford Kuga moves up the inside lane. Green car, I think, closing my eyes.

Chapter Twelve

It's bad luck

Figuratively, and almost literally, my engagement ring was bigger than I was. It had belonged to Constance's great-grandmother – possibly originating with the grandmother before that, the family history was hazy. It was a huge, platinum-set oval diamond, with emeralds either side. Heavy was the hand that wore the ring. As soon as it was on my finger, it immediately listed to the left. 'If I'm not getting that, I might as well dump Sam now,' said Brooke. Constance and Eva giggled. 'I wasn't joking,' she added, coldly.

'Is it OK?' said Ben. 'I know how you feel about, erm, recycling, and when Mum said she had the ring, I thought it would be perfect! That you'd rather have something old, that had a bit of history.'

'And Ben didn't have to pay for your Christmas present! Nice one,' said Sam. 'I had to spend eight grand at Chanel. Shit, sorry, Brooke. Pretend to look surprised.'

'Chanel?' said Brooke. 'But what about the necklace I showed you at Cartier?' She stormed off upstairs, leaving the rest of us to start the serious business of getting drunk.

Later that evening, after at least two bottles of champagne and a nap, I staggered to the kitchen. Somehow, I was simultaneously pissed and hungover, and I needed to get pints of water into my body as quickly as possible. I squinted at the ring. I was engaged! Unless I dreamed it? It was funny, that giant diamond was probably more valuable than Ben's car. But it looked like something that fell out of a cracker.

'Katherine?'

'Argh!' I felt a warm hand on my back and leapt into the air.

'It's OK, it's OK! Sorry to make you jump,' Constance slurred. 'Listen, while you're here, I really want to talk to you.'

I took a deep breath and tried to sober up. I knew what was coming. Hurt my son and I'll break your kneecaps before throwing your body into the Thames. No one would miss you. Or possibly something about how if I was joining the family, I needed to clean myself up a bit, and I couldn't wear the heirloom ring if I wasn't going to sort out my nails. Or ...

'Um, OK. I'm not pregnant, by the way! In case you were wondering. At least, I don't think I am ...' I patted my stomach, which was round with potatoes and something Constance claimed to have created especially for me: figs in blankets.

'No, no. Although if you are, that would be brilliant!' She giggled, hiccupped, and poured herself a glass of water. 'Sorry. No. Right. This is kind of awkward, how do I put this? Katherine, I know this must be bittersweet. This is happening, and your mum isn't around to help you with the wedding planning.'

'I honestly hadn't thought of that.' I tried to think of what Mum would have said, whether she would have liked Ben. I tried to place her face, to find an actual memory, not just something I was recalling from a photograph. It was hard to imagine her here, solid and human. Occasionally, I really wanted to talk to her, but I couldn't imagine having a conversation about place settings or flowers.

In fact, I hadn't even been to a wedding. I didn't have aunts or uncles or cousins, that I knew about. The only wedding I'd ever been aware of was that of a very posh girl called Aurora, who Annabel had been friends with at uni. And she came back in a very bad mood – 'The church was freezing. I've never been so cold in my life. Aurora's mother kept looking at my tits and shaking her head, and I got so bored and so drunk that I got off with someone who turned out to be Aurora's uncle ...' – so I never felt that I'd been missing out on anything.

Constance brought me back to the room. 'Katherine, I want you to know that I'm going to be here for all of it. I want to help. Venues, bands, food, anything at all. If you wake up at 3 a.m. having a panic attack about boutonnières, you can call me.'

What was a boutonnière? I knew what a panic attack was, I was beginning to have one.

'Right. Great,' I said. 'Thank you. Sorry. That's really kind of you.'

'It's overwhelming, isn't it?' she said, and hugged me. I squeezed back, politely, but she did not let go. 'I'm so, so happy you're here,' she murmured, into my hair. 'You're really good for Ben, you know that? I hope he tells you how happy you make him. He really needs someone to look after. I'm so glad it's you.'

Almost exactly eighteen months later, I was standing in the same spot in the kitchen, looking out into the garden. The world looked like it was made of poster paint; the sun had just come up, and it made the whole sky shine. It was almost 6 a.m. Constance had already gone down the road to the hired barn, muttering something about marquee men and bacon sandwiches. I was waiting for the kettle to boil.

I twisted the ring, which still listed to the side. It had been adjusted, but then I lost weight. ('Stress,' said Constance, knowingly. 'This always happens to women when we get engaged.' And I thought, why on Earth is no one doing something about this? What kind of institution am I entering, if preparing for that institution tends to damage women's bodies as a matter of course? Why is no one investigating this?) With each twist, I thought, he loves me, he loves me not.

I told myself it would be strange if I wasn't scared. Forever is, as Prince said, a mighty long time.

But did I really want to spend forever with someone who didn't understand why I'd objected to the hog roast buffet? Apparently, there were 'lots of vegetarian options', and that made it OK. I understood Ben's argument that it was the 'principle of the thing', that our guests would be hungry, they'd travelled a long way to spend the day with us and celebrate, and now was not the time for me to 'literally shove my beliefs down their throats', but what about my principles?

Poor old pig. Poor old me.

'Boo!' This time, a different warm hand landed on my back, and snaked around my waist.

'You look so beautiful,' Ben whispered into my ear, holding me from behind. 'And – holy wow, what are these?' He rubbed the strap of the silky white camisole between his thumb and forefinger, then pulled at the waistband of my shorts. 'I like these.' He reached down a little further, fingering the embroidery on the back, tracing the cursive curves. 'What does that writing say?'

'Um ... "Here Comes the Bride". Your mum got them for me,' I said quickly. I felt slightly embarrassed about how much I liked the shorts. I'd never have bought them for myself, but when in Rome. Or in Constance's case, when in Victoria's Secret ... 'Anyway, what are you doing here? Did you stay here last night? I thought you were at the Plough Inn with the boys?'

'Couldn't sleep,' he said. 'I know this is very bad luck ...'

'What is?' I asked.

'To see each other, before – but this feels like it can only be a good thing to me.'

Still behind me, he kissed the top of my head, before trailing his lips down the back of my neck. I moaned softly, and I felt that magic shiver. Ben's arms felt so warm, and so solid around me.

Of course I wanted this forever. It was Ben.

Slowly and deliberately, he pulled my camisole strap, so that it fell down my shoulder.

'You know,' he murmured, reaching for the other strap, 'you'll be a respectable married woman in just a few hours. You'll be Mrs Attwell.' I could feel that Ben was hard and getting harder. I wriggled, pushing into him, wanting to feel him swelling against me.

'I wonder what our guests would think,' he said, 'if they knew, when they're watching you coming down the aisle in your white dress ... ' Ben started to lift up the bottom of the camisole. Obediently, I lifted my arms above my head, and let him pull it off my body. He threw it to the floor.

He turned me around so that I was facing him. He exhaled, almost reverentially. 'Wow. You're ... God, I want you so much.'

Something shifted. Usually, I felt self-conscious when Ben looked at me. He was always telling me I was sexy, gorgeous and beautiful, but I struggled to believe it. I couldn't let go of my fear that he must be scanning for flaws. I didn't understand how someone with his body could find anything they liked about my body.

But in that moment, I felt happy to be looked at. I stood up straight. As sunlight flooded the kitchen, we were both golden. And I thought, he wants me, and I want him. This man wants to fuck me, and he wants to marry me. I want him to bite my nipples. I want him to pull my shorts to my ankles, and then pull me to the floor. I want his skin on my skin.

I pulled down my shorts and stepped out of them. For once in my life I felt elegant. The action was balletic.

'I wonder what our guests would think,' I repeated, getting onto my knees. 'If they knew, when they're watching me coming down the aisle in my white dress ... that I'd had a dick in my mouth before breakfast.'

Looking up at Ben, I smiled, sweetly and innocently, before pulling down his grey joggers.

'No underwear?' I asked, running my right hand up the inside of his thigh. 'I think that brings good luck. For me, anyway.'

I'd never felt like this with Ben before – greedy, impatient. He belonged to me, he was mine to touch, and I was so excited I didn't know where to begin. I gripped his dick with both hands, wanting the heat of him, the hardness of him, and he said my name like he was scared. Like he was calling me to stop me from running out into the road.

Of course, I'd done this before with him. Usually there was something excessively polite about it. Not quite trans-actional – rather, it was as though my brain was a bulletin board, layered with notices about things to be anxious about, things to be neurotic about. I couldn't completely enjoy giving head, because I knew Ben would be obliged to reciprocate, and I couldn't enjoy that because I knew that I didn't taste like an ice cream sundae, the way that women were supposed to.

But as I opened my mouth as wide as I could, breathing Ben in, I realised, for the first time, I was an animal. We both were. And the noises he made, the way he said my name, the way he clawed at my head and shook his hips, made me feel powerful. I felt as though I was falling into his body. I could dig my fingernails into his flesh. I could let reason leave me. I could do whatever the hell I wanted, right now—

I felt Ben trembling. 'Katherine, stop. Stop!' He pulled away. I started to lose my balance, and he reached for my hands, pulling me up to standing. He kissed me.

'Your pyjamas say "Here Comes the Bride",' he said. He stroked my inner thigh, slowly, his hand going higher,

higher, and then not quite high enough, before returning to my knee. 'We both know what has to happen.' Gripping my bare hips, he bent me over the kitchen table.

I turned around to look at him over my right shoulder. 'What are you going to do to me?' I murmured.

'Well, first – this.'

He bent down behind me and used the palms of his hands to pull my legs apart. I felt his tongue against my skin. At first, the flickers of pleasure seemed gentle, even sweet. But soon, the sensations inside me quickly became too big, too loud to bear. Ben wasn't doing this because he thought I'd like it; he was tearing into me, wanting me, trying to get to the centre of me. I felt as though I was being devoured. How strange – seconds ago, I had all the power, and I loved the way that felt. And barely any time had passed and I'd been pushed in the opposite direction, gripped by this force that made me into waves and water, something was crashing into me, and I was crashing out, and as Ben forced his tongue inside me, and his hands stroked and pushed and rubbed, I thought this is it. This is everything. This is why I must marry this man.

I'd had orgasms with Ben before, of course. There was always a point where the pressure built into something pleasant and pressing, there was a climax, a good feeling that got better. And I'd had guilty, awkward orgasms on my own. Quick, intense, shuddering affairs that lingered heavy in the pit of my stomach. But now, as the sensations built, I stopped being able to name what was happening to me, I just felt dense and weightless. The atoms of me were becoming tighter and smaller and harder, before they split apart ...

And I was still coming when Ben stood up. I had to grip the top of the table to keep from sliding down it, and I think he said 'I love you', and then he was inside me, pinning me in place. I tried to focus on him, on us, moving together, but I was wild and formless, drunk on him. And then I heard him saying, 'Oh God, oh God, sorry,' and slumping heavily against me. And then he got to his feet, and I started to laugh, and he laughed too.

Then he kissed me very gently. 'Can I marry you now?' he said. 'I could kiss you forever.'

'Good,' I said. 'Because soon you'll be contractually obliged to.'

Then we thought we heard a car, and I said, 'Constance!' and he said, 'Mum!' and we both said, 'Shit!' and started scrambling for our clothes.

'Get out of here!' I said. 'She'll bollock you. And then she'll make you help with the marquee.'

'You didn't see me,' he said solemnly. 'And next time I see you – we'll be getting married. I know this was supposed to be bad luck, but I'm glad. Because for the rest of today, there will be a wall between us, of aunties, and caterers, and hairpins. And I don't want to marry a lot of hairpins. I want to marry you. And I want to fuck you on the kitchen floor every day for the rest of my life.'

'Is that going to be in the vows?' I said. 'I hope so.'

'If not, I'll put it in my speech. I'll tell everyone that I've promised. Even when I'm ninety and my back has given out.' He kissed me on the head and walked out of the door.

Sometimes I look back and wonder whether I wish I'd known everything that was going to happen. On the day, everything felt like a good sign. For the first time in my life, I thought that maybe my luck wasn't always going to be bad. Maybe I was worthy of the cake, the dress, the ring and the man.

I do know that on my wedding day I felt happy. Even if I knew exactly what the future held, I wouldn't have changed a single moment of that morning.

Chapter Thirteen

Arrival

Cadwell Manor is a strange shape, like a snake made from Lego.

The main body of it forms a large grey L, but various red-brick outbuildings and attachments have been stuck on. This does not look like the work of an architect, rather the efforts of someone who thought architecture 'looked like fun' and thought they might 'have a go'. Or perhaps it rose, fully formed and bleeding, from the gravel. It seems to suck the sunlight straight from the sky. It looks like a place where cartoon villains would go for their reunion.

I know that professional photographers are very good at making houses look bigger, brighter and more welcoming than they really are. But the pictures I saw on the website could be images of a different building entirely. I have to bite my lip to stop myself from saying, 'There it is. The murder house.'

I'm being negative. Any minute now, Constance is going to say: 'My goodness, is that an original fourteenth-century Artesian well?' or 'If you squint, it looks a bit like the house where they filmed *Ghosts*.' I'll make a noise like a door creaking, to express my appreciation of the well, and I'll feel at least 5 per cent better.

I glance at Constance. Fix this! Work your magic!

She frowns at her phone, and then frowns out of the window. 'Is this definitely the right place? Did I put the wrong postcode in the satnav?'

Maybe this is my chance to escape! If I can get Constance to turn around and go back down the drive, we could easily spend the next three hours going up and down little country lanes. Eventually she'll give up and go home.

Instead, I hear myself replying. 'It says "Cadwell Manor" on that sign. This must be it.' I'm an idiot.

'Manor!' Constance snorts. 'This is not a manor to which I would like to become accustomed. Oh, God, sorry, Katherine. Don't listen to me. I'm being a bitch, I'm thinking as a sneery reviewer. I'm sure it's lovely inside. And I think Hema might have mentioned something about being in the middle of renovations. Come on. At least the setting is gorgeous. It will be lovely, a week out in the countryside.'

'And it's just a week!' I force my face into a smile. 'Seven days. That's not very long.' I try to think of something cheerful to say. 'I'm not even going to miss cardboard recycling! That's every two weeks, now! I'll be home in time to sort the bins out.'

'You would say that,' says Constance. 'And I don't think—' She is interrupted by a knock on her car window. This is especially startling because the window is open.

'Argh – hello!' says Constance.

The knocker leans in, and presses a (chipped, purple) fingertip to Constance's lips, before bowing her head.

I am reminded of the time a monkey stole one of Ben's

windscreen wipers at Woburn Safari Park. This woman is making it clear that this is her world. We're in her space.

Her long hair falls across her shoulders, coils of copper and pewter. She has a heavy fringe, pushed onto her forehead by a turquoise, beaded band – if I were to reach over and lift it up, I wouldn't be at all surprised if I found a tattoo that said I ♥ STEVIE NICKS. Her long black dress is covered in moons and stars. The silver thread glimmers in the sunlight. Real hippies don't look like this. This is what most people would wear if they had to be a hippy for a fancy-dress party.

Her eyes are small, round and grey, flecked with amber. They do not look especially friendly.

'I am chanting for the Goddess, and we require silence, in order to honour the celestial connection,' says the knocker. 'I must ask that you turn your engine off.'

Constance's eyes widen, and her lip starts to wobble. 'Oof, sorry, pebble in my shoe,' she whispers. 'Do excuse me. Katherine, maybe you can help?' She ducks, and yanks me down with her.

Noting her recently pedicured toes, I raise my eyebrows. 'How can you have a pebble in your shoe when you're wearing flip-flops?'

'I think that's Tamara! Her ghost, I mean! She looks just like her!'

'What? That is not a ghost,' I hiss.

Constance takes a deep breath, clears her throat and sits up straight, addressing the woman outside the car, who is now glaring pointedly at us. 'I'm Constance Attwell from the *News on Sunday*. I spoke to Hema on the phone. This is Katherine Attwell, she's checking in.'

'Hello!' I wave, wiggling my fingers at the woman. I've

never done that before, I think it must be some kind of subconscious, submissive signal.

Usually, Constance is able to wield her employer's name like a magic Access All Areas pass. Restaurant tables become available. Free drinks appear. Parking restrictions no longer apply. I've seen her charm her way out of a fine by implying that she was doing some top undercover reporting and urgently needed to go and speak truth to power. When the truth was she'd just run out of Eve Lom Kiss Mix and decided to reverse up Marylebone High Street so she could park right outside Space NK.

But usually, it works, and I'm left sulking in her wake as she skips to the front of the queue, with a complimentary glass of champagne. As the woman's frown deepens, I realise I do not like the alternative.

'Oh, I've gone right off them,' says the woman, presumably about the *NoS*, but she seems to be directly addressing Constance. 'The horoscopes used to be brilliant, but now they're useless. It's as though someone is just making up any old—'

'Sorry! Sorry, sorry, sorry!' Another woman runs out of the house and appears beside the hippy woman. She puts an arm around her. 'I see Cassandra came out to welcome you,' she says, pointedly. 'Cassandra is another guest, joining the programme. I'm Hema Bhal, the director. I'm thrilled that you've come to join us at Cadwell Manor.'

Constance shifts in her seat. Her spine seems to lengthen. 'Thanks so much for fitting Katherine in at such short notice.' Her voice has dropped an octave. She's looking at both women as though she's been invited to open Cadwell Manor, not leave her daughter-in-law here.

'Would you like the tour?' asks Hema. 'Constance, if you've not got to rush off, you're very welcome to join us.'

Hema is not what I pictured at all. Well, I didn't realise I was picturing anyone in particular, but I suppose I assumed she'd be something between Diane Keaton and Ina Garten. A big necklace, and crisp, classy linen. Subtle work, great eyebrows, Piaget watch. Successful Lady Therapist.

But this woman looks like she's run away to join the Scouts.

She's wearing functional-looking greige cargo shorts. You certainly couldn't see them in the undergrowth, and you probably couldn't describe them to a policeman ('What colour were the suspect's shorts?' 'I don't know! All the colours! None of them! What colour is a tree in the depths of winter, glimpsed through a dirty train window? Look, have you ever made a really bad potato soup?'). Although, for descriptive purposes, they have been helpfully adorned with zips. Festooned with them, in fact, as though she might have a sideline in sidling up to people in pubs and murmuring, 'You want to buy some fastenings?' If she doesn't have a Swiss Army knife somewhere, and a spare Swiss Army knife, I'll eat my hat. I'll eat a steak.

I'd guess that she's maybe in her mid-forties, but it's hard to place her. She could be Constance's age. She could be my age. Black hair, cut into a bob. Glasses with angular black frames. No make-up, sturdy boots, socks that come up to her knees.

There's something unsettling about her rawness, her pure functionality. Her stare is unwavering. I don't feel judged, but I feel seen. In fact, I feel X-rayed. I don't like it. Cassandra came out to put us in our place and tell us who we are. Hema knows.

I look at Constance, to see if she's similarly unsettled. 'I'd better go,' she says. 'I'm sure Katherine wants to ...' No! Don't abandon me! You can stay for ten minutes, Constance!

'Whoops! My sunglasses,' I say, bending down and nudging her in the ribs. 'You're supposed to stay and look at it, at least. Didn't Christa promise that you'd review it, or something? What happened to your journalistic curiosity?'

'I can just copy it off their website,' she grunts. 'And you weren't wearing sunglasses.'

I bob back up. 'Constance would love to come and look at your fabulous facilities!' I say, opening the car door. 'Shall we?'

Chapter Fourteen

Too many ghosts

'It's a really fascinating building,' says Hema, shepherding us up the stone steps. 'We've got Jacobean bits, Georgian neoclassical bits, and some interesting seventies bits. You might have heard about our bell tower, with the haunted staircase?' She leads us into a reception area.

'It looks like a rehab,' says Constance. Why is it that when she whispers, she sounds louder than a normal person is when they're just talking?

'It was a rehab, for a while,' says Hema, cheerfully. 'End of the eighties. It was set up by some record producer, I think, who made pots of money, then stuck it all up his nose – the irony! After that I think it was a youth hostel, for a bit. This is Sunny, my niece. She's on Reception, she'll get you checked in.'

'Stop telling people I'm your niece,' says the receptionist, darkly.

'Ooh, are you a goth?' says Constance. 'Is goth back? Fucking hell, I feel old. Sorry,' she says, doing her stage whisper. 'It feels a bit like swearing in church, doesn't it? Swearing in rehab. Or a youth hostel.'

Sunny taps her nose stud. 'No, this is darkcore. It's different. Name?'

'Katherine Attwell,' I say, apologetically. 'I like your hair.'

'She dyed it after watching *Beetlejuice*,' explains Hema. 'Apparently Beetlecore is also a movement, but not the one Sunny is doing. Sunny, Katherine is in the room at the top, with Elena. Could you bring her bags upstairs, when you've got a moment?'

'Sorry, no, I can't. I'm really busy,' says Sunny, in a tone I'd describe as 'unhurried'. She yawns and leans back on her chair. Her phone screen is flashing, and she sighs heavily, shaking her head. I'd love to know what's going on in her group chats.

Hema leads us into a sitting room. 'Some of these are original Jacobean beams,' she says, pointing upwards. 'The old windows were beautiful – they got ripped out in the seventies, but at least we still have the conservatory. Really, er, lets the light in.' We follow her gaze.

The room is the worst of both worlds: somehow dark, cramped, stuffy, yet then big, bare and cold. The walls have been painted recently, but the ceiling is patched with yellow. It's as if Michelangelo had been commissioned to paint an abstract mural that was supposed to serve as a tribute to smoking indoors. I can see a cracked and worn brown leather sofa, another that might have been pink once, and the most comfortable-looking one – royal blue, squarish, durable polycotton covers – could have been stolen from the reception area at Kwik-Fit.

'You could really do something with this space,' Constance says. Quietly, for once.

'You can't touch it,' says Cassandra. 'Too many ghosts

are here. Too much has happened. It's sacred. I can feel the energy build-up.' She turns to Constance and me, and frowns. Does she think we might be ghosts?

'It certainly does feel a little spooky,' says Constance.

Is that why it is so very cold in here?

I look at Constance, expecting a snort, an eye roll, or at the very least, a conspiratorial shrug. But instead she says: 'It would be an amazing place for a séance.'

'Oh, no, you can't just dial up the ghosts and tell them to come at eight o'clock on a Tuesday,' says Cassandra. 'That won't work at all.'

Hema claps her hands. 'As I was saying, this is a special space, and I'm still working out how to update it while maintaining the integrity of the house. The main spaces are being modernised, we've got a lovely up-to-date kitchen-pantry area, and the bedrooms and bathrooms are in full working order. Cassandra, why don't you let me get on with this, and finish doing your ... thing. Our sharing circle will be starting shortly.'

'Actually, I came out to find you because I've had an accident and I need some clean towels,' says Cassandra.

'What sort of accident?' asks Hema, warily.

'I am not at liberty to divulge.'

'OK.' Hema presses her fingertips to her temples. 'Ask Sunny. She'll tell you to ask me, so tell her that as soon as she's found you some towels, she can go home.'

'Also, there's a very strange smell coming from my toilet.'

'Open a window,' says Hema. Though I try very hard to avoid Constance's gaze, out of the corner of my eye I see that she's mouthing the words 'pillow menu' at me.

Chapter Fifteen

Trauma dumping

Even by my standards, Hema is odd. She spends a lot of time explaining the kitchen and utility room – although admittedly she endears herself to me enormously by telling us about the energy efficiency rating of the dishwasher. 'We ask our guests to clean up after themselves when it comes to drinks, snacks, et cetera. Please don't run the dishwasher if it isn't full. And please don't put your dirty mug into a clean dishwasher and run it again.'

I gasp. It's as though she's saying, *And by the way, please don't commit murder on the premises.* 'I would never do such a thing,' I say, defensively.

'I'm sure you wouldn't,' says Hema. 'But if you did, you wouldn't be the first. That's why I need to mention it.'

'Do you have a lot of people staying at this retreat?' asks Constance, as we climb the creaky stairs. 'Ooh, is that a Picasso?'

'What's the Wi-Fi password?' I ask simultaneously, itching to google how much water a dishwasher uses in a year.

'We're supposed to have five, including you, Katherine.

I'm afraid you can't have the Wi-Fi password. We can't stop you from using your phone, but we can definitely take advantage of the fact that the signal is terrible here.' Hema cackles. 'If it's an emergency, we can help you out in the office. But otherwise, we think you'll get the most out of this if you can't constantly check your emails. And what was the other thing?'

'The Picasso?'

'It's just a lithograph, we think. It might not be original. We've had a couple of other pictures checked out, and there are some very good forgeries dotted around the place. Cadwell Manor has a long and dodgy history; a couple of hundred years ago people kept losing it in poker games and buying it back with fake Fragonards.'

There's an enormous window on the landing, looking out into a wild, slightly parched garden, and the space is flooded with light. Hema and Constance have taken on a sort of celestial glow. 'Bloody hell,' says Hema, using a finger to trace the curve of the balustrade. 'You'd think we never dust.' She wipes her hand on her shorts, leaving a grey smear on the pocket.

Constance gives me a short, sharp nudge, and shakes her head. I know she's not impressed. She once told me that she didn't believe there was any point going away anywhere if the towels aren't at least slightly nicer than the ones you have at home. (And she sets herself a very high bar, towel wise.)

But at first glance, there's something almost magical about Cadwell Manor. Shabby, run-down, totally un-prepossessing from the outside – but secretly and strangely grand. Packed with ghosts. Bleak, then beautiful. And filled with the most environmentally efficient white goods I've ever laid eyes on.

Somehow there's something familiar about the space, even the smell. My body thinks I've been here before. It's that feeling you get when you enter a church, and you're transported to every church you've ever been to: it has that same waxy, solemn, dusty peace. A space for everyone. All my adult life, I've felt like a fly in the ointment, the stain marring the perfect surface of my surroundings. But here, I make sense. My stains could be part of a pattern. And I feel much more comfortable standing beside a fake Picasso than a real one.

'We've got a couple of single rooms, but most guests share,' says Hema. 'You're in with Elena. I'll introduce you now.'

We walk up to the first floor, and Hema knocks on a door. 'What?' says a voice.

'Your roommate is here!'

The groan that follows makes me wonder whether Elena is thirteen years old. Maybe I've interrupted her in the middle of gluing photos of BTS to a ring binder.

'I'll leave you both to it,' says Hema. 'Constance, if you come with me, I can get you a cup of tea. Or a glass of kombucha?'

'Lovely!' says Constance, cheerfully. 'And – will Katherine come down to say goodbye?' There's a slight wobble in her voice.

'You may as well do that now,' says Hema. 'We'll be starting in an hour or so, with the sharing circle.'

'Thank you for the lift,' I say, in a small voice. 'And for organising everything.'

Constance pulls me into a hug and grips me so tightly that the chain strap of her handbag digs into my arm. We rock, awkwardly, and then she kisses the top of my head. 'I'll miss you. And if you need anything at all, call.' I raise a finger to my cheek, which is now wet to the touch. Constance is pressing her fingertips against her eyelids, and shaking her head, briskly.

'It's only a week!' I call. 'Don't worry! I'll be fine! What's the worst that can happen?'

Turning, I open the door and paste on a smile, calling, 'Hello!' through bared teeth. And I realise the worst that can happen might be lying on a bed by the window, scrolling through a phone and scowling.

'Ugh, I was hoping you wouldn't turn up so I could have this room to myself. I can't believe I have to share. It's barbaric. Absolutely unbelievable.'

Glancing around the room, I have to fight the urge to say, *How old are you?* because my prediction wasn't completely off. This looks like the bedroom of a teenager. Admittedly, a very wealthy teenager, perhaps one who has been forced to appear on a reality show, introducing the ultra-privileged to the concept of youth hostelling.

The second bed – my bed, I assume – is covered in bags. There's a small Louis Vuitton wheelie case, a black nylon holdall, and several shiny shopping bags with cord handles. I count four bikini tops – pink, yellow, black and blue polka dots, all with the tags still on. Is there even a pool here? On the nightstand closest to Elena's bed, I see two mugs, an apple core, a packet of kale chips, and a pale pink notebook, embossed, in gold, with the words DREAM BIG. On the one by my bed, an open tube of pink lip gloss has left a sticky residue. There's another empty wrapper, and a faint dusting of white powder. Right. If she's been using cocaine in our room, I'm telling.

I get a little bit nearer, and my self-righteous rage lifts a little. I don't think cocaine has glitter in it. Still, I can't spend a week with this girl. She definitely doesn't want to spend a week with me. This is all wrong. I don't think I have it in me to stick this out. If I go now, I can catch Constance before she leaves, and beg her to take me home with her.

But I'm rooted to the floor, frozen in place. And furious. The rage feels random, and shocking. For the first time in my life, I want to fight. (Usually, I pick flight. Some people say it's a sign of cowardice, I say it's the only form of flying that's carbon neutral.)

'Maybe I should see if I can share with someone else,' I say. Then add, pointedly: 'Someone a little more *mature.*'

Mature is a funny word to choose, under the circumstances, because all I want to do right now is stamp my feet and say, 'It's not fair.'

I don't want to share a room, either. I don't want to be here. I want to be getting on with my job, and my life. I've never asked for anything, from anyone! I've always tried so hard to be good, and quiet, and efficient. And where has that got me?

Constance and Annabel don't want me at home. Shrinkr and the Jeremys don't want me in the office. Ben didn't want to be married to me, clearly. Now, this random woman is rejecting me from my own room. I have nothing, and nobody, and nowhere to go. The whole world is against me. I've always suspected it, and now I know it's true. 'Take some time, Katherine!' 'Look after yourself, Katherine!'

I've been farmed out to a healing retreat, cursed to spend a week with a woman who is looking at me as though I'm a giant, flaking scab.

Occasionally, I've wondered whether it would be useful to have a badge, something that says 'widow', or even better, 'widow and orphan'. Or a set of hazard lights that I could switch on and use as a clear signal. 'Treat this woman very gently, for life has been hard for her, and she has a lot of feelings. Give her plenty of space, and please don't eat crisps in it.'

The trouble is that I don't have it in me to be tragic, today. I want to scream. I want to flip the furniture and fling my arm out over the nightstand and knock everything to the ground. I can feel my nostrils flaring. There's an animal inside me, and she's stamping her hooves. I open my mouth. I want to shout, 'Get out! Get out of *my* room right now!'

Instead, Nanna comes out. 'It's an absolute pigsty in here.' I follow this with a yelp that starts at the back of my throat and emerges through my nose. A perfect Miss Piggy impression. How apropos.

As the air escapes from me, guilt and shame rush to fill its place. I shouldn't have said that. I've ruined everything, already. I'm a monster. Even my feelings are wrong. I'm supposed to be a sad girl, not an angry horse. I've been at the healing retreat for less than an hour, and I've already failed at healing.

I've got to calm down. Some long-buried advice from Grace the Therapist floats to the top of my brain. I need to breathe, before I react. Elena hasn't come here just to make mess and crumbs. Obviously she must be dealing with some awful, buried pain. For all I know, she's grieving too. Or she was abused or abandoned. Or her favourite Charlotte Tilbury lipstick got discontinued ... I could shake myself. Katherine, show some compassion. You're better than this.

'Look,' I try again, as kindly as I can. 'If you weren't expecting to share, you shouldn't have to. I'll talk to Hema. I'm sure we can sort something out.'

'No, we have to,' says Elena, dully. 'Believe me, I've begged Hema. There aren't any other rooms available. Which is insane, given the size of this place. It's got, like, a million bedrooms but apparently the roof might fall in on most of them any minute.'

'OK,' I say. 'Can we move your stuff off my bed, then? And clean up the nightstand?'

'In a minute. I'm busy.' Elena picks up her phone again.

'Do you have any signal?' I ask. 'Hema said there isn't much around here.'

'Not really.' Elena puts her phone down and shrugs. 'I keep picking up little bits, but it's slow.' She laughs. 'It never occurred to me that there wouldn't be Wi-Fi! I mean, what are we supposed to do? We're here for a whole week! I told Hema they really ought to warn people about it, that now it is technically a human rights violation.'

'What did she say?'

'She told me that in the event of an emergency I was very welcome to use a computer in the office. And I got the distinct impression that she was trying not to laugh at me. I'm already writing the review of this place in my head. Not that I could post one because there's no internet!' Elena throws her phone face down onto the bed. Then she sighs, picks it up, and starts to scroll again.

'My mother-in-law feels the same way,' I say. I must try

to build some common ground. 'She just dropped me off. I think she could be trying to break the speed limit right now, trying to get away from this place.'

'*You're* married?' says Elena. The emphasis reveals her disbelief. She might as well say, '*You* walked the runway for Alessandro Michele? *You* have a bronze medal for field hockey?' She looks at my hands, for proof.

I'm double-stacked, out of habit. The ridiculous engagement ring on top, my slightly less elaborate wedding ring on the bottom. Yellow gold, a band of five small diamonds, an engraving on the underside. BK and a date. (When I showed Annabel, she said it looked like I'd bought commemorative jewellery to celebrate my first visit to Burger King.)

'I was married,' I say, unmoored.

'So you're divorced, then.' Elena picks up her bag of kale chips. Apparently, she can eat and talk at the same time. 'I went on a retreat once, there was this woman there, and you'd think no one had ever got divorced before. Her ex was called Barry! Like, how desperate would you have to be to marry a Barry in the first place?' She waits for me to laugh, and I don't join in.

'Shit ... your ex isn't called Barry, is he?' She gathers kale chips in her palm, and drops them into her jaw, as though she's feeding a farm animal.

'No,' I say. 'He was called Ben. He died.'

I pause, waiting for the gasp. The flurry of ohmigodiamsosorrys. Maybe a tear or two. From me, as well as from Elena.

Because I wish I wanted to cry, right now, and that I had normal, appropriate feelings. A real widow would be shaking, sobbing, unable to speak. A proper widow wouldn't feel as though she was in the middle of a fight with her husband that will never end. Ben, you've made your point. You haven't spoken to me for months. I'm sorry, I want to fix this. But you need to fix it too. How are we supposed to do this together if you're not here? How many times do I have to tell people you died before I'm allowed to come back to life?

The tears come then, and they're all for me. I hate myself for using Ben's tragedy as a weapon, and a shield. For cheapening it, by presenting it to Elena and hoping it might make her treat me with kindness. For not being a better wife. For not having the chance to become a better wife. I miss Ben so much, but to be honest, I started to miss him while he was still alive, and I can't explain, or admit that to anyone.

Picking up a pillow, I sob softly, waiting to feel a comforting arm around my shoulder.

'Katherine, listen,' says Elena. She sounds serious. Maybe she's going to surprise me and say something incredibly wise and profound. I knew there must be more to her. We must be sharing a room for a reason.

I look up from the pillow, hoping that I look pale and pitiable, and not red and puffy.

'What you just did,' she wags a finger, 'was trauma dumping. I'm an empath, and I really struggle to make space for myself, and honour my own needs. We're all grieving. I've got an ex, too. I'm here to heal my broken heart. But you won't see me crying or feeling sorry for myself. You have to own your trauma, and you can't spill it all over me.'

Like your lip gloss is spilling all over my bedside table.

Elena's words feel like a sharp slap in the face, but they're strangely centring. A sharp blast of cold air. She's arrived, uninvited, at my pity party, cutting the music and turning the lights on.

This is why I've got to keep my feelings bottled up. Everything gets so messy when they bubble to the surface. Lesson learned.

Nanna's favourite book was called *Illustrated Lives of the Saints*. It was mostly pictures of people looking very calm and good, while being boiled in oil, or shot at with arrows. That's where the word 'beatific' comes from. You must show total calm in the face of adversity, in order to be beatified. I can do this. I can smile in the face of these arrows.

Even if Elena is the one with the quiver. She makes Lydia look like a fount of empathy.

'Right!' I say. 'Got it. No trauma dumping. Shan't happen again.'

'Well, you'll probably have to do a bit, we've got to go down for the sharing circle. Let's go.' Elena holds her bag of kale chips out to me.

'Um, thank you,' I say, stunned by this unexpected show of kindness. I peer into the bag. There aren't any left, but pointing that out would seem against the spirit with which the gesture is intended. I reach in, and mime taking a crisp. I'm sure St Sebastian would have done the same thing.

'No, put it in the bin, it's on your side. Come on, we've got to go.'

I take the packet and watch her walk out of the room. God, I'd love to be somewhere else right now, covered in arrows. I wonder whether they do archery here. I wonder what would happen if I shot a load of arrows at Elena. I'd go to prison, but at least I'd probably have a nicer roommate.

Chapter Sixteen

New friend

Just over a year after our wedding, I got pregnant. I still don't know whether I did it accidentally, or on purpose.

Ben and I had talked about it, in the abstract. In the way that we talked about taking a year off our jobs and living in Paris. (We talked ourselves out of it after a long, long weekend when we got the Eurostar and realised that we both thought the other one was able to speak French.) Or should we get an air fryer? (Yes.) Or solar panels on the roof? (Not in Ben's lifetime.)

He was open about wanting a family. 'Ideally, we'd have a whole crew,' he'd said. 'Imagine a lot of tiny sailors running around. And I'll be the captain!'

'Like the Von Trapps?' I asked. 'Does that make me Maria?'

'Seriously, I don't think it's too early to start thinking about it,' he said. 'Ed from work says he and his wife have been trying for a year now. It's probably going to take ages, so maybe it wouldn't hurt to start early. I'm not in a rush, but I don't want you to think I'm not keen. I'm really keen.'

At the time, I swooned. I believed him. And I let myself think that we had plenty of time.

Growing up, I knew, without being explicitly told – in the way that we suddenly know our left and right, and how to tell time – that sex makes babies, and babies ruin lives. After all, I'd been the baby that ruined my mother's life, and then her mother's life. As soon as puberty hit, Nanna started warning me about my fate. 'You'll end up just like your mother,' she prophesied, whenever I wanted to leave the house at night. 'You'll get in trouble, and I'm not going to look after your brat. It's bad enough looking after you.'

When I met Annabel, she was convinced that I must have been raised Catholic. 'I've never met anyone with so much guilt,' she exclaimed. Long before Ben, I was in the habit of taking a pregnancy test nearly every time I had sex – even though I used so many different methods of birth control I could have given classes at schools. It became a ritual, a superstition. If I was pregnant, I believed that instead of plus symbols, Nanna's ghost would fly out of the end of the stick. 'I told you!' she'd say. 'You've gone and ruined your life. That's what happens when you get up to funny business.'

Ben's suggestion that we might want to get pregnant, together, on purpose, was mind-blowing. It was exciting, and it was terrifying. For the very first time, I started to think that having a family, making a family, might be a choice and a blessing, rather than a problem and a curse. With a baby, we could become even more than the sum of our parts.

Sometimes I felt scared. I worried about big, abstract things like rising sea levels, deforestation, the fact that the planet would probably become inhospitably hot before my baby was eighteen. But my greatest concerns lay closer to home. How could I become a mother when I'd never really had one? I wouldn't know what to do! I bought books and read parenting blogs, and screamed inwardly when I came across the concept of the 'imperfect' mother, or the 'good enough' mother. Everyone was missing the point! I didn't want a book that told me I'd probably get it wrong, sometimes. I needed an instruction manual that explained, in detail, how to get everything right.

But the blogs made me feel even more determined. By the time I was pregnant, I'd be an expert, as long as I kept reading and learning. Soon, I started to believe in our hypothetical baby, and a version of me who would become unlocked by a new level of love. When Ben went away for the weekend, I waved him off, smiling mistily. *He should enjoy himself*, I'd think. *One day, these weekends will be a distant memory.* I became tender, saucer-eyed, treating him like the father he would become. Here's what breaks my heart; I have so many happy memories of our first year of marriage. But I can't remember what really happened, and what was just me daydreaming about all that could be.

It was a when, not an if. We both knew we wanted it to happen soon, but 'soon' was a vague point on the horizon, after Christmas, after the holidays, when work calmed down a bit. We believed we'd know when the moment was right. But we also believed we had time. Months and years to squander.

Constance was lovely about it, which surprised me. I expected that she'd be texting to ask about my basal temperature the moment we got back from honeymoon. 'I can't stop people asking,' she said, 'but I'm never going to ask you. I'm assuming you'll tell me as soon as it becomes my business. And until then, it's none of my business. If there's one thing required of a mother, it's that she stay out of her children's sex lives.'

'Oh my God, Mum!' said Ben, putting his hands over his eyes, then his ears. 'Please. Never say that. Never call it that. Never acknowledge that you know about such things.'

'I know more than you think,' says Constance. 'Katherine, did you know I had a sex column? It was 2005-ish, in *The Gentleman.* I did it anonymously, and the money was great. Then the *Daily Mail* found out who I was, and that wasn't so great.'

'Yeah, it wasn't so great at school, either,' said Ben, grumpily.

'I'm sorry, darling. Anyway, this isn't about you. Katherine is going to bear the brunt of this, now you're married. It might be OK now, but in a year or two, people she barely knows will be tripping over themselves to tell her she must get pregnant in the next five seconds because her fertility is about to "fall off a cliff".'

I looked around her kitchen wildly, half expecting to see a precipice, or a sign the earth was about to cleave in two.

'You know what else falls off a cliff?' she asked, and then, without waiting for an answer, 'Lemmings. You don't have to do what anyone else does. Some of my friends had their babies when they were thirty-eight, thirty-nine, forty!' She thought for a minute. 'I mean, I'm glad I didn't do that in a way because if I had, Ben would be, what, eighteen now, and my hall would still be full of stinky trainers. Katherine, you can only imagine how bad that teenage boy smell is. Even when it's your lovely teenage boys – pee-yew!'

Ben gave me a warning look. His trainer smell wasn't my favourite – and neither was tripping over them, when he abandoned them in the middle of the hall.

'Anyway,' Constance continued, 'people will be full of unsolicited advice. Recommending all sorts. Eat more pineapple. Take folic acid. Do it with a pillow under your bum. Smile, thank them, let it all wash over you. As your mother-in-law, I reserve the right to ask you once, shortly after your thirtieth birthday. But I'll do my best to leave you be.'

But Constance broke her promise.

Work had been getting stressful. It started over the summer. Ben and I had bickered about it. Not argued, exactly. We never argued, we never shouted. But it was difficult to make him understand how important work was to me. The company was growing, and that was exciting. The team was getting bigger, too.

'It doesn't make any sense,' said Ben. It was the third night in a row that I'd come home after 9 p.m. 'If there are more people there to do the work, there should be less work for you to do. You're at your desk for twelve hours a day. They're not paying you enough for this.'

'Yeah, well, they won't start paying me properly unless I put the hours in,' I muttered. 'You don't understand. You earn more than twice as much as me—'

He cut me off and put his arms around me. 'It's our money, you know that. For our life together. You don't even spend anything! You get all your clothes from Oxfam!'

I shook him away. 'That's not the point.' I knew that couples were supposed to argue about money. That was why I wanted to earn my own.

It would make sense if Ben shouted at me for feckless

spending, or racking up debt, or not pulling my weight. Those were things to be upset about. But I was very, very careful not to do any of those things. I didn't understand why he didn't seem to care or mind about my paltry wages, when I minded deeply. And he didn't understand that I couldn't let myself depend on him for any kind of financial or emotional security. He'd changed my life, and given me everything, which meant he could just as easily take it away.

'Katherine, I do understand,' said Ben, in a voice I didn't like. The last time he'd used it, he was refusing to pay the plumber who broke our toilet. 'You're being exploited at your crappy job, by your crappy bosses, and you won't stand up for yourself. But if you can't do it for you, I want you to do it for your new husband who misses you and wants to see you occasionally, when there's still some daylight.'

'You're right.' That was something I'd learned from dealing with Nanna. If I protested my ill treatment, and claimed innocence, a telling-off could go on forever. Submission always brought things to a swift conclusion. 'It's a blip, a bumpy bit while the company grows. And because I've been there for so long, I've got to be there smoothing things over. But I'll be working late for a week or two, and things will be back to normal. I promise.'

'Good,' said Ben. 'They better be.'

And we had sex, and we both felt better.

But the week or two quickly became a month, which turned into months.

Before long, it was a Sunday night in October, and I was heading to Constance's house for dinner. Ben had been sailing in Cowes, and he was going to meet me there. As I walked up her road I thought, it's dark. It's not 7 p.m. yet, and it's dark. Did I miss a whole summer?

I felt ill, too. Not awful, just worn out. As though I was fighting a bug, and I couldn't quite shake it off. It must have been creeping up on me, I'd been going to work and coming home and sleeping a lot. In fact, if Ben announced he was off sailing for the weekend, it came as a relief. I didn't have to yawn my way through friends and walks and pub lunches. All I really wanted to do was sleep, with nothing but a giant bag of crisps for company.

Standing on Constance's doorstep, I cupped my belly, and thought 'Are my thighs getting wider, too?' Then 'I hate hating my body, I hate myself for hating my body, and I'm too tired to be a feminist today. I'm too tired for Constance. I'm too tired to do anything apart from sleep, and my back hurts, and I think I might have aged twenty years overnight.'

When the door opened, I was yawning. 'Sorry,' I said, hurriedly, after bringing my hand to my mouth. 'I'm knackered. There's something going round the office, maybe I've caught it.'

I waited for Constance to hug me – which she did, after a beat – and when I leaned in to kiss her, she took my face in her hands and tilted it from side to side, squinting slightly. 'Are you pregnant?' she said, with pure joy in her voice.

'What? How?' I blinked.

'You are! Come in! Sit down! I'll get some herbal tea, I've got some sort of hormone lady tea somewhere! Oh my God, oh my God!' She hopped from foot to foot, trapping me in the doorway. 'This is wonderful news! Who else knows?'

I put my hand on my belly, again. 'Well, I didn't, thirty seconds ago. I can't be, can I?'

Constance looked concerned. 'When did you last have a period?'

'I can't remember. I've been using this new tracker app.' I fumbled for my phone. When had I last put anything into the app? I'd been too tired. 'I think I must be due on soon, I've lost track a bit. I can't think when we last ...'

She raised her eyebrows. 'The point of a tracker is that you don't lose track. Give it here. Ah, so you had sex at the end of your last period – which was a while ago.' She raised her eyebrows. I almost bit a hole into my lip, trying to stop myself for apologising for not having enough sex with her son.

'It looks like you were due on over two weeks ago.' I tried to snatch my phone back, and she held it away. 'Are you logging every time you had sex? Suzie just did something about these apps for the *Telegraph*, and they only work if you ...'

This was embarrassing. 'Yes, I know, Ben's been away so much with these sailing competitions, and this week I've been feeling a bit off ...'

'Because you're pregnant!' She took me by the hand and led me into the warm.

'Hold on, I've not done a test yet. And if I am, I should tell Ben ...'

'You have talked about it, though?' said Constance. 'I raised my son to understand that with great penis comes great responsibility. He knows how it all works!' She raised an eyebrow. 'You're very pale, Katherine. It's fine to feel shocked. It's a big deal! Ben was a surprise. Then I tried to get pregnant again straight away, and Sam took nearly two years. Anyway, it's OK if you weren't expecting it.'

Constance was right. I thought we had another year or two, at least. I'd sort things out at work, Ben would want to spend more time at home, and we'd be able to get ready for a major life change. Tomorrow, and tomorrow, and tomorrow.

We were still children ourselves, playing house. I couldn't look at our wedding presents, sets of bowls and plates and cups, without thinking of the miniature versions you'd expect to find in a dolls' house. Whenever I wrote anything on the kitchen calendar – usually BEN SAILING, with an inky line etched across two or three days – I thought, *How strange. This is what grown-ups do.* We had all the props and trappings of an adult life. If – when – the officials inevitably came to check on us ('Officer, we're worried about the kids across the street, they look like they're going to work and paying the bills but we think they must be toddlers in trench coats'), even they would be forced to admit that everything appeared to be in order. But I wasn't convinced. Any minute, the wolf would come and blow the house down.

But then, when I'd suggested coming off the pill and trying to track my natural cycle, when I told Ben I was bored of being bloated by hormones, worried about the health risks – did I mean that? Perhaps my body was thinking for itself, moving faster than my mind. Maybe I knew I'd never be ready, but I was as ready as I'd ever be. And Ben didn't stop me. I was waiting for him to freak out, to insist I take extra pills, to appear in the bedroom wearing a full body condom. But he smiled, he shrugged, he said, 'Great idea, babe.' Then: 'Is there anything apps can't do?'

Was there an app that would tell me if I wanted this baby?

If I was allowed to have this baby? I'd been preparing for this moment for so long, and I still wasn't ready. I'd never be a perfect mother. I might not even be a good enough mother.

Constance left me propped on a pile of cushions, a soft, pink rug over my knees, while she marched to the Tesco two streets away for 'pregnancy tests and supplies'. The plural concerned me. Everything concerned me. Was I going to spend the next few months here, getting rounder and slower, rendered immobile? Maybe there would be some amazing new technological advance that meant Constance could have the baby for me. She'd know exactly what she was doing. She could probably get a column out of it. I felt as though I should be on the news. 'IRRESPONSIBLE WOMAN TO BIRTH CHILD. Katherine Attwell took four months to finish writing thank you letters after her wedding. Also, she forgot to cancel her Tidal subscription and paid over £100 just to listen to one Beyoncé album. What is the country coming to?'

Then I cupped my belly again, rubbing a thumb over it. Surely that couldn't be a whole baby? It felt like premenstrual bloating, or a third helping of dhal. 'Hello,' I said, cautiously. 'Is anyone there?'

Was there a little person, making themselves at home, in me? I felt terrified. Then, excited. There was a tingling in my core, cutting through the tiredness. This baby wanted to be here. It wanted me to be its mother.

Maybe they would be brave, like Ben. Not scared of waves and water. And not waiting for 'a good time', not offering to drop in 'but only if it's convenient'. Jumping in, coming alive, making themselves known and feeling confident that the world was ready for them.

And I loved them, already. It was a beam, a ray, warm and pure. 'Hello,' I said again. 'I love you. I'm your friend.'

I thought of my mother, then, and her pregnancy. She had been so young. Sixteen, going on seventeen. Her whole body must have felt so new and unusual that she couldn't separate out discrete feelings. Filled with hormones and strangeness, raised in a home where every urge, desire and impulse was wrong. She must have been so scared. There I was, growing, sending signals and messages of love, and how they must have confused and frightened her. Did she know, at some subconscious, cellular level, that she wouldn't be around for long enough to protect me and look after me?

I thought of Ben. The bravest person I knew. Or, rather, the least scared, which wasn't necessarily the same thing. I hoped this baby wouldn't be scared. But this baby would probably be given to messing about in boats. I'd never know a moment's peace.

'Hello,' I said, for a third time. 'Are you a sailor? Of course you're a bloody sailor, you're bobbing about in a large body of liquid, right now. I hope your daddy will teach you to be safe on the water. And I will teach you to be brave. Because I'm not brave at all, but I am going to learn, for you. I'm so scared right now, little baby. But I'm going to become very strong. That's exactly what you deserve.'

When Constance came back, I was weeping into the blanket. 'Hormones! Of course!' she said, knowledgeably. Then Ben walked in, his hair sticking out in all directions, the sea still seeming to cling to his coat. 'Honeys, I'm HOME!' he bellowed, before taking in the scene. Me, pale and weeping, his mother standing over me. 'What did you do to her?' he asked Constance, before seeing the boxes in her hands.

He turned white. 'Oh my God, are you sure?' he asked me.

'Pretty sure,' said Constance. 'But that's what these are for.' She handed me a test. 'Are you, ah, ready to go, now?'

It was not the longest two minutes of my life, but I had time to run through plenty of possibilities. I already loved our baby so much! But could there really be an actual baby? I was probably just tired, dramatic, on the brink of flu. Chances were that the test would be negative and I'd get my period tomorrow. I was just weepy with PMT. At least I'd have a chance to find out how I really felt. I was much more ready for a baby than I realised.

Or would it be somehow inconclusive? A frustrating non-result, a total anticlimax. A very, very faint line – or a question mark. More information needed.

And yet, when the time was up, the second line could not have been clearer if I had drawn it on with a biro.

I almost fell out of the downstairs loo with excitement, I just about managed to pull everything up and wipe everything down. 'Look!' I shouted, bursting through the door of the sitting room before I remembered to put the cap back on the test.

'Ha! You peed on that!' said Ben, snatching it from my hand. Then, 'Holy crap!' I couldn't read his tone. Was he angry? Was he scared? Maybe this was the one risk he was afraid to take.

'Are we ... Is this OK?' I asked, cautiously. 'I'm as surprised as you are. I know it's much earlier than we planned.'

Constance hovered, waiting to say something, desperate to tell her son how he was supposed to feel.

'Oh, Kit Kat.' Ben pulled me to him, and I buried my head

in his chest. He smelled of salt, sweat, woodsmoke. 'It's a shock, but a really nice one, I think!' He squeezed me, then released me. 'HA!' he said again, pointing at Constance. 'You're going to be a granny! In your face, old lady.'

Constance raised an eyebrow, forehead like a millpond. 'Darling, I can't wait to be a granny. A young, fabulous granny!' She opened her arms wide and hugged us both. 'This is the best, best news.'

And in that moment, something I hadn't realised was even missing finally slotted into place. Finally, I had a point. I had a purpose. This was what family felt like. Connection. I'd be bonded to these people forever. I couldn't be cast out into the cold, now.

I knew there were infinite things to worry about. The world was burning. Soon, the seas might not be safe for my baby to swim in. One day, my baby might get fired, or dumped, or lost. In fact, this was inevitable. I was going to have a human baby, one that would inevitably, eventually, graze its knees and feel anxious for no reason and get hangovers.

But for the next nine months or so, I had a brand-new job. My baby depended on me. I would keep it safe from harm. It was as though a hidden spring of confidence was bubbling up inside me. My clever baby knew how to get the best out of me. Pregnancy was going to be my first proper adventure, and for once, I was ready for it.

Chapter Seventeen

Make good choices

I follow Elena down the stairs, and back through Reception. I make a point of stopping at the desk.

'Hey, Sunny,' I say, smiling. 'How's it going?' Elena is ahead of me. She hasn't turned around to watch me setting a good example and being friendly and polite. Even though I'm speaking quite loudly.

Sunny does not look up from her phone. 'You need to go through there.' She jerks her head infinitesimally. 'Please don't ask me for anything, my shift finishes in three minutes.'

Elena finally turns to me. 'It won't do you any good, you can't friend her into getting that Wi-Fi password.' We go into the sitting room, where Hema is waiting, and smiling. She waves us into the conservatory.

Right, Katherine, you can do this. After all, you only get one chance to make a first impression. Earlier, with Elena, you lost control, which means it's even more important to charm the rest of the group. For the rest of the day, you will stay positive. You will be interested in everything, and see the good in everyone.

After my mini meltdown earlier, I'm determined to keep it together.

'It's nice and cool in here,' I say. 'So refreshing!' It's so refreshing that I might have to go and put a jumper on. I sit on the nearest sofa, which sinks beneath me. There is so little resistance in this cushion, I'm sure I can feel the ground against my bum. I smile at Hema, waiting for her to suggest I try another seat. One where I don't have to sit with my knees up by my face, like a frog. Elena takes an armchair as far from me as possible. Surely she's not being mean? She's just trying to be comfortable.

I shift and find a spring that lifts me up a little. 'Who are we waiting for?' I ask Hema.

'The rest of our guests should be coming down now.'

We all look back at the doorway, just as another three women enter, murmuring and giggling quietly. They already seem to have made friends. Even mad Cassandra is part of the gang. I've just got here, I've only met one person who doesn't work here, and I've already rubbed her up the wrong way. I wrap my arms around my body, ostensibly to warm up – but if I'm honest, I need a hug. It's just a week. It's just a week.

Elena watches the women walking in. She's sitting up very straight, craning her neck. As the women get nearer, her focus grows, until her gaze lands on a striking woman with glossy black hair and glossy black lycra leggings. Her trainers have no identifiable logos, which is usually the hallmark of a secret millionaire. She has a few other 'secret millionaire' tells too – there's a collection of bangles, beads and bits of string, running from her right wrist almost to her elbow, and a single skinny braid trained over one eye, with a white feather woven into the bottom.

Is she famous? Firstly, she looks incredibly polished and confident. Secondly, Elena is bouncing in her chair with such animation that I fear for its springs. I can see the thought bubble over her head, and it reads 'CAN I HAVE A SELFIE?'

'Oh my God,' Elena says. 'We've met, yeah? I think I went to your Soul and Spirit webinar last year! I only saw the first twenty minutes, but they were amazing. I was in a café with intermittent Wi-Fi.'

'Sorry, hon, that wasn't me,' says the woman. 'That sounds like my kind of webinar, though, mystical. I'm imagining a gathering in a cobwebbed cave, spangled with dew, everyone drawing nourishment from the womb of nature ... to hell with those corporate Zoom drones. Anyway, I'm Anya.' She smiles sweetly, and sits down beside me. Miraculously, the knackered sofa does not collapse.

'Let's all grab seats and do names and introductions,' says Hema. 'We begin every retreat with a sharing circle. We introduce ourselves, we talk a little bit about our path, and what we hope to get out of this experience. All I ask is that you're as honest and clear as possible. And then, we'll have time for a bit of a Q&A. I know some of you have been on retreats before and others are new to this.' Hema looks directly at me, and I look away, wishing I could produce some perfect homework to show her. 'All I can tell you is that you're here to heal. You can help each other, but above all you'll be learning how to help yourself. There is work to be done, and you're the only ones who can do it. It's not exactly magic, but it can be magical. Also, will someone remind me to stick the dishwasher on before we start the Q&A or there will be no clean glasses at dinner.'

I cannot begin to solve Hema's mad riddle, but I can be the one who reminds her about the dishwasher. Challenge accepted.

'Anya, as you've introduced yourself, why don't we start with you, and go round,' says Hema, smiling. Great! If they go clockwise, I'll be the last to speak and I'll have plenty of time to work out what I'm supposed to say.

Anya smiles. 'Hello, I'm Anya and I'm a lawyer – I mean, I used to be. I was a specialist in reputation management, the youngest partner in my firm, sixty billable hours a week, and it was prison. And now I'm free. This is my gap year! I've been suffocating, strangled by my own ambition. I quit my job six weeks ago, and now I'm going to become a reiki healer, on course to be certified by October. I've already trained for over fifty hours. I've signed up for a training course in psycho-aromatherapy and one day I'd like to open some sort of wellness recovery centre for former lawyers.' She pauses, and smiles. 'My ex accused me of being an overachiever and a perfectionist, *as though those were bad things to be.* But obviously, I can't be either of those things, because I'm here, with all of you! And I just got a Hamsa hand tattooed on my—'

'Great, thank you, Anya!' says Hema, cutting her off. 'We'd better keep things moving.'

I like the look of the next woman; she seems warm and round. She has dark eyes, and tiger-striped hair, cut into a blunt bob. She looks almost as glossy and put together as Constance, but slightly older. There's an irrepressible squishiness, a sexiness. An air of mischief.

'Hello, I'm Rachel, and I'm also here after a break-up. My ex is a shit. We were married for twenty-three years, he got done for sexting, and I'm in the throes of a horrific divorce. I say sexting, he was sending pictures of it to young women who worked for him, and I don't think they wanted to see it. Well, most of them didn't. Anyway – my life is falling apart, although when I think about it, it's been falling apart for ages. I've been on the odd spa day, but as my mother would say, it's a long way from spas I was raised. My friend Liz came here and loved it. I'm trying to keep an open mind.' Rachel looks around at us, as if any one of us might give her a reason to snap her mind closed again. 'But if I'm honest, I'd really like to be anywhere but here. Ideally with a bottle of cold white wine and some cigarettes. I miss Marlboro menthols. One of my kids is vaping. He's sixteen. He says it's to help him cope with the stress of the divorce. And I know I should be worrying about his growing body, his little lungs, but I'm more worried about how my own child could do something so cringey.' Though she has the air of someone who might be about to cry, Rachel laughs. 'I suppose I'm hoping to come away with a sense of possibility. I keep thinking about the beginning of my marriage, wondering whether I'd have gone all-in if I'd known what I do now. Obviously, of course I would have done, because of the kids. But I was an optimistic person, once. I'd like to feel optimistic again.'

I'm nodding. I've never, ever been able to describe myself as an optimistic person. But it must be nice to know you're capable of it, of feeling hopeful and looking on the bright side. Although isn't 'optimistic' just a euphemism for 'irresponsible'? Divorce, or death, aside, how can anyone look at the state of the world and feel hope?

Cassandra, sitting beside Rachel, responds animatedly.

'You're to get over him once and for all. No accidental pocket dialling. No walking past his house and hoping to manufacture a coincidental bumping into him. No more creating fake profiles on dating apps, and catfishing him. Have you tried rose quartz?'

Hema says, 'Let's stick to introductions for now, Cassandra. What would you like to share with us?'

'I'm Cassandra, and I'm an astrologer and poet. I'm also an experienced ...'

Let me guess. It would make my life if Cassandra said 'chartered surveyor' or 'economic analyst'.

'... psychic medium.' *Obviously*, I think. Clearly I don't have any psychic powers. Although, I should have been able to work that one out without them.

Cassandra lowers her voice. 'It felt like a good time to come, after a dramatic change in my personal circumstances, which is somewhat complicated. You know Guru Toby?'

Seven heads shake, and seven mouths make polite, apologetic noises. No one in the sharing circle seems to know of Guru Toby, apart from Elena, who gives a non-committal grunt.

'@SpiritualTobes on Insta?' Cassandra continues. 'He's got over eight thousand followers. Anyway, I met him at his ashram in Axminster, I went out to Goa with him to help him set out his retreat. Stuff happened. I shagged some people, he shagged some people, I was struggling with non-attachment. The welcome centre burned down. I wasn't not responsible. Technically, I didn't burn it down,' she said, hurriedly. 'But in another way, I suppose I did. You know. It happens. So here I am.' She shrugs.

163

Annabel would *love* this, I think, sadly. She'd love Cassandra. She's terrifying – her life is clearly a total mess, and yet, she somehow seems totally in charge of it. In fact, everyone here already seems to be capable of rising above their mess. They know exactly who they are, and what has happened to them. I'm the only one who has been drawn by a pen that's almost out of ink. I'm defined by my widowhood because I don't have anything else. These women are going to be fine. If I was Rachel, coming to the surface after decades of a difficult marriage, I'd be like a mole, small and scurrying, desperate to get underground again. But she's making jokes. She has expensive highlights. She worked the sharing circle like it's an open mic night.

Elena is next, and I give her an encouraging smile. I'm desperate to fix things, after our bumpy start, and make her like me. We're roommates. We have to get along.

Still, I can't imagine what she's in here for. Maybe she's still sad about getting bad grades on her GCSEs. Maybe someone laughed at her TikTok dance.

'Hi, I'm Elena,' she starts. 'And I'm also here because of a bad break-up. I was – am – in love with someone I met at work. Who happened to be my boss. And I know that we can't be together until I do the work. When I'm the very best version of myself, he will come back to me. I'm here because I believe I can manifest the love I want, if I'm surrounded by the right energy.' She breaks off to scowl at me. 'The trouble is that the energy in this house is all wrong. How can I love myself if I'm not giving myself the best of everything? Surely I can't be expected to focus on myself if I have to share a room. And I saw a weird blue stain on the bath mat,' she finishes.

What a nightmare. She's the worst— Wait, I'm meant to be channelling St Sebastian, I remind myself. Maybe I can be a good influence on Elena. I have a week to lead by example. I won't get cross, I won't get frustrated. I'll keep all my feelings locked away, and eventually she'll see there's more to life than bath mats.

That's not to say I don't feel a little glee when I catch Hema's eyes, and see her raising her eyebrows. For less than a second, darkness seems to flash across her face, but it doesn't settle, and her features soften into something bland and vague. 'I'm sure Sunny can get you a replacement bath mat,' she offers. 'And sharing a room is part of the programme. Give it a chance, you might learn to like it.'

'Well, the website didn't make it clear enough,' says Elena. 'You could get sued for this. Also, the bottle of Aesop hand soap in the bathroom has clearly been refilled with Dove.' She folds her arms, as if to say case closed.

To be fair, Constance would be complaining about fraudulent hand soap. The last part of Elena's rant has made me feel homesick. But I'm expecting some sort of reaction from within the circle. Isn't anyone going to say anything? Why is no one calling Elena out for being so rude and obnoxious? But Anya has tilted her head to one side, and she's nodding gently. Rachel looks like she might be trying not to laugh. In fact, I half expect her to start clapping her hands and chanting 'Fight, fight, fight!'

Hema says, 'Thank you for letting me know about the hand soap. It's a serious matter. I will investigate.' Elena flushes, and my schadenfreude flashes across my face. But then Hema says, 'Katherine, it's just you to go. What would you like to tell us?'

Nothing! I've got nothing to tell! What's my name? Where am I?

I take a deep breath and pretend I'm about to deliver a client presentation. Which was a terrible idea. Now I feel even worse.

'Um, I'm Katherine, hello. I'm here because my best friend and my mother-in-law – well, she's not really my mother-in-law, any more, as such. They ganged up on me.' I coughed and took a deep breath. 'My husband died, in a freak accident. He went sailing in a storm and fell off his boat and drowned. I'm fine though,' I say, hurriedly. 'I'm seeing a therapist, sometimes. I've kept busy ... but then work ... I love my job, but I just got fired. Well, they've told me to take the summer off, not to come in for a bit. I made some stupid mistakes, I'm so ashamed.' I can't do it, I can't do it, I can't do it. 'I think I've been making mistakes for a long time. I don't know what's wrong with me. I want to be good. I want to be OK.'

Ugh. That was horrible.

I want to run away, but I don't think I can get out of my sofa hole fast enough.

I think I'm about to cry, and that is not happening, so I hold my breath, and start to hiccup instead. Hema has started to speak. I sit up to listen, trying to hiccup quietly into my hands.

'Welcome, everyone. Thank you for sharing. I'm Hema, and I'm going to be your director and counsellor for the next week. As you know, here we specialise in Holistic Integrated Wellness. What that means is we offer you a range of sessions and therapeutic practices which have been designed to begin to build resilience, and mental and emotional strength. Healing isn't about curing. Our aim is to help you help yourselves.'

'That reminds me, I have a question about the breakfast buffet,' says Elena. 'Because I can only eat bread if it's sourdough, and no one replied to my email ...'

Hema ignores her. 'Helping yourselves, in this instance, means ownership and responsibility. And if nothing else, by the end of the week, you'll be excited about taking responsibility. I think it's interesting that most of you spoke about something bringing you here, whether it feels like you were called by a force or by a family member.'

She looks at me, and I look away, not wanting to make eye contact.

'Something I want you all to think about is choice. Every single thing you have ever done, leading up until this moment, has been the result of a choice that you've made.'

'That's true, actually,' says Cassandra. 'After a lot of therapy, I'm able to say that I can't blame Guru Toby. I didn't start that fire, but suppose I commissioned it.'

'Thank you, Cassandra,' says Hema. 'That's an extreme example, but a valid one. My point is that you'll get the most out of this experience if you all embrace the idea that being here is a choice. Every one of you will be asked to leave your comfort zones. Some of the therapies and experiences will feel awkward, exposing, overwhelming or downright ridiculous. Choose to embrace it all! Choose to throw yourself into every moment. And trust the process.'

'Namaste,' whispers Anya, reverentially.

'After dinner tonight, we have free time, but I strongly advise you to get an early night. Tomorrow, we're getting up bright and early for sunrise primal screaming. Which means you're all going to choose to be up at 4.30 a.m.' Hema laughs. No one joins in.

'Anyway, thank you for sharing so honestly, we'll be coming together like this, and talking about our growth throughout the week. I'll see you all soon for dinner.'

As she stands up, Rachel says: 'Oh! We were supposed to remind you about the dishwasher!'

Damn. I wanted to be the one to do that.

'Thanks, Rachel,' says Hema, giving her a grateful smile. 'I'll see you all shortly.'

This doesn't feel like a choice, at all. Annabel has been known to say, 'There are no accidents', usually after she's pocket dialled an ex, or spent £200 on skincare after popping into Selfridges to use the toilet. But I don't think I've heard her say it since Ben died.

Have I really chosen to spend a week of my summer out of work, stuck in a draughty conservatory, with a newly minted hippy, a sext divorce case, a psychic fire-starter and a selfish brat? It's like *The Breakfast Club*. Even the goth on Reception is giving serious Ally Sheedy. None of those kids chose to be in detention, did they?

I do make choices, but they always seem to be the wrong ones. I can't be trusted to choose for myself. I didn't even pick the right chair. I certainly didn't pick the right husband ... I wince. I can't think about that right now.

It's only a week. Surely I can survive any amount of anything, for a week.

Chapter Eighteen

Unmothered

I was really surprised by how much I enjoyed being pregnant. It felt a little bit like joining a cult. There were so many rules to follow. There was a new vocabulary to learn. And there were rituals, and mini sacrifices. I liked saying a hard no to soft cheese. I liked waiting in long coffee queues, arriving at the front and murmuring, 'Just a peppermint tea, please.' Just meaning 'I am currently engaging in a great act of self-sacrifice, and denying myself caffeine for the sake of my unborn child is more energising and refreshing than an oat flat white could ever be.'

Privately, I wondered whether pregnancy might unleash some great, maternal longing within me – I was scared that it might trigger an unstoppable torrent of grief for my own mum, or even for Nanna. There were no generations of wise women who had any biological imperative to look after me, or my baby. All my proper family was contained within my body. But instead of feeling vulnerable, I felt fierce and strong.

Being pregnant made me feel as though I was a key part

of a duo, a team – even more than marriage did. I was my best self, for my baby. I couldn't engage in any of the grubby, scruffy mean things that I did or thought when I was alone, because I was never alone. I stopped eating strange crumbs I found on the sofa. I stopped using foul language. (Constance told me she laughed so hard 'a little bit of wee came out' when we just missed a bus and I shouted, 'FIDDLESTICKS!')

Even the sickness didn't bother me too much. It helped that Constance was on hand to guide me through my daily game of 'Normal/Not Normal?' (And shield me with her jacket during a trip to the Surrey Sculpture Park, where I threw up in the grass because one of the sculptures reminded me of a boiled egg.)

'It's absolutely incredible, when you think of what your body is doing,' she said. 'All of that energy is engaged and diverted, there are all kinds of confusing physical signals and symptoms. It's fascinating. And it's knackering.' She was a fierce advocate of ginger tea and naps.

I was nervous about telling Annabel. Not because I thought she'd be jealous, exactly. It just seemed wrong that it was happening this way around. For as long as I'd known her, she'd held my hand and led the way. She was my big sister, to all intents and purposes. Whenever something new and scary loomed on the horizon, she'd go on ahead and check that it was safe. Surely I could only be pregnant if she produced an actual newborn baby from her own handbag. ('By the way, I have some news too!')

The other thing that baffled me was the fact that there were guidelines and debates about when you were supposed to tell people. That was the one rule I couldn't quite fathom.

I definitely didn't want anyone else to know before I told Annabel. But how long did I have to wait? Also, no matter how many times people tried to explain the months and numbers – I was supposed to count from my last period, and I was six weeks pregnant when I took the test – I couldn't make the idea stick. The nine months started in August. But as far as I was concerned, I 'got pregnant' in the middle of October in Constance's downstairs loo.

I avoided talking to Annabel until my first midwife's appointment, communicating almost exclusively in GIFs, occasionally meeting her at the cinema, where I could slip in once the film had already started and it was dark. (It didn't matter what we were watching, I always fell asleep.) Work was always a solid excuse – and then she had a big presentation at an AGM somewhere odd, like Ghent. And then her great-auntie died and she had to go to Scotland for a whisky-soaked three-day wake.

Eventually I realised I couldn't put it off any longer. If I didn't tell her soon, I'd have to start thinking like a sitcom producer, and editing my life so that Annabel only ever saw me from the neck up. On a rainy Saturday at the end of November, we met up at the Brockwell Lido Café. It was officially three months. Technically I was allowed to tell everyone. But I still felt overwhelmed by anxiety, convinced that I must be breaking some sort of secret, hidden rule.

I was too nervous to concentrate on anything she was saying. I didn't remember ordering anything, but pots and plates arrived on a tray. I blew the steam off my tea (chamomile and lavender, this time; it was revolting, but it smelled nice), and poked at my polenta cake with a fork. 'Annabel,' I said, looking everywhere but my friend's face. 'Annabel,'

I started again. Why didn't I write this down beforehand? Oh, yeah. Because I'd tried and I kept falling asleep. There were several entries in the notes bit of my phone that just said 'Annabel'.

She squashed her cake (toffee apple) under her fork. 'We're not OK, are we? I feel like you've been avoiding me. Have I done something wrong? I could feel it, you know, even in Scotland. I've upset you, and I don't know why. What have I done? Is it because I didn't call when I was in Ghent? Is it because I didn't tell you that I got off with Tom again?'

'Oh my God, seriously? Tom?' I didn't mind but this was good gossip. 'It's not that, but I want to know about that. It's ... me actually. This is quite big, life-changing, even ...'

'Shit! You're not getting divorced, are you?' The fork, loaded with cake, hovering by her mouth, returned in slow motion to the table. 'I think I might be about to cry.'

'No, I'm pregnant.' I started laughing, and Annabel started crying, and neither of us could stop.

'Sorry, sorry.' She waved her hands in front of her face. 'This is great! I'm really happy! This is incredible! Happy tears!'

'You're not cross?' I said. 'I was worried you'd be ... I was worried.'

'Katherine, you're always worried. But you seemed so distant. Separate. I suppose it never occurred to me that it might be good news! But this is the best news! You're having a baby! When? What kind? Can I start buying tiny trainers?'

I told her about the midwife appointment, and how Ben had surprised me by saying he wanted to be surprised, and the midwife saying that, anecdotally, she felt she'd seen a little bump in couples choosing not to know the sex – but her colleague said the opposite. And that I was excited about having a summer baby, and how Constance was already making plans for the baby's first Christmas. And that I thought I'd be scared, but apart from the constant state of either puking or feeling as though I was going to puke, I never felt better or happier.

Annabel enjoyed my pregnancy almost as much as I did. We'd hang out at Constance's house, with or without Ben, lying down on the sofa, eating biscuits and talking nonsense. 'I wish you'd got knocked up years ago,' she'd said. 'If only I'd known how much fun having a pregnant friend can be. This is so much nicer than drinking horrible white wine at Be At One.'

I got very, very comfortable with breaking wind in front of my mother-in-law, without apology. 'I was exactly the same,' said Constance fondly. 'When you fart,' asked Ben, 'is the baby farting too?' And Constance would throw her hands up in despair and calculate the cost of Ben's education, and I'd laugh, and fart again.

It happened just after Christmas. I think my baby was a little bigger than an avocado, and a little smaller than a turnip.

I woke up, feeling, as usual, like a deep-sea diver who had broken through the surface too quickly and left her brain under water. No change there. I kissed Ben, I stood in the shower, I thought, *Ooooh, I could murder a coffee,* and then, *Ah, no, better not,* just as I had done for the last few months. The journey to work woke me up slightly – the cold air was sharp and exhilarating. Since I'd got pregnant,

I always felt a little too hot. This was the only time of day when I felt comfortable and calm. I loved dark mornings in London. There was something about being up before sunrise that made me feel as though I was in on a secret. And we were at the very end of winter. The days were already becoming a little longer. I was seeing the last of the bare branches. The brighter days were coming, and they would bring warmth and joy. I had so much to look forward to.

It was a busy day. As soon as I told Jeremy that I was pregnant, I'd been determined to prove that pregnancy wasn't going to make me any less productive. I felt a pressure to prove myself, and I'd taken on too much. I tried to push through the tiredness, knowing that if I stopped, I'd never catch up again. At around 4 p.m., I realised I couldn't remember when I last took my eyes away from my screen. I stood up at my desk and stretched and then winced. I could feel a little cramping in my lower abdomen, as though something was contracting. Weird, I thought. Must just be period pains. And I turned my attention back to the meeting, which was about whether or not we could work with a company who made plastic recycling bins, when only 80 per cent of the plastic they used was recycled. The odd burst of discomfort was jarring enough to bring me back into the room. 'There's a good environmental impact report on polyurethane,' I said. 'It's a very effective insulator, and it's far from perfect, but the best of a bad bunch. I'll email it to everyone.' I remember being relieved I'd made a contribution, thinking that I could probably leave soon. I could send the report from bed, once I'd taken some painkillers.

Shortly afterwards, as I was packing up, I reflexively patted my bump, my friend – and remembered that I couldn't possibly have period pains. Like the coffee I kept forgetting, then remembering. I wasn't worried. I assumed it was a trimester shift, the baby getting more turnip-like.

Once I was home, I went straight to bed. I was exhausted. The tiredness was strange. There was no gradual creep, no slow lowering of energy levels. I'd feel fine, great, even – and then it was as if I'd taken a step and fallen down a hole. Ben was trying to be understanding, but I knew he was struggling to make sense of it. My condition had stopped being a novelty, and the realities of impending parenthood were slowly sinking in.

'You're sleeping all the time,' he'd said, accusingly. 'And this is our very last chance to do stuff. We need to go out, have fun.'

I'd felt simultaneously sympathetic and defensive. 'Look, my body is doing all the work, of course I'm tired,' I'd said. 'I don't love this either. I'm sure I'm supposed to feel a bit more energetic during the later stages. It would be nice to hang out more at the weekends, when neither of us have work.' I didn't want to tell him to sail less. I wanted him to want to sail less.

Ben promised me that we'd have a weekend together, just the two of us, as soon as he'd got Padstow, and Falmouth, and Portland, and Dartmouth out the way.

As I pulled the covers up, I thought about this. Marriage was supposed to involve a lot of compromise. Maybe I wasn't doing my bit, either. We could go out that night, we could try the new wood-fired pizza place near the Tube station, I could wear a dress. A proper date, just like we used to have. I just needed to close my eyes for half an hour.

The pain woke me up. I'd been sleeping so heavily that I hadn't noticed Ben getting into bed, next to me. Opening my eyes, I could just make out an arm, in a blue tartan pyjama sleeve, flung out over the duvet cover. Instinctively, I squeezed Ben's hand. 'I'm sorry,' I whispered. I realised I'd gone to sleep in my work clothes. Were my trousers wet?

Then, there was a clenching, a cobra squeeze in the pit of my stomach, and I thought I might be sick. Still holding Ben's hand, I grabbed it again.

'Bloody hell, Katherine! That hurt!' he said, sitting up, rubbing his eyes. Then he frowned. He touched my forehead which was also wet. He turned on his bedside light. 'You're so pale,' he said, and he sounded frightened. I didn't think he was scared of anything.

We went to hospital. I started crying when he suggested it, and I couldn't stop. I thought I was going to die, and I wanted to do it at home. I just wanted to lie in bed, bleeding, aching, vomiting, praying for unconsciousness. When I staggered to the toilet, the blood looked black. It made me think of oil spills, disasters. Something had poisoned my landscape, everything was tar and ash.

Ben drove. I wore his old jogging bottoms and jumper, two pairs of knickers with an entire toilet roll bound around both. I sat on a pile of newspapers that he found in the boot. 'Why do we have newspapers?' I'd asked, and he shrugged. 'No idea.'

The doctor was gentle, but infuriatingly calm. 'It's going to be OK. It's nothing you've done, you're young and healthy and you have nothing to worry about. It's your very first pregnancy, and sometimes the first one is complicated.' I remember Ben asking, 'But why? There must be a reason why.' But not what the doctor said in reply. She did say, 'We advise women to come back within six weeks to talk about next steps.' Women. We don't just have the burden of growing the baby, but the burden of facing the future.

I didn't want to talk about next steps. I wanted to sink to the floor and never get up again.

My baby. My friend.

'I'm so sorry, I'm so sorry,' I murmured, over and over and over. Physically, there was pain, and yet I wasn't in pain; I was vaguely aware of cramping, burning, nausea, but I'd checked out of myself. I'd left my body, just like my baby had. I didn't blame the baby, I didn't want to hang out in me, either.

Ben was terrified but I couldn't seem to bring myself to care. We were like two ghosts in separate realms. I remember the doctor talking, explaining things slowly, becoming frustrated. Giving us piles of pamphlets. She told me that it was safest to let any remaining tissue pass out naturally at home. It took days for me to work out what she meant – to connect that phrase with my baby. Our baby.

When Ben drove me home from the hospital, he almost collided with a white van. The driver honked and shouted, before driving off, and Ben pulled over for a few minutes to get his breath back. Usually, he was a cheerfully sweary driver – but he didn't even scream and curse. He just turned pale. 'I'm so sorry,' he'd said. 'I don't think I'm with it, I've never done that before. Are you OK?' I nodded, but really I wanted to scream: 'Coward! Why didn't you finish this? End me, now. Make me bleed out.'

The next day, he called in sick for me. He said: 'She's had a family emergency.' What family? Now I didn't have a link to a single soul that I shared blood with. I'd failed as a mother, just like mine had, and hers had before that.

I cried without stopping for three days, until I felt sick from it. My whole skull ached. I talked to my baby constantly. Please tell me there has been a horrible mistake. Tell me you're still there. Tell me you're OK. Tell me what I did wrong. I'll do anything to fix it. Anything at all. The screen of my phone became smeary and unreadable as I searched and searched and searched for anything that might help me make sense of my pain. There was nothing. I saw photos of smiling women, who'd endured countless miscarriages before having 'my four beautiful babies' and think, *But I'm not like you. I'm broken.*

Even Constance couldn't help. 'Katherine, I don't think I know a single mother who hasn't been through this,' she said. 'I promise you will have your baby. I promise everything will be OK.' I didn't believe her. I would never have my baby, because I could never let this happen, ever again. I could not bear this much grief, and this much pain.

Because what if my baby was born, and then something happened to it? What if I happened to it?

And as I threw myself into work, trying to numb the pain, trying to shut it down, I began to realise that the world is no place for a baby. What would become of the sea, and the sky? Would there be tall trees, and fresh fruit, and soft grass? How many babies were already being born to people who were in pain, desperate, anxious, struggling? How many other babies would I have to hurt through my own careless consumption, my greed, my selfishness, my need to nurture and protect my own?

I started to think that maybe my purpose was not to be another bad mother, but to end the line of bad mothers.

I was able to present my plan as a protest. At work and

online, I found, if not kindred spirits, exactly, like-minded people who were also scared about how our scorched planet might be able to support the next generation. We had the facts at our fingertips. Even though we were relatively privileged, we had no space, not enough money, inadequate healthcare, spiralling bills. At one party, I heard myself saying, 'I have reduced my carbon legacy. I could drink petrol and do less damage to the planet than I would if I had a kid.'

During the day, I thought of myself as a kind of activist. My baby had wanted me to be brave – well, this was bravery. I was stepping up and making a sacrifice for the greater good. My smugness, my self-satisfaction kept me warm. (It's a carbon neutral heating system. You don't have to switch the radiators on.) It became a barrier between Ben and me. 'Katherine, will you shut up about wanting to make the world a better place?' he growled, after I tried to sign us up for a city farm composting scheme. 'The world is a horrible place. What has it done for us lately? What's the point?'

I felt so lonely. We slowly stopped reaching for each other, started stepping around each other. We rarely had sex – and when we did, it felt savage and mechanical. I frightened him. I went back on the pill. I chose to feel the artificial, hormonal emotions, instead of my own raw ones. If I woke up in the early hours of the morning, I'd talk to my baby, my friend. I'd weep for them.

I hope you're in Heaven. I'm glad you never had to know how bad things got down here.

I wish I was up there with you.

Chapter Nineteen

The screams

Am I in a car?

I can hear engine noises, a motor running, something heavy, choking and guttering itself to life.

Or maybe it's a lawn mower outside? That would make more sense – only it isn't coming from far away, it's here, in the room, with me. Where am I, and why is there a lawn mower here?

Peeling open one eye, I piece the evidence together. The piles of clothes, and snacks, and suitcases. The sticky puddle of lip gloss on my nightstand. The overwhelming smell of vanilla and candyfloss. And the woman in the bed beside mine, Disney pretty. Hair fanned out on her pillow, black and glossy as treacle. Full lips, resting in a perfect pout. Eyelashes that look as though they were drawn by a calligrapher. And she's making a noise like an industrial chainsaw. In fact, if you bought a chainsaw and it sounded like that, you'd take it back to the shop.

According to my phone, it's 3.42 a.m. The sun isn't up yet, but brightness is beginning to creep into the room, straight through the voile curtains. Why didn't I bring an eye mask? Maybe I could fashion one out of Elena's discarded bikini tops. I close my eyes and pull the duvet over my face. If I think of nice things, I can trick myself into going back to sleep.

Sinking down into the sheets, I allow my thoughts to drift. Being sleepy is a little like being drunk – my subconscious is suspending all judgement. There are no rules. I can think of anything, or anyone I like. I start to circle my left nipple with my right thumb, letting myself remember the last time I was properly, thoroughly kissed. I imagine a bra dropping to the floor, soft, warm skin, the curve of a bare shoulder. Maybe I'll have the dream, again ...

'OM HANUMATE NAMAH!'

In my half dream, two bodies spring apart, panicking. And half a second later, my real body is sitting up and blinking.

'What?' I say, stupidly. 'Is there a fire?'

'Shhh! Don't disturb me. I'm meditating.'

Elena is sitting cross-legged, at the end of her bed. Her eyes are closed, and she's holding her hands up, pinching her thumb and forefinger together, making A-OK signs. This is not OK.

'Do you need to do that in here? Elena, it's four in the morning!'

'I GIVE MYSELF PERMISSION TO PROSPER AND GROW. OM HANUMATE NAMAH!' She flicks two Vs at me, before rearranging her hands back into their spiritual configuration.

And Elena thinks that not being on the Wi-Fi is a violation of her human rights! This is torture. It's certainly cruel and unusual.

Once again, it's one rule for everyone else, and one rule for poor old Katherine. Elena just walks around littering, leaving crumbs, shouting, complaining, being bitchy and rude and entitled and even managing to meditate offensively. I mention the genuine tragedy that has befallen me, and I'm accused of trauma dumping. How am I meant to be a good person in these conditions?

But … No. I can't think like this. I've got to try. I've promised myself that I'll try. I need to be the bigger woman here. I'm not going to judge Elena. I'm going to help her. I'll set a good example. I'll be gracious, and forgiving, and just lovely. Then when her guard is down, I'll say, 'So, what are your thoughts about the climate emergency?' and subtly persuade her to change her consumerist ways.

'OM HANUMATE NAMAH! THE MONEY IS COMING. I BELIEVE I AM WORTHY OF GREAT WEALTH, AND GREAT SUCCESS! OM HANUMATE NAMAH!'

Maybe I need a mantra too. Today is a new day. Today, I will lean in. Today, I will have a great attitude. I'm resolving to smile, and say yes, and do anything that is asked of me, and keep an open mind. Constance has sent me here to heal, and I am grateful. I can't remember what we're doing first, but I vow to commit completely. I'll do whatever it takes. At least I'm wide awake now.

What was it? A sun salute? Something to do with the sun, or something outside …

Oh, shit. Sunrise primal screaming.

I shower to a soundtrack of OM HANUMATE NAMAH. The water comes out freezing. I yelp and hear an angry 'DO YOU MIND' through the door. I don't mind, really, once I get past the initial shock. Cold water is supposed to be very good for you. I'm becoming a different person already. I won't know myself by the end of the week.

My towel is small and scratchy – so good for the circulation! – and I dry and dress quickly. This is great. When I think of all the time I've wasted, lying in bed at 4 a.m., feeling absolutely wretched, I feel ridiculous. I should have just got up and taken a freezing shower. This is what gives the evil tech bros all that confidence!

'Is that what you're wearing?' Elena has stopped meditating and is frowning at me.

'Yes, why?' I say, suddenly self-conscious. I tug on my shorts.

'That T-shirt . . . ' Elena throws her hands in the air, as if to say, *Where do I begin?* 'It looks like lost property. Like you were in a fire and went down to the local church hall for emergency clothes, and you were the last person in the line.'

'Hey!' I say, defensively. 'That's . . . ' I look down at the T-shirt. It's almost as long as the shorts. It was white, once. The pink logo was red, once. It reads, MARCHMAIN INSURANCE HALF MARATHON, 2019.

I think this used to belong to Constance, but I have no memory of her running anything other than a bath.

'It belonged to a friend,' I say, coolly. 'She wasn't using it, so I thought "waste not, want not." I try not to buy new clothes.' Now, Elena will ask me why, and we can have a conversation about conservation.

'Well, I think you should try,' she replies. 'It's a matter of self-respect.' She looks at me almost kindly. 'If you need money, you should try doing my meditation. It's for wealth manifestation. I learned it from this fantastic woman on

Instagram, I'll find you the details. Honestly, Katherine, it's changed my life. And it could change yours too.'

I don't trust myself to speak. Luckily I don't have to.

'As soon as my wealth starts to grow – and I should see results in ninety days – I'm buying a whole new wardrobe. Have you seen those Saint-Laurent slut boots, with the buckles? If I dress like a CEO, I can become the CEO, right?'

'CEO of what?' I manage, at last.

Elena rolls her eyes. 'My life. Obviously.'

She gets out of bed and starts pulling clothes out of a bag. I see a scarlet lace thong and a matching bra. There's a bright white tank top, and a denim headband. Everything has a price tag attached, which she rips off with her teeth. As she dresses, I realise the bra is fully visible through the tank top. She shakes out the headband and steps into it – oh, those are shorts – before dabbing a finger in the puddle on my nightstand and smearing it over her lips. 'Right. I suppose we better go and start screaming.'

By the time we get outside, everyone else is already in the garden, standing in a small circle. 'You're the last ones down,' says Hema, pointedly. 'We were just about to start without you.'

'Elena was ...' I trail off. If I'm already in trouble, I don't think blaming someone else will help. 'Sorry, it won't happen again.'

'Don't worry,' says Elena, adjusting a bright red bra strap. 'I'm used to people waiting for me. I don't mind.'

I look around at the group. Anya is tapping an Apple watch and doing some squats. Rachel is yawning – and I'm pretty sure she's still wearing her pyjamas. I hop from foot to foot, suddenly self-conscious. Right now, I really don't feel like screaming.

'We're beginning the day – and our programme – with a great release,' says Hema. 'This exercise is especially important for women because we're all socialised to hide our feelings. Many of us struggle to express anger. This is an opportunity to connect with our breath, to access and embrace buried, trapped pain, and to start the new day feeling light and free. We're stimulating the vagus nerve, which will give us a full body boost.'

Before Hema has finished speaking, Cassandra throws her head back and screams. 'Aaaaaaaaaarghhhhhhhhhh!' She sounds like she's done this before. The noise is almost musical. She sounds like a didgeridoo.

Hema looks slightly pissed off. 'That's great, but if any of you have done similar exercises before, I'm going to ask you to wait, so we can all go together.'

Rachel yawns again. 'Sorry, that wasn't a scream, I'm just knackered. To be honest, after that barley salad last night, I'm just really hoping not to do a primal fart.'

'I've got some charcoal tablets you can have if you like,' says Anya. 'I find they help with my stress IBS.'

'Have you got any carnelian crystals?' says Cassandra. 'If it's bloating, they're very good.'

'Everybody, please,' says Hema. 'Let's focus. Listen to me. Now, I want you all to start by joining hands, opening your mouths as wide as you can, and saying "Ah." Make that sound as long and slow as you can. Release everything you've got. All that air, all of that old sleep, anything stuck in your system, everything that might slow you down today. Let it go!'

185

Elena gives me a look of horror, as I grit my teeth, grin, and grab her hand.

This is fine. I can get through it. It's no worse than being trapped between Jeremys in a conga line at the Shrinkr Christmas party.

I'm late eighties Princess Diana, doing humanitarian work. It doesn't matter that Elena is staring at me as though she thinks I'm going to infect her with something. Old T-shirt disease, perhaps? Anya takes my other hand, and together, we say, 'Ah.'

I close my eyes. I can feel the sun getting warmer, and slightly stronger, as I lift my face up to the sky. Our sound gets deeper, and I can feel myself falling into it, getting swept away by it. A rising tide. The darkness behind my eyes is tinged pink. We make a weird choir. We're not quite in tune, but I feel like part of a group. It's glorious. My shoulders start to drop. There's space in my body, where everything has been hunched up and tightly packed.

'Good,' says Hema. 'You can stop now. You're ready for the real work.'

We let our hands fall. That wasn't so bad. I think I can manage this. There's safety in numbers, after all. It won't be too humiliating if we're all doing it together. Come to Cadwell Manor, where no one can hear you scream. Because they're already screaming.

'We're going to be working on breath techniques throughout the week. In fact, there's an optional breath-work seminar after dinner tonight,' says Hema.

Great! Sign me up! I'm already pretty good at breathing. I mean, I must be. I've done yoga, I don't smoke, I should have very healthy lungs.

'So this morning I can guide you through the process, but you don't need to worry too much. It's all about the release, there's no right or wrong. And we're miles away from our neighbours, you're not going to disturb anyone. I'm going to ask you to go around the circle, and pick something, or someone, to scream at. It doesn't matter how trivial or how big. It can be the first thing that comes into your head. In fact, it's better if you don't think about it too much, just let the energy flow through you.'

Yes! I know exactly what I'm going to scream about. I bounce on my tiptoes, feeling very pleased with myself for coming up with the right answer so quickly.

'I just want you to be as honest as possible, and as loud as possible,' continues Hema. 'When it's your turn, step into the middle of the circle, and let rip. Move as much as you like. I'll go first and demonstrate.'

Hema steps into the circle and squats down, pressing her palms against her thighs.

'FUCK YOU, ALISON SNAPERLY,' she shouts. 'FUCK YOUR SQUIRRELS. I HOPE YOU GET DRY ROT AND JAPANESE BINDWEED. AHHHHHHHH! AHHHHHHHHHHH AHHHHHHHHHHH AHHHHHHHHHHHHHHHHHH AHHHHHH RAHHHHHHHHHHHHHHHHHHHHHHHHHH!' She rocks on her heels, kneeling forwards and backwards, completely uninhibited. The noises she's making are extraordinary, industrial. A challenge for Elena's snores.

Hema leans over into a forward fold, her arms hanging in front of her like a marionette's. She gives herself a shake, and grins. Her shoulders are lower. Her forehead looks smoother.

'Ah, that was brilliant. I feel fantastic! Ready for the day!'

'Who's Alison Snaperly?' says Rachel, and I am deeply grateful.

Hema laughs. 'She sold me a house in 2009. There were squirrels nesting in the attic. I lost my mind. I've moved twice, but I haven't been the same since. Sometimes I like to scream at a politician, or someone making the world worse, but an Alison Snaperly scream always works a treat.' She looks at us. 'Right, who's next? Elena?'

My roommate steps into the ring, and I start to feel a little queasy. Surely she isn't going to scream about me?

'I HATE YOU, CADWELL MANOR!' roars Elena. 'I SHOULD NEVER HAVE COME HERE! YOUR TOWELS ARE SHIT! MY ROOMMATE IS SHIT! I WANT MY OWN ROOM WITH A NESPRESSO MACHINE! HOW AM I MEANT TO MANIFEST MY BEST LIFE, STUCK HERE WITH THESE FREAKS? HOW AM I MEANT TO GET PAUL BACK? ARGHHHHHHHHHHHHH! ARGHHHHHHHHHHH   ARGHHHHHHH ARGHHHHHHHHHHHHHHHHHHHHHHHHHHHHHH!'

I gasp, audibly. I'm embarrassed for her. That wasn't a primal scream. That was a tantrum. Elena's rudeness is so shocking, it's almost exhilarating. I realise that I feel angry, disgusted, awkward – and jealous. I could never, in my wildest dreams, be so free with my fury. If that sort of scream stood between me and cardiac arrest, I'd suffer in silence and take the heart attack.

But how would it feel to be Elena? How would it feel not to care, at all?

She's still screaming. Her arms outstretched, her hair is flying. She looks quite frightening. With a final 'AARGHHHHH' she comes to a stop.

'Elena,' says Hema. 'That was ... '

I patiently wait for the onslaught. Elena is going to get a bollocking, and then she's being sent home. Wonderful. This is better than reality TV. (Not that I'd know, of course.)

' ... really, really powerful. Well done. I could feel the pure rage leaving you. Do you feel looser?'

'Actually, yes, thank you,' says Elena. She sounds surprised. 'It's like I'm all cried out. Everything has been building up, and building up, and now all the feelings have vanished.' She smiles. 'Although I'm sure it says something on the website about Nespresso machines.'

'Really sorry,' says Hema gently. 'There's just one in the office. We try to encourage you to cut down on the coffee, while you're here.'

'I've got a spare travel kettle, if you want to borrow it,' says Anya. 'I'm sharing with Rachel, and she brought one too. And you can have some of my valerian tea – it's pretty hardcore. It's *blissful*, but I warn you, it's stinky.'

Elena nods, but she does not say thank you. My jaw stiffens, and my shoulders start to lift up again. 'Thanks, Anya, that's really kind.' I speak through gritted teeth, trying and failing to catch my roommate's eye.

'Katherine, you're up.' Hema nods, and I walk into the circle.

It takes two short steps for my stage fright to hit. I look around. Cassandra gives me a tight smile. Rachel nods encouragingly. Anya does a double thumbs up. 'Don't be frightened!' she whispers.

I open my mouth, put my hands on my hips, and lean back. I don't feel very well.

189

I'm angry because Elena has been rude, and selfish, and entitled, and no one has called her out on it.

I'm angry because women like Elena get everything they want, and they still complain, and I get nothing, and I have to be brave and strong.

I'm angry because I worked so hard, and my work doesn't want me there.

I'm angry because my heart is broken and no one can fix it.

But it's not OK to be angry about any of those things. I can't justify it. I can't admit it. Out loud, it will sound trivial and ridiculous. Screaming about it won't be empowering. I'll be horribly, horribly vulnerable.

I put on a big smile. I stand up straight and clear my throat. My hands are still on my hips, but the stance feels too aggressive, too confrontational, so I let them dangle by my side.

'I'm angry about the climate emergency!' I say, in a clear voice. 'I'm angry about the rising sea temperatures. I'm angry about species loss. I'm angry about the government's failure to address this very serious problem. AHHHHHHHHHHHHHHHHHHHHH!' I want to scream, but I can't release the sound. It's stuck in my throat. This is more like a primal trip to the dentist.

'AAAAAAAARGHHHHHHHHHHHHHHHH!' I close my eyes and try again. I was waiting for a powerful feeling of release, I thought I'd start screaming and never want to stop, but I can't do it.

'Katherine, let me stop you there,' Hema says. She addresses the whole group. 'This is a perfect example of what not to do.'

Pure, acid mortification burns in my cheeks, my chest, my belly. It's the first day, and I'm already the worst one. I've failed at healing. It's not even 5 a.m. I can't bring myself to look at anyone. I bet Elena is delighted.

'Do you want to try again?' she asks. 'Think local, not global. This isn't *Question Time*. It's not about picking a cause. You need something you're connected to, passionate about. Something you genuinely care about. That's how you let rip.'

'I am truly passionate about the sea,' I say, quietly. 'I want to scream about the climate emergency. I care, a lot. That's what I do. That's who I am.'

'You need to scream from a place beneath your head,' says Hema. That doesn't make any sense. 'This week, we must all be very, very honest with each other and with ourselves. This isn't you, is it? We couldn't hear any you, in that scream.'

How can she tell? She's known me for about twelve hours.

I look at the ground, for a long time. I want to say, 'Hema, I can't hear any me, either. In my life. I haven't been able to hear myself, see myself, or even truly touch myself for some time. I can't find me. I don't know where to look, I don't know where to begin. I'm trying so hard. And this is why I was scared to come here. Not because I was scared of what I might find, when I lifted the rock. But because there might not be anything underneath, any more. Like I said, I'm trying. That's all I have. This is my best, and I'm so ashamed that it isn't good enough.'

Instead, I whisper, 'Sorry.' I squeeze my eyes tightly. A tear rolls down my face, and off my chin. I watch it hit a dandelion. Immediately, an ant crawls into it. It's a pathetic version of the Butterfly Effect. I failed Screaming 101 and drowned an ant.

'Why don't I go?' says Rachel. 'You can go again in a bit. Believe me, I can show you petty and pointless. I'm planning to scream about an argument I had in Waitrose over some sausages four years ago. I reckon it's hard to start screaming about the big things first, we need to build up.'

I cannot bear their kindness. It's worse than being corrected by Hema. It's even worse than watching Elena being the star pupil.

'Thanks, Rachel,' I say, without looking up. 'Sorry, I just need to go to the toilet. I'll be right back.'

I don't wait to see if Hema stops me. As soon as I turn away from the circle, the tears fall and fall. I run back to the house as fast as I can. When I get to the room, I throw myself onto the bed and howl into the pillow, screaming and crying and punching the bedding, until my throat aches and my kidneys hurt. I kick against the wall. I wail. I bite the air. My rage is nameless, and it's so much bigger than me. It wants to choke me, it wants to drown me. I've been fighting this thing for so long. Right now, we're on the same side.

Chapter Twenty

Curiosity

Eventually, I was fine. Well, I learned to be. I focused on my work, telling myself that I was grateful to have a job to go to. The office was boring and quiet, sterile and safe. Every new project was an emotional painkiller, and focusing on global horror took my mind off my personal hell.

At home, I prayed for Ben to reach out for me. Instead, he retreated into himself. I wanted to believe that we just needed a little bit more time before we felt like ourselves again. But the weeks stacked up and made months. I didn't have the language to talk about how sad I was, or how scared I was. And our house was haunted, now. The ghosts were oppressive, making a mess in the kitchen, stretching out over the sofa. I was heartbroken for our baby, and heartbroken for our future ghosts – the parents Ben and I would have been. And in our efforts to avoid the ghosts, the present, corporeal Ben and I avoided each other too. I saw him less and less. It was horribly easy for the two of us to abandon our shared world, and step into our separate spaces. Sometimes, I wanted him to stop me. I even missed arguing with him about how much I was working. He didn't seem to care enough to call me out. I wondered if he wanted me to beg him to stop sailing and stay at home at the weekends. I missed him, desperately, but I knew I missed a version of Ben who might never come back.

At Shrinkr, I became nihilistic. The relentlessly bleak news cycle didn't bother me as it once did. I used it to reinforce my confirmation bias – the world was an unbearably awful place and nothing good ever happened within it – and I became numb to horror. If you wanted a quick report on the possibility of everything ending in fiery disaster by 2070, I was your woman. If an international charity hired Shrinkr to pull together a document about a humanitarian aid response following the Rwandan genocide, I was the one who got called into the meeting. I was constantly working above my paygrade, and I didn't care any more. Frankly, I would have paid them if it meant I could stay in the building and keep hiding from the rest of my life.

I was especially furious about the fact it was suddenly summer. It was as though I'd spent six months watching a very sad film in a very dark cinema. I'd stepped out as the end credits rolled, face puffy, eyes downcast, into the glaring sunlight. And everyone else seemed to be shrieking, giggling and wearing espadrilles. Every single newspaper announced HEATWAVE! RECORD TEMPERATURES FOR BRITS! SCORCHIO! and no one except me seemed to care. Every pavement was filled with smiling men and women, in short-sleeved shirts and floral dresses, enjoying cold drinks, saying, 'Apparently it's hotter here than it is in Florida right now!' My clothes were sticking to me, my marriage was falling apart, the world was burning, and my baby was dead. The end was nigh, and I looked forward to it.

Most days, I was the first one at work. This was how I liked it. I didn't want to chat to anyone about how their evenings were, or what they were having for lunch. And that morning, I was in such a bad mood I was exhilarated from it. I was utterly sick of other people. All I wanted to do was get to the office and drink a cold cup of water before throwing myself into a day of spreadsheets and solitude.

But one day when I got to my desk, there was a strange woman sitting there. Spinning on my chair. Eating one of my rice cakes.

My first thought was that she must have broken into the building. Very occasionally, a homeless person would come in overnight, and hide out downstairs in the lobby. Cyrus on Security was as kind as he could be, without getting fired – a few of us helped him to maintain a stash of clean towels and shampoo, so our visitors could have an early shower before the Jeremys arrived, and they had to be smuggled out.

But my liberalism had its limits. I didn't begrudge anyone a rice cake, but it would be nice if she asked first. *For goodness' sake, Katherine. This is a starving, vulnerable person. That packet has been open for months. Let it go.*

She was wearing some of the worst trousers I'd ever seen in my life. Pale, baggy cotton, patterned with purple concentric circles, and yellow lightning bolts. I was a dedicated charity shop trawler, and I'd wear pretty much anything that was clean and didn't have too many holes in it. If I thought those trousers were bad, they must be heinous. She had tanned feet, and brown suede Birkenstocks. Proper ones. And pretty, pale pink toenails.

But, wait … A homeless woman wouldn't have a pedicure, would she? Unless it was some local nail bar initiative. That seemed like a poor use of community resources. But who was I to judge? If it cheered a person up, and gave them their dignity back …

'Hi, I'm Lou.' The woman put my rice cake down on my desk and offered me her hand. (No manicure, a lot of silver rings, bitten nails, splodges of what I hoped was ink.)

'I'm Katherine,' I said. 'Um, sorry, but you're in my chair. This is my desk.'

'That is a very bourgeoise notion of possession,' said Lou. 'Our human experience is transient, we're on this planet for a very short amount of time, do you want to be defined by your desk, or by the person you are?'

'Right,' I said, clasping my hands and squeezing my knuckles. It was far too early for this. 'The thing is that I need to get on with my work, which is on my computer, which is there. Where you are. Do you know where your own desk is?' I knew I was sounding shrill, and I tried to slow down. I could already sense that arguing with this Lou was going to be like reasoning with a toddler. I would get nowhere if I acted like a toddler too.

What was she doing here? I started to formulate theories. Lou would turn out to be Jeremy's sister, and the new COO. Or she'd been sent here to do some kind of exposé for reality TV. She'd act like an idiot savant and shame the employees who were mean to her. I'd fallen at the first hurdle.

Lou showed no signs of getting up. I gave it one last try. 'Is it your first day? Do you know who's doing your induction?' And how did you get in, where is your key fob, and were all of your other trousers stolen from a washing line?

'It is!' said Lou. She spun in her chair, completing a near perfect circle, before beaming at me. 'Jeremy told me to come in early, and report to one Katherine Attwell. He said she's always in hours before anyone else. Is that you?'

I nodded.

'Great! Do you want a cup of tea? Don't worry, I've found the kitchen, I don't need a tour. Builders, or herbal? I've brought a great horny goat-weed one, actually, but it gets a bit intense. It's not trippy as such, but trip adjacent. Let's wait until the afternoon when we're bored.'

'A peppermint tea would be lovely, cheers,' I said. 'There should be some in the cupboard.'

Lou finally got off my chair and bounded over to the kitchen. Her bum, I noticed, resentfully, was perfect. It looked amazing in those horrible trousers, luscious and rounded. I realised I was staring. I looked away, before my eyes drifted back to check it out again. Something unfamiliar pulsed in the very pit of my belly. Jealousy, maybe?

I hadn't really thought about my body since winter ended. It had stopped being useful. It hadn't done its job properly, so I was trying to punish it, by ignoring it. When I looked at Lou's body, I felt a brief flicker of life, an awareness of myself, my skin. Something within me had woken up. My pilot light still worked.

But I'd never been in the habit of staring at strangers. And this felt different from a simple comparison, I wasn't just looking at Lou and vowing to start doing squats . . .

It was the heat. It had to be. And I could not think about my colleagues' bodies. It was completely unprofessional.

Rubbing my eyes, I turned my computer on, silently apologising to my cushion pad as I sat down. It had briefly known first-class buttocks, and now it had to put up with my economy ones again.

Ah, there was an email from Jeremy, sent about twelve minutes ago. The subject head was one of his favourites. FORGOT TO MENTION ...

```
New starter, Lou, going to be working
with you on the Woodland Trust project.
Need you to show her the ropes. J
```

Brilliant. Wonderful. Delightful. Great. This was exactly what I signed up for. After all, I was a team player, an open-minded, collaborative, flexible employee who loved working in groups with people who had complementary skill sets. My CV said so.

I breathed out, picked up a Biro and snapped it in half. Then I looked at the trail of shattered plastic, gleaming under the glare of my screen, and felt sick with remorse.

'Couldn't find the peppermint tea, so I did you a hot Ribena.' Lou was standing over my desk, holding two steaming mugs. 'It's a bit like Ayurvedic medicine and it's Toothkind.' She put them down and sat in the chair beside mine. 'Right, hutch up, show me. Tell me everything.'

She gathered her loose, tawny hair up in her right fist, and secured it with a pin. The action released a scent, something spicy, fresh and green. It evoked cool air and pine trees, and for almost a second, I could believe in a world away from the office. Somewhere with natural light, where no one had ever heard of Microsoft Outlook.

But work was meant to be flat, grey and shapeless. This was my safe space. My fortress! I didn't come here to make friends. I didn't have the resources to do anything apart from my job. An area where I was only expected to operate within two dimensions. And now, this woman with her fancy shampoo and her stupid trousers had come along to ruin everything.

'So, where were you before Shrinkr?' I asked, politely.

She trailed her hand through the air, expansively. 'Here and there, this and that. Doing a bit of volunteering in Asia, backpacking . . . ' She broke off, and laughed. 'Wow, Katherine, you should see your face. It's OK. I used to be in corporate law. I was a solicitor. I'm not a total flake. I'm not going to make you lick toads or anything.'

Quickly, I shook my head. 'Sorry, it's not you, it's the heat. Let's get started.' I had so many questions, and I didn't trust myself to ask any of them, for fear of what they might unleash within me. Why did you go to Asia? What was it like? Did you go alone? Were you scared? Why did you quit law? Where do you live? Are you seeing anyone? I was worried that if I started listening to stories of Lou's adventures, I couldn't trust myself not to run to the airport to buy a one-way ticket to Bhutan.

I told myself that it was the sheer novelty of meeting someone with a story. I hadn't felt truly curious about anyone, or anything, for a while. She seemed friendly, and fearless, and inquisitive and new. There was something hopeful about Lou. Briefly, she made me feel as though I could hope, too. I could quit and start over. I could explore. I could be brave. For a moment, it was as if a shooting star suddenly burst out of my body and made me look up. Then everything immediately faded to black.

I felt very old. I'd tried to be a mother, and I failed. I had no energy, and no life. I couldn't run away to Asia and start again. I needed to work out how to fix my marriage – and I wasn't sure I even had the energy to understand how badly it was broken. Looking at Lou didn't fill me with a sense of life's possibilities. It made me feel as though I was too late, although I wasn't sure what for. And what was the point of always being ten minutes early for everything, if I was too late to live?

I thought about asking Lou if she had lunch plans, and whether she'd like to come to the noodle place around the corner. Then I thought of the gritty rice salad in a Tupperware box in my bag and sighed, resigning myself to leftovers. I didn't deserve nice things like noodles.

Chapter Twenty-One

The emotional emergency

When I wake up, I'm alone. The room is oppressively hot, and my face is stiff, and sticky. I feel as though I've been baked.

Something bad happened. I'm stiff with a sense of shame that I can't quite place. My skin is prickly – I feel as though I'm coming down with the flu, a Post-It note of a symptom from my body, reminding my brain that it needs to deal with something awful.

Oh my God. I failed at screaming. I've not been here for a full day, and I ran away. Everyone knows I ran away. Everyone saw how embarrassed I was. And I pretended that I had to go to the toilet, which is the most cowardly, least believable excuse of all time.

Sitting up quickly, I blink, trying to work out what to do. I'll have to leave. Should I call Constance? No, best if I just make my own way home. There must be a train station somewhere. I can hide out at my house, and maybe I'll pretend I'm getting a lift home with someone, so she doesn't come and pick me up at the end of the week.

I look around the room, wondering whether I could make a rope ladder out of bedsheets, before realising that solves nothing. And if I'm embarrassed now, how bad will it be when Hema finds me swinging across the house, or stuck in the guttering?

All I can do is apologise, and try harder, and promise that it won't happen again.

Standing in the shower – freezing, again – I wish I could produce some sort of character reference. 'This isn't who I am!' is the sort of empty defence made by terrible people, after they have been caught doing terrible things. Rachel's husband probably said it when everyone found out about the sexting. What if this is exactly who I am? I've spent my life trying to be good, trying to do the right thing, always. As soon as my circumstances get a tiny bit difficult, I become a craven, lazy idiot who can't follow a simple instruction.

Everyone downstairs is probably judging me, right now. I wonder what they're saying. I bet they think I'm really repressed.

Grace the Therapist had used that word, more than once. 'It's normal,' she'd explained, gently. 'No one wants to sit with their pain or examine it, but it needs to be done. It can't be locked away. And I wonder whether you have a lot of emotions locked away. Would you say you struggle with shame?'

And I'd sat on my hands and looked down and said: 'Not really.'

Because I didn't know what to tell her or how to begin. Yes, the shame was especially bad, after Ben died, but it had always been there. I'd been ashamed for so long that I couldn't remember a time when I hadn't felt it burning under the surface. I couldn't tell anyone the reasons, and I couldn't begin to explain the feelings, even to myself. I'd lived so carefully. I'd been so desperate to tip the balance to good. And where had it got me? Alone, tired, sad, embarrassed, bad at screaming. And about to face a lot of people I barely knew over chewy muesli.

I sigh heavily, and feel a little bit better. So I try an experimental scream, a brief 'Wah!' and that helps too.

I get dressed again, in a plain tee and a pair of brightly coloured cotton trousers, taking a tiny amount of pleasure in the fact that the outfit will most likely horrify Elena. I make my bed. Then, because hating her is making me hate myself, I try to atone by making Elena's bed too. Even though I doubt she'll notice.

I really ought to make much more of an effort with her. I think about trying to tidy up the mounting piles of clothes, the gleaming tubs and tubes, and wonder why she has so much stuff. Why has she brought all of this with her? I understand the urge to feel fully prepared, but Elena has packed enough clothes and make-up to stock a small department store.

I know I'm an outlier, shopping-wise. I've seen Constance and Annabel talking in their secret, special language, trading tiny packages and asking each other about SPF and retinoids. I know how capitalism works, I've seen adverts that have left me wondering which part of my body will collapse first, and which cream to apply. I've even paid well over the odds for a beautiful vintage seventies sundress, only to discover it's Topshop deadstock with the label cut out.

But the sheer volume of Elena's possessions is startling – and they're all new. Maybe, if I were to start rummaging around in her cases, I'd find some underwear or a pair of socks that was more than a week old. But I can't see any worn, loved, normal person stuff. It looks as though she had to construct a whole life, in a hurry, from the top floor of a shopping mall. Is she in witness protection? Maybe she wasn't making a joke about my T-shirt. Maybe she really was in a fire.

She's here because she's been through something, just like the rest of us. She's a mystery. A vacuous, messy, entitled, irritating mystery. And I'm just curious enough to want to stick around and see if she solves herself.

It's still morning. I can start this day all over again. The nap helped – I probably just needed more sleep. I'll go down to breakfast, make amends, sort things out, and cheerfully eat my mea culpa on toast. If I stay polite and positive, I can do anything.

'Good morning, Sunny!' I say, stopping at Reception. 'How are you doing?'

'Don't ask me for anything,' says Sunny. 'I'm going to the dentist.'

'Are you OK?' I ask. 'Is it just a check-up, or are you having something done? I hate the dentist, but I always feel so much better afterwards! It's always great to get it out the way.'

She shrugs. 'I go to the dentist all the time. She sells me nos.'

'Oh!' I'm not sure what to say to that. 'I hope she gives you a sticker!'

Sunny does not reply.

In the dining room, Cassandra is holding half a croissant

aloft. She looks tense. 'And no one is worrying about ions,' she says. 'And they should be.'

Anya nods and says, 'Have you heard—' but Cassandra makes a squeaking noise and brandishes the croissant at her. Is she using it as a conch shell, *Lord of the Flies*-style? I'm never going to be able to make my big apology if I have to fight Cassandra for a crumbling baked good.

'You can get devices that remove ions,' she says, as a smattering of flakes drifts down from her hand. 'But some of them are made by people who also sell machines that cause ions. Coincidence? I think not!'

'Hello, everyone,' I say, pouring myself a cup of coffee. Oh, God. 'I just wanted to say, about this morning. I'm so sorry.'

Rachel turns to me and smiles. I think she's simply re-lieved that I've changed the subject. 'Oh, love, don't be. It wasn't even 5 a.m.! No one is at their best in the morning. It was good, though. I cried.'

Anya smiles at me. 'Hema didn't like my thing, either. I wanted to scream about the hell of my old life. In order to make my point, I had to explain the basics of international tax law. Basically, I was working with this client who has a residence in Switzerland, and there's a monetary convention that only applies to certain parts of the Schengen area ...' She shakes her head, briskly. 'But that's not who I am, any more. Obviously. Screw the man.'

'By the time Anya had explained her tax thing, we'd all forgotten where we were and what we were supposed to be doing,' says Rachel. 'Look, Liz told me it was a bit like this. She said that Hema would really challenge us, especially the "good girls", if you know what I mean.' She wiggles her fingers. 'Liz said it had something to do with forcing us to claim our space and advocate for ourselves. It's easier for some of us than others.' She glances at Cassandra, who is still waving her croissant and saying something about 'force fields'.

'I think I'm going to find Hema and apologise,' I say, standing up. 'The whole thing is really hanging over me, it's a horrible way to start the day.'

'Things can only get better!' says Rachel. 'I think she's in the kitchen.'

And that's exactly where I find her: standing in front of the dishwasher, a checked tea towel wrapped around one hand, a glass tumbler held aloft in the other, up to the light. She's rotating it, and muttering. 'I just cleaned the filter,' she says. 'I don't understand.'

'Do you want me to help you to unload it?' I offer. This is a way for me to get back into her good books.

'What's the point?' says Hema. She sounds utterly defeated. 'They'll all come out smeared. I'll have to try a power cycle.'

She puts the glass down and looks at me, as though she's just realised who has walked into her kitchen. I notice that she doesn't smile and shame floods my system with a vengeance. Am I ashamed because I cried, or because I didn't scream properly? Or because I don't cry about the right things? Is it because I feel guilty about Constance organising this, and about all of the energy and money and time she's invested in me over the years? Is it survivor's guilt?

'Hema,' I say. 'I want to apologise.' No, that won't do, it sounds meaningless, unfelt. I put my hands in the pockets of my ridiculous trousers and try again. 'I am really sorry about this morning,' I say. 'I was tired. That's no excuse, I realise. I wasn't trying hard enough. I really want to get this right and give it my all.' Rocking on my heels, I try to think of other words to say. 'I'm confident I can learn from my mistakes, and I'd really appreciate a chance to move forward.'

She still isn't smiling. I grin, trying to encourage her. It hurts my face.

'Katherine, tell me what happened this morning.' She sounds neutral, calm. In a way that makes me think she could be seconds away from screaming at me.

'I was late,' I say, dully. 'And we held hands, and we did the breathing, throat-clearing thing, which I liked. And then it was my turn and I flopped . . . ' I trail off.

'Do you know what was going on in your body?' asks Hema.

Is that a trick question?

'I don't know,' I say, slowly. 'I think so?'

'Katherine, you strike me as a woman who might appreciate the nerdy background,' says Hema. 'Primal scream therapy had a real moment in the seventies. It was largely debunked, its therapeutic properties were overstated, and it fell out of fashion. But in the last couple of years, I've talked to women who have started doing it, on their own, for fun. Well, not fun exactly' – she rolls her eyes, and then scowls at the dishwasher – 'it's more that women's lives are hard. We have to put up with a lot of bullshit, and so many of our concerns are dismissed as trivial. We all have huge, universal, heavy fears, crushing amounts of sadness. But to process them, we have to unearth them. And to do that, we have to start by clearing out a lot of the surface-level nonsense.'

'Right,' I say. 'I wouldn't really know where to begin. It isn't that I don't get annoyed about things' – I think of Elena and her mess, Constance and her dozens of keep cups – 'it's more that I can't. It doesn't help and it doesn't change anything. The world is still in crisis. And the serious stuff, well, you know!' I laugh. 'You don't want to get me started on that! I might never leave!'

I make a noise that implies I've made a hilarious joke. Hema shakes her head.

'This week, let's focus on the stuff you can control. Forget about the climate emergency. You need to start worrying about your emotional emergency.'

Chapter Twenty-Two

Naming ceremony

Soon, Lou started to get under my skin, in a way that disturbed me. Sometimes I realised I was conducting silent conversations with her in my head when I was alone. Outside the office – not that I was outside the office often – I'd read something, or see something on TV, and wonder what she thought of it. And I felt restless. I found myself picking up my phone as though I was waiting, but I didn't understand what for. Sometimes I woke up feeling almost excited, thinking, *It's today!* What? What was today? I told myself that this was a positive shift. Maybe the grief was easing.

Also, I kept reminding myself that Lou evoked intense feelings in a lot of people. Everyone at Shrinkr adored her immediately. Ray in the postroom nicknamed her 'Lovely Lou' before the end of her first week. He didn't know my actual name – every so often, I'd go down to the basement to retrieve a missing package and Ray would frown and say, 'I always thought you were called Kathleen. Or Karen?' (Sometimes he'd frown at me and say 'Katherine Attwell?

Are you sure?' And I'd have to stop myself from saying, 'Well, I am permanently in the throes of an existential crisis so in all honesty, no.')

When she was formally introduced at the team meeting, Jeremy recited her potted biography. 'This is Lou – Louise. She joins us from Cambodia, where she was heading up a sustainability programme for the Voluntary Service Overseas.' I was deafened by impressed noises. Everyone was fascinated by her.

'Did you make it to the Preah Khan temple whilst you were in Cambodia?' asked Lydia. 'Because I spent a couple of weeks out there, and I thought it was just incredible. Stunning architecture. Everyone goes to Angkor Wat for some reason ... but you get such a better feel for a place when you go off the beaten track, don't you?'

'Mmm, yes!' said Lou. 'Down with the beaten track. And top marks for the architecture! Ten out of ten!'

As we walked back to our desks, she muttered, 'Did that Gen Z foetus just ... Cambodia-splain to me?'

When she took the piss out of Lydia, I felt myself beginning to melt. But this was work. I couldn't start slagging off my colleagues. 'Lydia's great ambition is to go out and work with VSO. I'm sure she'll be grilling you for tips before long.' Then, I said: 'What was it really like? Apart from the stunning architecture?' I stopped myself from asking my big question. What made you go? How did you find the courage to leave your old life?

Lou grinned. 'My job was basically making juice, showing people how to bottle it, and chatting with anyone who wanted a chat. We were outdoors, almost always. And I didn't really have to wear shoes. I loved it.' She looked down at her Birkenstocks and made a face. 'I am not looking forward to winter.'

'Do you think you'll go back out there one day?' I probe. 'It sounds ...' Not incredible, not amazing, not fun. I did not have a word for the longing Lou had unleashed in me. Could I go? Could I walk away from all of this, the sadness, the loneliness? From my haunted house? I even wanted to escape Annabel. She'd been trying so hard to cheer me up, and I know I made her feel like a failure. I was bringing everyone down.

Instead of finishing my sentence, I started to sob.

'Oh, love, you're ... hey, hey ... come here. What's wrong?' I didn't realise I'd started crying until Lou gathered me into her arms. 'Let's get out of here.'

'But we've got to do that deck for the Woodland Trust!' I said, and she rubbed my back.

'Never mind the Woodland Trust. We'll just have to tell the badgers there has been a personal emergency.' She squeezed me tighter. 'And you know what badgers are like. They'll assume it's code for your period, they'll freak out and they won't ask any more questions.'

I snorted. 'And if they do,' she added, still holding me, 'we'll tell them your Mooncup got stuck. And I had to retrieve it.'

'How did you know I use a Mooncup?' I said. I was half joking – I hardly knew Lou. I wanted to be silly and light-hearted, but my question sounded more intimate and provocative than I meant it to. Let's both think about my vagina. I don't know why I was feeling so weird. I talked to Annabel about this kind of stuff all the time. It might have been because I couldn't remember the last time I'd been hugged with such care. Lou held me like she didn't want to let go. And I didn't want her to, either.

'Katherine, you've got a Mooncup vibe. You're even more Mooncup than I am. In fact,' she added, 'if you could, you'd probably use a small birds' nest, woven from twigs and feathers. And that's how you get thrush!'

I laughed hard, and then cried harder again. She led me out of the building, down a side alley, to a small, cheerful coffee shop.

'I fancy an iced coffee, do you? You grab us a table, and I'll get the drinks in,' she instructed.

I sat at the back, and watched the barista greet her with a 'Hey, girl! We missed you this morning!' I prodded the napkin dispenser, feeling jealous. What would it be like to skip through life, knowing you were that charming and that loveable? The Lous of the world could gambol off to Cambodia whenever they wanted, confident that they would receive a warm reception. If I went, I wouldn't make a single friend. I could live there for ten years and everyone I met would think I was called Kathleen.

I was going to cry again. I was so sick of myself, and so sick of feeling sorry for myself. I had a good job, and a lovely husband, and a very nice life. My sorrow was crushing, but it wasn't unique. The doctor had said I wasn't even the only woman she'd seen that day. Since I'd lost our baby, all over the country hundreds, maybe thousands, of women had lost their babies. For some of them, it probably wasn't even the first time it had happened. Were they on the floor? Did they sometimes wake up, only to find that grief had come out of nowhere and flattened them – as though a car had inexplicably come off the road and driven straight through their house?

'I hedged my bets and got a flapjack and a brownie. Everyone loves a brownie, and you look like you might be fond of an oat.' Lou put a tall glass in front of me, and indicated the pink, striped paper straw. 'Sorry, the straw was a mistake. I thought it would cheer you up, but ...'

She gestured to the crumpled, snotty pile of napkins in front of me. 'We don't have to talk about anything. But you can tell me anything, in confidence. I'm in AA, so ...'

'You can fix cars?' I whispered, a little perplexed and picturing her emerging from under a bonnet, oil slicked photogenically across her cheekbones. Maybe she thought that meant she could fix anything.

Lou laughed so hard that she rocked the table. I loved the sound of her laugh, it seemed to come from somewhere deep and warm. 'The other AA. Alcoholics Anonymous. So I've had loads of practice when it comes to listening to people telling me the worst, most painful, most embarrassing things you can possibly imagine. And then not telling anyone else. Safe space.'

She held her palms up, and I wondered about her rings. Where did she get them from? Who gave them to her? Did she take them off before she went to sleep?

'OK,' I said. 'This is probably going to sound incredibly trivial, compared with some of the things you've heard. And, I guess, what you've been through.' I felt shy. I'd assumed Lou must be younger than me, that she was another typical Shrinkr employee. A loud, posh girl who'd been on a gap year for a decade who had confused a basic grasp of the shortcomings of capitalism with a social conscience. But I let myself look at her, and I noticed the faint, feathery lines etched around her eyes. There was a tiny scar above her left temple, half an inch of silver, testifying to some accident or misadventure. Lou's youth came from her kindness, her curiosity. I realised she was probably older than me. She'd known real pain, real struggle. She'd lived a lot.

'Have you heard the expression, "there is no hierarchy of pain"?' Lou asked, pulling off a corner of brownie. 'Everyone has a different reason for being in AA, but you'd be amazed by just how different we all are from each other. And we all end up in the same room. You don't have to earn the right to be sad. Right now, you're in the sadness, and that's OK. But you might feel five per cent better if you talk about it.'

I pulled at the opposite corner of the brownie. 'Right. OK.' I looked at Lou, and then started to speak to the brownie. 'I just had a miscarriage. Almost six months ago. It was my first pregnancy. I didn't even think I wanted to get pregnant yet, until it happened, and then it was all I wanted. The sadness is drowning me.' Gulping, I squashed the brownie between my fingers. 'I'm submerged, over-whelmed by these feelings I can't even articulate. Every day, I'm trying to swim to the surface and break through it. I just want to get back to the air and light and normal, but I'm so, so tired. I can't talk to my husband. I've tried. He's underwater too, in a different ocean, and we can't find each other. I don't think he's ever been sad like this before. I have, not that it helps. My mum died when I was little. My nanna raised me, and she died, too. So this shouldn't be such a shock. I don't understand why this loss is so hard to bear.' The tears returned, and I didn't bother to stop talking. Oh, this was the ocean. I was in so deep that it was spilling out of me. 'What's that stupid thing people say about loving something, letting it go, seeing if it comes back? I know that if you love someone, they will leave you. It happened with my mother. It happened with my baby. And now it's happening with Ben.' I smacked my head against the table and let my tears pool on the Formica. 'Sorry, I'm sorry, I'm so sorry.'

A warm hand was stroking my head. 'Jesus, Katherine.' My hair was getting trapped in Lou's rings. It hurt a little, but I didn't mind. 'Sweetheart, you've really been through it. I'm not going to say it's OK. I'm not going to say it will get better. Because that's not what you need to hear, now. You're grieving. Of course you're grieving.' She kept rubbing my hair. 'And I bet you haven't been signed off work or anything because that would be hell for you. You don't want to sit in your house and try not to think about things. You need to be distracted. You need to be numb. And sometimes it gets too much.'

I nodded, exhaling heavily. She knew. Lou knew. She was the only one who had seen me, in my grief. She was the only one who had made me feel a little bit better – because she wasn't trying to make me feel better.

'I'm going to ask you a question,' she said gently. 'And you don't have to answer it. Had you thought about what you were going to call your baby?'

Gathering my strength, I sat up. I was surfacing. 'Well, we wanted to be surprised. Ben thought that we had to meet our baby first so we could find a name that fit. And I agreed. But my mum was Margaret, so if she'd been a girl ... ' Lou took my hands in hers, and nodded, as I tried to steady my breath. 'If she'd been a girl, she would have been Maggie.'

'I love Maggie,' said Lou, solemnly. 'That's beautiful.'

She lifted her glass in the air. 'To Maggie! Cheers.' I raised my own, and we toasted baby Maggie. 'Here's to you, and here's to your lovely mum.'

'Thank you,' I said. 'That did help. I feel different. Since it happened, I've felt as though I was disintegrating, turning transparent. And now ... I feel like I have a little more structural integrity, or something.'

'We don't have the right rituals, any more,' said Lou, tugging on a skein of hair. 'In Cambodia, I noticed that they are so much better at death and grief than we are. We need to honour our losses and make space for people to be sad.'

When Lou looked at me, she made me feel steady. There was no pity on her face. I didn't feel the usual, nagging need to impress her, or please her, or tidy myself up. I could only describe it as a kind of unconditional steadiness. Serenity. She looked at me as though I made sense. *It's OK*, I thought. *You're here.*

Chapter Twenty-Three

Silent alarm

Hema's words are bothering me, like a crisp caught between my back teeth. I want to forget they're there, but every few minutes I find I'm fidgeting, poking and prodding at them. Emotional emergency. What does that even mean? It's a ridiculous expression.

So I cried. But, come on! Who doesn't want to cry after a telling-off? I'd been publicly humiliated. Surely it would have been much more worrying if I hadn't reacted at all! And I'd barely had any sleep, and I'd been woken up by the world's loudest woman.

It's outrageous for Hema to suggest I'm experiencing some kind of crisis. I'm fine, really. What kind of retreat is she running, anyway? How does this help me heal? How does this make me feel better? Maybe it's a scam. I'll get to the end of the week, and she'll say, 'It's much worse than we thought. You're going to need to stay for a month. We have an emotional emergency package. By the way, it costs ten thousand pounds.' But what did she say in that introductory talk? Something about taking responsibility, and choosing to be here.

Fine. I choose not to have an emotional emergency. I choose to put Hema out of my mind. I choose to be good at this. At least, good enough to stop anyone shouting at me.

'Katherine?' I realise Anya has her hand on my shoulder. 'Where did you go? Are you OK? I said, we're going to be late for yoga.'

'Sorry,' I say, leaping to my feet. 'I'm fine. Let's go.'

'Emergency' implies some sort of collective responsibility, I think, before wobbling out of my tree pose and falling to the floor. *I can't deal with this alone. But who is going to help me?*

'Make sure you're concentrating, Katherine,' calls the instructor. 'Everybody, let's move into Downward Dog.'

I'm *not* having an emotional emergency, I think, hours later, mindlessly chewing my Mindful Raisin, but if I was, I'd want a summit. People in grey suits, shaking their heads and producing pie charts. A modest buffet.

'Guys, I want you to call out some of the dominant flavours of your raisin,' says the bearded man at the front. 'What is it evoking for you, in a sensory way? No wrong answers!'

'Confusion!' I call, as Elena shouts, 'Sweetness' and Anya says, 'I think you've given me a sultana.'

What are you supposed to do in an emergency, anyway? Stay calm. That's always the first instruction. Keep calm and . . . eat lunch? I have no memory of entering the dining room, but I'm pulling out a chair, and everyone is laughing.

' . . . and he said, deadly serious, "We've been burgled. Someone has taken my golf clubs." And I smiled and shrugged and said, "No, darling, I sold the lot on Vinted for seven pounds fifty!"' Rachel grins.

'You *didn't*!' Anya is struggling to breathe. 'That's evil genius.'

'They say the best revenge is living well,' adds Rachel, 'but I think you have to get creative. And petty.' She reaches over and hands me a bowl of something. 'This is the chicken salad, the avocado one is at the end of the table. Do you eat meat?'

'No, not usually,' I say, squinting at the salad as though there might be a message for me in the leaves.

'Hon, are you feeling OK?' asks Rachel. 'I wondered if you were a bit light-headed, in yoga. Did Cassandra make some of her special mushroom tea?'

'Hema said I'm not allowed,' says Cassandra, sulkily. 'Apparently it contravenes the insurance.'

'Oh, we've got to be very careful about that sort of thing,' says Hema. 'You'd have to fill in a lot of paperwork, and you wouldn't like that.'

'What about giving readings?' says Cassandra. 'I'd like to share my gift – and surely there's no paperwork required for that!'

A vein briefly bulges in Hema's forehead. 'If we've got time at the end of the week, it might be a possibility. But we've got quite a full programme already, there's lots to coordinate.'

Elena looks up. 'Do you use tarot cards? Is it like an energy reading?' It's the first time that I've heard her sounding curious about anything.

'That all depends on you,' says Cassandra. I suspect she's trying to be mysterious, but I wonder whether she could read me. And whether I'd want her to.

'Can you talk to people who aren't here?' I ask, nervously.

'If you're struggling with signal, there's a phone in the office—' says Hema, but Cassandra holds her hand up to stop her. 'I believe Katherine is talking about communicating with the spirit world. That very much depends on whether the spirits want to visit.'

'I mean, they might be busy.' Rachel looks as though she's trying very hard not to laugh. 'They might be having their annual two weeks in Mallorca. Or waiting for someone to install a washing machine.'

'Or getting a massage,' says Anya. 'You know what, sometimes, during my reiki course, I've wondered about that. If you give reiki to someone, and they're haunted, the ghost could just be lying on top of them, getting a free massage, and you'd never know.'

'Of course you'd know!' says Cassandra, crossly. 'They'd make their presence felt! People come from the spirit world with *messages*, they're not going to drift around the world getting free treatments!'

'But that's exactly what I'd do, if I were a ghost!' says Rachel. 'And ghosts aren't idiots!'

Hema has her head in her hands.

'I'd love to talk to you about the energy readings,' Anya says to Cassandra. 'It's something I'd really like to learn to do. Have you thought about teaching a course?'

Cassandra sighs, heavily. 'My gift cannot be taught! Maybe *you* should sign up for a course that teaches you not to try to make everything into a course.'

Maybe an energy reading is exactly what I need. In a way, it doesn't sound woo at all. If my house can have an energy reading, so can I. It's just a tune-up, a spiritual MOT. I'd rather have that than let Cassandra summon any ghosts who might want to tell tales on me.

'How does it work exactly?' I ask, hesitantly. 'If your problem was that you didn't know what your problem was, could you guide them to it? Or is it like going to the doctor, where you have to make a list of your specific symptoms?'

'And even doctors aren't that great,' says Anya. 'I was having an awful time with my bowels, the scans didn't find anything. In the end the only thing that sorted me out was some acupuncture. It's all about flow.' She looks thoughtful. 'And almond croissants from Gail's. It was the acupuncturist who pointed out they might be making me a bit bunged up. I walked into an appointment while eating one, you see, and she figured it out straight away. Which just shows the power of alternative medicine.'

Cassandra nods. 'You need to be as clear and cooperative as possible. I'm just a vessel, a channel for the higher powers to work through.' She shrugs. 'I can't look you up and down and say, "You live near water, you're allergic to walnuts and your Auntie Betty says hello."' She blushes and looks almost modest. 'Well, on a good day I can, but not for everyone.'

She catches my eyes for a second, and gives me a look that startles me. I didn't think Cassandra was even *aware* of me – but her face is briefly filled with tenderness, and sorrow. Then her eyes seem to flash and shrink. She knows something. She might know even more than I do.

'Coming back to the here and now, for a minute,' says Hema. 'This afternoon, we've got a treat for you. You're all finding your inner joy and strength through music and movement with Millie in the conservatory!' Under her breath I hear her add: 'God, I wish she'd think of a better name for it, it hardly trips off the tongue.'

Do I have any inner joy and strength to find? The emotional emergency is ongoing. I'm on red alert.

Chapter Twenty-Four

'Don't you know how hard I've been trying?'

'What's going on with that weird girl at your work?' said Annabel, holding the door for me. 'Ugh, it smells even sweatier than usual in here.' Annabel was a hot yoga regular, and I went whenever there was a special offer. This meant I was restricted to off-peak classes – going in my lunch hour, a real gesture of hope over experience when I considered the fact that it took me a good forty minutes just to get in and out of my special stretchy shorts.

'Who, Lydia?' I said, trying to breathe through my mouth. 'Oh, she's not done anything especially awful for a bit. Although she did tell Jeremy that she thought he was going through the male menopause and sent him some recipes for a sweet potato curry. I don't know how she gets away with it.'

'Not Lydia, the other one. The new one, who tried to nick your desk on her first day. The gap yah acid casualty one, you said she had mad trousers and Birkenstocks. Lucy, or Linda?'

'Oh, Lou!' I said, smiling. 'Oh, she's fine, she's great!

She's really sweet actually, and incredibly smart. She's a massive hit with the Woodland Trust. We're heading up a hedgehog initiative.'

'Don't you mean hedging up,' said Annabel, putting one arm into her bralette, and elbowing me in the face. 'Or maybe spearing, because of the spikes. Although is it hedgehogs that aren't actually spiky? They're supposed to be quite soft when you pick them up.'

'Please don't pick up any hedgehogs,' I say. 'They won't like it. In fact, I should probably make that our top line. No hog fondling.'

'You don't need to be a fact hog, I know all about hedgehogs,' said Annabel, grumpily. 'I know you're supposed to check bonfires, before you light them, to make sure that they haven't wandered in. And ... the most famous one is Mrs Tiggywinkle.' She bent down to reach for her bag, tripping over her trainers. 'I know I moan about this every time, but I've never, ever been to a yoga studio with a changing room that had space for actual humans to get changed in.'

'It's quite pessimistic of the yoga people,' I said, 'as though they think that only two or three people will come. Teeny-tiny people. I can't fit one of my shoes in the lockers. These are pegs for a nursery school, not for adult yogis.'

'Created to trigger body dysmorphia before you've got your leggings on,' said Annabel, sighing. 'It's probably because petite, perfect yogis have no attachment to possessions. And it's humbling to start the class, feeling like a fat cow with too much stuff.'

I nodded. 'Although Lou was saying something really interesting about that earlier. She gave all her stuff away before she went to Cambodia. Literally all of it. She pretty much went out there with two pairs of trousers, some sandals, and some vests. She said it was horrible, and scary, but she was so freaked out by the idea that she knew she had to do it. That there was no point going if she was going to come back and be locked into her old life.'

'Right,' said Annabel. 'If we're quick, we can get on the back row.'

'Lou is really impressed that we're doing lunch yoga. She says she's never been able to do it – everyone assumes she would be, but she always falls over. She said she's been mistaken for a yoga teacher more than once.'

'God, what a wanky thing to say,' said Annabel, pulling me through the studio door. 'You hold those spaces, I'll grab our mats.'

'No, no!' I said, hurriedly. 'She told me because she thought it was funny, she's not the sort of person who shows off about things. Kind of the opposite, really. She's sort of . . . not humble, because that makes her sound very dull. But she's really funny, and really wise. She reminds me of Kate McKinnon.'

'Kate McKinnon from SNL?' said Annabel, whispering quite loudly. 'The one you have a girl crush on? When was she ever known for her wisdom?'

'What about Weird Barbie? She was wise!' I hissed, as a woman in a tiny pink crop top, with gleaming abs, made her way to the front of the room. Oh, shit. It was a Kita class. Kita hated us. Admittedly, she had good reasons. We were the naughty girls at the back of the room who could not stop talking. Well, Annabel was the naughty girl at the back of the room who could not stop talking, and I was the anxious, twitching nerd, watching her grades go down the drain and wishing her friend wasn't such a bad influence.

'Good afternoon, everyone. Let's all focus and set our intentions before we start the session. It's time to settle ourselves and really commit to the flow.' Kita gave me a pointed look.

'Yes, miss,' whispered Annabel, and I made a face at her.

'OK, we're going to start in mountain pose. Now take a deep breath, go slow and steady, and we'll meet in Downward Dog.'

Upside down, I met Annabel, who caught my eye. 'Do you fancy Weird Barbie?' she mouthed.

'Her name's Lou,' I said, thinking it's funny how much more vulnerable you are, when your bum's high in the air. Then I clapped my hand over my mouth and immediately fell over.

'Katherine, stay in the pose. Be in your body, not your brain,' sang Kita. 'That's very good, Annabel. Beautiful frame.' God, why did I always get picked on? Why did everyone else always get away with everything?

'Now we're all going to flow into triangle pose.' Kita's ponytail bounced and shone under the studio spotlights, as she folded her limbs into equal angles. Perfectly folded human origami. In contrast, my body looked like something bound for the wastepaper bin. I felt tightly crumpled, unable to remember my original shape.

I didn't have a crush on Lou, that was ludicrous. Ludicrous! I thought, smiling.

Oh, fuck. Oh, fuck fuck fuck.

No. Annabel was just jealous because I had a new friend. She was teasing. Ben was my crush. Ben was my love.

226

The thing about Triangle Pose was that it only worked if every bit of your body came together in a state of harmonious balance. It was a strengthening exercise in muscle recruitment. Every point of the triangle was supposed to support every other element. It was powerful, but delicate. If you got it wrong or didn't work at it, it wouldn't support itself. It would collapse.

Just like a marriage.

Was my triangle about to fold in on itself?

This was ridiculous. A phase. A symptom, a sign that I urgently needed to sort things out with Ben. I'd ride it out, and soon I'd have a lovely, easy friendship with Lou, just like I did with Annabel.

But I'd never blushed with pleasure when I'd heard Annabel's name. I'd never fantasised about spending time with Annabel when she wasn't there. I'd never sprayed perfume on the back of my neck and wondered whether Annabel would notice it.

I hadn't meant for this to happen, I hadn't even been aware of it happening. It was like getting lost. I'd had the map upside down, I'd been singing along to the radio, I'd suggested stopping by the lake and having a picnic. Now it was dark, and cold, and terrifying and I didn't think I could find my way back if I wanted to. Did I want to? I was a cheat. I was committing adultery. I was a worm. My husband was grieving for our child, and I was falling in love with someone else.

My breath started to get fast, and shallow. I was going to have a panic attack, at yoga.

Lou doesn't love me, I thought. *I mean, she loves everyone. Everyone loves her. I'm not special. What we have isn't special. She's magnetic. I've seen her in action. I'm a silly girl, with a silly crush, and if I were to tell her, she'd laugh. She'd take my hand, and squeeze it, and say she really appreciates my friendship, and that would be the end of it.*

The thought was supposed to be comforting. It made me howl, out loud. I gulped down a sob, and another one came out.

'Warrior one now, lovely full body stretch,' sang out Kita.

I had to focus on the yoga. If I could get this right, I could redeem myself. I'd prove this was just a blip. Like millions of women before me, I sought comfort by silently reciting the list of logical reasons for feeling as though I was on the brink of disaster. My feelings weren't facts. I wasn't going to blow my life up. It was work stress. Something to do with my period. Maybe a peri-peri menopause? (It was certainly making things spicy.) Perhaps this was because I'd run out of my magnesium supplement. I'd start a course of high grade CBD oil, and I'd be *fine*. This would go away.

I swung my body up, from horizontal to vertical – and watched one of my own tears sailing in front of me. It travelled across space and time. It seemed to swell in the light, getting bigger and harder to ignore, before it landed on Kita's bare ab. She looked utterly disgusted.

Out of the corner of my eye, I could see Annabel watching the tear's trajectory.

She looked at Kita's face, then at mine, and said, loudly and clearly, 'We need to get out of here.'

We'd always walked past the pub at the bottom of the road, but when Annabel paused outside the grimy, etched-glass windows, I nodded. If I was about to detonate my life, I might as well do it in a place that looked demolition-ready. She pushed the door open and held it for me.

It was almost empty – a man with a grey face sat on a table by the door. His coat was zipped up, and his phone was flashing. We walked straight up to the bar, and Annabel said, in her clearest, loudest voice, 'Hello, two large glasses of white wine, please. Pinot Grigio, if you've got it.'

The man behind the bar spun around, almost dropping the glass he was drying. 'Jesus Christ! Sorry! No one usually comes in this early. Apart from . . . ' He nodded at the man we'd seen. 'Anyway, yeah, no problem. Weirdly, it's actually cheaper if you buy the whole bottle, is that all right?'

Annabel nodded, thanked him, tapped her card and picked up the bottle. I took the glasses and followed her to a table at the back of the room. Before we sat down, she filled both glasses to their spilling point and said: 'What are you going to do?'

I gulped at my wine. It was horrible, but that didn't matter. It was what I deserved. I was a bad wife, and a bad person, drinking bad wine.

'I don't think I can do anything,' I said. 'I don't think I should do anything. Nothing will fix this. Nothing will help.'

'Do you think this Lou feels the same way?' I didn't like the way Annabel called her 'this Lou'. It made her sound like a dodgy character, someone who let herself into my home and stole my heart on the pretext of installing some cheap double glazing.

'None of this is Lou's fault,' I said sharply. 'Leave her out of this.'

'We can't though, can we?' said Annabel. 'Logically. Have you talked to Ben?'

Change the record, Annabel. She always gave the same stupid advice. 'Of course I haven't talked to Ben,' I snapped, draining my wine. 'I didn't know until fifteen minutes ago. And Ben won't really talk to me, any more, about anything. We're ships in the night. He's busy with work. When I try to spend time with him, he says he can't because I'm too busy with work. In fact, he literally is a ship in the night because he's sailing. He doesn't even tell me he's going any more, he just puts it on the calendar.'

'Have you thought about couples counselling?' asked Annabel, gently.

'Annabel, I've begged him to come to couples counselling. I've phoned Relate. He said he's fine. "I don't have a problem if you want to see a counsellor but leave me out of it."'

'What?' Annabel looked shocked. 'That doesn't sound like Ben. I mean, I don't doubt he said that, but he's not OK.'

'I know,' I said. 'I keep telling myself that we just need time. He doesn't even touch me any more, Annabel. He barely makes eye contact with me. I think he blames me for what happened. Our baby.'

'But that's ridiculous!' Annabel banged her elbows on the table. 'You're grieving, too. It happened to you! In your body.'

I shook my head. 'I think that might be the problem. My guess – and I don't know because he *will not talk to me* – is that he's furious with my body, and me. Honestly, he looks at me with contempt. Disgust. If he looks at me at all, I think he's just too sad. I can't reach him. And I kind of hate him, too! Because I needed him, and he hasn't even tried to reach me ...

I started to sob and slumped in my seat.

'And I should be fixing this!' I said, angrily. 'I can't just say, "Oh, look, the man I promised to love forever has gone mad and now hates me. I'll just fall in love with this random woman at work! JESUS.' I banged my fist on the table. The man by the door turned around. 'Annabel, in the time you've known me, how many crushes have I had? I never fancy people! Definitely not real people, who aren't on TV. Why now? Why her?'

Annabel put her arm around my shoulder. 'This is what is giving me pause for thought,' she said, quietly. 'You're not that sort of woman. You don't have that sort of marriage. You're not flighty. If you had a new crush every week, I might roll my eyes and say, "Oh, there she goes again." But – it sounds like this might be something.'

'Well, I'm married, and Lou probably doesn't feel the same way, so there's no room for it to be something,' I said firmly.

'Katherine, how would you feel if Ben was in love with someone else?'

'Oh, God, I don't know. Relieved, probably.' As soon as the word was out of my mouth, I clapped my hand over my face. 'No, that's not right. I just meant that it would make sense of what was going on. I'd understand why he was shutting me out.'

'You see?' Annabel nodded. 'If – and this is a big if, I appreciate that – if you are in love with Lou, and it sounds like you might be, is it fair to Ben to try to stay married to him, while you're dreaming about someone else? And more importantly, is it fair to you?'

'If we got divorced' – I'd never said that word out loud. I was going to be sick – 'I'd be lost. I'd be no one. I wouldn't have anywhere to live. I wouldn't have Constance. I wouldn't have a family.'

'You'd have me.' Annabel sounded faintly hurt.

I clutched her hands. 'I know, and that's everything. But ... I'm Ben's wife. That's what makes me a proper person.' I twisted my wedding ring. 'If I got divorced' – acid rose in my throat, and I tried to swallow it down – 'it's as if there wouldn't be anything tethering me to the Earth any more. I've already lost one family. Ben gave me a whole new one, I don't want to lose them too.'

'Listen,' said Annabel. 'I know this is really scary. Change is really scary. But you've got to do something, before it's too late. You need to decide whether you can stay married to Ben. Because if you do, you've got to start fighting. Equally, if you don't, you need to leave. But you have to choose, Katherine. You need to take responsibility for what happens next. There isn't a reality where you get to think about Lou until your marriage drifts back to a better place.'

I couldn't believe what I was hearing. Annabel was meant to be my best friend. Surely it was her job to reassure me, and make me feel better? *'That's* your advice?' I snapped, angrily. *'I've* got to fix this, alone? What do you think I've been doing, with Ben? Don't you know how hard I've been trying? For the first time in months, I feel happy. I feel human. Maybe that's why I have a silly crush! You're meant to tell me that this will blow over!'

Annabel put a hand on my arm. 'I'd be a bad friend if I told you that. You're the only one who knows how you feel, and I want you to trust your feelings. I want you to be happy. And no, to be honest, I don't think this will blow over! I don't think it's a weird blip. I think you're in the middle of an emergency!'

'WHY ARE YOU BEING SO DRAMATIC?' I shouted, leaping to my feet. 'I just want to do the right thing, be a good person. For better, for worse, remember? You were there on our wedding day. I can't leave Ben. And why are you making me feel guilty about Lou? I haven't done anything. We haven't even kissed!' Well, once. In a dream. And it was more of a feeling than something I could see clearly, or really remember. And sometimes I dreamed about women. But surely everyone did that! Again, it was just a stress thing, or a vitamin deficiency, or a sign of me embracing my own feminine power, or something.

'This isn't about being a good person or a bad person,' said Annabel, angrily. 'Just, be a human being, for once in your life! There's nothing noble about sacrifice. You don't get points for staying with Ben because you're unhappy. Whatever the ghost of your bloody nanna might have to say on the matter. This is really hard, Katherine! This is scary, grown-up stuff. But you can't cast yourself as the victim and hope the situation resolves itself. Otherwise a lot of people are going to get hurt. It's not just about you.'

It was as though she'd slapped me. 'You don't understand,' I said. 'It's never about me. I never do what I want.'

'And yet somehow, it's always about you,' said Annabel. 'You're seeking everyone's approval and validation. It's exhausting. I'm sorry that you're going through this, but I can't tell you what to do. And I can't tell you that it's all going to be fine. You need to listen to yourself. Give yourself a break. And give me one.'

'I'm exhausting?' I stood up. That was a horrible thing to

say, but she had a point. I was exhausted. I was exhausting myself. 'Well, I'll leave you alone to recuperate. You've given me a lot to think about.'

'K, wait a minute.' Annabel stood up too. 'I hate arguing with you. You're upset. This is big. Let's go outside, get some air.'

'You do what you like.' I gathered my jacket and my bag. 'I'm leaving.'

Chapter Twenty-Five

How to fix a marriage

I couldn't go back to work. Not with Lou there, wanting to know how yoga went. Lou was a little bit psychic. She wouldn't call herself that, in so many words, but she knew about people. She'd know about me. In fact, she probably knew that I fancied her before I did. Right now, she was probably working out ways to let me down gently. I rang Reception and said I thought I might be coming down with a bug, I'd just been sick. This was almost true. And while it was probably a symptom of guilt, shock and bad white wine, there was an outside chance that it was stomach flu.

I had to fix my marriage. Surely there was something I could do that would set us back on course. When were we good together? I just needed to remind Ben that he loved me, once. And I loved him. What did I love, about him? I concentrated hard. I couldn't quite conjure his face in my imagination, the image kept misting over.

This was Ben. My Ben. We had to pull through. This man was tender, funny and kind. I tried to think about our high points, our happy days. Our first time together, on the water, when he made me feel as though we were both made of magic. Our wedding morning, on the kitchen floor ... my Ben was *so loving*. Nothing like the stranger I was living with.

But Ben had pulled away before. I thought about the months before he proposed – and how I'd misinterpreted his anxiety, and believed we were heading for an ending, not a beginning. Maybe this was all in my head. Just a bump in the road, and in ten years' time we'd look back on this strange, sad period and laugh.

He might surprise me. We'd have a vow renewal. Perhaps he'd want to try for a baby again. I knew I was supposed to want that, too, eventually. Every single pamphlet and blog I'd read had *promised* me that the urge would come back when the time was right. But I had a horrible feeling that I'd never want to have a child with Ben, now. I could tell myself that this was because the world was on fire, and having a baby would be a betrayal of my principles. But I had deeper, darker fears. If I got pregnant again, that might fix us for a few months, or a couple of years. And then what happened? What if life got hard again? Our baby might get sick. I might get sick. We could lose our jobs. The house could fall down. And Ben might check out of our marriage, again, and abandon me.

Thinking about it made me feel tight and trapped. The stakes were too high for a baby. And if it didn't work, there was no way we could survive that much loss again. If it did, I'd spend the rest of my life holding my breath, waiting for Ben to shut me out.

What would life with Lou be like? Could I dare to let

myself dream about it? I could summon her face, straight away. I could see us somewhere green, in a park, or woodland. I could feel the sun on my skin. I could hear her laughing.

No. I didn't want to be divorced from Ben. We'd made promises to each other. I had to stay with him, in sickness, and in health. We were sick, and I needed to make us better. I wasn't the sort of person who acted on whims and instincts. I wasn't the sort of person who threw things away. Everything could be reused and repurposed. I never wasted anything. Of course I was going to save my marriage.

As I walked up the road, I made a vow. Starting from tonight, I was going to do better. I'd cook. I'd spend the rest of the afternoon making a very elaborate vegetarian lasagne. Ben would come home, and I'd greet him at the door in my underwear. Different underwear, I thought, trying to remember exactly what was under my clothes. That was the problem, I couldn't remember where my sexy underwear was, let alone when I last wore it. Things were going to be different around here!

When I opened the door, it took me a moment to realise the house felt odd. Someone was there. Perhaps it shows how bad things were, that my first thought wasn't 'Ben' but 'burglar'.

'Hello?' I called, cautiously, gripping my keys with my hand. What on earth could I do to stall a burglar? Throw my shoe at them?

Before I'd had time to think of a decent weapon, the door of the sitting room opened. I was expecting to see someone in a mask, and a black and white striped jumper – OK, if

I'm completely honest, I was also picturing them holding a sack full of hamburgers. But it was Ben, and I screamed.

'Katherine?' he said, as though he didn't quite recognise me.

He was wearing grey joggers, a grey T-shirt, and he had a grey face. He looked drained, like VHS footage of himself. 'What are you doing here?'

I felt very self-conscious. For the first time in a long time, I saw him.

Usually, Ben blurred into a composite of all of his different selves. I still saw a handsome man emoji when he was watching TV, wearing nothing but pyjama bottoms and a sharing-sized bag of Doritos on his right hand, like a snacking gauntlet. I could see the ruddy, cheerful Ben, his hair spiked with saltwater, returning from a sailing trip. I could see him when he was off to work, smooth and serious in his good suit. It was as though I'd always looked at him through a love filter, a kaleidoscopic fracturing of light through which his goodness shone out.

Now, I was confronted with a sad, tired man, who took absolutely no pleasure in being surprised by his wife. I felt self-conscious, gaudy. I was glowing with rage, and fear, and love. I wasn't happy, but I was animated. Confronted with Ben, it seemed vulgar of me to be breathing, and three dimensional. I should flatten myself against the wall, or fall through a hole in the floor, out of respect.

Panicking, I got hold of myself. 'I came home early because I felt a bit sick after hot yoga. It was probably the heat. Ha! I'm feeling better now though. Are you OK?'

My words were falling out of my mouth too quickly. I was trying so hard not to say the wrong thing. Like, 'What are you doing here?' 'Why aren't you at work?' and 'Is this the first time you've said you're going to work and you've stayed at home, or has this been going on for a while?'

'My meeting got cancelled,' said Ben. 'So I decided to work from home.'

'Oh.' I didn't know what to say to that. 'This is a lovely surprise. I'm really happy that you're here.' I had promised to love this man, no matter what. I reached for his hand and squeezed it. Look at me, Ben, I begged silently. This will all be OK, as long as you look at me.

When his eyes met mine, I breathed out. 'We've not had a night in together for ages!' I said, hopefully. 'I was thinking about cooking, but maybe we should just curl up on the sofa. Get a pizza, or something.'

Ben pulled his hand away from mine. 'I thought you'd come home because you were sick.'

'Honestly,' I said, 'I feel a lot better now. And it's so nice to see you. I've missed you.'

'You know, now that you're here ...' Ben said, and trailed off. His eyes did not meet mine. 'We need to talk. I've been thinking about us. It's been hard, hasn't it? And we ...'

I should have read the room. I should have seen Ben, the man in front of me, in all of his anxiety and vulnerability and sadness. Instead, a vintage *Cosmo* tip flashed up on my internal autocue. Something about 'irresistible ways to surprise your lover'.

'We should talk,' I said, slowly. 'But right now, there's something else we could do.'

Maybe this had been the problem, all along. I'd always been too passive. I'd let Ben do the wanting. I had to want for both of us, and prove my desire to him. I looked at him directly, trying to send him a signal. Trying to make him feel as beautiful as he once made me feel.

It was up to me. I felt powerful. I felt excited. My marriage was going to be fine. This was how I'd fix it. Before, this was how we stayed connected. This was how we came back to each other. I didn't want Lou, of course I didn't. I wanted my husband, and I just needed to remind myself of how good we could be together.

I looked at Ben and started to unbutton my jacket. In any other reality I would have muffed it, fumbling and cursing, as sweaty and awkward as usual. But on that day, of all days, I popped the buttons in single, smooth, fluid movements. The jacket fell to the floor, the weight of the fabric making the sound of a boot pressing against freshly fallen snow.

'Katherine?'

'What?' I smiled, lazily, as I reached for my hem, and pulled my dress over my head. Standing by the mat, in my black shoes, black knickers and black bra, I thought, I am a sex goddess. I am doing marriage right. We're not in trouble. We're fun and wild. We're going to do it in the hall.

'I don't think ...' He was shaking his head.

I walked to Ben, reached up so I could wrap my arms around his neck. I pressed my body to his, and the fabric of his T-shirt felt warm against my bare skin.

'I want you so much,' I murmured, barely brushing his lips with mine.

His hands were warm on my waist, and for a second I thought, It's OK. It's going to be OK. It took me a moment to realise he was pushing me away. I'd oriented my body towards his and I stumbled, falling against the wall.

'Ben? What? Why?' All of the smoke and huskiness had vanished from my voice, every syllable was going up by a full octave. 'But we ... '

'I don't feel like it,' he told the picture hanging twelve inches above my head. 'I don't think it's a good idea.' He stooped to pick my dress up from the floor and handed it to me.

'Oh,' I said. 'Right.'

I thought a thousand things, then.

Just say you don't love me. Just tell me it's over. Don't you want to fix this? Don't you want to try? We're married. I've been trying, so hard, to keep all of the promises I made to you. Are you trying, at all?

Because I'm choosing you. I have feelings for someone else, and I'm trying to push them away, for our marriage. Can't you see that? Can't you see how lonely you're making me?

Fuck you, Ben, for abandoning me. With a hallway, and a universe between us.

I wasn't brave enough to say any of those words out loud. I weighed up my options and picked my jacket up from the floor.

'You know, the nausea has come back. I might just go to bed,' I said, avoiding Ben's eyes.

When I got upstairs, I had two messages. The first was from Lou.

Love! Lydia said you were poorly, this gastric thing is a nightmare. Have you got any ginger tea? Feel better

soon, let me know how you're feeling in the morning.
DO NOT WORRY ABOUT W TRUST. I will badger them
for you!

A badger, three hedgehogs. Three kisses.

Oh! I hugged my chest and bounced up and down on the bed. Then the firework faded, just as quickly as it had exploded. That was a work text. From my colleague. I had a problem. A big, bad, inappropriate problem.

I replied.

Great, thank you. Will try ginger tea, hopefully back
tomorrow. XXX

The other message was from Annabel.

I'm sorry! I didn't mean to upset you. I hate arguing with
you. DO NOT WORRY ABOUT THINGS. It will be OK.
Let's talk soon with better wine. XXX

As I read it, my phone buzzed again. Lou had added: 'I can't believe how much I missed you this afternoon. It feels like you've been gone for days.'

I stopped breathing. Three flickering dots appeared. I held my phone, tightly, watching, waiting, wondering. Hoping. The dots vanished.

When I woke up a few hours later, face down on a damp pillow, there were no more words. Just a single kiss.

Chapter Twenty-Six

Spartacus

'I think we did music and movement at school,' says Rachel, as we walk towards the conservatory. 'That's what they called it then – you know, about a thousand years ago, when the war was on. I remember pretending to be a squirrel, and a lot of flute music, and Mrs Anderson complimenting me on my imaginary tail.' She pats her tailbone and grins. 'I'm so crap at yoga, I've been losing the will a bit. Finally, it's my time to shine.'

I'm surprised to see Sunny at Reception. 'Oh, hi!' I say. 'I thought you were at the dentist!'

'I am,' says Sunny. 'I'm not here. You're imagining me. Or, more likely, I am imagining you.' She sinks down below the desk, and I remember what she was doing at the dentist. 'I think she's on, um, laughing gas,' I whisper to Rachel.

'I love that stuff,' she whispers back. 'One night, when the kids were away, I got my mate Polly to bring some over, it was great fun. Of course, when they came back the next day and found the canisters in the garden, I had to pretend that some local teens must have broken in. I was panicking, and I said, "Ruffians came"; I sounded like Mr Burns. I have not lived it down.'

I start to wish I had some drugs of my own when we walk into the conservatory. A very small, very blonde, very pink woman is waiting for us. She's in a fluorescent fuchsia satin one-piece, with a black leotard over the top. I've never understood that look, from a functional perspective. Is it for warmth?

Do I know this woman from somewhere? Maybe Instagram, or something Annabel sent me? Or something on TV ... *Made in Chelsea*?

She has pigtails and piercings. I see lots of tiny, twinkling golden rings, a constellation of wealth in her right ear. A scattering of swirls and circles on her left bicep. She's wearing a lot of golden necklaces – and I think I see an ornate, diamond 'C' dangling from a chain.

Camilla! Millie is Camilla! Oh my God. Camilla Ponsonby.

The last time I saw this woman was at Ben's funeral, in a black cocktail dress. Working the room, as though she was at a book launch or something. But what's she doing here? I thought she was a jewellery designer. Although I might be getting her mixed up with another one of Ben's friends. He stayed in touch with most of the girls he went to school with – and every single one went on to become a jewellery designer, or something to do with wellness. (Apart from the small subsection that doesn't need to work. They spend their time buying and renovating Portuguese farmhouses, and taking lots of photos.)

What do I remember about Camilla? That day was so strange, most of it is still shrouded in fog. But when I close my eyes, I can feel her hands digging into my forearm. She didn't cry, she wailed, while rocking backwards and forwards. 'It's a tragedy for our whole generation! I don't think we'll EVER RECOVER!' Then she introduced herself to Eva, who had come over to rescue me. 'Hello, I'm Camilla, a VERY CLOSE FAMILY FRIEND. Have you met Katherine? Ben's wife?'

Eva ushered me away, muttering something about Constance needing my help. 'Was it me,' I asked, 'or did she somehow say the word "wife" sarcastically?'

Eva squeezed my shoulder. 'That's funerals, kid. Everyone thinks it's about them. And the people in the eye of the storm are expected to nurse these random idiots through their grief, and hand out tissues. But yeah, she did sound sarcastic.'

When Camilla found me again, and she did, she was even louder. 'I don't know HOW YOU'RE GOING TO COPE!' she cried. 'KATIE!'

'It's Katherine,' I said, through gritted teeth.

'Kath, WHATEVER YOU NEED, just let me know. I'll drop EVERYTHING. I'll COME AND STAY WITH YOU. Actually,' she sounded slightly brighter, and opened her handbag, before handing me a flier, 'I'm hosting a necklace-making workshop in Ibiza, you should come! I'll DO YOU A DISCOUNT!'

I had completely blocked this exchange from my memory, until now. It's staring me in the face, in neon pink.

This is a very weird coincidence. Unless it isn't a coincidence at all.

I'm being ridiculous. This isn't a sign from the universe, this is a sign that I was married to a posh person. Women like this turn up everywhere – at parties and Pilates and Peckham pop-up cocktail bars. And I'm only at Cadwell Manor because Hema is a friend of a friend. I'm a posh interloper too.

'Haiiiiii, everyone! Welcome, welcome, welcome! It's an honour to invite you all into my special space today!' Rachel snorts and jolts me out of my reverie. 'I'm Millie, and I'll be showing you all how to move towards joy! Please pick up a hula hoop and follow me into the garden!'

Millie bends over, thrusting her tiny bum high in the air – why? No one naturally bends that way! She's just showing off! – and picks up a large pink hoop from the top of the pile. Even the way she walks annoys me. She moves as though she's thinking *Boing, boing, boing!*

'I know her,' I say to Rachel, trying to talk out of the side of my mouth without moving my lips.

'What? You know her? Is she a friend?' Rachel picks up her own pink hula hoop and regards it morosely. 'Christ. To think I was feeling quite optimistic about this session, five minutes ago.'

'No,' I say. 'She's a . . .' Friend of a friend? Distant acquaintance? She kissed my husband when they were both three years old, and reminded him of this at our wedding? (And then got drunk and tried to snog him and instead of apologising, said, 'Oh, that's just what weddings are all about!') 'Cunt,' I finish, forcefully. Then I gasp. I didn't mean to say that out loud. I'm a bad person. The worst person.

Rachel laughs. 'You know, I thought so,' she says. 'She seems like a real cunt.'

We walk out into the garden. The sun is fierce today, the

246

heat hits me, as though I've walked into a wall. I wouldn't be confident about hula-hooping on a cool day. But I'm already starting to sweat – I don't think the hoop will stay on.

The sweat is gathering so rapidly at the top of my thighs that I start to wonder whether I've wet myself. It's the sort of weather that makes you wish you could wash under your skin.

I bend down, pretending to scratch my ankle, but waiting for everyone else to assemble, so I can stand at the back. Cassandra is talking to Millie – or rather talking at Millie; from my vantage point, I can see Millie is desperate to escape. I catch odd words. 'Marrakesh', 'acupuncture', 'lawsuit' and 'John Lennon had one'.

The sun is starting to burn the back of my neck. I hope Ben is wearing sunscreen, I think, automatically. And then I remember. This is the first summer that I don't have to nag him about SPF. The first summer where I don't worry about Ben turning pink, the first season when I'm not anxiously monitoring the mole on the back of his knee. Ben loved the sun.

Watching Camilla, or Millie, swivelling her hips and smiling, I think of Ben, and his world. The women he grew up with, confident and uncomplicated. They were his people. Not me. Perhaps he should have married a Millie, or a Sophie, or an Anouska. (She was one of the Portuguese farmhouse ones.) When tragedy struck, Millie wouldn't have failed him. She would have jollied him along, she'd have the key to the cure. Or rather – tragedy would have swerved her, entirely. She's lucky – a talisman. #Blessed where I am cursed.

If Ben is here, somewhere, watching – and I don't think he

is, but I don't know that he isn't – I need to show him that I can hold my own with Millie, and women like Millie. I hate the idea that he's constantly looking down and thinking, 'Her? Really? I picked the wrong girl. If I'd known that I wasn't going to be around for so long, I'd have made some very different choices.'

So I pick up my hula hoop, and step into it, holding it against my waist. And for reasons I cannot fathom, I blurt the words, 'WOO! Let's go!'

'Kat, Kath, is it – is that you?' Millie looks straight at me. 'Oh, wow, you look . . . anyway, how are you?' She tilts her head forty-five degrees to the right.

'Great,' I say, determinedly. 'Really, really good. It's Katherine, by the way.'

Millie starts to set up a Bluetooth speaker, and fiddles with her phone until sound pours out. It's generic dance music – a drum beat, and someone singing about feeling good.

'KATH'S HUSBAND DIED JUST AFTER CHRISTMAS IN TRAGIC CIRCUMSTANCES,' bellows Millie, over the music. 'HE WAS A VERY CLOSE FRIEND OF MINE.' She smiles. 'VERY CLOSE,' she says again, thrusting her hips out.

I hear a sharp intake of breath. I think it came from Rachel.

I *know*, in my blood and bones, that Ben did not have a fling with Camilla Ponsonby. I also know, because Ben told me, that Camilla once threw up, in a taxi, while she was kissing a boy called Josh. And Josh didn't want to pay the fine, *so he swallowed it.* The woman in front of me can be as bossy, glossy and condescending as she likes, but she's not perfect. I'm certain my husband did not fancy her. In fact, Ben once described Camilla as a vampire. 'I know she doesn't want to literally suck my blood, but there's something about her that's very draining,' he'd said. 'I'm not even religious, but when I see her coming, I have a strong urge to make the sign of the cross.'

Yet *she's* looking at *me* with pity. Then she beams, wiggling her tiny bottom and punching the air. 'Anyway, IT'S TIME TO ACTIVATE OUR JOY CENTRES!'

Maybe I could have made my marriage work, with an active joy centre. Maybe there was a middle way – in which I managed to be a little bit more Millie. Five per cent cheerier. Five per cent more loveable. And then, even though it's a cloudless day, even though I can feel the sun burning the backs of my legs, I feel very cold.

Is there the slightest outside chance that Millie *isn't* lying?

Even when our marriage was at its worst, it never occurred to me that Ben might cheat. But how would I know? Maybe I wasn't paying attention.

I think of all the times Ben said he was sailing. I never checked to see where he was going. I just believed him. Sometimes he'd come home late, and get into bed when I was asleep, or nearly asleep. And sometimes, he'd kiss my forehead, or wrap his arms around my waist, and pull my body towards his. But in the months before he died, I'd be aware of him rolling to the very edge of the bed, to get as far from me as possible. I asked him about it once, and he said he didn't want to wake me.

'Now, MARCH TO THE BEAT,' says Millie, 'and really THRUST THOSE HIPS. Back and forth, around and around! Don't be afraid to GET SEXY!'

I try to picture Ben and Millie, Millie and Ben. Naked, breathless, somewhere secret. Back and forth, around and around. I could murder her.

Only – it doesn't make sense. Even my vivid imagination isn't quite buying it. Millie fancied Ben, I believe that. Millie definitely wasn't shy about letting Ben know she was keen and available. But if Ben had been sneaking around, I think he would have seemed happier. More purposeful. There would have been a secret spark, a lightness. He would have had something to look forward to.

Ben wasn't cheating. Not with her. I'm sure of it. I'm sure of him, still.

So why do I feel disappointed?

'Now, everybody, I want you to get your HANDS IN THE AIR and SHAKE YOUR BUTTS! Stir it up!' I want Millie to make me feel angry, but she only makes me feel guilty. Maybe she could have made Ben happy. And he suffered, in frustrated silence. Because he was a good guy. And I hate him for it.

I shake my butt as hard as I can, and I feel a little better. I'm astonished that my hula hoop is staying up.

'GREAT WORK, KAT,' shouts Millie.

Why didn't he cheat? Why couldn't I have found him in bed with an entire netball team, or something? Why couldn't he have done something flawed and human, instead of shutting down completely?

I believed Ben knew the secret to happiness. He was an optimist, and I broke him. I made him sad. I failed to fix things. But he didn't help himself, he just stopped collaborating with me. I would have done anything to make him happy, and he knew that. If he'd given me any clue, any indication of anything that might have made our marriage work, I would have done it. He stood back and let me take the blame, and the shame. That's not what good guys do.

Now he's left me this impossible legacy. He's Beloved Ben, taken too soon. He's perfect, I'm tragic, and trapped. I can't tell anyone the truth about myself, about us. And the infuriating thing is that Millie thinks she knows him. She thinks that he could only resist her charms because he was such a good guy.

'COME ON, EVERYONE! LET'S GO FOR A BIG FINISH!'

Do good guys ignore their wives, Ben? Do good guys use their pain like a shield, a way to protect themselves from the demands of the people who love them? Are they unable to face themselves, or their partners, when the worst happens? When someone who loves them reaches for them, do they keep pushing them away? When I felt as though my whole body was rotten and broken, when I was starved of tenderness, when I just needed the crumbs of touch, Ben punished me, he withdrew, he went numb, he took himself away. He didn't need to die to abandon me, and he didn't need to cheat to break the promises he made for me. He was a good guy, and a bad husband. I was a bad wife. And I'm bewildered, and hurt, and angry with him, and maybe that doesn't make me such a bad person ...

And then, I throw my hands up to the sky and scream.

I have never made a sound like this before. It's desperate, uncontrolled. My screaming register is much lower than I realised. It's more grunt than howl, quite *National Geographic*. If someone were to play me a recording of this and tell me it was the sound of a warthog having an orgasm, I'd believe them.

Two things are happening. Firstly, I realise that the scream is now in control, carrying me along with it. I'm not thinking poor me, my sad marriage, my heartbreak, my tragedy, it's not fair. I'm just in awe of the noise that's coming from me. And the fact that I'm screaming like this, while hula hooping.

The other thing is that I'm not the only one screaming. Rachel started, followed by Cassandra. Anya is wailing, quietly. Only Elena looks confused. And Millie is annoyed. She's waving her hands, turning the music off. 'EVERYONE,' she bellows. 'Please, STOP! What was that?'

'Primal screaming,' says Rachel.

'Why would you do that in *my* class?' Millie says.

'Because ... ' Rachel looks around. 'Because we've got to ... '

'Because Hema told us that we need to cultivate a screaming practice,' says Anya. 'It's very cleansing. In fact, I've just been reading some research on choral screaming. It's very bonding. It's a sign of how we're all learning from each other and becoming closely aligned.'

'Why would you all start screaming at me though?' says Millie. 'It was horrible.'

'You should take it as a compliment,' says Rachel. 'It's a sign of how your work was helping us align and cultivate a shared energy.' She looks at me, and mouths, 'I am Spartacus.'

'OK,' says Millie. 'We'll leave it there. Now, I offer a range of workshops, and I'm always happy to see private clients. I do a chakra cleanse for beginners ... '

'Ahhhhhhhhh! Ahhhhhhhhh!' Rachel begins again. 'Once you start, you can't stop. It's like Pringles.'

'I'll leave my leaflets at Reception,' says Millie. 'Kath, call me, yeah? I'd *love* to see you! You must miss Ben so much. I can help you remember the old times. Actually, I've got a friend who does past life regression, that might be something you're interested in . . .'

'Ahhhhhhhhhhhh!' I say. 'Rachel, you're right, it is addictive. Thanks, *Cammy*, I'll be sure to get in touch!'

Once Millie and her hula hoops have left the building, we gather in the conservatory. Anya and Cassandra offer to do a tea round. 'Bring biscuits,' shouts Rachel. 'If you can't find any, I'll take a rice cake.'

'That was weird,' I say. 'That was a very strange place for her to show up.'

'I'm trying to be open-minded, but she definitely had an air of bullshit,' says Rachel. 'Even by my newly woo standards. She was just a glorified aerobics instructor, really.'

Hema walks in. 'How was that?' she asks. 'I really should have warned you, Millie was a bit of a last-minute replacement. We were going to have a talk on the basics of Buddhism and embracing impermanence, but the guy's car broke down. He was very zen about the lessons we could all learn from this, but I wasn't quite so mellow.'

'Well, I suspect Millie had last-minute availability for a reason,' says Rachel. 'She wasn't great. And she was a bit inappropriate with Katherine.'

'I thought that, too,' says Anya. 'It was a weird coincidence – she knew Katherine's husband, or claimed to, but she wasn't very sensitive about it. It affected the vibes of the class a bit.'

'Sorry about that,' I say. 'I didn't mean to put anyone off.'

'I don't think we missed much,' says Elena, darkly. 'It was

mostly just a posh woman screaming at us about energy. I spent most of the class dropping my hoop and picking it up. She didn't even teach me about core strength.' She taps at her phone. 'She's got, what? 19k followers? Who cares, really?'

'There's definitely something going on, though,' says Anya. 'This Millie wouldn't have been here if it wasn't for a Buddhist with a broken-down car. And she made Katherine scream.'

'*Did* she?' Now Hema's interested, and I don't like it.

'I just got the urge, I suppose,' I say, feebly. 'Maybe it was from the hooping.'

'It was as though it had got lost in the post,' says Anya. 'It was the sound of birth, or something finally arriving.'

'Thank you for saving me with all of that communal screaming nonsense,' I say, gratefully.

'No worries! Any time!' says Rachel, just as Cassandra says: 'It wasn't nonsense.'

Chapter Twenty-Seven

Just a cold

Google was no help.

I wasn't really sure what I was searching for.

I suppose what I wanted was a couple of case studies from married women who had fallen for their colleagues, ideally examples where the husband had been told, and said, 'Great news! Now I can pursue my ultimate dream, in which I move to the mountains for a solo lifetime of quiet contemplation. But I would be happy to attend your wedding, and be a doting, if distant, uncle to your future children.'

But in reality 'work crush out of hand' brought up some fairly bleak-sounding court cases, and even bleaker images of the Rana Plaza disaster. 'Feelings for colleague normal?' was worse. The advice was, more or less, 'tell HR and then be prepared to get fired'.

I knew it wasn't just a crush. Using that word was an attempt to contain the feelings and tell myself that it was all circumstantial and silly. Despite the mounting emotional evidence that was piling up in front of me. I suppose I felt crushed *by* it. Completely knocked out. I was a woman in denial, struck by debilitating love flu. It had turned into full-blown pneumonia, and I was still telling myself it was just a tiny romantic cold.

Sometimes I managed to convince myself that my feelings were a strange symptom my brain had generated to cheer me up and get me through the darkest period of my life. Annabel was wrong! The only solution was to sit tight and let the situation resolve itself. Every time my thoughts drifted towards Lou, I tried to picture myself laughing about it with Ben, in five years' time. 'I never told you this before, but I almost ran off with a woman from work! Thank goodness I saw sense!'

When that didn't work, I reminded myself that Lou flirted with *everyone*. She was always warm and tactile, it was just her way. I told myself it couldn't mean anything. I was just so starved of attention that I was misinterpreting her. I poured as much energy as I could into resisting the impulse to think her actions might mean anything. When Lou grabbed my hand, or touched my knee to demonstrate a point, I'd recite the alphabet backwards in my head.

We started to see each other outside of work. I went out with Lou's friends for pizza, and tried not to think about what it might mean when her mate Sally said, 'So you're the famous Katherine.' We all ended up going out dancing in Dalston. I felt awkward and self-conscious, until Lou lifted my hand high in the air, and spun me around until I was dizzy. Laughing, we walked to the bar holding hands. *This doesn't mean anything, this doesn't mean anything*, I thought. *It can't mean anything. It's just been a long time since I held hands with anyone. That's all.* Then I made the mistake of catching her eye.

'Oh!' she said. 'Sorry.' She dropped my hand, and we both looked at my wedding ring.

Still, it was fun to spend time with someone who didn't have any history or context for me. She wasn't mired in the heaviness of the last few months, even though she was the only person I could talk to about any of it. Things were becoming slightly strained between Annabel and me. I couldn't tell Annabel how much time I was spending with Lou because I knew she'd have opinions, and I didn't want to hear them. So I told her work was crazy, I had so much on. I had to work at weekends. And if I was seeing Lou, we'd probably talk about work, so it wasn't a lie, exactly.

I relished the slow creep of joy, the lightness returning to my body. The days were getting colder and darker, but I felt perversely energetic. I woke up smiling, rather than thinking, 'Oh, no, not this again.' Sometimes I sang in the shower. I didn't actually iron any clothes, but I thought about it.

This, I told myself, was the very best thing for our marriage. Maybe Ben would feel better if I was busier, and more cheerful. I thought he'd notice that something was going on, with me, and he'd at least be curious about it. After all, I didn't have the energy left to keep asking about counselling, or date nights, or for any display of affection or attention. I told myself that Ben needed me to give him space, and then he'd come back to me.

I waited for him to ask where I was going, or who I was with. Or anything at all. But he worked, slept and sailed. Occasionally, we'd be summoned for an awkward lunch with Constance. He'd turn up late, and grunt at us.

'It's like he's turned into a teenager again,' said Constance. 'It's freaking me out. Is he like this at home?'

'Pretty much,' I admitted. 'We don't see a lot of each other at the moment. It's probably my fault for being so busy with work,' I added, guiltily.

Constance shook her head. 'No, I've seen you together, I know you're trying to reach out to him. I talked to him about getting counselling, and he snapped and said, "You're as bad as Katherine." Look, he might get this from his dad. Peter can be a nightmare, in that way. He just shuts down, inexplicably, whenever anything feels too hard. And Peter struggles with empathy. He can be very kind, but when he's down, he doesn't believe anyone could possibly have it as bad as he does. That was the main reason for our divorce.'

The word made me shudder. 'You don't think that's going to happen? I don't want to lose Ben! Or you!' It felt like a horrible omen. I remembered my argument with Annabel. I couldn't think clearly, the idea of life without Ben made me feel panicked and trapped. Even though I was living a life with barely any Ben.

'My son is the light of my life, and the beat of my heart, of course he is,' said Constance. 'But from where I'm standing, right now even I can admit that he must be a bugger to be married to. I've been where you are, and as your friend, my heart is breaking for both of you. I can see how hard you're trying, and . . . ' I didn't hear the rest of what she was saying, as I was crying so hard.

'Look, we'll make it work, I know we will.' She hugged me and I cried harder. There was so much I couldn't tell her. She wouldn't love me any more if she knew what I knew.

Chapter Twenty-Eight

Still alive

'OM HANUMATE NAMAH! I DESERVE WEALTH AND HAPPINESS! OM HANUMATE NAMAH!'

Wait, what? What's happening? I sit up in bed and see Elena, arms outstretched, eyes closed, and start to piece it all together. I'm still at Cadwell Manor. I'm still sharing a room. Once again, Elena is still beginning her day, and mine, with a great big blast of entitlement. At least she didn't wake me up with her snoring.

Why shouldn't she have wealth and happiness? I've got to be less grudging. I will learn to like Elena. And I'll make her like me, if it kills me. Maybe I should find a chant for that.

Elena yawns, and I think the chanting is over. I have to ask. 'What does it mean, when you chant that? Does it do anything?'

She smirks. 'It doesn't really translate. It's a sacred ancient prayer, summoning resilience, power and strength. But, you know, you really have to know about chanting in order to use it properly.'

'Oh wow,' I say. I will get through to her. 'So you've

learned about sacred chanting. Have you done a lot of travelling? Did you go to India? I've never been, I'd love to know what that's like.'

Elena flushes a little. 'Well, I've been here and there, but I haven't been to India exactly.' Exactly?! Does she mean she's been to the Star of India on the Edgware Road? 'But I've done a lot of research.'

'Oh, right? So is there a book you'd recommend, or—'

'YouTube, Katherine. I found it on YouTube. GOD. I don't know why you're making such a big deal of this. It doesn't matter how it finds you, as long as it finds you, OK? This might be it finding you now. I might be your guru.'

'Um, great,' I say. 'Why not?' I must have slept well. 'I agree. It doesn't matter how things find you, there isn't necessarily a right way to learn. I work for a non-profit, and we're always tying ourselves into knots about our clients and their ethical credentials. Everyone is trying to do better, and certain people at work expect the clients to be perfect before we take them on.' Now that I think about it, I'm one of the certain people. Damn. 'I could be better at letting people be better, maybe. Anyway, I'm rambling, sorry. Remind me, what is it you do?'

I wait for Elena to tell me she's an aspiring TikTok creator, or that she sells crystals on Etsy. 'I'm ... well, I was a project manager. Junior project manager. Now I'm a fired project manager.'

'I'm sorry,' I say, cautiously. 'Did you like your job?'

'Yeah, I really did. I started on the graduate scheme, and my boss – Paul – was really impressed by what I was doing, and we started to work together. He promoted me. I was really happy, it was going brilliantly, and then he ... ' She shakes her head briskly, and exhales. 'We slept together. We were drunk. I was drunk. I don't think I realised that I liked him, until that happened. He's married.'

I fiddle with my ring and try not to think of all the things that word does and doesn't mean.

'I'm sorry,' I say. 'I mean, it's not a good look for him, is it? It sounds like he took advantage of you. Your married boss, hooking up with you when you're drunk.'

Elena frowns. 'God, you sound like my friends. He wouldn't have done it if he didn't feel something. But the trouble was – he wanted to keep it a secret. He wasn't sure whether he wanted to stay with his wife. It came out, I went kind of crazy, messaging him, hanging around him. Eventually his boss said that if he wanted to keep his job, he had to fire me.'

'What a bastard,' I say. 'What a horrible thing to do.'

'You don't understand! He didn't have any choice!' Elena sighs. 'Anyway, it's fine. I'm being really proactive and doing as much work on myself as I can. It's really important for me to invest in myself.' She puts a hand to her heart and closes her eyes – before reaching up and patting her lashes with her fingertips, to check that they're secure. I suspect that being Elena probably isn't easy – and in her own way, she's trying as hard as I am.

'What sort of work?' I ask. 'Is there anything that's help-ing you to get over Paul?'

She looks at me as though I've just told her that I've murdered Paul, and I've got his body in a blanket under my bed. 'Why would I want to get over Paul? I'm going to get him back! And I think I'm making great progress.' She starts to list things on her fingers.

'There's manifestation, energy cleansing – I really want to do this Love and Wealth programme. Last week, I found the most incredible healer on Instagram. You get a twenty-minute one-on-one video call with her, and she tells you what to do. She tells you it's going to be OK. And it's only £250. She even takes Klarna and Clearpay.'

'Elena, there are plenty of people who will give you advice and tell you things are going to be OK, for free!' I say, thinking guiltily of the number of times Annabel has done it for me. Would her advice have been any more effective if I'd paid her hundreds of pounds? I suppose I would have been more likely to take it. 'It sounds ... ' Dodgy? Ethically dubious? Like a great big massive scam? 'Expensive,' I finish.

'She's totally worth it,' says Elena. 'In fact, when I have a bit more money, I might buy a block from her. For a thousand pounds, you get five sessions.'

'How are you funding this, if you're not working?' I ask. 'How did you pay for ... ?' I trail off, sweeping my hands around the room. I'm not sure if I'm indicating Cadwell Manor in general, or the piles of new clothes carpeting our room.

'Well, I had some savings,' says Elena, 'which covered this. It was my emergency money, but as soon as I heard about the retreat, I thought, "Well, this is a love life emergency." And there's always credit cards. Have you heard of the Law of Attraction, Katherine?'

I'm going to, aren't I? 'It rings a bell.'

'Well, this is where a session with a healer could be incredibly useful for you. See, you're unhappy because you're attracting bad energy, with your lifestyle and general demeanour.'

She points at my nightie. A giant green Woodland Trust T-shirt. 'If you, say, stopped sleeping in that thing, and bought yourself some beautiful silk pyjamas ...' She points to herself, resplendent in electric pink satin. She rubs the fabric between her fingers. Don't do that, Elena, you'll set fire to yourself. 'You would change your energy. Professionally, erotically, everything in between.'

Elena smiles and turns her palms up, as if she's delivering the closing point of her TED talk. 'See, everything I spend on myself is an investment that will come back to me double or triple, at least. So it's OK to borrow money to build the life I deserve – in fact, not just OK. It's vital. Because once the lifestyle is created, the money will flow towards me, to support it. I'm not going to be the sort of woman who accepts second best. I'm living my best life.' She smiles – it's the warmest and most genuine I've ever seen her. 'I'm gaming the universe,' she says. 'Maybe you should start.'

'You've given me a lot to think about,' I say. Meaning, 'It's as if you took off the top of my head and went at my brain with an immersion blender.' Obviously, it's bullshit. But it's such compelling bullshit. It's like meeting a cult member. We've all dabbled in the woo. I bought Constance hipster tarot cards for her birthday. Annabel drops a lump of rose quartz in her bra when she's feeling terminally single. But I've never met anyone who believed in anything quite so hard. Or anyone who invented their own logic and built their own version of common sense.

'I don't know why everyone isn't doing it!' Elena smiles happily. She leans out of her bed and rummages in her bag. 'See this shower gel? It's called Goddess Daily, it costs forty-eight quid and I heard that Gwyneth Paltrow uses it.

Now, I'm going to get in the shower, and the universe will see a woman taking care of herself, and it will rise up to meet me, energetically. I don't see why Gwyneth should get all the gifts!' She tears some plastic wrapping from the full bottle, and walks to the bathroom.

I feel unsettled. Yes, Elena is completely mad, and I can't believe she's getting into debt over video chats and shower gel. But maybe she's right about the T-shirts. The trouble with wearing old clothes is that they're always covered in old memories. This conversation has made me tense and restless. I've never felt less like a goddess. Maybe I should ask to borrow the shower gel. I suspect I'll have to make do with a large cup of coffee.

At the breakfast table, the mood seems charged. 'I guess today's the day!' says Rachel, reaching for the milk. 'Who's ready?'

'I am!' says Anya. 'I got up early to read all about it, and it's meant to be incredibly powerful. Apparently, sometimes it's possible to ... you know. During.'

'Possible to what?' I ask. I've completely lost track of what's on the schedule today. 'What are we doing this morning, anyway? Is it foraging?'

Rachel snorts. 'In a manner of speaking, that's exactly what it is.'

Hema walks in with a tray of glasses. 'Girls, I've put these through twice now, I promise they're clean, they don't look as shiny as I'd like them to, but they'll do for juice. It's erotic meditation today, Katherine. I thought I'd try running the session in the morning, as everyone is fairly focused. For some reason it doesn't work quite so well after lunch.'

'Right,' I say. Shit. I travel back in time to the other day, when I was sitting at Constance's kitchen table. She warned me then. She said something about erotic meditation. And I thought I'd rather die. In fact, I will fake my own death before I willingly attend an erotic meditation session. Life comes at you fast.

'How, um, erotic is it?' I say, haltingly.

'Well, that's really up to you,' says Hema, and Rachel smirks.

Why am I so poorly prepared? This isn't like me. If I'd have been on top of things – oh, God, what an expression – I would have organised some kind of briefly calamitous accident or injury. A 'Whoops, there goes the breadknife, clumsy me!' moment. I could at least have gone for a walk in the grounds and found some stinging nettles to roll around in. I wish I'd got primal screaming right on my first attempt. That way I'd have some credit. I could run away now, but you can't run away twice.

After breakfast, we're sent upstairs to the 'atrium' – a bright, glass-walled room at the very top of the house. I haven't been up here before, but I'm relieved that the erotic limits of the conservatory have been recognised. I don't think I could be in the same room as that sofa and think of anything sexier than a smear test.

It's far too late to get out of this.

A voice in my head is whispering *What are you so afraid of?* I don't see why I should have to explain myself to myself. I've not had sex for months. I'm a widow. My sex life is completely bound up with my grief, it's embroidered with it. I'm so, so good at facing all my other fears. I check my bank balance regularly, I never kill wasps and spiders, even the really huge ones. I stay on top of my laundry. I know exactly what's in my kitchen drawers because I took all my old phone chargers and dead batteries to be recycled. Why can't I be allowed to fail at one thing? Where am I supposed to find the energy to be good at sex, when I feel obliged to invest so much of it in being good at admin?

As the door shuts behind me, and I enter the room, I realise exactly what is frightening me. I was good at sex, once; or rather, I used to love it. I used to crave it. It used to make me feel alive. And I suspect I'm about to discover that my odd dreams and brief flickers aren't enough to warm me. That my sexual self died with Ben. From the waist down, I'm dead as a recycled battery.

I don't think I can escape. I must go through with it. As I make my way to the grey mat on the end of the row, I make myself a promise. I'm going to cut myself a deal. If this is as bad as I think it's going to be, I'll leave immediately. I'll walk straight out without packing. I'll hitch-hike if I have to.

Dusk pink blankets have been folded into squares and left at the bottom of our mats. I can also see a rounded pink shape – oh, it might be an eye mask. Anya is my nearest neighbour, but she's quite far away. I think we could both stretch out our arms and there would be a good few yards between our fingertips. I watch her shake her blanket out over her body. She gives me a little smile. 'See you on the other side,' she says, softly, putting her eye mask on. 'Good luck!'

I do the same.

Hema stands by the door. 'Is everyone settled? Do you all have your weighted eye masks? I won't stay but let me know if you need anything. You'll be guided by Shala, who'll be coming in very soon. I did a session with her on a retreat I attended last year, and I was very impressed.'

I love the weighted eye mask. The sensation against my lids is delicious. It mimics that feeling of sleep seducing you, pressing down upon you, making you too heavy to care. When you're so tired that you can feel whole, stressful sentences orbiting your buzzing brain and then shooting out of your ears, leaving anxiety cobwebs that your pillow will clear away.

The blanket is great too – soft, and slightly silky. I'd assumed it would be stinky, or scratchy, but it's luxurious. It's in far better condition than the towels in the bathroom. Once, I'm sure I could see what was sexy about a nice blanket. My body responded to the way it felt. My brain didn't run the numbers and ask about the factory it was made in, or how many gallons of water it wasted, and whether you could get it second hand, or make do with a repurposed hessian sack.

Constance would love this. Oh God. Do not think about your mother-in-law during a sexy meditation. Maybe thinking about Constance will help to keep the sexy thoughts at bay. *Why do you want to keep them at bay?* says the voice, again. *I'm going to ask you one more time. What are you afraid of?*

I sigh and pull the blanket under my chin. I can't hear you! I'm sleeping.

You're not dead. You're buried alive. You still have cravings. And you're worried that you can't keep them under control.

I'm almost tearfully grateful to Hema for interrupting

my internal monologue. 'One last piece of advice from me,' she says. 'Lower your expectations. Or let go of them altogether. This is about pleasure, and pressure is the enemy of pleasure. You don't know what's going to come up for you. Hopefully, Shala will be able to guide you to your fantasy world. Some people find it very relaxing – but the erotic part manifests days, weeks or months later. And someone always falls asleep, so don't be embarrassed if it's you, and try not to laugh if you hear someone snoring.'

That's me! With any luck, I'll be fast asleep in minutes. Thanks, Hema!

'Also, Shala uses sound-bath techniques, which can be overwhelming. Please try to stay in the room, and keep an open mind, but if you absolutely need to leave, I'll be outside with water. Enjoy!'

I lie very still. I close my eyes, and then open them. No light is getting through the mask, so I close them again. I hear murmuring, and the creak of the door.

'Welcome, everyone, and thank you for having me. I'm Shala, and I'll be guiding you through this erotic meditation session. We'll be here for about forty-five minutes.

'Firstly, I want to reassure any of you who are nervous, and new to this. It's a practice of sensual recentring. This is a beginners' session, and I'll be going very slowly and gently.'

She stops, I think, to take a sip of water.

'There are plenty of misconceptions about this practice, so here's what you can expect: I'll be asking you to recall touch, pleasure and sensation. The sounds you hear will enhance that sensation. I will ask you all to remain still, and not to touch your bodies during the session. As I said,

268

this is about recentring. It's not a sexual practice, but it has been created to enhance your sexual lives. Now, does anyone have any questions, before we begin?'

I have many questions. What did any of that mean? It's erotic meditation, but it's not actually erotic? Schrödinger's sexy meditation?

Still, it's a relief, I guess. Shala will tell us to think of flowers blooming, or trains driving into tunnels, and I'll ignore her and drift off without thinking about my non-existent sex life. It helps that her voice is so soothing. It's beautiful, low and modulated. She could be a BBC radio announcer, or a transatlantic movie star. Or a pilot. It's a hypnotic sound. My head feels a little heavier. My shoulder blades are sinking. I'm going to sleep, and it's going to be delicious.

'I want you to breathe in through your nose, for three counts,' says Shala. 'Then out through your mouth for three counts. Feel your chest rising and falling. Start to notice what you're feeling in your sex centre – whatever that means to you.'

What does sex centre mean to me? I picture a naked gym, filled with cheerful, healthy, possibly Swedish people bouncing nudely on treadmills. A pool filled with people ripping off each other's swimsuits, with a large old-fashioned sign that reads HEAVY PETTING MANDATORY. A café, where one naked person is telling another naked person that they can't have a smoothie because it isn't safe to use the blender.

'If you're struggling to find your centre, you may tilt your hips, very gently, in rhythm with your breath,' says Shayla. 'Try to catch the wave, then release it.'

I follow Shayla's instructions. Oh.

'Don't worry if you feel a pulsing, or swelling,' says

Shayla. 'That's totally normal. Now, I want you all to feel safe. If you can, think of the last time you were intimate with yourself, when you were alone. Or imagine it happening in the future. No pressure, no expectations. Just you.'

Well, that's probably my cue to start nodding off. The last time I was all alone, with no expectations, I probably had a lovely nap. There's something deeply soothing about the breathing and hip tilting. I'm drifting away from the day, sinking below the waterline of consciousness and . . .

. . . what the hell was that?

When Hema mentioned 'sound-bath techniques', I thought there might be the odd tinkling bell. I've been dragged to enough yoga classes and breathing workshops with Annabel where the session begins and ends with something like that, the vibe being very 'Santa's sleigh, in the distance'.

This was more 'lying in the middle of a flight path'.

'Some of you may experience some tingling,' says Shala. 'Breathe through it. Breathe with it. If your body is starting to feel warm, that's OK. Slow your breath if you can.'

I can feel something, on the soles of my feet, and the backs of my thighs. Can I slow my breath? The warmth is creeping, sending tendrils up my arms, and down my collarbone.

I don't want to fall asleep. I want her to bang the gong again.

'Can you think of a colour?' she asks. 'Don't worry if it doesn't come straight away. You might not see it in your mind's eye, but you might feel something. You're alone, safe and warm, feeling good in your body. You're surrounded by bright light. If it helps, imagine the light is pure gold,

270

and let the colour reveal itself slowly. Relax, wait for the colour to come.'

Wait for the colour to come. Wait to come.

There's a haze, shimmering through the dark of my vision, curls of smoke in pink and orange. Am I just thinking about pink because of my blanket?

I wait for Shala to give us another instruction. A 'By now, you should see a flower, which represents your vulva'. Or 'If you see orange, seek medical attention'. Nothing. I'm sure I can still hear the dying, floating notes of the gong. And the sound of five women, and me. Our breath is soft and steady, choral. We're breathing together. Alone, together. Sharing an experience, but all floating and separate. Seeing our own colours.

That's ... sexy, I guess. All of us, connecting with ourselves. Maybe remembering moments of intimacy and pleasure. Maybe constructing them especially, building those moments anew. I wonder about Rachel. Is she thinking about her marriage, her husband, what it used to be like when it was good? Or is she having a filthy fantasy about someone new, someone who doesn't know her habits and patterns? Someone who makes her feel wild.

Shala bangs the gong again.

This time, the vibrations spread straight through me, like a fire.

'If you can, let the colours travel outside your mind and spread all over your body ... perhaps the colour is strongest in your sex centre. Can you feel that colour spreading to other parts of you? Your fingertips, your toes, your ankles? Your lips?'

All the blood in my body seems to rush to my mouth,

271

and I start to remember what I've been trying to forget. The kissing.

It was the kissing that made me feel wild. It was urgent, it was electric. It turned me on – and made me realise how completely meaningless that expression usually was, how overused. Because it was as if every scrap of my skin had its own dial, and every single dial had been turned further than it was supposed to go.

It was too much. More than I could cope with; more than I deserved.

'Welcome every sensation that you're experiencing,' says Shayla. 'Let it in. Feel it all. Breathe it in.'

The waves of vibration are still travelling through my body. They hit the back of my neck, and I gasp. I can feel my nipples buzzing, hardening through my top, through my blanket.

God, the heat of you, the weight of you, your mouth on me, I want you, I want you.

The vibrations are lapping and breaking over me, moving down, and all I can think about is the way our bodies fit together, an arm brushing my waist ...

I'm not sure what's happening. There's the sound of a gong, and Shala's voice, and my whole body buzzes. I'm an animal, I'm a flower, I'm the ocean, and I'm not waiting for the colour to come any more because I'm coming, and I'm shaking and crying under the blanket, and I don't understand how my body could be moved in this way. How it could betray me, again. But as the stillness sinks into me, I realise that I feel better than I have done for a long, long time. And I'm not sure that I'm ready to go home yet.

Chapter Twenty-Nine

Giving gifts

Divorce, the 'D' word, became my Scottish play. Every time it was mentioned on TV, I flinched. I had to do something to counteract the bad luck. Christmas was looming, too. Ben had asked me to marry him at Christmas. It made symmetrical sense, to me, that he would ask to leave at Christmas. A bleak, frightening version of *Carol of the Bells* went around and around in my head. 'Hark! It's the end! End it with Ben! All seem to say! He'll walk away!'

Our marriage felt liminal, and transitory. I thought it was my final destination, but we were both passing through. Although where could we be going? Sometimes, when Ben snored beside me, I'd google things in the dark. 'What is a happy marriage?' 'How do you know if your marriage is working?' I deleted every search. Nothing brought me comfort, nothing brought me hope. 'How do you even know if you're happily married?' I thought, angrily. Presumably you need at least three marriages under your belt just to understand the nature of the union. How much anxiety and low-level misery is a cause for concern, because surely some is ... normal?

The brilliant thing about being depressed and scared in December is that you never have to face your feelings sober. I went on my work night out. I went on Annabel's work night out – it was easier to be around her when I was pissed. And when she held my hair back, and I tried not to throw up on her shoes, we both said, 'It's jus' like old timessss.' Even though our roles were reversed – I'd always been the one to stay sober for the taxi driver, and to force pints of water and ibuprofen on everyone else.

Ben was out a lot and drunk a lot. Occasionally we'd bump into each other in the kitchen at the end of the night, making toast and opening cupboards and drawers. We could be kind to each other. He'd ask me about my night, I'd ask about his. Neither of us made much sense. Once, we almost talked. I was standing at the sink. He walked behind me, he put his arms around me and said, 'I miss you, K. I really miss you.' He sounded lonely, and far away. I leaned into him. Maybe we just needed to have drunk sex on the kitchen floor. Then the smoke alarm started beeping, and the moment was lost.

We just had to get past Christmas, I told myself, and the curse would be lifted. It was almost twelve months since the miscarriage, since that awful January when everything started to go so badly wrong. If we could make it out of that shitty year intact, I'd give our marriage everything I had. I'd make some truly radical New Year's resolutions. It was no wonder Ben was sick of me. I was sick of myself, fed up with being dreamy, and difficult. So what if I felt amorphous, floating, unfixed? I could change! Out with the old Katherine, with her to-do lists, her plans to find an ethical investment pension, to start the day with a freezing shower, and to take out the recycling for the neighbours that couldn't manage. I was going to learn to be a good and cheerful wife. I would take life less seriously. I would plaster a convincing smile on my face. I would commit to commitment. I was young and healthy. I was married, with a nice house, a good job, and nothing to worry about. There was no reason for me to plod the Earth with a set face, waiting for something awful to happen.

I cured my hangovers by scouring the internet, looking for the perfect Christmas present for Ben. I became obsessive. He always needed sailing gloves – but that wasn't exactly romantic. And he always needed them because he was always losing them. Our marriage was too fragile for my big gestures to be lost at sea. He loved crisps, all crisps. Could I write him a love letter in crisps? Could I work out how to make a ship in a bottle, with a tiny Ben and Katherine on deck, and preserve our love in miniature, for ever? I was getting panicked and furious. Our relationship depended on this present. And I was going to get it wrong. And I hated myself for folding, and thinking capitalism and commerce held the answers. That, in spite of everything I stood for, part of me still believed that we could be fixed with more stuff.

The week before Christmas, I found myself beside the window of an antique shop off Brick Lane, gazing at it so intently that it might have been a Magic Eye picture. The answer must be here, somewhere. I'd get him a silver tankard! No, I wasn't going to get him a tankard, what was I, his uncle? My eye was briefly drawn to another silver piece. A delicate nest, with two little birds peeping out. I longed for it; there was something about the way the twigs and feathers were rendered that made me ache. Sure, Katherine, buy yourself a present. That will really help your marriage. I shook my shoulders and told myself to focus.

On the same shelf as the bird's nest, next to some demitasse spoons, I saw a compass. The card beside it said it was late Victorian. It was plain but stylish, with a cream enamel face, and sturdy blue hands. A great gift for a sailor. 'This is a beautiful piece,' said the salesman, as he wrapped up the package in navy tissue paper. 'One of my favourites. You obviously have a very good eye.' Even though I realised he said that to every person who spent money in his shop, it felt like a sign. I had vision. I could see clear waters ahead, we just needed to finish navigating our way out of the storm. This was a good omen. I still loved Ben and knew him well enough to surprise him. And maybe the compass would help us to find our way back to each other. I couldn't wait for Christmas morning.

When the last day of work arrived, I felt almost festive. I wasn't even annoyed by Lydia's choice of Christmas jumper, which came with its own battery pack and played 'Jingle Bells' off-key.

Jeremy called me into his office for a final meeting. I gathered my notes, assuming that he wanted to make sure I hadn't left anything hanging, and that our clients had emergency out-of-hours contacts. 'I just wanted to say that you've done a fantastic job this year,' he said, once I'd shut the door. 'You've worked really hard, and I'm really impressed. Well done.'

He asked me what my Christmas plans were. 'I hope

you're having a proper break, you definitely need a rest. Don't look at the socials, all the content is scheduled. I can't imagine that anything will come up that we need to respond to. You've been doing a lot of overtime, Katherine. Your commitment is commendable, but you deserve to spend a week with your feet up, eating mince pies.'

I made a vague noise of assent. What could I say? 'No can do, boss! I've got a week to save my marriage!' I was thinking of Christmas as a series of exams that I had to pass, no matter what. I tried, and failed, to concentrate on what else Jeremy was saying. Instead, I remembered my very first Christmas in Dorset, and how nervous I had been. How hard I tried to win everyone over. Why did I never get to relax? Why did I have to try and try and try?

'. . . a really good team,' said Jeremy. 'So impressed with how you've hit it off, and how welcome you've made her. I think she's on her way, so send her in if you see her. Now, get on out of here. Go home! Merry Christmas, Katherine!'

'Merry Christmas, Jeremy! Have a good one!' When I left, I saw Lou waiting to go in.

'Good, I hoped I'd catch you before you go,' she said. 'Because I got you a Christmas present. And I didn't want to give it to you when we were at our desks, in case you hated it, and it got awkward.'

She pressed a small, pink tissue-wrapped parcel into my palm. It was tied up with silver ribbon. My hand seemed warmer, and extra sensitive where her fingertips had brushed my palm. This was just a Christmas present from my work friend. It wasn't anything more. No matter how badly I wanted it to be.

'Lou!' I said. 'I didn't get you anything! I'm so sorry!' I

was flustered, and flushing. Maybe it was a trap, and Ben was in on it. I was going to say too much, and embarrass myself, and she'd say, 'Oh my God, you fancy me.'

'Yeah, you did,' she smiled. 'Anyway, don't say that, just say "thank you". You can open it as soon as I've gone in there.' She jerked her head towards Jeremy's office. 'Merry Christmas, Katherine.' She kissed me softly and briefly on the lips and walked away.

Did that really happen?

I walked out of the office and opened the package. It was the little birds in their nest from the antique shop, attached to a silver chain. On a tiny card, she'd written,

For your thrush. Lx

Chapter Thirty

Nature

Something has shifted in the group. I was expecting Rachel to be the noisy one, to do the whole Wife of Bath routine, but she seems subdued. It's Anya leading the lunchtime chatter. The meditation seems to have changed her. It's the first time I've seen her looking truly relaxed. Her skin looks as though it's been illuminated from within.

'It was extraordinary,' she tells the table, holding a salad tong aloft. 'It was this full body gong orgasm that just kept going. I took MDMA once, after my finals, when I knew I'd got a first – and it was even better than that. Feel my arm!' She holds out her forearm to Elena, who gives it a reluctant squeeze. 'Doesn't it feel like hot buttered dough! I feel like hot buttered dough all over!'

'Good for you,' says Cassandra, sulkily. 'I ended up on a sort of astral plane, having a very depressing conversation with one of my ancestors about drowning in a well.' She frowns. 'Awful morning.'

'Love, I think you nodded off and had a bad dream,' says Anya.

'How dare you? I'm a very experienced astral traveller!' Cassandra bangs her fork on the table, for emphasis.

'I'm sure you are,' says Anya, gently. 'But I did hear you snoring.'

'This feels like a good opportunity to remind you all to keep open minds,' says Hema. 'It's very human for us to come to these practices with great expectations, and to compare our experiences with our neighbour's. But try to take it all one moment at a time. Don't judge yourself for judging yourself, it's inevitable. But try to remember that there's no right or wrong. Cassandra, as you know, any meditation we practise can lead to moments of transcendence after the event.'

'I do know, thank you,' says Cassandra. 'But I think my ancestors need to learn about respecting boundaries, all the same.'

Hema looks like she wanted to say something, but Elena gasps, and waves her phone in the air. 'What the fuck? Paul's wife is having a baby!'

Anya catches my eye, and mouths, 'Paul? Remind me?'

'I'm supposed to get him back!' Elena is screaming. 'I've been trying so hard … I've spent so much money!' She picks up a piece of sourdough, and sobs into it. Her pain is visceral. Something inside her has snapped. 'Why doesn't he want me? Why hasn't he chosen me? What am I doing wrong? I don't understand!' She howls, and then folds in on herself. It's as though every one of her muscles has snapped, and every bone has crumbled.

Poor, poor Elena. She's so lost, and so sad. Behind all of her front, and bluster, she's desperate. She's broken.

Without thinking I get up and walk to her chair, and put

my arms around her. 'I'm so sorry,' I murmur. 'I'm so, so sorry. You poor love.'

'Screw you.' Elena shakes me off and stands up. 'I hate this place. This is all completely pointless. My whole life has been pointless. He doesn't love me. Nobody loves me. Nobody gives a shit about me.'

She hurls her water glass at the wall, and it shatters. She turns to Hema. 'It's OK, you don't have to throw me out. I'm leaving.'

'Elena, you're not going to get thrown out,' says Hema, evenly. 'You're upset. Why don't you take the afternoon to calm down, and then we'll have a chat in a couple of hours.'

'No!' she screams. 'I want to leave now!'

'OK,' says Hema. 'That's fine. Why don't you go and pack? I'll talk to Sunny and organise a taxi to the station for you.'

Elena has her hands on her hips. She's shaking. I know she wants to keep shouting and screaming. She keeps opening and closing her mouth, as though she's struggling to find something to say. 'This is all your fault!' is what she lands on. I'm not sure if she's speaking to one of us, or all of us.

'Do you want me to help you pack?' I offer, weakly.

'NO! Stay away from me!' She runs from the room.

The sunlight is shining on the carpet, where Elena threw her glass. I can't tell the difference between the shards, and the droplets of spilled water. That was awful. And strangely exhilarating. Watching Elena was like an out-of-body experience. I'd never, ever do anything like that. But sometimes, says my brain, you really want to.

And didn't I lose it on my first day here? Didn't I just scream at Millie the wannabe marriage wrecker? And didn't it feel good?

281

Outside, it's hot, bright and clear. But in the dining room, it feels as though a cloud has burst, a storm has broken.

'Don't worry, it happens every single time,' says Hema, mildly. 'It's all part of Elena's process. I probably shouldn't say this, but I can usually predict the person who snaps and starts breaking crockery.'

'If I hadn't had that massive orgasm, it probably would have been me,' says Anya.

'I've already said too much,' said Hema. 'But please don't worry, I know it's very unsettling. I doubt Elena is going anywhere. If she's desperate to leave, I'll give you a chance to say goodbye. But if I had a pound for everyone who said they were leaving, and stayed until the end, I'd be able to replace the dishwasher.' She sighs and looks at the carpet. 'Still, I suppose that's one less glass to worry about.

'Anyway, you have an afternoon of self-directed healing practice.' Five blank faces stare at her.

'That means free time. There's optional yoga in the conservatory, it isn't guided but the mats are out. You're welcome to use our library and read anything you like. Just make sure you return it before you go, back to the shelf where you found it. Or come out and explore the grounds. We're on five acres here. It's a bit of a walk, but you can even go down to the lake. If you're lucky, you might see a frog or two. If you need me, I'll be outside doing a bit of gardening.'

'I'm going to be preparing for my readings,' says Cassandra, grandly. 'In fact, Hema, I need to speak to you. It's all confirmed, for the last night, yes?'

'Sure,' says Hema, wearily. 'That's fine.' I suspect Elena has accidentally done Cassandra a favour. Hema will probably agree to anything now – no one has the energy for another glass-smashing.

The lake is calling to me. Rachel and Anya have both said they're going for a lie-down, but I think they have very different agendas – Anya mentioned something about going via the library and looking for some Jackie Collins.

I go to Reception, hoping to find a map of the grounds, or anything that might give me a vague sense of where the lake is.

'What are you looking for?' I hear Sunny's voice, but I can't see her. 'I'm down here!' she calls, and I peer over the desk. She's squatting on the floor, and she looks a little peaky.

'Are you OK?' I ask. 'Can I get you some water?'

'I'm fine, I had a late one. I just woke up from a nap.'

'Under the desk?' I ask. 'Isn't it a bit cramped down there?'

She shakes her head. 'This is the best place for me, really. Close to the ground. The only way is up.'

'For sure,' I nod. 'I was looking for a map or something. Do you know which way the lake is?'

'Are you going for a walk?' she asks. 'You'll need a hat.' She rummages under the desk, and pulls out a baseball hat, waving it over the top of the desk. Eagles of Death Metal. Of course. 'Take this,' she says. 'I don't have any sunscreen, but you should wear some. I think I'm going back to sleep for a bit. If anyone asks, tell them I've gone to the post office.'

'I didn't know there was a post office around here,' I say.

'There isn't.' Sunny nestles her head against a pile of Manila envelopes and yawns, before closing her eyes. 'Don't

lose the hat, I stole it from my ex. The lake is that way.'
She makes a vague circling gesture at the space behind her
shoulder.

I feel very grateful for the hat. The sun is fierce – it feels
even stronger than it did yesterday. Once again, I think
about how Ben would have loved this weather. And then, I
think, *But Ben didn't love me.*

'Oh!' I say it out loud. The thought is shocking, icy water
splashing the back of my neck. And refreshing.

I think about Elena's shock, and rage and sadness. I'm
really not so different from her. We both tried to make the
wrong people love us, because we thought their love meant
we were worth loving.

Ben and I had loved each other so much, once. Until I
couldn't reach him, and he didn't want to be reached. Ben
felt more present at his funeral than he had done for the last
six months of our marriage, because the congregation was
able to bring him back to life by remembering a handful of
sunny days and barbecues. The Ben they were mourning
was not the Ben I had to live with in that last year.

The year before Ben died was one of sadness. Grief for
the child I'd lost, and the husband I was losing. And then
guilt when I did have hopeful happy days. When joy returned, I believed Ben's death was a punishment for that
joy. I wanted to punish myself. And it isn't working. I think
I want to start to seek joy again. If I can forgive Ben, for
hurting me, then maybe I can start to forgive myself.

It doesn't make any sense. My thoughts are still dark, and
heavy. I should be ashamed. I failed to make Ben love me. I
should have tried harder. But my feelings are light and easy.
My body has changed since this morning. My leg muscles

feel soft and supple. The tightness in my hips has dissolved. It's as though the composition of my cells has changed. They used to hold pain and tension, and now it's passing through.

'Katherine?'

Hema is a few feet away from me. She's wearing a visor and holding a pair of secateurs. 'Come and help me with this buddleia!' She's standing beside a bush filled with purple flowers. 'I really should have done this months ago. But you know what they say. The best time to plant a tree is twenty years ago. But the second best time is now.'

I feel a bit awkward. 'Are you sure? I don't really know what I'm doing. I mean, all my plant knowledge is hypothetical. I don't want to mess it up and do the wrong thing.' I picture me, an hour from now, standing in a desolate, treeless wasteland while Hema cries.

'There is no wrong thing,' Hema says. 'Everything grows back. Now, some of these blossoms have had their day, I'm going to do a bit of deadheading. Could you bear to get down to the roots and start getting rid of any knackered branches? There's a pruning saw down there somewhere.' I squat. The pruning saw must be that big knife. I see a thick, grey, lifeless branch, and tentatively cut at it. Hema doesn't scream at me to stop, so I keep sawing.

We're silent for a little while. I can hear the odd bee, and a hum that rises and falls. I think it might be the sound of crickets. A bright green creature lands on my saw, and I stop, and gasp. 'I think I've got a grasshopper!'

Hema crouches down to have a look. 'So you have! I love grasshoppers. Can you see that flash of yellow on its belly? It's a meadow grasshopper, I think, we get loads here. That's what happens when you don't cut the grass.'

I wait for her to ask about the retreat, or how I'm finding things, but we keep working in silence. The sun seems to be getting hotter and hotter. Sweat is running down my shoulders, and gathering in my elbow creases, and I'm sawing away, in rhythm with the crickets. I don't know how much time has passed.

'Oh, I never used to see blue butterflies, and now they're everywhere.' I break the silence, as I watch a pair chasing each other around the flowers. 'I love being in nature.'

'You're never not in nature, though,' says Hema. 'It's not good for us to think of it as something we go to. We don't drive around and go shopping and go to the office and think "Oooh, better have some nature now." You are nature. It took me a long time to learn that, even though it's very simple.'

'But you're always in nature.' I pull at a thick root, and it comes away in my hand. 'You're here. Surrounded by green space, close to water ...'

'And people,' says Hema. 'I need people. I'm fascinated by why we do what we do. And by the way that we fetish-ise nature and celebrate its wild qualities, while we seek to stamp out those qualities in ourselves. Nature does exactly what it needs to do and that's what taught me to accept my own messiness.'

I look at Hema, surprised. 'How are you messy? You seem so calm. So controlled. I can't imagine you throwing a glass against a wall.'

She laughs. 'Katherine, I think I've thrown a glass against that actual wall. You know why I first came to Cadwell Manor? I was in rehab here, in the nineties, just before it closed.'

'What for?' I say, unable to conceal my shock. Ordnance Survey maps? Kendal mint cake?

'Alcohol, mainly,' says Hema. 'I mean – whatever I could get my hands on, but alcohol was my biggest problem.'

'I have – had – a friend in AA,' I say, falteringly. 'Sorry, I'm probably not supposed to say that. But she was very open about it. I think she still goes, most days. She said it really helped her.'

'Same,' says Hema. 'It's great that you can attend meetings online now, it makes it much easier when we have retreats. It's not for everyone, but sometimes I think it kind of is. We all need to be reminded that we're largely powerless, and it's comforting. We all need to be reminded to take things one day at a time. It helps with grief,' she finishes, simply.

'Right,' I say. 'But sometimes I feel as though the grief will never end, and sometimes I worry that I haven't started grieving properly. And when I do feel it, I'm doing it wrong. I'm supposed to be sad. And I feel ashamed, and angry, and confused. I am sad. But if I'm really honest about it, I think I'm saddest about what I'm not feeling. About all the ways that I'm getting it wrong.'

Why am I telling her all this? 'I'm fine, though,' I add, hurriedly. 'I'm seeing a therapist. I know what I'm supposed to be doing. Mindfulness, journaling, that sort of thing. I mean, I haven't had much time to journal, I've been so busy with work. But I'm definitely going to do it.'

'Like I said, I try to go one day at a time,' says Hema, mildly. 'I don't know what your friend has told you about her experiences, but it takes the pressure off. You don't have to commit to doing everything perfectly, for ever. You just promise to do your best by yourself, for twenty-four hours at a time. Like, now. I bet, when you were studying that grasshopper, you weren't thinking, "I should be journaling about this", were you? You were just absorbed in watching. Getting curious.'

'I guess.' I feel exposed, caught out. Hema has noticed me slacking off. I've accidentally shown her who I am, when I stop striving, and forget about who I ought to be. But I also feel relieved. 'Maybe when I retire, I'll watch bugs all day long. If there are still bugs to watch.'

'Why wait? You can't pause nature. If there's a grasshopper right in front of you, you can't say, "Work's crazy right now, how is your September looking?"' says Hema. 'If you're worried about the world burning, I'd watch all the bugs you can, today.'

Another grasshopper lands on the hem of Hema's shorts, before pausing for a second and jumping off again. 'We've got a journaling workshop coming up tomorrow,' she says, eventually. 'So if it's something you're interested in, hopefully it will be helpful.'

We saw, and snip, and stop every so often to look at something small that has wandered into the path. I think about Ben, but my attention keeps being pulled to the present by the scratch of grass on my shin, or the shadow of a bird on the ground. It's just a day. A day off grief. A day of watching, without waiting. I'm not hoping for change, and I'm not afraid of it. I'm just here.

Chapter Thirty-One

Loved

After Christmas, we seemed to turn a corner. The worst year of our lives was coming to an end. If we could get past January, we might survive.

It was subtle, but steady. Ben hadn't quite returned to glorious Technicolor, but he no longer looked like an old sepia photograph. He wasn't out of the house all the time. Sometimes, he'd cook meals for the two of us, using actual ingredients. The day he made a tomato sauce out of tomatoes felt like a tiny triumph.

I was careful not to ask him for anything. I waited to be touched. He did not notice the tiny silver nest pendant I wore on a chain. I usually tucked it under my top. If he did, I'd have said it was a present from a friend, a little Christmas thing. It wasn't a big deal, it didn't mean anything, and that was why I hadn't told him. He'd loved the little compass, although he'd asked, anxiously, 'Does it actually work? Is it functional?' The noise-cancelling headphones he had given me functioned perfectly. I told myself they were not symbolic in any way. Not all gifts had to be.

We both went back to work on the same day. I was in the kitchen, drinking coffee, and he was chanting, 'Keys, keys, keys, who stole my keys, someone took my keys.'

I got up, walked to the coat stand by the door, and pulled them out of his jacket pocket. 'Ta da!' I said, as I dropped them into his hands, and then, taking a risk, stood on my tiptoes to kiss him on the cheek.

'What would I do without you?' he said. 'Hey, that reminds me, I meant to ask. You don't have plans on Saturday, do you? I'd like to ... spend some time with you.' It was the first time that he'd looked into my eyes for a long time.

'Great!' I replied. 'I'm around. That would be really nice.'

After he left, I noticed the calendar said HAMBLE with a line that started on Saturday and crossed into Sunday. Which meant Ben was choosing to sack off sailing to spend the day with me.

On the way to work, I started to wonder why Ben was bothering, now. It seemed sudden – and, pathetically, I thought, almost unfair. I'd tried so hard with him. My heart had been broken too. Why did this all have to be on his terms? I fingered the nest under my jumper and felt guilty. I could have tried harder.

But that didn't matter. I'd made my resolutions, perhaps Ben had too. Marriage was hard, but so were we. This was going to be a better year. As I queued at the coffee shop I gave myself a motivational speech. I wasn't going to worry about my marriage any more. I was going to be grateful for all the wonderful things about Ben. Instead of wishing the past was different, I was going to focus on the future.

By the time I reached the office, I was full of resolve, and over-caffeinated. (I'd focus on my marriage, I thought, but

I'd make a second resolution, and try to get down to one coffee a day.) Lou was already in, and she hugged me.

'Happy New Year! I have so much to tell you! Mostly because I went to a silent retreat for three days, so there's a lot of backed-up chat. I wasn't allowed to text in there, sorry. I'm so glad you like your birds!'

Shyly, I lifted the pendant up to show her. 'I love them, they're perfect. Thank you.'

'Listen,' she said. 'There's a new veggie bao place opening in Clapton on Saturday, do you want to come? We could go out out after?'

'I'd love to!' I said. 'Oh, shit, sorry. Saturday. I can't. Ben wants to do something. I think it's a surprise.'

She stopped smiling. 'Ben. Of course. Sorry.'

'I think he's cancelled sailing for it.'

'He's cancelled sailing?' said Lou. 'Oh, in that case it must be a big deal.'

She was hurt, and I hated it. 'I'm sorry,' I said. 'Maybe we can do something on Sunday? I'll come east! We were talking about going to the Bethnal Green V&A. Or maybe we could go for a walk on the marshes—'

'Oh my God, stop!' Lou held her hand up. 'I see you, Katherine. You can't be everything to everyone. You can't keep compromising, and you can't fix everything. Don't do what Ben wants, don't do what I want. Do what you want.'

I'd never heard Lou like this before. I didn't think anything could upset her or annoy her. And she wasn't making any sense. I wanted what Ben wanted, and I wanted what she wanted. There wasn't anything else left for me to want. I sat down, awkwardly.

'Look, ignore me,' she said, eventually. 'I'm just feeling

a bit January, and I think my period is due. No Mooncup jokes, I'm not in the mood. If you want to cheer me up, you could make me a hot Ribena.'

Over the next few days, she was friendly enough, but distant. I saw her laughing with Lydia, and it made me want to weep. It had to be hormonal, seasonal, some other secret stress. I didn't want anything to change between us, but I felt as though I'd lost something very precious.

On Saturday, I woke up alone. Ben had left a note on the pillow.

Gone for a run. Meet me at the Strand Palace hotel at 11 a.m. X

I was a little disappointed. I'd been looking forward to spending the whole morning with him. Pulling the duvet around my shoulders, I looked down at my black silk slip. It was very cold in the house, and I'd worn a nightie to bed, hoping that we might have sex in the morning. I could have worn my pyjamas and been a lot warmer.

Still, it was exciting that he wanted to meet at a hotel. Were we staying overnight? He hadn't mentioned anything about packing a change of clothes, but perhaps that was implied.

I dressed carefully – a red silk wrap dress, a treasure from the Shelter shop at Coal Drops Yard. I unearthed a black lace bra. The matching knickers felt a tiny bit tight after Christmas. I hoped Ben wouldn't notice. This is bound to feel strange, I told myself. We've got to get used to each other again. I've got to get used to myself again.

Sitting on the Tube, I squirmed in my seat. Was this

excitement, or nerves? I remembered waiting for our first date, pacing the floor of Annabel's room, and worrying about my hat. That felt like a beginning. Maybe this was a new beginning, and Ben wanted to start again, with a grand, extravagant gesture. Perhaps I was being wooed, and this time Ben was going all-out with hotels, champagne, acts of seduction. I wished he was picking me up in his crappy car. I wished we were going somewhere quiet, where we could really talk. I didn't want to be in a hotel, surrounded by other people.

As I walked into the building, I reminded myself of my resolutions. I had to focus on the future and be open-minded.

'I think the reservation is for Attwell,' I told the maître d', scanning the room for Ben. It was gloomy, despite the high ceilings, the brook-babble of chatter. I wondered who else was there on a Saturday. I heard a cork pop and listened for the whoop. Every group of girls was, I assumed, there for a hen do. I was looking at the world through a weird filter. To me, every woman looked like a bride-to-be, they were my ghost sisters, reminding me of my past. Now I'd seen things. I knew things. What could I tell them? 'Marriage. It's tough. But it's worth it!'

Was it really?

I realised I'd looked through Ben several times before I saw him. He seemed different. There was a hardness to him. He didn't seem sad, but he didn't seem warm. Maybe it was the running. I realised that I was looking for a man who had dressed for a special occasion, but he was still in his joggers and a hoodie.

'I'm surprised they let you in like that!' I said, sitting down opposite him. 'How was your run?'

'Katherine, I don't really know how to do this, or how to say this. I'm so sorry. I wanted to come somewhere we've never been before, somewhere neutral. I didn't want to do this at home. I've been thinking ... ' He picked up a glass of water and drained it. 'Thinking about us.'

I think I knew, then. I think I'd known for a very long time. But I still said, 'No! NO!'

The room seemed to tilt, turning sideways, before righting itself. I gripped the side of the table. This was what it felt like to be on a sinking ship. Everything was shaking and sliding. If you managed to get out, there was a chance you'd drown. If you stayed, there was no chance of survival. 'It isn't your fault,' said Ben, 'and I don't think it's mine, either. I haven't felt right, since ... since our baby. I've been trying to find the right moment to talk to you for weeks. It just isn't working any more. I need a fresh start. And I think you do too.'

'What are you saying, exactly?' I asked. Like an idiot. 'Ben, it's been awful. But it's been getting better, hasn't it? And this is life. Awful things happen, and you don't think, "That's it. I give up."'

'Katherine, every time I look at you, I think about what happened. And I can't do it any more. I loved you so much—'

'Loved?' I cried, my voice getting higher and louder. 'LOVED?'

'And I will always love you, in so many ways. But I don't think that's enough. It's not fair to either of us. I was sure you felt this way too. I thought you knew it was over. Please be honest – do you really want to stay married to me?'

'Ben! Of course I do!' I said. I didn't want to lie. I didn't know it was a lie until I said it out loud. I wanted to want it. 'I just don't think this can be the end,' I said, quietly. 'It doesn't feel like the end.' But I was remembering my conversations with Annabel and Constance, and how upset I felt when they talked about the hypothetical end of our marriage. If someone suggests you might divorce your partner, you don't get upset if things are going well. But if you feel anxious, and panicked and defensive – you're probably heading for divorce.

'Like I said,' he took my hands, 'I will always love you. Don't think this isn't breaking my heart, because it is. And please don't worry about the practical stuff. You can have the house. You can have everything.'

'Is it because you've met someone else?' I said, as the ground continued to roil beneath me.

'No.' Ben's gaze was steady. 'Have you?'

I looked away. I listened to the clatter of cups and cutlery. I prayed for a waiter to come with a wine list, for a neighbouring hen do to get out of hand, a Thames tidal wave. Anything at all that would save me from having to answer.

'I don't know,' I said, eventually. It was the most truthful I'd been all day.

'Listen, I've got to go, I'm going to Hamble. But take my card. Order anything you like!' He stood up.

'I don't want anything,' I said, standing. 'Have you told Constance?'

'No!' Ben sounded shocked. 'Of course not!'

That was when I started crying. My lovely, lovely almost-mum. My friend. We'd just had our last Christmas together, and I didn't know. We might not even send Christmas cards after this. Her son was breaking my heart, and she had to take his side. She was obligated to. And maybe that was correct. Maybe I broke his, first.

'Please, please don't cry,' said Ben, as I felt around for a napkin, knocking things over. 'That was why I thought it would be good to do it here. I hoped you wouldn't get upset.'

'Ben, this isn't a Noël Coward play! I'm not going to stiffen my upper lip and suggest we have one last game of tennis!' I wasn't just crying, I was wailing.

'It's OK! Half of all marriages end in divorce! Mum's divorced. I'm a child of divorce! And it was a good thing that my parents split up! They're fine. I'm fine!'

'Are you?' I said, acidly.

'Look, Katherine, I don't think there's much more to say, right now. I've got to go. It's Hamble, this weekend. I'll be home tomorrow night, and we'll talk about the details when everything feels a bit calmer. You're going to be fine. You're a coper.'

We got to our feet. Ben hugged me, and I stood stiffly. I wanted to memorise his touch. And I wanted to shake him to the ground and then kick him repeatedly. Before I could breathe him in, he was running away, practically dancing to the exit.

I can't remember how I got to the toilet. I have a sense of flickering black, bumping into people, apologising to a waiter who looked at me and asked if I needed help. I know that walking was difficult, that I had to fight the urge to get on the floor and crawl. It was as though I'd forgotten everything I knew about staying upright.

I remember seeing the attendant and feeling bad because I

didn't have any change. I remember falling to my knees, and retching. I remember thinking that I should have ordered something, because I hadn't eaten anything since dinner last night, and my body wanted to throw up and up and up, and there wasn't anything there for it to eject.

I remember the sweat, rolling off me like weather. My knees sliding on the tiles, my hair sodden and burning. I remember struggling, between heaves, to take off my dress, not being able to get my fingers to untangle the knot of the belt, ripping off my stockings, thinking that not much more than an hour ago I'd put those stockings on to be ripped off by Ben. I was naked, soaked, and failing to be sick. This was the worst a person could feel. This was the miscarriage of my marriage, and I was all alone. No one was going to take me home and put me to bed.

When the sweating stopped, I felt a little better. I put on my cold, wet dress. I wedged my bare feet into my boots. I gathered my coat around me and walked out of the building. The air was damp and chilly. I couldn't work out whether it was actually raining, or just about to, but I hailed a cab quickly. I didn't have the energy to feel guilty; this was an emergency too.

As soon as I was home, I took off all my clothes, and went back to bed. When I woke up, it was starting to get dark. What was I going to do? What would my life look like, now? I wanted to call Annabel. I wanted to go straight to Constance's kitchen, and weep all over her kitchen island.

Is there someone else?

I picked up my phone and made a call.

Chapter Thirty-Two

Honesty

Eventually I leave Hema to her gardening. I think about trying to find the lake, but I realise that I'm really craving a cool shower. I head back to the house, and when I open the bedroom door, I remember what happened after lunch. Elena is face down on the bed. Is she crying? There's a whimpering sound – little puffs of air, escaping from some-where. I know that noise, it's the sound you make when you're beyond tears. When the grief is so black and heavy that you've run out of the physical means to express it.

I should back away slowly before she sees me and leave her in peace. I'm probably the last person she wants to see. Maybe I can have a shower in someone else's room.

But I can't fight my instincts. I walk over and sit beside her. Should I stroke her hair? It seems a little creepy, so I put the palm of my hand on her back. 'Hey,' I say, quietly. 'How are you feeling?'

I hold my breath and wait for her to tell me to get out. She rolls over and raises herself up on one elbow. She's wept off most of her make-up – it makes her seem older, and younger at the same time. She seems frail. The shiny face, the confidence, has gone. 'Why does nothing ever work?' she says. She doesn't look at me. 'I'm trying so hard. I'm trying everything. But it's as if I'm climbing this mountain, every day, and whenever I make a tiny bit of progress, there's a landslide.'

'Oh, Elena,' I say. 'That's such a familiar feeling. I know exactly what you mean.'

'How could you?' She shrugs me off. 'Katherine, I'm twenty-four, and I don't feel as though my life will ever, ever begin. Paul was the best thing that ever happened to me. He won't take me back. I loved my job. I ruined everything, and I still don't understand what I did wrong. And now I'm back at my mum and dad's. Working in a café. I hate myself. And that's after spending eighty pounds on an email course of self-love affirmations.'

'You can't really hate yourself,' I say, impotently. 'You seem so confident. So assured.'

Elena talks over me. 'I'm in so much debt. And all I do is work on myself. It's like a full-time job, on top of my real job, and I'm so, so tired. I wake up early, and I chant, I journal. I did a juice cleanse, and I worked out that each individual juice costs more than I make in an hour. And it was supposed to make me glowing, and energetic, and it made me hangry and sad, and I got a massive spot on my chin that still won't go away. Sometimes I think that was the real reason why Paul broke up with me. Because of the spot.'

'Elena, no one who was worth your love would ever break up with you because you got a spot,' I say. 'It sounds like Paul took advantage of you. And I'd rather be you, than his wife. You're single. You're free. She's having a baby with someone who cheated, with a vulnerable, much younger colleague. She's stuck with him. You're the lucky one.'

'How would you know?' she says, shaking her head. 'You've been married. You know someone loved you. Someone saw you.'

I shake my head. 'My marriage really wasn't a good marriage,' I say. 'Not at the very end. My husband wanted to leave. I wanted to leave. We ended up making each other very unhappy.'

'But at least everyone is sympathetic,' says Elena. 'You're a widow. You have a right to be sad. I'm just another dumb girl who needs to get over it.'

I smile. 'You weren't sympathetic,' I say, as gently as I can. 'You told me off for trauma dumping!'

Elena puts her head in her hands, and shudders. 'This is so embarrassing, but I was jealous. I know, I'm a bad person. But all I could think was "no one will ever love me enough to marry me". And I thought everyone would feel sorry for you, and be kind to you, because your tragedy is real. And they'd all think I was young and stupid.'

'You're not a bad person.' I hug her. 'I promise. And I don't think you're young and stupid. No one does. I promise that everyone here has been hurt, and they're getting better.' I think of Cassandra. 'And whatever you think you've done, and whatever you feel guilty about, at least you haven't set fire to anything.'

Elena gives me a small smile. 'God, when you arrived, I felt so claustrophobic. Living with my parents has been such a nightmare, I just wanted a bit of space, you know. They're always shouting about the mess, about why I keep buying new clothes, and how I'm not paying them rent. And then you're this saintly woman, you seem so contained. You don't need all of this stuff. I've maxed out credit cards on a new wardrobe, just for the retreat. And you clearly don't give a shit about what you wear.'

I look down at my sweaty, grubby gardening clothes, and shrug. 'Thanks.'

'Sorry, but come on, it's true. You make me feel even worse about myself.' She sighs. 'I get it, I do. I know they don't want to live with me, either. It's hard though – I've got friends whose parents are buying them houses. Their parents still look after them, take them shopping, treat them to lunch. Sometimes I don't think my parents love me, so it's no wonder Paul didn't. No one will.'

She starts crying again.

'Listen,' I say, tentatively. 'I'm not a saintly woman, at all. I'm just like you. I feel terrible all the time. I'm always trying to do better.'

Elena stops crying and frowns at me. 'How?'

'I don't know.' I fidget with the hem of my T-shirt. I do know, but I'm scared of saying it out loud. 'I'll try to explain. Sometimes I feel as though I was born bad, and I need to be extra good, just to level out. It's almost like a superstition. I'm obsessive about recycling in the way that other people get obsessive about avoiding the number thirteen. And sometimes I think that my luck is so awful, there's no amount of good deeds that can turn it around. I'd be better off if I practised a few superstitions.'

Elena shakes her head. 'That doesn't make any sense. That's really sad.'

'It is, isn't it? You know – here's something I've never told anyone. Not even my therapist. I was – am – sad that Ben died. I was shocked, and confused and angry. But the last time I saw him, before he died, he told me he wanted to get divorced. And that felt worse.'

Elena gasps. 'I'm angry with Ben,' I add. 'I felt so hurt. Sometimes, I don't think I have any grief left, because I spent the last year of our marriage grieving him, grieving the baby we didn't have, grieving us. And sometimes it feels like there's a lot of grief, backed up behind my rage, but the rage is too heavy for me to lift.'

'Oh my God.' Elena looks shocked. 'Why did he want a divorce? What happened? Did you want to break up?'

'I don't know! It's complicated!' I'm starting to regret this.

'Was he cheating?' Then, with some incredulity, 'Were you?'

I don't know where to begin. 'The point I'm trying to make is that I don't want you to look at me and think you'd be happier with some version of what I had. All relationships are really hard. What if Paul had chosen you – and then in a few months, or a few years, he ended up cheating with another woman he was working with? What if everything Paul has done had nothing to do with you, and everything to do with Paul?'

'Maybe,' says Elena. 'I just think that if I'd been different – better – we'd still be together, and he wouldn't cheat. Now I'm rejected, and humiliated. All my friends know that he didn't pick me. I wasn't good enough to be chosen.' She looks thoughtful. 'At least no one knows you were going to get dumped! You've got nothing to be embarrassed about.'

I want to gasp, and weep, and say how very dare you. I

cannot believe you have the audacity to trivialise my tragedy. But I laugh. I laugh, and laugh, and I can't stop.

'What's so funny?' Elena asks, as I try to get my breath back.

'I don't really know,' I say, wiping my eyes. 'Maybe it's the relief of finally talking about it.'

'It's true, though!' says Elena. 'Everyone feels sorry for you. No one is laughing at you.'

'But you know,' I say, cautiously. 'Are you laughing at me?'

'Not really. It's made me feel confused, I suppose.'

'And what about Rachel?' I ask. 'She's not a widow, she's going through a horrible divorce. Are you laughing at her? Do you think she should feel embarrassed?'

Elena shrugs. 'Well, I think she is embarrassed. I'd be mortified if I found out Paul was sexting other women. But she didn't do anything, did she? She's got nothing to be ashamed of.' She looks slightly more hopeful. 'You know, I feel a lot better. You could charge people for this.'

'I don't think I should start monetising advice. I was just being' – I try to think of the right word – 'friendly. But I'm happy to hear that it helped. If you're feeling better, will you stay?' I look around the room. I don't think Elena has made any attempt at packing, but it's hard to tell.

'I'll sleep on it,' says Elena. 'And there's the journaling workshop tomorrow. I'd like to come to that.'

When I finally get in the shower, I think about Elena, and Paul, and Rachel, and Ben. All of us, taking risks, betting on each other, hoping for better and landing on worse. As the water hits the back of my neck, I think I can feel my grief under my skin, changing shape. I'm so sad that Ben died, but I'm even more sad that our marriage died first. And maybe there is no reality in which it could have lived.

It isn't the first time I've cried in the shower, but it's the first time I'm aware of my tears being washed away.

Chapter Thirty-Three

The storm

Was I making a mistake?

In the last ten hours, nothing, and everything, had happened. The sky had fallen in, but I'd travelled back in time. I was standing in the entrance of a restaurant at a smart hotel, excited, confused and terrified, scanning the room for a familiar face.

But this time, I knew, straight away. She was strange, and she was familiar. Her tawny hair was clipped up, and shone old-gold in the lamplight. I saw the nape of her neck, and I had to suppress the urge to gasp, or cry out. 'That's just your friend,' I told myself. 'Your friend from work.'

She was sitting at the bar, on a tall stool. I tried to hug her hello, and she half climbed, half fell off. 'This was the most sophisticated place I could think of,' she said. 'I thought it meant we'd absorb some of the elegance of the place, and we wouldn't embarrass ourselves. So much for that. Oh, love, I'm sorry. I'm so sorry.'

Lou hugged me, and I let myself relax against her body.

'I'm sorry that we're not at the bao place in Clapton,' I said. 'If I'd just said yes to that, we could have saved ourselves a lot of trouble.'

'I'm not,' said Lou. 'Firstly, we'd still be queuing, and it's too cold for that. Have you seen the forecast? It's supposed to snow, or something.'

'The climate emergency has no chill,' I said, solemnly. 'Or, perhaps too much chill, if it's going to snow. It cannot take a weekend off.'

'How are you feeling?' said Lou. She put her hand on my knee and looked into my eyes, solemnly. 'I've been thinking about you a lot, and I have come to the conclusion that you must be cursed! Anyway, you need a drink.'

'I'll have what you're having,' I said.

'Are you absolutely sure? Because I'm having a Diet Coke. If you want to drink a vodka Martini, I don't mind. Have ten vodka Martinis.'

'I'm sure,' I said. 'Being with you makes me feel better than vodka.' Then, I felt my whole body turning red. My toes were blushing. 'I mean,' I stammered. 'It must be a sober thing. The effect sober people have – showing us all we can have a nice time without alcohol.'

Lou smiled. 'I spend a lot of time with sober people and no, that is not the effect that most of them have on anyone. But I drank a lot of vodka in my time, so I wouldn't be surprised if it's still coming out of my pores. Being with me is probably like passive smoking, for booze.'

'It's a theory,' I said. 'Anyway, thanks for choosing this place. I can't believe it's so calm and quiet on a Saturday night.'

'You're not supposed to come to your old haunts, but

I used to love getting drunk in here,' said Lou. 'I started because I hoped it would slow me down. I thought that if I was paying a lot more money for drinks, I'd drink less. Obviously, that didn't work, and I realised I loved it because I could drink alone, without being judged. I'm sure people were judging me, frankly, but I didn't feel judged.'

'Liminal spaces,' I said. 'Hotels are temples of impermanence, we're all just passing through.'

'That's true of everything, though,' said Lou. 'I don't want to get all "the destination is the journey" on you, not today, but nothing is for ever, not really.'

'My marriage certainly wasn't,' I said.

'Oh look! Our drinks are here!' she said, loudly. 'Lovely, we get more snacks!' She picked up a green olive and started chewing.

'Are you OK?' I frowned at her.

'Yeah, yeah, fine.' She took a sip of Coke. 'Just … I'm here for you, you know I am. But I don't know that Ben was making you happy. And you deserve to be with someone who does.'

She looked at me intently.

'I …' I picked up an olive. Maybe I could choke on it, and paramedics would have to be called, and we could forget this whole thing. 'I don't want to make you feel awkward. I have some feelings that won't go away.'

'Katherine, I think I know what you're trying to say,' said Lou. 'But I need you to say it. And I need you to mean it. Don't do this if you're confused about Ben, or about your marriage. Don't do this if you're only doing it because you're scared of being alone.'

I put the olive down. I leaned towards her and kissed her

softly on the lips. I felt my heart beating against hers, both our pulses quickening.

'That's what I'm trying to say.'

Leaving the bar, in the lobby, on the pavement, in the taxi, I wished it felt wrong. I wanted it to feel wrong. I wanted Lou to say 'No', to tell me I'd made a mistake. I wanted to be able to blame her – or Ben. To say I was vulnerable, and overwhelmed, and I didn't know what I was doing. Or even that I was powerless to resist, that desire existed outside of me, and it was too strong for me, that it was capable of picking me up and carrying me away.

But I was making a choice, deciding. These were my desires, and I was in charge of them. We held hands. I don't know who reached for who first. I remember thinking that I didn't understand I'd been scared, until the fear drained away. I remember that I wasn't worried that Lou would let go, or that I would want to.

The roads were becoming treacherous. The promised snow materialised, and a thin, unbodied sleet was spilling out of the sky. The wind was picking up. We sat in traffic and watched a heavy wooden board slide down the street, and out into the road. Shop awnings bulged and billowed. Even the buses were buffeted by it, swinging and wiggling. It looked funny, if you forced yourself to forget that it was a sign of the impending apocalypse.

We hadn't discussed where we were going. I think I gave the driver my address, because I needed to bring Lou into my home. Ben had said I could have the house – as though that was any compensation for the pain. I didn't want to take it. But that night, I wanted to claim it. I wanted something good to happen in that space, where it had felt so dark and lonely for so long. I needed to make love in my bed. I didn't want to come home in the morning, anxious and exhausted, and think, *And here is the place where I cried, after Ben left me.*

When we stepped into the hall, Lou kissed me, soft and slow. I was starving for kisses. I couldn't get over her smoothness, her sweetness. I didn't realise how much I wanted to touch her hair, until it was satin in my hand. She broke away to trace my collarbone with her finger. It was like an electric shock. I almost fell to the ground.

'Katherine, you have no idea – I never thought this would happen. I never dared to let myself think it might happen,' said Lou.

'I thought I was going mad,' I whispered. 'I've been holding everything in. Hope, even. Now ... ' I paused. If I told Lou that it was as though she'd brought me back to life, surely she'd run straight through my door and home again. No, she wouldn't. I could tell her anything, everything, and she'd stay.

'Now,' said Lou, and I knew she knew.

We went upstairs. For maybe the first time in my life, I hadn't made the bed. The curtains were open, and I could see the sleet making trails across the sky. The wind shook the trees. I felt exposed, self-conscious. I started to straighten the duvet.

'It's OK,' said Lou. 'Leave it.'

I walked over to the window. 'Do you want me to close the curtains?'

'No! I want to seduce you in the moonlight.'

'I think that's mostly street lamps and light pollution.'

Lou pulled off her jumper and sat on the bed. She had her back to the window, so the light seemed to shine through her hair, and outline her body as though she were a saint in a stained-glass window. A saint in leather trousers, and a sheer black bra.

I wanted to do everything, then, to lick, and stroke, and bite, and feel. The alacrity of longing shocked me, I didn't know I was capable of wanting so much, at once. She looked perfect, to me. What could I possibly offer her in return? She couldn't want me. No one did.

'Are you OK?' she asked. 'We can go very, very slowly.'

I nodded. I pulled my jumper over my head. This was a terrible mistake. I stepped out of my skirt and tights. She was going to reject me. It was inevitable. My body was no good to anyone, it was a broken home. This was it. I wasn't ever going to do this again. I wasn't ever going to be this vulnerable with anyone, ever again.

Lou stood up and walked towards me. 'I knew you were beautiful,' she said. 'But you're really beautiful.' She kissed me, and her hands were on my hips, my bare back, my neck. 'Tell me if you need me to slow down,' she said, sliding a bra strap off my shoulder. 'Because I'm not very good at being patient,' she unhooked the bra, 'but I'll try. I'll learn.' Then her mouth was on my nipple, and I was pushing her down on the bed, wrapping my legs around hers, and scrabbling for her zip with no patience and less dignity.

'Sorry.' Lou kissed my shoulder, and sat up. 'I couldn't have picked worse trousers for this.' She pulled them down, until she could kick them off her ankles. 'You know, this is when I miss drinking the most,' she said. 'It's been a long time since I've been with someone new. This is so awkward when you're sober. Realising your clothes don't magically fall off.'

'Can I help?' I asked. Lou lifted her legs in the air. 'Please do.'

I wish I'd slowed down, that I'd acted with some reverence and awe. But I pulled Lou's (black, lace) knickers down as though I was about to perform an emergency operation. I think I closed my eyes. I knew she'd be perfect, and I was afraid to look. She'd be a flower, a porn star. She'd have the body all women are supposed to have.

When I looked, she was beautiful, and she was normal. There was a birthmark at the top of her left thigh, no bigger than the tip of my thumb. It looked like a squashed star. There was hair – maybe a little more hair than I had. She was unique, I realised, and so was I. There was no right way for either of us to be, and no right way for either of us to do this.

And so I let my dream self take over. I decided to stop worrying about doing it wrong, and just do what I'd been longing for. Lou was just as nervous as I was, so maybe I could be bold for both of us.

When I touched her, delicately, tentatively, she writhed against me, so I moved faster and harder. I touched her in the way I wanted to be touched – as though I found her whole body fascinating. I did. I'd never seen myself up close, even when I was pregnant. Lou was bright, vivid, alive. And when she screamed, and gasped, and reached for me, it felt delicious. I couldn't believe I was capable of bringing another person so much pleasure. I couldn't believe I had so much power.

Holding my breath, trying not to be nervous, I kissed her

311

birthmark – and then her. This was what I wanted, what I'd missed so much. To know someone, to be able to tell them how you felt with the way that you touched them.

Lou seemed to tremble and buzz. She stopped moaning for a moment, before calling out something without syllables. She closed her eyes and stayed very still. She was smiling.

'Katherine Fucking Attwell,' she said, at last. 'Who knew?'

We fell asleep, holding hands and talking nonsense. I woke up with a dry mouth, and underwear still on. Lou was naked, her body seemed silver in the dark, curled into a perfect gleaming S.

My husband left me today, I thought. And maybe that was exactly what was supposed to happen.

Still sleepy, I closed my eyes, and pulled my knickers to one side. They were soaked. I thought of all the times I'd wanted to touch myself, and felt scared, and strange, and guilty. I thought of the times I'd given into my urges and cravings, and felt better, then worse.

Now, there was something about my body that felt voluptuous to me, it was pulsing and magical. I wanted myself, and the more I touched, the greedier I got. I stroked, slowly. I wanted to make myself wait, I wanted to drive myself crazy.

Lou snored gently, and I breathed out hard. I didn't realise I was grinding my hips until I noticed the rise and fall of the bedclothes. I couldn't do this now. I should try to get some sleep. I moved my hand away, and noticed my inner thighs were slippery. I moved it back, and moaned, quietly. But not quietly enough.

I felt another hand on top of mine. 'Wow,' said Lou. 'So you're awake.'

She sat up and moved between my legs. 'I suppose we might both be dreaming,' she said, thoughtfully. I felt her tongue through the lace of my underwear, and then it was inside me. She gripped my hips hard, as though she was trying to earth herself.

'Oh God, oh no, please, yes, no, that's it!' I didn't know what I was saying but I needed this, I needed her, I grabbed her hair and pushed against her and surrendered. I'd never been more, and less, in my body, overloaded and on fire. In that moment I knew nothing but 'yes' and 'there' and 'more'.

By the time I'd got my breath back, Lou had rolled off me. 'Sorry, I don't think we'll get back to sleep for a while,' she said. 'At least it's Sunday tomorrow.'

'I'm going to go downstairs and get us some water,' I said.

In the hall, I tripped over the strap of my handbag. I must have dropped it on the floor. Picking it up, I reached for my phone, more out of habit than anything else. It took me a moment to realise it was lit up, flashing and buzzing away. I had a lot of messages and missed calls. Why was Constance calling me? As soon as I picked it up, it started buzzing again.

'Oh, Katherine, thank God.' Constance was sobbing.

'Constance! Where are you? Are you OK? Do I need to send an ambulance? I'll come and get you!' My mouth took over, while my brain thought, *Emergency! Emergency! There's an emergency and I have no idea what to do.*

'Katherine, I need you to stay calm,' she half screamed. 'There's been an accident. A sailing accident. Oh God. I don't know how to tell you this. Ben's dead.'

'No,' I said, calmly. 'Constance, I think there must have been a mistake. He can't be. He's ...' I caught myself just before I said 'left me'. I took a breath. 'He wouldn't have gone out, would he? The weather is too bad.'

The wind shook the glass panes in the front door, making a fluting noise as it came through the gaps in the frame. Ben was a good sailor. He didn't have accidents. Please let this have been an accident. A mix-up.

'I'm at the hospital now. I'm so sorry, Katherine. I don't know how this happened or why he was on the water, but he was. He got caught in the storm, and he went overboard and he drowned.'

Chapter Thirty-Four

Telling Ben everything

'I've been rethinking my original plan.' Anya's eyes are sparkling. I wonder if she's been at the erotic meditation again. 'I don't need any time off from work. I think I needed a complete career change. I love this space. I love this week. I want to work in this world! I want to be the Steve Jobs of wellness!' She rubs her hands together. 'I've got so many ideas, I'm sure I can get some investors together. I could spend my forties absolutely killing it, retire when I'm fifty and then just go on retreats all the time! I move some investments around, sell my flat . . . ' She beams. 'It's all falling into place for me.'

Hema has suggested a post-breakfast 'check-in' – a sharing circle before our journaling workshop, to focus our minds.

'How old are you now?' says Rachel. There's an edge to her voice. She's been in a bad mood since erotic meditation. She's barely spoken to anyone. I miss her. I miss having a friend to be silly and sarcastic with.

'Thirty-six,' says Anya. 'So – I've really got to crack on,

get back to it, make some plans. Now that I've found my calling.'

'Do you, though?' says Rachel. 'Anya, the last time we did this, you told us that you had left the corporate world because you were a workaholic.'

'But I'm not a workaholic,' says Anya, patiently. 'I've just told you that I'm going to retire when I'm fifty! Being here, with all of you, has inspired me. And imagine what I can achieve in a new industry!'

'Hema, tell her,' says Rachel. I have to bite my lip to stop myself from laughing. 'Tell her she's doing it wrong.'

'Rachel, Anya's plan seems to have got under your skin,' says Hema, gently. 'Do you know why that is?'

'Because it's such a waste!' Rachel throws her hands up. 'My God, I'd do anything to be thirty-six again, and I wouldn't shut myself in an office for twenty hours a day. I wouldn't have pottered along in my stupid marriage, just trying to get through Christmas, or half-term, or the summer holidays. I would have taken the kids out of school and gone to Marrakesh. I would have had an affair!'

'What's stopping you?' says Anya. 'Surely this is a wake-up call! Don't waste a single second! Go to Marrakesh right now!'

Rachel looks like she wants to hit her.

'I tell you what you should have done,' says Cassandra. 'I bet you've got a lovely house. You could have burned it to the ground, with hubby in it, and cashed in the insurance. Then you could have bought a whole riad and filled it with young men. Mind you,' she adds, 'did you have insurance? Because you should always check before you burn anything down. Don't ask me how I know.'

'I don't think we need to ask,' says Anya. 'But Rachel, you really could go now. You could go anywhere. Any of us could.'

'Well, ideally not by plane,' I say. 'But I bet you could get a train to Marrakesh. Maybe you could go from London to Paris, then on to Spain . . . '

'Will you SHUT UP.' The rage in Rachel's voice is frightening. 'You're worse than my kids. I'm sorry that I'm almost sixty. I'm sorry that it's all my fault. I'm sorry that I bought you all of those iPhones and trainers and computers. I'm sorry I bought an expensive car to chauffeur you around in. I'm sorry I didn't make you wait at a bus stop in the rain. I'm sorry I forced you to come to Mauritius. I should have taken you camping in Rhyl – because that's what I did when I was your age!'

'Everyone, take a breath,' says Hema. 'It's OK, sometimes things get a little heated. Remember, you're about to do some journaling, and that's a great way to work through these big feelings.'

'I'm sorry, Katherine,' says Rachel. 'I know I've never driven you anywhere. Listen, I'm as scared as everyone else about the state of the world. I think about it a lot – what's going to happen to my kids, and their kids. I feel powerless. Not just about what's happening. About my whole life.'

'What would make you feel powerful?' I ask. Oh! Hema is looking at me, slightly startled.

'That's a good question, Katherine,' she says. 'Maybe we should all try to answer that, when we journal.'

Elena is very quiet. I think she's keeping a low profile after her outburst yesterday. I keep looking over at her, but she's always looking at her phone. I hope she's not reading the pregnancy announcement, over and over. At least she's still here.

'OK,' says Hema. 'Let's leave this for now. We'll meet in the atrium in half an hour. I've got pens and paper up there for you, you don't need to bring anything.

'Apart from your innermost feelings,' she adds, thoughtfully. I feel slightly sick. I wonder if I can write about that.

A trestle table has been set up, with chairs, exercise books and biros organised along one side, Last Supper style. Hema stands in front of the table and waits for us to take our seats.

'Has anyone here done any journaling before?' Anya's hand shoots up. Rachel rolls her eyes.

'This is something I love doing, and I love teaching,' says Hema. 'Firstly, this is an activity that every single one of you has probably done without realising. Whenever you make a list, or write a message, or send an email to yourself – you're journaling.

'Today, there's only one rule. Just write whatever comes into your head, until the session ends. And you can't get up, wander around, check your phone or go to the toilet in the middle. It's OK to write "I hate this, I can't do this, this is horrible", but you have to keep writing.'

'What's the point?' says Rachel. I think there's some bitterness in her voice.

'For me, it feels like clearing leaves out of a swimming pool,' says Hema. 'Our heads are filled with profound things, trivial things, joyous things, and things that terrify us. And quite a lot of clutter. This is one way to sort through them, to throw some light on them. Over time, we feel less scared of ourselves. More powerful.' She looks at me and smiles.

'No one else needs to see this,' Hema finishes. 'After this, we have a fire ritual, where we can all burn our pages together.'

I should say something about domestic fire hazards, how fire poisons the atmosphere and threatens garden wildlife. But the idea of burning my words is deeply appealing. I feel calm – but giddy. I can say anything I like and release it. I can purge my most poisonous thoughts, and no one needs to know.

There's a murmuring, a collective sigh, a tapping of pens on the desk, but I'm already in my head, and the words are flying out. I know exactly what I have to do.

Dear Ben, I write, immediately smudging the ink with my arm. I don't care. My pen is moving at speed.

I want to tell you I love you, and I miss you, but I'm angry with you too. Part of me thinks I should tell you that I'm sorry about what happened with Lou, but in all honesty, I'm not sorry. I don't regret it. You hurt me, before I did anything to hurt you. And that's no way to conduct a marriage, but you stopped trying, before I did. You didn't have to protect me from pain. But you did have to talk to me.

In a way, I wish you were still here, because I wish we could get divorced. Is that crazy? I don't know how to grieve you. How do you grieve someone you were already grieving? Ben, it wasn't my job to make you happy, and it wasn't your job to make me happy. But you had to share your feelings. You had to give me a chance.

I spent most of our marriage in a state of disbelief. I was so shocked that you chose me, and that you wanted me. For so long, I had been alone, and suddenly I had a life and a family. There was a safe space for me, and, in your world, I felt held in place. I thought I owed you everything, and I'm sorry about that. I think I should have remembered that I chose you, too, and I could also choose myself. I wanted to be perfect for you. And I lived in fear of what would happen when you discovered I wasn't perfect. It was more catastrophic than I could possibly imagine.

Do I believe there's a heaven, and that you're there? I don't know. Maggie – that's the name I gave our baby – makes me want to believe. And the idea that you might be up there, together, is too hard for me to bear. But maybe that's just this version of events, and there's another one in which we're not together, but we're with Maggie on earth. Our baby wouldn't have saved us. I know that now. Life would have happened, because life always does. As soon as things got hard, you would have checked out. And maybe that would have been too much for a child. Maybe it was too much for you. Your dad ran away, too. He made himself a fortress out of work and money and hid behind it. We both thought I was the abandoned one, the orphan. I'm sorry I didn't fully understand the ways in which you were abandoned too.

But you had your lovely mum, and so did I.
Constance feels like my family. I might never feel
worthy of her love, but I've never doubted it either.
Ben, I'm the most scared about losing her. Because
I can't see how she can stay in my life in the same
way, as I try to figure out a path. I don't know how,
but I want to forge forward.

    I did meet someone else, and everything felt
different with her. She didn't make me feel as though
I'd slotted into a gap, as though I was tethered to the
world. She makes – made – me feel as though I'm
floating in space, and I'm not scared of the silence.
With her, life seemed bigger. I'm sorry I didn't tell
you. I'm sorry I started falling in love with her as
I was falling out of love with you. I used to think
the guilt and shame of it would kill me. But now
I'm here, with a load of mad women, and we're all
angry and ashamed and confused and making stupid
decisions about how we spend our money and our
time. We're all just trying to live in the right way.
Maybe I've been looking at everything through the
wrong lens.

    Because I worry, all the time, about what I
might do wrong. What I can do better. If I knew
what was going to happen, I wouldn't have felt
so scared during our marriage. We couldn't have
worked. I would have set you free. I wouldn't have
blamed myself. And I would have done Christmas
in Australia, and I wouldn't have nagged you about
recycling batteries.

    After writing all of this, I don't feel so angry

with you. I loved you, very much, and I hope you
know that.

'How's everyone getting on?' says Hema. 'Got three pages yet?'

I look up. Everyone is crying. Everyone is covered with ink.

Together, in silence, we walk out of the room and down the stairs. We follow Hema out into the garden.

Is it hotter than yesterday? The heat seems to make the sky shimmer. We walk past the pruned buddleia and I count three blue butterflies. We walk a little further and I tread carefully, listening for crickets. The grass is getting longer. No one says a word, but the space is alive with sound.

There's the water. The surface of the lake is electric green, reflecting the sun shining through the leaves. Hema pauses in front of a small wooden jetty.

'It's a bit rickety, but it should hold all of us,' says Hema. 'Although if anything happens, we might need to tell some small lies to the insurance people.'

I realise she's carrying a metal bucket with a lid. She opens it and pulls out a small bottle of lighter fuel. 'Oh,' I say, 'I was worried we were going to have a big bonfire.'

Hema rolls her eyes. 'Come on, after we saw all the grasshoppers yesterday? No, the only thing that's going to be harmed here is your handwriting. Now, don't feel obliged to burn your pages. Does anyone want to hang on to their journals? For their memoirs?'

Everyone stays quiet, apart from the crickets.

'OK, I'm going to start the fire. Get ready. I'd suggest ripping out the pages and keeping the notebooks for future journaling – but if you feel as though you need to burn the whole thing, do whatever you need to do.'

I pull out my words and fold the paper into a neat square. Then, I kiss it.

'God, I love fire,' says Cassandra, dreamily. 'So cleansing.'

We line up behind Hema and take turns to drop our pages into the flames. I see my words disappearing into blue, brown, bright gold. Winter warmth on a summer day. Everything Christmassy will always remind me of Ben. And that there are ways to love him, and to honour him, while acknowledging that it's an imperfect, complicated love. Because love always is.

'Katherine, you need to stand aside and let Elena get to the bin,' says Hema. 'It's getting too hot to hold.'

I step back and look out at the water's edge. The lake is ebbing and swelling very gently. Go on. You know you want to. A bead of sweat starts to gather at the back of my knee. My face feels raw from fire. And from the big cry.

'Wouldn't it be lovely to jump in?' I say. And then, I take off my T-shirt. I step out of my shorts, and my flip-flops. I walk to the end of the jetty and jump. Briefly, I am airborne. I land with a splash, just as Hema shouts out, 'Katherine!'

The water is thrillingly sharp. I feel a shock of cold, and then pure joy. For seconds, I feel safe, held, new.

'You know you've still got your bra on?' says Hema. She crouches down and lets me hand her the wet bra. 'Trust me, it gets really uncomfortable after ten minutes,' she says, smiling. I swim away, watching the dragonflies at the water's edge. It's amazing how many things you can hear if you listen carefully . . .

'Wheeeeee!' Anya is holding hands with Rachel and

Cassandra, and they're running towards the water. Hema offers Elena a hand, and they jump.

'This swim wasn't on the schedule,' says Hema, picking a reed out of her hair. 'So lunch might be a bit late.'

Chapter Thirty-Five

The end of the beginning

I sat at the bottom of the stairs for some time, waiting for Constance to call me back. I thought about Maggie, and how the blood and pain had almost helped. That was a disaster I had to confront, physically and immediately. I knew exactly how I felt, or rather, my muscles and bones and guts knew for me.

It didn't feel like shock. I simply couldn't believe it. The phone would ring again, and it would have all been a mistake. Or this was a guilt dream. My subconscious was punishing me.

I thought I was more resourceful than this, I thought I knew how to be good in a crisis. I should go straight to the hospital in Southampton. Constance had said something about coming to pick me up, but there was no way she should drive. Should I wait for the first train? Call a cab?

The panes of glass on our front door were turning from deep purple to blush pink. The sun was coming. The storm had passed.

When I heard my name, I realised how cold I was. Why was I still naked? Lou was standing at the top of the steps.

'Hey,' she said, tenderly. Then: 'What happened? Oh my goodness, Katherine. Are you all right?'

'Ben,' I said, without turning around.

'What?' said Lou. I could hear panic in her voice. 'Is he here? Does he want you back? Does he—'

'He's dead.' I stood up, and faced Lou, the flight of stairs between us. 'He drowned. His mum just called. He's . . . his body, I guess, is in the hospital. I have to go.'

She ran down to me and threw her arms around me. 'Katherine, I'm sorry. I'm so, so sorry. What do you need? I'll take you to the hospital.'

'No,' I said. 'Thank you. I think I need to do this alone.'

'You've had an awful shock,' she said. 'Quite a lot of awful shocks. I don't think you should go on your own.'

'I have to,' I said, in a monotone.

'But, will you come back?' asked Lou. 'When will I see you again?'

'I really can't think about that right now,' I said. I heard the edge in my voice, and I felt ashamed of myself. In every way. This was all Lou's fault. *No*, I thought. *It's all yours.*

'I'm a widow,' I said, testing the words, weighing them. My tongue felt heavier in my mouth. A widow. It didn't fit.

I ran up the stairs, pushing past Lou, heading for the bedroom. Where was my underwear? I picked up a soft, grey jumper from a chair, and pulled it over my head before I realised it belonged to Ben. It felt wrong to wear it, fraudulent. But I couldn't bear to take it off.

I sat on the edge of the bed, and Lou sat beside me, putting an arm around me.

'I was just about to start coming to terms with being a divorcee, and I'm a widow.'

'Love, this is a lot. I can only begin to try to imagine what you must be going through right now. But I want you to know that I'm not going anywhere. You know how I feel about you. And I'm here for you.'

I wriggled away. 'I appreciate that, I do, but – Lou, I can't do this right now. I'm still married. But I can't be married, can I? Oh, God, I don't know what I am any more. This feels like a sign, a bad sign. The timing is all wrong.'

'It always is,' said Lou. 'OK, we need to get you out of here. At least, let me take you to the train station. And if you want me to come down, I'll come down.'

I shook my head. 'No, Lou, I can't do this. I can't start this now. I don't know what I want, maybe we should never have done this.'

She turned away from me. 'Oh.'

I didn't think I could feel any worse, but I turned colder. It was as though the sun had gone in, and the sky was solid with dark clouds. I couldn't be with Lou, of course I couldn't. But I couldn't be with anyone else, and I couldn't be alone.

'I'm so sorry,' I whispered.

One night. I wasn't even allowed one night. I'd ruined everything.

'I was so afraid that this would happen,' she whispered, quietly. 'I really hoped that this' – she gestured at the bed – 'was the beginning. But it's the end, isn't it?'

'I'm sorry,' I said, again, pointlessly.

'Katherine, please don't hate me for asking this. I know this isn't the right time, but I need to know – was this real to you? Or have I just been a rebound? Did you call me because you knew I would make you feel better?'

'No! Of course not!' I was in tears. 'You know how I feel about you!'

'So let me stay! Let me be with you! Katherine, I want to be part of your life. *Please.*' I could hear her voice cracking, and it broke me. I didn't think there was anything left to break.

I shook my head. 'It wouldn't be appropriate.'

Lou sighed, and got to her feet. 'That's you all over, isn't it. That's your problem. You're very appropriate, Katherine. Everything has to be done right. But I can't be with someone who needs permission to love and be loved. I can't wait until it's appropriate.'

I jumped up. I felt furious, hurt, wounded. What did she want me to say? *No, come to the hospital, meet my mother-in-law, meet Ben's family! They'll love you.*

'Don't you get it?' I said. I was straining to control my voice, shuddering with the effort. 'Ben's dead. Dead.' I repeated it, hoping I could make myself believe it. 'We have to wait, don't we? What else can we do?'

'Katherine, last night, I asked if you were sure about me. About us—'

I erupted. Shock, rage and fear bubbled up and spilled over. Of course I was sure. But the world was different now. 'COME ON, LOU! YOU KNEW I WAS MARRIED! YOU KNEW IT WAS GOING TO GET COMPLICATED!' I screamed.

'YEAH! I DID! AND I FELL IN LOVE WITH YOU ANYWAY!' she shouted back. We both gasped. Her eyes met mine, and I had to look away.

'Lou, I'm sorry. I've got to go ... I need time.'

'Yeah,' she said. 'So do I.'

She gathered her clothes and walked out of the room. Shortly afterwards, I heard the front door opening and shutting.

When I got to the hospital, I didn't recognise the tiny, haggard woman on the plastic chair, until she said my name.

'He's in the ...' she said, sobbing. 'The mor— He's not here. We can go to him.' I hugged her tight, and she felt tiny in my arms. I was going to look after her. I had to. I couldn't burden her with anything that had happened over the last twenty-four hours. Her pain was palpable, crushing. Nothing could hold it, nothing could contain it.

After a while, she peeled herself away from me. 'They found some things in his pocket. I thought you might want ...' The sound that came from her made me think of animals, going alone into the forest to die. I would have drowned myself for her then, if I thought it could have done any good.

The clear plastic bag contained an uncapped biro, a bank card, and a small enamel compass.

I remember very little of the next few days. I stayed with Constance. We urged each other to eat and sleep, but I don't know that we managed much of either.

Once an hour, I thought about calling Lou. Sometimes, when I was staring at her old messages, I'd see the three flickering dots. I didn't know what she wanted to say, or whether I wanted to hear from her. I missed her. I was angry with her. I blamed her. I wanted her.

*

When I eventually got back to my desk, she wasn't at work. At first, I assumed she was punishing me, or that she felt too shocked, or strange to come in. On the third day, I asked Jeremy.

'It's a real shame, she's decided to move on,' he said. 'Her contract was up in a couple of weeks – of course, we'd have renewed it, but she's gone on to Chatham House, to work with the Southeast Asia team. She'd accrued a bit of holiday, so she's taken that in lieu of notice. She said they wanted her to start straight away.'

'What. An. Incredible. Opportunity. For. Her,' I bleated.

'Surely she told you? I thought you were inseparable,' said Jeremy. 'Are you not in touch? I guess, with the stress, and everything ... ' He patted me on the head, and I flinched. We both looked at his hand as though it was a rat emerging from his sleeve.

'Sorry,' he said. 'I never know what I should say about these things. So tragic.'

In the fog that followed, I must have opened a hundred cards, a thousand cards. I thought I was numb to sympathy and kindness, until I opened a lilac envelope. The card said, simply, WITH SYMPATHY. It said, 'I am thinking of you, always. LX'

I put it back in the envelope. Then I took off my pendant and put that there too.

Chapter Thirty-Six

A message

'I'm really nervous.' Elena is fidgeting in her seat. 'I don't know, I feel as though I'm sitting outside the headmaster's office. The universe is about to give me a report card, or something. Maybe it's because it's our last night here. It feels a bit like the end of term.'

She winces, and I reach for her hand and give it a squeeze. I can't believe I hated this woman, a few days ago. She's changed so much. Maybe I have, too.

'I don't think there's anything to be nervous about.' I force myself to smile. Because this is just a final bit of fun. Cassandra can't really be psychic. She's definitely not going to summon a lot of ghosts with messages for me.

Although if she isn't, why am I here?

I try again, attempting to reassure myself as much as Elena. 'Look, Hema wouldn't let Cassandra do this if she thought that she was going to upset us. Would she? I can't believe Cassandra managed to wear her down. Maybe she does have special powers.'

Elena shudders. I knew I should have skipped this and gone to the yoga session.

'I just feel so guilty,' says Elena. 'I keep thinking about Paul, and how I could be with a married man. I was so jealous of his wife, and I've started to feel sorry for her. Since we spoke, I'm thinking of all those times when he was with me, and he should have been with her . . . ' She shrugs. 'I think Cassandra is going to say that I have toxic energy. Homewrecker energy.'

'Elena, you fell in love!' I say, forcefully. 'It didn't work out. You got hurt. You fell for someone who didn't treat you well, someone who took advantage of you. I'd suggest that you don't go round looking for married men in the future – but give yourself a break. You loved Paul, and you're falling out of love with him. It's really painful. You're allowed to be vulnerable, you're allowed to be confused. Hopefully Cassandra will guide you through this.'

'Thanks, Katherine.' Elena still has my hand, and she squeezes it tightly. 'You're as good at giving advice as you're bad at choosing clothes.'

'Always a pleasure,' I say. I decide the compliment is too heartfelt for me to take offence from it. Elena has a point. And my own words are looping and echoing around my mind. *You fell in love. It didn't work out. You're allowed to be vulnerable. You're allowed to be confused.*

Anya emerges from the dining room doorway, looking quite cross. 'All done. Who's next? By the way, you should know that *Cassandra doesn't like to work collaboratively*,' she shouts, behind her. 'And she isn't a *team player*. I'm going up to the atrium. If you want a reiki session, *I'd be very happy to share my knowledge.*'

She stomps off. I look down. If I catch Elena's eye, I'll start laughing.

We turn to each other at the same time. 'Are you—?'

'Katherine, *please* go first. I'm still deciding. I'm not ready.' Elena twists her hands. 'Go in there and tell me everything. And if it's awful, I'll just go and do some reiki with Anya or something.'

Reluctantly, I get to my feet. 'Fine. I don't think there's anything to worry about. Cassandra will probably just tell me to drink more water. Or not to sign a contract when Mercury is in retrograde.'

I open the door. What's the worst that could happen? I think back to the moment I met Cassandra, when she was rude to Constance, and stifle a giggle. This is all just a bit of fun. And I don't want the full psychic works, just a quick energy reading.

'Sit.' I hear Cassandra before I see her. She's placed herself at the head of the table, and I can just about make out the wooden chair on her right. This room feels so different, in the dark. It takes me a moment to reconcile this space with the places where we've all been eating, drinking and laughing. The dark, velvet curtains have been drawn, and there isn't a single shaft of light to expose us.

In here, Cassandra has a real presence. Usually, she seems like a caricature, a throwback. But this is her domain.

'Please could I have an … energy reading?' I say, hesitantly. It feels a bit like going to an old-fashioned hardware store – another place where I have absolutely no idea what I really need, or how to ask for it.

She puts a hand on my shoulder and closes her eyes. 'I've had a message this week. I think it might be for you.'

'Right,' I say. A small shiver runs through me. Of course,

Cassandra already knows I'm a widow. She's going to assume that's why I'm here.

'Do you want your message?' says Cassandra. 'Because some of this might be hard to hear. Not everyone is ready to be receptive.'

Not really. She's spinning this out. This is all very end-of-the-pier, basic, psychic nonsense, surely.

Surely?

'OK,' I say. 'Let's get this over with.'

'This is from someone who loved you very much. And she knows you loved them.'

She? Oh my God, has Lou died? Am I really *that* cursed? Wouldn't someone have told me?

'She says she feels guilty about leaving you, and she watches you, she knows you feel guilty about everything. She wants to free you from that guilt. She says that she knows you're good. And that whatever you choose, you'll always be good. You'll always be loved by her.'

'Right,' I say, trying to ignore the shivering. It *can't* be Lou. It definitely can't be Nanna.

Of course I feel guilty about everything. It's obvious. And Cassandra has had a week to watch me. Although she's never given me the impression that she's been paying much attention.

'Do you know who it is?' I say. 'Because I thought – I hoped . . . ' I can feel the tears coming, and I fight for breath. I was hoping for Ben. I didn't realise that I wanted to hear from him so badly. I couldn't admit that I needed to say goodbye. I badly, badly wanted to say sorry. And to forgive him. To tell him that I never meant to hurt him, and I know he didn't mean to hurt me. We were just a pair of humans, muddling through. We'd been so unlucky – but we'd been really lucky to know each other. To have loved each other.

I take a breath. 'Can I leave a message for someone?'

Cassandra shakes her head. 'For goodness' sake, I'm not the parish bulletin board.' Then she looks me in the eyes and wipes my face with her thumb. 'Oh, he knows, love. I promise. Don't worry.'

'How did you know that I—'

'But this isn't your husband. This is ...' She frowns. 'Hang on, is that an N or ... no, M! M! M!'

'M'. M for Mum. M for Margaret. M for Maggie.

'What?' I don't trust myself to breathe. 'M? Are you sure?'

She shrugs. 'To be honest, Katherine, it's impossible to be sure. There's always a lot of static, there's not much clarity. She's saying "love" a lot. I guess it might be an Em, Emmy, Emily? Does that make any more sense?'

'The letter M makes sense.' I stand up very slowly. 'I think I'm going to go.'

When I open the door, Elena whispers loudly, 'That was really quick, you weren't in there for five minutes ... Katherine, you're *white*. What happened in there?'

I put my hand to my face. 'Am I?'

'Should I go in? Is it safe? Is it scary?'

I shrug. 'It is scary, but I'm glad I did it. You should go.' I smile at her. 'I'll be waiting for you.'

Elena opens the door, I sit down, and take a breath.

Maybe Cassandra was just telling me what she thought I needed to hear.

And maybe I really needed to hear it. I have loved. I am loved. I am good. Perhaps everything is that simple.

Chapter Thirty-Seven

'Thank you for telling me'

'Well, it's been real,' says Cassandra, hugging me. 'I guess I'll see you in the group chat.'

Rachel catches my eye and murmurs, 'Real? Cassandra?' and I snort. She goes in for a hug. 'I'm sorry I was such a dick at the end. And I'm glad we're all staying in touch. It's been good fun.'

'Please don't worry about it. You've been through a lot. Will you be OK?' I say.

She smiles. 'I think so. I'm definitely going to Marrakesh. Or somewhere. I might even look into getting the train,' she says, giving me one last squeeze.

Elena taps me on the shoulder. 'I'm really going to miss you, roomie. And thank you. Last night – Cassandra told me some things that really helped, but so did you. I think I've changed, this week. You really helped me.' She looks embarrassed, and starts to turn away, before turning back and giving me a hug. 'I'm going to miss you too,' I tell her hair. And I mean it.

Anya is giving out business cards. I take one, and she

tells me to message her. 'I'm so excited! I've finally decided what to do with the rest of my life – set up an erotic healing centre for stressed women. I've already opened up the first funding round. And I want you all to be the first to come.'

'Pun intended,' says Rachel.

'Marvellous,' says Hema. 'It's simply not a retreat unless someone decides to go off and start their own retreat.'

When it's time to say goodbye to her, I feel a little weepy. 'It's as though I just started to get into it, and now it's time to go home,' I say. 'I'm sorry that I was bad at screaming.'

'You're so welcome,' she replies. 'And you got there in the end. It was a pleasure to spend time with you and get to know you. Come back any time. Keep journaling and look out for grasshoppers.'

Then I see Constance's giant tank of a car coming up the driveway, and I have to fight the urge to run to her and fling myself across the bonnet. She opens the door and I throw myself into her lap before she's had a chance to get out.

'I really missed you!' I say, and she kisses the top of my head.

'Did you have fun at camp, sweetie?' she asks. 'Did you make some nice new friends?'

We've been in the car for five minutes when Constance says, 'Katherine, I need to tell you something.' She turns the music down and takes a deep breath.

She is driving very, very slowly. As soon as we turned out of Cadwell Manor, we immediately got stuck behind a tractor, on a narrow country lane.

'What?' I say, anxiously. 'Have you heard from Shrinkr? Have they told me not to come back? Or is it something to do with Ben? Or ...?' She's spoken to Lou. Oh, God.

'I've sorted out some of Ben's old things. I've given quite a lot of his stuff away to charity shops. I know that you told me you'd deal with it, and not to just give it to Oxfam, so I rang someone up, and they came to sort it out. A lot of the technical clothing is really useful, as a donation.'

Her words are coming out hurriedly. 'I kept a few jumpers, I know there will be some things you want to keep. But – it was all over my house, and every time I saw it, I fell to pieces.'

'Thank you,' I say, eventually. 'That's really kind. I'm glad you did it, it was the right thing to do.' I swallow. 'Actually, I need to tell you something too.' I can't do this. But if I don't do it now, I never will. 'Ben – the day he died – told me he didn't want to be married to me any more.'

I wait for the sky to turn dark and fall in. Nothing happens. The tractor's trajectory does not alter. Constance looks at me and looks away.

'Can you bear to tell me what he said?'

I think. 'He took me out for breakfast. He told me it wasn't working, that he couldn't look at me and not think about what happened. Our baby.' I gulp, and gasp. 'Sorry.'

'Oh,' she says. 'Thank you for telling me.' She doesn't sound shocked. In fact, she sounds relieved.

'I just feel so guilty. I feel so guilty about … a lot of things. I'm a fraud. And I let Ben down, and I let you down …'

'I knew,' she says, softly. 'Oh, love. I didn't know that it happened that day. But I knew it was on his mind. And it was up to him to tell you. You were both so unhappy, Katherine. It wasn't your fault.' She takes her hands off the steering wheel, and swipes at her eyes, sharply. 'My heart was breaking, for both of you. His father did the same thing to me. It turned out to be the best thing for both of us. But I knew Ben was going to cause you a lot of pain ... '

'He's your son,' I say. 'Your beloved. He will always be your boy. It's OK. Constance, I loved him so much. And even though that love wasn't enough to hold us – I'll never stop loving him. Or you.'

The woman beside me has made me feel so loved. She's given me so much. And she's funny, and fun, and smart. She's been more than a friend. She's mothered me. But she owes me nothing. And I owe her freedom. I owed it to Ben.

'Listen,' I say, a lump rising in my throat. 'You have been so kind to me. And I understand if you don't feel that it's appropriate to have me in your life any more. Because if Ben was still here, I probably wouldn't be in your life in the same way.' I tilt my face towards the sky, hoping the motion will reverse my tears. It only makes me snottier. 'If you ever wanted to go for lunch occasionally, though ... ' I'm bawling now, 'I would really love that.'

'What are you talking about? Here, let me find you a tissue, or something.' She reaches into her pocket, and pulls out a crumpled bit of paper. 'Sorry, that might have choc-olate croissant on it. Katherine, are you trying to break up with me? I'm not going anywhere. We'll always be family. You're stuck with me. And you might not believe this, but one day, sooner than you know it, you'll meet someone great, and *they'll* be family too.'

She's right about the tissue. I get a bit of icing sugar in my eye. I take a breath. 'I'm just so sorry that I wasn't good enough for Ben, or you. I'm so sorry that I couldn't make it work.'

'You have nothing to be sorry for, Katherine. But believe me, I know that feeling. This is pretty much all I talk about in therapy. I'm ashamed that my perfect son wasn't perfect. I'm ashamed that I'm still angry with him, sometimes, even though he's dead. And I argue with him, and he can't answer back.' She shrugs.

'What does Jonathan say?' I ask. 'About the shame, and the anger?'

'He tells me that it's normal, which is annoying. But he also asks if it helps. And when I let it all out, it does. I will always be able to feel the bit of my heart that Ben broke. But one day I'll trace the line, and it will feel solid, and smooth. It won't start bleeding all over again. I don't know if this makes sense, but if I had to choose between this utter agony, and a world in which I'd never had a boy called Ben, I'd pick the first one, every time.'

I think for a few seconds. 'Same,' I say. 'I feel exactly the same.'

Chapter Thirty-Eight

Seeing the future

I'm excited. I'm definitely excited. They say that physiologically, excitement and anxiety are almost identical. You just have to *choose* excitement. There's a fluttering sensation all over my body, a mild tingling. Heat in my cheeks, even though the air feels a little cooler and crisper today. It's definitely turning autumnal. Time for the true new year.

It can't be anxiety. I've been off work for weeks. I've never had so much time to rest and relax. I've been on a healing retreat. I'm *healed*. If I'm feeling a little scattered, a little keyed up, it's just a sign that I'm happy to be back.

I chain up my bike and squeeze my beautiful brown leather satchel. A perfect gift from Constance, who said it was a present to celebrate *'la rentrée'*. 'This is what they do in France, darling. It's very civilised. You take the whole summer off, and then going back is a big deal. Something to celebrate.'

She presented it to me last night when she took me and Annabel out for dinner. They ganged up on me, again, but I really didn't mind. 'Go easy,' Annabel urged me. 'You've changed, this summer. It's been wonderful to see. But don't let work take over your life again.'

'It will creep back in, if you let it,' Constance agreed. 'Make sure you talk to Grace the Therapist about having good boundaries.'

I think about the coming winter, and shiver. I don't want to come here, in the dark, and leave in the dark. I don't want to be the last to leave, either. This time it's got to be different.

My first job for the day is a meeting with Jeremy Senior. That's probably why I'm anxious – I mean, excited! And I'm being ridiculous. I think I'm expecting My Jeremy to jump out from under a desk and ambush me with a lot of impossible tasks. He wasn't even on my return-to-work email. Jeremy Senior is so vague that he probably doesn't even realise I've been away.

As the lift ascends, and the fluttering feeling increases, I try to steady my breath. I just need to get used to this again. It was my life, for so long. By lunchtime, I'll be back to normal, at last.

Stepping out of the lift is startling. Was the office always this bright, and this noisy? I'm overwhelmed by the whir of fans, the grinding, blinding light and sound. I take a deep breath and head to Jeremy's office. What's the worst that could happen? They'll say they've been managing fine without me, and they'll fire me? I'd love that. No, I wouldn't. What am I talking about? What would I do all day?

I must remember what Grace told me – my body has a feeling, and my brain finds a thought to match. It's fine to feel anxious, but the anxiety isn't giving me any instructions. My knock is loud, and it surprises me. I'm about to apologise, but before I can get the words out I hear a cheery 'Come in!' Jeremy Senior is there, with Akila, who is smiling and wearing a powder blue trouser suit.

Is this good, or bad? Maybe Akila has just come out of kindness. After all, she's the one who looked after me after I fainted. She's the one who was nice to me. I'm surprised she's able to make time for this. For me.

She smiles, and I smile back, and I'm certain that I have a whole bush of spinach in my teeth.

'Katherine! Great to have you back! Pull up a pew! Welcome, welcome!' Jeremy Senior indicates the wobbly blue swivel chair on the other side of the desk, and I perch. 'So, delighted to have you back in the office. And you've had time to really refresh, revitalise, reconnect with yourself!'

'Since you've been gone, we've had a few team changes.' Akila grins. 'We've never worked together directly before, but that's about to change! We've had some fantastic news!'

'Right!' I say. 'Lovely!' Did you fix the climate emergency while I was gone?

'Google!' says Akila.

'You want me to google the fantastic news?' I ask.

'Google wants to work with us! It's a joint campaign. We'll be consulting with them, exploring ways that they can be more sustainable. But we'll be brand partners too. There'll be some filming, some spokesperson work. A lot of travel – we'll be going to California!' says Akila. 'It's great that we could give you some time off to rest up, because things are going to get quite intense.'

I feel faint. I think I need to sit down. Oh, I already am.

'Intense?' I echo.

Akila smiles. 'We're absolutely confident that you're the perfect woman for the job. You can handle this. That Mayburn presentation aside, you've always impressed the whole management team. There isn't anyone else here with your work ethic, and your commitment to quality. And you know Shrinkr inside out.'

'You're long overdue a proper promotion,' says Jeremy. 'Jeremy – ah, the other Jeremy – kept begging me to wait, because he felt that he depended on you. But now he's gone ...'

'What do you mean, he's gone?' I ask, shocked. 'Is he OK?'

'Stress,' says Jeremy, gravely. 'About a week after you left, there was an incident over some coffee. He threatened Lydia with a stapler and took voluntary redundancy.' He chuckles.

'Ah, I think that's confidential,' says Akila.

'Sorry, wildly indiscreet of me,' says Jeremy.

'Right,' says Akila, wearily. 'Katherine, this is basically a whole new role, so we've got a contract drawn up for you. Take your time to look it over – but we've got a press conference at the end of the week, and we need to get your flights booked. There's a corporate induction and retreat in Mountain View.'

'What about my old clients and things?' I say. 'What about the Woodland Trust? I've got so much to sort out.'

Jeremy makes a face. 'Ah, I hear that hasn't been going so well. Young Lydia didn't hit it off with them, and I don't think they're going to renew their contract. Even though we let her go, too. To be honest, though, Katherine, they're not big payers. It's not going to hurt our bottom line too much.'

'But we don't have a bottom line, do we?' I say. 'I thought the point of Shrinkr was to help organisations like the Woodland Trust.'

'I know.' Akila nods. 'But ultimately, priorities change, funding is always a challenge – we grow or we go under. We need Google to be able to afford to work with the Woodland Trust. I'm sure we'll get someone else on that account, don't worry. Meanwhile, Google also pays for you to have your own office, and a new assistant. And a significant salary bump.'

She scribbles down a number on the top of a piece of paper and pushes it over the desk.

Before I see the number, I read the words KATHERINE ATTWELL, CONTRACT.

I skim down. 'Additional duties ... extra hours when required ... a minimum of twenty-four hours' notice for mandatory international travel ... fixed term with performance reviews every six months ...'

No. 'No,' I say. 'No, thank you.'

Akila laughs. 'Obviously we can make that number move,' she says, scribbling something out and writing something in its place. I don't want to look at it.

'I'm sorry,' I say, and stand up. 'I can't.'

'Why not?' says Akila. 'Katherine, you're clearly smart, dedicated and ambitious. This is a dream job. It's a chance to take your career to another level. And surely you can't say no to that salary jump. What on earth do you want?'

'That is a very good question,' I say. 'And it's one I've been afraid to ask myself, for a long time. I don't think I want to work in an office. I don't want to worry about the world all the time while hiding from it. I don't want to live in fear of myself, or my mistakes. I don't want to always worry about being better, being perfect.'

I pick up the contract. I see the number, and swallow. But it's not enough. I'm worth more than that. I want big skies, and green trees, and true love. 'Thank you,' I say. 'But I think my future is out there, somewhere.'

I smile, and walk away.

Chapter Thirty-Nine

You are good

What's wrong with me?

I've just been offered a second chance. In fact, not just a chance – the most exciting career opportunity I could ever hope for. After a lifetime of late nights at my laptop, and weekends spent worrying about work, all that effort was finally seen. I was going to get my big reward. And I said no. This might be the most irresponsible, least Katherine-ish thing I've ever done in my life. And yet, it feels like one of the very best decisions I've ever made.

I've never felt more like myself. I'm free. It's as though there's more room for my lungs in my chest. I was heavy and solid. Now I'm molten, elastic. When did I last feel this way?

It was the last time I did something irresponsible and un-Katherine-ish.

Sighing, I try to push that memory away. Because I want to be present for this. I want to sing. I could leap into the air and click my heels, or cartwheel from the watercooler to the yucca plant. I'm free! My future is wide open. There's no point dwelling on the past. I *do* have a handful of happy memories at Shrinkr, but I'm not ready to look at those yet. I'm too raw; it's too soon.

Who knows, maybe in fifty years I'll be beside Annabel, on the porch at a nursing home, and she'll turn to me and say, 'Do you remember when you were in love with that girl from your work?' And we'll laugh. Maybe I'll tell her about our night together, and how I never knew I was capable of that kind of connection, or that sex could be so explosive, yet so tender. And one day, I'll feel lucky to have loved Lou, in the way that I feel lucky to have loved Ben.

Even though Lou is the only second chance I'd love to take.

As I walk across the office, I let myself wonder what she's doing now. Maybe she went back to Cambodia. Maybe she met someone. I hope she's happy. I hope she thinks of me, sometimes, and smiles. I hope she knows I loved her.

Love her.

Because I've been stuck. I haven't begun to grieve her. But I think I've learned how to start. When I leave the office, for good, I'm going to be leaving the part of my life that belongs to Lou. It will hurt. Closing my eyes, I remember our first meeting – how this gorgeous, vibrant, bold, smart, courageous woman seemed to fall out of the sky, at a time when I was so lost, so broken. And I wish I'd acted sooner, I wish I'd been braver. I'll never make that mistake again. I'll never choose fear over hope.

When I open my eyes, I see a woman at my desk. Sitting on my chair.

Her tawny hair is piled up, and I can see gold chains glistening against the back of her neck. She's very tanned. As I get closer, I notice that she's writing something on a piece of paper. Her hand is moving furiously. Her rings are glinting and flashing. She throws her pen on the desk and sighs, before grabbing a rice cake from a packet, and snapping it in two. 'This is impossible,' she mutters.

Am I hallucinating? Did I *manifest* this? Is this a weird side effect of all that chanting with Elena?

'Lou?' I say tentatively. My heart isn't beating any more, it's *vibrating*. I could take off and start hovering above the carpet. 'What are you doing here?'

She spins around to face me. 'I don't know. I really don't know.'

'Did you come here . . . for me?' I'm not sure what I want the answer to be. I might be sick.

'Katherine—' Lou looks at me for less than a second, and then drops my gaze. She snaps the rice cake into quarters. 'I've been trying so hard not to think about you. About anything. I went back to Cambodia and it was awful. I missed you every single day. I hated you. And I hated myself for not being with you. I didn't know what to do. I got so desperate that I asked Akila if I could come back and freelance – at least, that way, I could see you. She told me you'd been away – that you're coming back today, and you were going to get this amazing promotion . . . '

She tents her fingers, and exhales heavily. 'Now that you're here, I don't know what to do. I've been dreaming about seeing you for months, but I didn't think about what would actually happen when I did. If I did. I tried to write down how I felt, what I want to say.' She shrugs, and points at the piece of paper. I see my name, in blue ink, over and over again. 'I can't do it. I don't know where to begin.'

'I'm not coming back,' I say. 'I'm leaving Shrinkr. For

good.' In spite of everything, I can't stop myself from smiling. 'I'm going now. But will you come with me? We can get coffee, or … something.'

Lou nods and stands up. We walk out of the office together. Standing in the lift, I can't let myself look at her. I want to touch her. My hand is itching, burning from the absence of hers.

Neither of us says anything, until we're standing outside the coffee shop – the place where I told her about Maggie.

'You grab a table, I'll get the drinks in,' I say. Just like the first time we were here. But then, Lou took the lead. I remember her confidence, as well as her kindness – the way she seemed to charm everyone in the café.

'Cupcake?' says the barista. 'Sorry, I mean, would you like a cupcake? Not, as in the term of endearment. Not that you're not a cupcake! Anyway, they're new, cherry and mascarpone. God, sorry, it's my first day.'

I smile. 'Sold! Two cupcakes, cupcake!' She beams at me, and giggles. I glance over my shoulder, and notice Lou, staring at us intently. She's frowning.

'You've changed,' she says, as I approach the table. 'The way you talked to that woman – that was banter! You're a banterer! It's as though you're not afraid any more.'

I put down the cupcakes. 'Oh, I'm still very afraid,' I say. 'But the fear isn't bigger than I am.'

Lou's eyes are wide. 'That's funny because I've never been more frightened in my life. And before I say anything else, I want to tell you that I'm so sorry. And I'm sorry that I didn't know how to reach you, that I couldn't begin to understand what you were going through. Katherine, until I met you, I thought I was brave. But you scared me.'

I try to speak, but she holds her hands up. 'Listen, the way I felt about you, the depth of it, the weight of it – it frightened me. I was in way over my head. In a way, Ben's death gave me an excuse to run away and hide. If things had been different,' she swallows, 'our lives would have become incredibly complicated. I told myself it might even be for the best – that maybe, the pain of being without you would be easier to bear than the pain of worrying that you might go back to Ben. That I might lose you to someone else. But . . . '

She pauses, and I can't bear to breathe. I can hear the radio, the rattle of cups, and my own blood pounding in my ears. But what?

'I always find a reason to run away, when things get serious,' she finishes. 'With you, I wanted to stay. I knew that no pain could possibly be worse than the pain of being without you. But more importantly – the warmth and joy I feel when I'm with you is bigger than anything else. Being scared of losing someone is just part of loving them. It's always going to be a risk. I can't do anything to fix the fear. I know that now.'

Sitting down, I take her hands. 'Lou, I'm always frightened. I'm so frightened of failing. I'm so frightened of getting it wrong. But I'm even more frightened of what I might lose if I'm not bold enough to try.'

Looking into her face, I realise just how vulnerable I am. The stakes are high. It's one thing for the two of us to be apart and broken-hearted, missing the idea of each other. It's another for us to be brought back together, sitting in front of each other, putting a bet on the future.

A thought bubbles up, and spills straight out of me. 'You know, I could never, ever get tired of looking at your face,'

I say. 'Whatever happens next, I want you to know that. I missed you, I thought about you all the time – but the you I dreamed about doesn't compare to you, here, now.'

'I feel the same,' Lou says, slowly. 'I feel exactly the same.'

'And you're right, Lou,' I say. 'I have changed. I've lost so much, and I've gained so much, and I'm still here. All I'll do is lose if I don't find the courage to do this.'

'Do what?' Lou whispers so quietly that I can barely hear her over the hiss of hot water and hum of grinding beans.

Maybe I don't have any courage. Maybe I can stay in this moment for ever. Perhaps it's not worth the risk.

But I was brave and bold with Lou, all those months ago. And it was magical. It was perfect. It was the best thing I ever did.

So I kiss her. Leaning over the table, I take her in my arms and breathe her in. The scent of her hair, the curve of her waist – touching Lou feels like remembering a forgotten favourite song.

When we pull apart, she's smiling. 'Lou,' I say. 'You make me brave. Brave enough to tell you that I want you. Brave enough to ask – can we start all over again?'

I don't know whether I deserve a happy ending. But this could be my happy beginning. Because I'm just a girl, standing in front of a girl, deciding she doesn't have to be good, any more. Because she is good. Good enough to live a big, bright life.

Acknowledgements

Every time I write a book I feel more aware of, and grateful for, the many, *many* people who make it possible. If you're reading this – hello! – and thank you for taking some time to 'watch the credits'. If you've enjoyed *Pity Party,* and I hope you have, it really is thanks to the following people.

Enormous thanks to the team at Sphere – my excellent, insightful editor Molly Walker-Sharp, marketing genius Brionee Fenlon, and the publicity dream team Stephie Melrose, Beth Wright and Gaby Drinkald. Also to Sophie, Liz, Zoe Carroll and the incomparable Jon Appleton (especially for the spirit boosting, generous emails!). Bekki Guyatt, thank you so much for another beautiful, brilliant cover – and for all the beautiful, brilliant covers. Thanks also to illustrator Becki Gill.

'Agent' Diana Beaumont – my goodness, I feel so lucky and proud to have you in my life. Thank you for being a kind counsellor, a top pal and a mensch. Please never ever retire. Most of all, thank you for the feedback that saved this novel – 'it needs to be much funnier and much sexier'! Much love and thanks to the Marjacq team, Guy, Leah, Imogen, Phil, Catherine and Sandra.

A huge thank you to my generous early readers, Sophie Morris, Livvy Peden, Lauren Bravo, Louise O'Neill, Sarah Knight, Caroline Corcoran, Lucy Vine, Julia Morris and Marina O'Loughlin. And love and thanks to Dolly Alderton, Marian Keyes, Lisa Harris, Jo Ouest, Lou Sanders, Sheryl Garratt, Nikki May, Julie Owen Moylan, Holly Bourne, Emma Gannon, Penny Wincer, Lucy Werner, Antonia Taylor, Helen Lederer, Chris Neill, Lindsey Kelk, Isy Suttie, Sarah Ellis, Helen Tupper, Helen Thorn, Annabel Rivkin, Emilie McMeekan, Bryony Gordon, Holly Williams, Ana Fletcher, Heloise Wood, Elizabeth Neep, Joel Morris, Jilly Cooper, Amanda Butler, David Nicholls, the Queen's Reading Room team, Nina Stibbe, Cathy Rentzenbrink, Donna Freitas, Jade Beer, Pandora Sykes, Andreas Loizou, and the Margate Bookie crew, Tom Ryan, Harriet Ryan, and the HLF gang, Ronnie Traynor, Jo Neary, Nell Frizzell and Rebecca Humphries. Thank you all for your generosity, support and friendship.

A special thank you to the South London Lovers, Authors Anonymous and the Crispy Lads. And much love and thanks to my parents, for raising a clan of readers, and to my sisters – my favourite main characters – for everything, especially for recommending that I read Susan Sontag and Lisa Jewell.

Huge thanks to all the literary nosy parkers who listen to You're Booked, and to every guest who has generously shared their reading story with me. Huge thanks to my wonderful Substack community, the Creative Confidence Clinic, and all of the students who I've worked with on a Write Like A Reader course. Every single one of you has taught me to be a better writer.

And most of all, thank you, Dale. You inspire me every single day with your curiosity and kindness. You make my world richer, brighter and *so much funnier*. I'll never write a love story that's better than ours. And I want to write books that make people laugh – but I will always want to make you laugh the most.